THE O'MALLEYS OF TEXAS

DUSTY RICHARDS

THE O'MALLEYS OF TEXAS

PINNACLE BOOKS
Kensington Publishing Corp.

www.kensingtonbooks.com

PINNACLE BOOKS are published by

Kensington Publishing Corp.
119 West 40th Street
New York, NY 10018

All Kensington titles, imprints, and distributed lines are available at special quantity discounts for bulk purchases for sales promotions, premiums, fund-raising, educational, or institutional use. Special book excerpts or customized printings can also be created to fit specific needs. For details, write or phone the office of the Kensington sales manager: Kensington Publishing Corp., 119 West 40th Street, New York, NY 10018, attn: Sales Department; phone 1-800-221-2647.

PINNACLE BOOKS and the Pinnacle logo are Reg. U.S. Pat. & TM Off.

ISBN-13: 978-0-7860-3923-4
ISBN-10: 0-7860-3923-X

First printing: October 2017

10 9 8 7 6 5 4 3 2 1

Printed in the United States of America

First electronic edition: October 2017

ISBN-13: 978-0-7860-3924-1
ISBN-10: 0-7860-3924-8

PROLOGUE:
THE LONG DRIVE
TO SEDALIA

Easter Coble walked through the cold dark night keeping the long wool coat tightly wrapped around her. The celestial sky projected outlines of the towering oak trees that cast long shadows and patches of starlight on the ground. A tall girl of seventeen, with blond braids coiled on her head, she was headed toward the man she loved—Norton Horsekiller. He waited for her in the log shed full of hay that her father called a barn. The snugly built cabin behind her was dark—her parents were sound asleep. They wouldn't miss her during the short meeting with him.

Her father never approved of Horsekiller as her suitor. Said he was too wild to ever be a real provider and would never furnish her needs as a wife and mother. But the six-foot-tall young woman had her own ideas, and, headstrong, she snuck out to meet her lover.

In the barn's darkness, he shocked her by sweeping her in his arms and kissing her. She swooned in his hug. After their kiss he went to quickly telling her how he and three others were going to the buffalo land called the Cherokee Outlet that the tribe owned farther west. He would come back rich with wagonloads of hides and meat, and then he would marry her.

"Tonight we can begin our married life. I will return shortly with many wagonloads piled high with meat and hides. Even your father will be impressed by my wealth when I marry you. Tonight I need your body for good luck on my hunt. It won't hurt you, and we will be bonded as man and wife forever."

Beguiled by his words and skills at arousing her, she agreed and did as he asked, both of them wrapped inside the blanket he'd brought, lying together on top of the sweet-smelling hay. After he'd kissed her good-bye and was gone, while sneaking back into the house she wondered about his words. Once inside, she felt disappointed that her transgression that night with him was not as uplifting as she had expected. But she was to be his wife when he returned triumphant from the big hunt, so the path of her life after this night was cut and dried. She was to be Horsekiller's woman for better or worse when he returned.

From that day forth she prayed a lot for his safety and success. To escape her discouraging thoughts she read from the Bible, more to submerge her worries and the questions from her mother and father about where he went off to. But when morning sickness struck, Easter alarmed her mother, who sat her down and asked her if she had a baby in her womb—did she?

Easter collapsed in tears and told her mother the entire story about her hopes and dreams. But her mother shocked her, saying no simple Indian like him could ever go out there and get rich killing buffalo without money and wagons. He had most certainly lied to her.

That night she imagined that Norton's son inside her belly kicked her while she was crying on her wet pillowcase. She sat up, stiffened her back, and decided, by damn, she'd have the baby and raise him, no matter what happened to her personally.

Border gangs made up of both renegade Indians and outlaws raided settlers and small settlements up and down the Arkansas-Indian Territory line, striking fear in everyone during those years before the Civil War. The scattered families slept with their guns ready night and day. Her mother even became proficient with a shotgun that Easter could quickly reload for her.

One day a tall, big strapping man named Hiram O'Malley came by. His long blond hair was shoulder length and his face clean-shaven. They said he was near thirty years old and the head of the Home Protection Society. This organization was made up of the farmers, storekeepers, and residents around Cincinnati, Arkansas. Hiram rode a fine horse and recently had become widowed when his wife had drowned during a picnic on the Illinois River. Easter also learned, from gossip, they had no living children at the time.

A so-called newly formed band of bushwhackers struck first north of Easter's folks' farm at a mill on Brush Creek. They kidnapped two young girls after they slaughtered several other people on the site and set fire to the water-powered mill.

Word spread fast after the incident. Hiram came, himself, to tell her father about the raid and for them to be ready for more trouble. Her father had his black powder single-shot rifle leaning on the log fence where the three of them worked in their bountiful garden—her pa, her mother, and Easter.

Easter recalled the head bobbing, powerful red stallion that O'Malley rode by there that day. His mouth at the bits lathered like his shoulders from the fast trip his rider made to get there and warn them. The great horse kept half rearing as if anxious to run again. But she also saw the glint in Hiram's blue eyes when their glance met and he tipped his hat to Easter and her mother. "Good day, ladies."

"Good day to you and thank you, sir," Easter said proudly.

"I wish these were better times, ma'am. But they aren't," he apologized almost singly to her, then galloped away to warn others.

What a bright brilliant man bravely sacrificing his life for all of them. She felt very impressed and also lucky he could not see the obvious swell of her son's form in her belly under the generous-size new dress that her mother had sewn for her.

Two days later she walked the two miles to the store in Cincinnati, with her mother, to get a few items they needed like baking powder and a block of tea. Coffee beans were too high priced for her mother to charge on their store account.

At the store a young Cherokee woman approached Easter and pulled her aside. The woman told her mother that Easter would be along shortly but that she had some words for her first. Her mother frowned but went on with her shopping.

"What words do you have for me?" Easter asked her.

"I am sorry to be a bearer of such bad news. But your man, Horsekiller, is dead."

"Horsekiller is dead?" She felt light-headed at the shocking news. Her knees buckled and she fainted.

When she woke up she found herself seated on her butt, and both her mother and Lily Four-Oaks, who had given her the bad news, were staring at her with shocked looks on their faces.

"Easter, what is wrong?" her mother asked.

"Oh, Mother. She said he is dead."

"Who is dead?"

"Horsekiller. He and both of his companions were shot, killed, and robbed out in the Cherokee Outlet," Lily answered.

"Are you telling us the truth or is it some rumor you simply heard?" her mother demanded of Lily.

"No, the truth. My cousin was with him and he is dead as well. I knew she didn't know."

"Oh, dear, this is bad news," her mother said, hugging the sobbing Easter. "Baby, I am so sorry, but this, too, will work out for you."

"But, Mother, he will never see his son."

"My dear, there are many things he will be deprived of ever doing. But we, the living, must survive."

"Do you have his baby?" Lily asked quietly as she knelt beside her.

Easter nodded.

"I am so sorry. My cousin Rose Big Star is carrying one of his, too."

Easter glared at her. "Are you certain?"

"Why would I lie?"

Easter struggled to her feet. "It was a good thing they killed him out there or I would have killed him myself for lying to me."

Lily looked more shocked as Easter's mom stood up and said, "We don't need to make any more gossip or threats for the entire world to hear, my dear. Tonight you and I will tell Father and make plans."

"Mother, he will be so mad at me."

"No. You are his only living child. He worships you. He will worship the boy, too, when he comes."

"You know you are having a boy?" Lily asked, wide eyed.

"Some things you know in your heart," Easter's mother said.

"Oh, Easter, I hated to tell you about him, but you needed to know."

"Yes, and I am grateful. Quietly tell your cousin I am sorry for her, too," Easter said.

"Oh, I will." Lily took her hands and squeezed them. "May the Great Spirit be with you and with him, too." She meant the one in Easter's belly.

"I hope so. Thanks, Lily."

Her mother turned to Easter. "Rest here a moment; I will get my things and we can go home."

"Oh, Mother, I hate to tell Father my plight."

"Don't hate anything. Charles is an understanding man when you get past his crusty side." She handed her a hanky made from an old bed sheet. Skirt in hand, Jenny Coble went up the steps and inside for her items.

Lily had gone on, too.

What would she do? No man to marry and support her newborn. How had she ever been so dumb to let him love her that cold night? He did the same exact thing to Lily's cousin. Another ignorant stupid country girl probably just like her, and him convincing two of them to let him sow his wild oats inside both of them before he ran off.

Well, she'd know from here on that it took very little for a man to plant a seed in her body. Little good that knowledge would do her at this point in time. His lies, his fabrications, all came back to her. He either practiced his prepared speech on Lily's cousin or her. Either way they'd worked for him.

All her dreams and plans evaporated into the cloudy sky. Someone was talking to her, and she turned to see that a great stallion and a blond-headed man—Hiram—on his horse had stopped right beside her. One thing was certain. He wouldn't make that mistake again, to stop and talk to her when he learned the news that she had a breed in her belly.

"Your name is Easter, right?"

With her hand she shaded her eyes against the bright overhead sun. "Yes, and you are Hiram O'Malley."

He bounded off his horse. "Glad we have that straight now. I must warn you that gangs are raiding again, and I want you and your folks to be ready in case they raid your place."

"We will try our best. Mother is in the store."

"I wanted to talk to you if I may. You've been crying. Is it serious?"

She shook her head. He could not be interested in her problems, not in the least. And if he knew her true condition he'd spur that great horse and ride off as fast as he could, to get away from such a wanton woman. Soon everyone would know about the foolish whore from Cincinnati. She couldn't be seen in public. Shunned for her sinful ways and to be avoided by all good men. But, not knowing, he simply stood there before her with his hat off.

"I am going to ask. Would you go to a social at Cane Hill with me next Saturday night?"

"No."

"Why not?"

"I can't say, sir."

"I have honest intentions."

He would not be convinced of anything she told him. So damn persistent. She finally leaned over and jerked him by the sleeve up close. "Because I am pregnant."

He looked at her so funny and asked, "Who is the lucky man?"

Damn him anyway. "He's dead."

"Then you have no excuse not to attend that social with me. I am alive."

"Why would you want a-ah stained woman?"

"Easter, we both live in a violent world. I lost my own wife six months ago. She drowned in a river and I couldn't save her. You have lost your man and I bet you could not have saved him, either."

"But you were married to her."

"I will be by your place for you about four thirty Saturday with a buggy. That is a nice enough dress for you to wear to that event. Now will you go with me?"

Before she could answer him her mother walked up, obviously hearing his words.

"Easter, tell the nice man your wishes, please."

Her hands clasped before her, she broke them apart. "Mother, I already told him I was with child. He won't listen to me."

"I heard, ma'am. Her ex had died and I would not take that as an excuse."

"We learned that only thirty minutes ago—here. Easter, tell the man yes or no."

"If he's that hardheaded I will go with him."

"There, Mr. O'Malley, she will attend your social."

"May I be presumptuous?" he asked.

"How is that?" Jenny asked, amused at his insistence.

"I want to kiss both of you on the forehead for being so generous with me."

"Won't bother me, sir."

He kissed her mother and smiled, then turned to Easter.

She shook her head in disgust. "Go ahead. Chances are good you'd do it anyway."

After his quick kiss, which still burned on her forehead like a brand, he leaped into the saddle, reined his horse around, mentioned some things he must do, and repeated the time that he'd be there for her on Saturday evening. Anything past noon was evening in Arkansas.

"Well, now he knows; let's go tell your dad and hope he is so forgiving."

"Mother, I was not bragging I swear. He was so persistent for an answer, I told him my condition." She threw her hands up like tossing chicken feed. "That didn't bother him one bit. He is a tough man to tell no to."

"Remember that Saturday night when you go with him."

"What could it hurt? He can't get me with child. I already am that."

"My dear, you are not some scarlet woman."

"Who decides that?"

"The man you might marry."

"He's not going to marry me. Not him. I don't believe he wants to marry anyone."

"Just sit tight on your butt and keep your legs crossed."

"I will try."

Their talk with her father went smoothly enough. They never mentioned Lily's cousin's similar condition, only that Norton had been killed. They did tell him about Hiram and the invitation, and that, even with him knowing the information of her condition, it had not shocked O'Malley away from asking her out.

"I can hardly believe you told him and never told me?"

"I was coming home to tell you, Father. That straw-headed gentleman would not take no even after I told him."

"I can see why he would not take no for an answer."

"Why?" She frowned at him.

"Easter, baby and all, you have blossomed into a lovely young woman. His last wife drowned, and he sees in you the beauty I see in you. Jenny looked like you when I married her."

"But she was not with another man's child."

"I really think he is a frank, honest man. But you will learn more about him, right?"

"Saturday night. The first time he hugs me he will realize and know for sure, won't he?"

"I am sure then he will."

"I am sorry I hid this from you, Father. I was

ashamed but I believed Norton would come back rich and marry me. I am a dumb stupid daughter who could not wait or listen. I must pay the price, but I thank you for your support and your promise to help me and my son when he comes."

On Saturday evening, O'Malley drove up with two fancy, sparkling black horses and a luxurious buggy to take her to Cane Hill. Easter's dress, washed and ironed, looked very nice on her. Her mother pinned her hair up, and the black wool shawl would keep her warm going and returning.

She knew, when his powerful hands were on her waist to easily lift her up on the buggy seat, he could tell her son was hiding there. But he was unshaken by anything, and once Easter was safe on the seat, he waved at her parents, ran around the buggy to the other side, and took command of the horses.

"Well, how are you today?" he asked.

"I feel like a fairy-tale princess sitting high up here on this seat and those wonderful horses pacing along to the jingle of the harness taking me to a castle in the Alps."

"You write storybook fables?" he asked.

"No, but these are not your horses or rig are they?"

"No. I borrowed them to impress you as to how serious I am."

"I am impressed. I never saw a rig this nice or fancy on the road before in my life. Be careful. If we wreck it you will spend the rest of your life repaying the owner."

"I could have hired a driver, but I wanted us alone to talk with no one around. I have no crazy ambitions or needs, but I feel you need to know that nothing in your past bothers me—tomorrow will be a new day and I hope we can walk hand in hand down the path of life together. I knew that day I saw you in the garden, I wanted to know you better."

"You don't understand it all."

"I know you told me he, like my Ruthie, is gone. So the living must continue."

"I agree, but he was a Cherokee. His son—" He'd swapped the reins to his other hand and put his finger softly on her lips to silence her.

"His son will be our son, red or white. Our son. I will never let him know he isn't mine and yours. And when he is grown I will tell him or you can tell him about his true father. That is not an issue for me. If you have children that are half out of their heads, you love them. His skin color will not bother me."

"Hiram O'Malley, you are so persistent that I am beginning to believe all you are saying."

"Good. When will you become my wife?" He halted the team where the road passed through some dense hardwood forest.

She blinked her eyes at him in utter disbelief at his words. "I have no idea."

"There will be a minister there tonight. Marry me tonight. We can go back and tell your folks we are married and go home to my house and farm."

"You have not even seen me and what I look like. You may be shocked."

"Why?"

"I look horrible." She searched both ways and found the road hidden by woods, and no one stirred. She unbuttoned her dress, then raised the slip to show him. "My bulging belly is disgusting to look at. I saw it so in the mirror in Mother's room."

"May I touch it?"

"I guess that won't hurt him, but don't you see how ugly my body is?"

"Oh, honey." He swooned. "It is gorgeous." His calloused hands were softly running over all her skin. His fondling of her belly almost made her sick. She couldn't understand his joy.

"Marry me?" he said, sounding excited.

"You will regret it all your life."

"Never. Never. Never."

"Folks will think we're crazy . . . What are you doing now?" she asked.

"Kissing your wonderful belly."

Oh, my God, he did, and she about peed. What a wild crazy man.

They were married an hour later. Two hours afterward they drove back and relayed the news to Easter's folks. They acted a little set aback but wished them good luck. Three hours later she was in his wonderful feather bed and she let him kiss her all over wherever he wanted. Here was where she also found out what real love was like—oh, she would always regret her one transgression from before, but she was so excited about the real man who loved her homely swollen belly and her. She thanked God that night for his deliverance of her from her sorrow and depression.

Hiram taught her how to shoot and load a .30-caliber Colt Paterson. She learned she had to cock the hammer back on the pistol to get the trigger exposed. It didn't take long before she could shoot it and bust all the bottles set on a rail fence. Her being alone worried him when he was gone trying to stop the raids by outlaws on country folks in western Washington County, Arkansas.

Her pregnancy went well and a midwife delivered her son easily.

Long John O'Malley was born on May 5th that year. The afterbirth was buried and the midwife sent home that evening. The baby boy was in the bed with them, but she knew Hiram wanted her and despite being sore, she wanted him. She decided not to say that she had heard that nursing a baby was good birth control, and good that she didn't. Nine months later, February 5th, in a snowstorm, her second son Harper Alan came in their world screaming. Another long baby son, with blond hair this time. Two babies nursing at the same time was enough for any woman, but she had the milk so they flourished.

Easter and Hiram couldn't be apart, but it was three months later when she realized that nursing two boys must have made for birth control. Apparently God said that was enough. They laughed about it but kept trying for more though none ever came. Both sons, at age six, went to the first grade in the three months' school held in the one-room schoolhouse near their farm. But when the teacher moved on to another rural school, by the third year, Easter had already taught them to read aloud from the Bible, do the multiplication charts, and write in a good penmanship. They read every book they could find, beg, or borrow.

One day Easter was home alone. The boys and their dad had gone to buy a horse for one of them, when an outlaw came by and dismounted at the yard gate. She saw and appraised him out of the small window and immediately went for her loaded Colt Paterson.

He pounded on the door.

Holding the cocked pistol out ready, she warned him, "I am going to blow your head off if you come through that door."

"Bullshit, you whore—" He broke the door down and it fell inside on the floor.

She saw the shock written on his face as he saw the gun and right before the fiery blast came from the gun's muzzle. He wore the look of a man who really regretted what he'd both said and done. She shot him again in the chest before he slumped down in the doorway. With the room full of gun smoke, she decided to go out the back door of her house because she didn't want to step on him to get outside.

Later she harnessed their gentlest mule and

tied a lariat to the dead man's feet. She clucked to the mule, and Jasper began to drag him out of her doorway and to the yard gate, making sure he didn't block the gate. Unhooking the rope, she coiled it up, drove Jasper back to the barn, unharnessed him, and laid the harness in the hay. When Hiram and the boys came home, they could put it up on the holder. Then she turned Jasper loose in the pasture again, went back into the now smoke-free house, and finished her dishes. Hiram could fix the door, too.

Her men came running into the house shouting, "Who was he? Are you okay? What happened?"

"Some bad-mouthed man broke in my front door. I warned him I'd shoot him. Now he believes it. You boys can repair the door, and you need to hang up the harness that I used to drag him out to the gate."

"Why did he do that to you do you reckon?" Hiram asked her.

"He called me a whore. I knew he had the wrong house."

Her husband wrestled her into his arms. "Baby, he sure was at the wrong house."

Not long after that Hiram heard about Texas. Nothing could change his mind, so he sold their place and the four of them loaded up—lock, stock, and barrel—and headed there in two wagons. The homestead land Hiram found for them was west of Fort Worth right in Comanche country.

To tell the truth, in Easter's opinion, Texas was no richer farmland than Arkansas.

Those boys grew up fast. They became Texas Rangers at fourteen. Oh, they didn't go chasing down outlaws, they were part of a poop patrol on the outlook for Comanche that snuck down in their country and killed folks, kidnapped teens, and generally raised hell.

The brothers rode all around looking for scattered horse apples, which meant Comanche were in their midst. They learned quickly that a barefoot range horse stops to poop in a pile and an unshod Indian pony scatters his as his rider goes on. If that sign showed up, they and their neighbors were fixing to have a whole lot of trouble with war parties.

They wore .30-caliber Colts and had a Spencer under their stirrup. Of course by then the Civil War was on, and most of the men and even boys had been called up. Hiram and his team of rangers were left at home as point people to protect all the manless settler families living in their county. Hiram didn't like it, but someone needed to be in charge.

Coffee got so high priced they did without it. And sugar, too. Even cloth for new clothing became extinct.

One day, when the boys were attending a three-month school session, they came home all beat up, and one of Long's overall suspenders even had been torn loose. The sight of them shocked Easter. Black eyes, noses bloody, their clothes in rags.

Her hands on her hips she demanded to know what they had been doing.

"Mom, three grown men rode up and called Miss Shepherd a-a whore," Harper said. "And for her to come outside—I remembered the man called you that and made you so mad you shot him. Well, my gun was out on my horse, so me and Long went outside. We had to clean their plows."

"Who won?"

"We threw them on their horses and they left bawling," Long said.

"What did the teacher say?"

Harper answered. "She said she didn't think them men will be back."

Long nodded. "They got the worst of it from us I am sure."

"Let me dress your cuts and then you two change into some work clothes. I am sure I can fix these to wear again."

"Mom, there wasn't a thing else we could do."

"You boys did the right thing. I am just not used to seeing you two so beat up."

"They were big as Dad."

"I understand. Let's wash those cuts. I'm proud of you two. I bet the teacher is, too."

"Oh, she told us so," Harper said.

She was proud of her boys.

Around then, rumors started that the dreary war was going to soon be over and maybe things in everyone's lives would improve. Texas was broke and sinking. Hardly anything was on the shelves in stores, and what little could be found was at sky-high prices. No one had any money left. Hiram traded for another place farther from the persistent Comanche threat, to near Camp Verde above Kerrville.

A nearby rancher, Captain Emory Greg, had been by talking about taking a large herd of Texas cattle to the nearest railhead up at Sedalia, Missouri, and sell them as soon as the armistice was signed. But if the war did not end he said he thought he could get past those Federal troops who might stop him up around Fort Smith, Arkansas.

The former Confederate captain said that during the war they had eaten up every chicken and hog in both the north and south parts of the country. Yankees had money, and if they wanted meat it might as well be Texas beef. But the trip to Sedalia would not be an easy one. Lots of outlaw bands and free holders roamed the mountainous region of Arkansas and Missouri and would surely try to steal a large herd of cattle—or anything worth ten cents for that matter.

"Can he deliver them do you think?" Easter asked her husband.

He shrugged. "I don't guess that anything can't be done. And with enough good help he might get there and sell them for a profit."

She shook her head, bewildered. "Cattle sure are not worth ten cents apiece around here."

He hugged her and kissed her like he did all the

time even though she had been his wife for eighteen years. "We will survive."

Bless his heart, she decided, but when her two sons came home that night and told them both they were going to Sedalia, Missouri, in two weeks with the Greg herd, her heart stopped.

"You boys may be able to beat up some sorry ranch hands, but you two are not going to Missouri and get killed by angry Yankees," she told them.

"Aw, Ma, we are only going to herd some longhorns up there. The war is about over. Why Greg's going to pay us fifteen bucks a month if we get them up there."

"Who will bury you?"

"Ma," Long said in a voice she could hardly tell from his brother's, "we aren't getting killed. We're just going to be herding some cows."

She looked up at the underside of the split shingle roof for help. "Hiram! Tell them no."

He hugged her like he always did when he wanted to change her mind about something. "Darling, you have to let go of the boys some time, even when you don't want to, so they can fly from the nest."

"I don't want them to fly anywhere. They don't have wings to start with, and they'd need them to ever get those crazy cattle north of even where we came from."

"Aw, darling."

"Don't aw me." But even as he kissed her she knew

she'd lost another battle to this big burly man she loved so much.

Ten days later, teary eyed, she watched her only two wonderful sons ride off. That was the worst day in her entire life. She felt she might never ever see either of them again. Her husband hugged and kissed her. "Those boys are plenty tough to survive."

May God help them.

CHAPTER 1

Harper rode a red roan horse his father said was a Comanche buffalo-hunting pony. The powerful former stallion they'd neutered to save fighting with, as a stud was a tough enough horse. Harp, as his brother Long called him, felt comfortable he had the steed to carry him to Sedalia, Missouri. Both boys were wearing new shirts their mother made from pillow ticking material. She said it was the best material to last for the drive.

The memory of the tears on his mother's beautiful face still stabbed at Harp, but both he and Long were going north for good or bad. He reset the .30-caliber Colt in the holster on his hip. His father said the revolver was a plenty big enough hand gun, plus he could put five of the five bullets in a bouncing tin can with it, and with a larger gun he would need lots more practice to be that accurate with it. The lever-action Spencer rifle under his right leg was another weapon he knew all about. Stirrup to stirrup he rode beside his brother Long, headed for Captain Greg's ranch. They were going to be grown-ups soon and people would have to accept them as men.

"Long, what do you think Missouri will be like?"

"Mother said they've got more rain and the trees were bigger than Texas. I want to see them."

"What about those big rivers we have to cross?"

His older brother shrugged as if they'd be nothing. "We can swim. Lots of Texas boys sure can't do that."

"You reckon those cows can swim?"

Long shook his head. "There ain't a cow in the whole lot of them. They're all steers."

"Ah, you know what I meant."

"Yeah, I bet them steers naturally know how to swim."

Harp agreed and vowed he'd never say *cows* again. Among real cowhands he might sound dumb. Last thing that he wanted to happen was for anyone to think he was a dumb farm boy. They rode on to Greg's Bar 87 Ranch that day.

The place was abuzz with activity. They dismounted at the headquarters office. A man with a quirley in his mouth came out onto the large step. "You boys are the O'Malley brothers?"

"Yeah, where do you want us?" Long asked.

"The herd is two miles west. Report to Matt Simons. You've got bedrolls and war bags?"

"That's what they told us to bring," Harp said, patting them tied on behind his cantle.

"Good. Some boys coming ain't got nothin'. You

guys been around cattle, Simon needs both of you to hold them steers in a herd."

With everything said, the two O'Malleys turned their horses and rode west.

Harp heard the cattle bawling long before they rode out of the cedars into the meadow. Most were grazing and bawling between bites of grass. Their incisive loud calls hurt his ears, but like it or not he knew he'd hear them clear to Missouri. Several mounted herders on hard steering horses were trying to keep them contained in the large meadow. They found a rider about their age and asked him where the boss was.

He waved them north and took off after another wild steer headed for the brush. The horse the boy rode didn't look up to the job noted Harp. In disgust he shook his head and his brother agreed by making a disapproving face after the rider.

They found Simons. An older man with gray sideburns who greeted them and told them to unload their bedrolls and things in the second canvas-covered wagon. He had watched them ride in. "I am damn sure glad some real cowboys got here. When you get your things put up, I am going to split you two up. Harp, go right?"

"Yes, sir."

"Go help them, boys. I'll send some replacements later. Long, you ride north. Those boys up there are not cattle-wise at all. They ask, you tell them I said both of you are in charge and you tell them what they must do to keep them cattle together."

"Are there some better horses for them to ride?"

Harp asked him, pained about the mounts they had seen so far.

Simons shook his head. "Not many of them."

"If Mr. Greg's going to herd these cattle very far, he better find some." Harp shook his head in concern and parted with his brother.

Harp spent the rest of the day keeping the herd quitters in the large meadow. His buffalo horse could work circles around the mounts the rest of them rode. By late afternoon they finally had them settled down some. The steers were mostly lying down and chewing their cuds when Simons brought some fresh hands on more horses not ever used before for herding. Harp noted that about the mounts the moment they rode up.

"How did it go, Harp?" Simons asked him.

"None of them got away since I got up here, but if I didn't have Comanche here, I couldn't have held them."

"Simons, ain't there any trained horses like his?" a boy named Carl asked him.

"What you're riding is what we've got."

Carl dropped his head. "Man, you'll have a real mess coming when we hit the trail."

"Harp, you get some supper and a fresh horse. I'm putting you in charge of the night guard."

"Sir? How many men do I have to do that?"

"Oh, five or six. Why?"

"Will they all come in for supper?" Harp asked him, concerned how he'd meet them and figure it all out.

"Who will watch the herd?" Simons asked.

Harp pushed his lathered horse in closer. "Some need to sleep. How will I set up that order?"

"I guess ride by and tell them who stays and who goes to supper."

Harp had no idea how many men were even working on containing the herd. He told two to stay in that group and four to go eat supper and report to him when he got to camp. On the north side he found Long on his sweaty horse still busy working his section of the herd.

"How many guys are working here?"

"Why?" Long set his using horse down beside Harp.

"I am in charge of the night riders."

Long looked at him in disbelief. "How did you get that job?"

"Brother, I don't know that I want it, but I have it. Hell, Simons just handed me the job. Now you choose two to stay and tell them I will send replacements in a little while. The rest need to go get supper. They must report to me in camp. Meanwhile I'll start a list."

Long narrowed his dark eyes at his brother. "Good thing. He'd handed that job to me, I'd have shoved it up his ass."

"Long, that ain't no way to work for a man. I can see there is going to be lots more to this trip than I thought about as being our problems."

Warily, Long shook his head. "All the damn cheap horses in Texas and the boys have the scraps."

"You're right, brother, but now I need to make a list and figure this herd guard business out."

They had boiled beans for supper in camp. No

bread, no dessert. Harp took an instant dislike to the grubby-whiskered guy named Chester doing the cooking. He had the list of the hands named on a tablet.

> Randy Hamilton
> Chadron Turner
> Chaw Michaels
> Darvon Studdy
> Red Culver
> Carl Kimes
> Eldon Morehouse
> Kevin Doones
> Norm Savoy
> Doug Pharr
> Long O'Malley
> Harp O'Malley

Simons had gone somewhere, the camp cook told him, seated on a log and smoking another quirley. Harp was busting to ask him what was coming for breakfast after the sorry showing that he served that evening, but he kept the matter to himself. He did take the alarm clock, wound it, and set it for three hours to get his next shift out on time. Simons must have gone to town. No sight of him. Harp felt a little like he'd been abandoned. In an effort to make sure he had help, he'd saved the last shift for himself, Long, and Chaw, the only other real cowboy in his book.

The herd didn't run off, and dawn saw them back in camp for some watery oatmeal—nothing else.

When he assigned the crew to go ride herd, they all were disgruntled about the food. No Simons at noon, either. More plain brown beans for lunch.

"Harp, we're going to have to move them steers. They've eaten or shit on all the grass up there," Chaw told him, hunkered down on some run-over boot heels, making frowns at each spoonful of beans he shoveled into his mouth.

"I know it's bad food. I'll try and do something about it."

"I'd like to go north but I ain't going on this crap." Chaw rapped the metal plate with his spoon.

"Stay tight; I'm saddling up and going to where they hired us and ask some questions. If things aren't fixed, Long and I won't be staying, either."

Chaw nodded. "I'm with you two."

Harp saddled Comanche and rode back to Greg's outfit. No one was around and so he dismounted at the yard gate. A nice-looking woman in a blue dress came to the door. "May I help you?"

"Yes, ma'am, is Mr. Greg here?"

"No, he's gone to town on business. What's wrong?"

"You expect him back pretty soon?"

"Not very soon. Is something wrong?"

"Ma'am, I hate to worry you, but I was put in charge of the cattle drive, and the cook they hired is lazy and—ah, well—as sorry an excuse for one as I've ever seen. I haven't seen the boss in twenty-four hours, and the boys are beginning to get upset. I guess cowboys are worth about two bits today, but he might miss them when they all leave. And besides we've run out of grass for the steers and need to move them."

"What is your name?"

"Harp O'Malley, ma'am."

"I've met your mother—Easter?"

"Yes, ma'am."

"Well, she should be proud of you. You could explain all that and not cuss once."

He smiled, amused. "I know better than that, ma'am."

She straightened her shoulders. "Harp, I'm sending Emory, the minute he gets back, over to the herd. You will have results when he gets there."

"I didn't come to upset you."

"You didn't. But Emory will be displeased when he hears all that is happening."

Harp tipped his weather-worn felt hat and remounted his horse. On the trip back he short-loped him. Long cut him off short of camp. "You do any good?"

"Emory Greg is coming. Why?"

"Your boss come back drunk as a skunk. Asked where you were. I told him tending steers."

"Where's he now?"

"Snoring in his bedroll."

"I spoke to Greg's wife. He was in town on business. I mentioned the cook, the feed, and the men to her. The man who sent us up here was nowhere around."

Long made a scowl. "What did she say?"

"She said Greg'd be here when he got back."

"You reckon he will?"

Harp nodded, looking over the camp for Simons.

"He's over in the shade." Long pointed him out.

"Let him sleep." He dismounted and undid his saddle.

Scratching his belly, the cook came over. "The boss wondered where the hell you were, boy?"

"I don't work for you. Mind your own damn business."

"When he's not here I'm in charge." Chester rapped his chest with his fist, and in Harp's opinion that was a challenge. Without a word Harp stepped in and knocked the cook on his ass in a one-two punch. Chester never saw his fists coming until they struck him. Spilled on his ass, Harp pointed at him. "Load your gear and get the hell out of here."

"You can't fire me."

But then there were six cowboys with sticks in their hands backing up Harp. Chaw stepped in. "You heard Harp. We've had enough of your bad cooking. Load your ass up or we're lynching you, mister."

Chester took the hint, loaded his stuff in a tow sack—cussing under his breath—and left. Harp told three of the boys to wash the cooking utensils, rinse, and dry them while he mixed flour and baking powder. Long greased a Dutch oven for him. Carl had a sharp hunting knife he washed and then sliced bacon. Norm ground some beans for coffee. Another hand put on the water to boil, and they all acted like they were relieved at last to have that nasty cook gone.

"There's some dry apples and bugs in the supplies, will that make something sweet?"

Harp had Norm looking for supplies. Harp answered him, "Yeah, we can make something. Long, grease another Dutch oven for us to bake it in."

"Got her."

The baking powder, he hoped, would work in his dough. Some of his mother's own sour dough starter would be better, but they didn't have much choice in this case. The beans were almost boiled. Carl's bacon was frying. Using some of the grease, Harp was frying some chopped onions in a big skillet.

Long was tending the biscuits in the Dutch oven and the second one with Norm's slurry of dry apples, raisins, flour, sugar, water, and baking powder. Things were going all right in Harp's opinion. They took a break for some good coffee, and everyone stood around looking smug. He had his list of hands to replace the herders after they ate. Maybe the captain would get there shortly.

The biscuits worked, but in his case he decided his mother's were lots better. The fried onions and crisp bacon made the beans tolerable, and Norm's dessert wasn't café fine but they bragged on it. The herders coming in reported the herd was becoming more upset without much to eat. Those boys could hardly believe they'd run off the cook and had some real food. They were soon bragging on the grub when Captain Greg arrived.

He stepped off his horse and motioned to Harp. "What's going on up here?"

"We planned to wait for you, but we run off the cook and cooked ourselves supper."

"Anna said you told her he wasn't very good. Where is Simons?"

"Sleeping it off over there."

"Looks like you've handled it, Harp. What else?"

"We need to move the steers to better grass, and most of these horses are junk."

Greg chuckled. "Where should we go with the cattle?"

"North I guess. They're out of feed here," Harp said.

"We better ride up there and find a place in the morning."

Harp nodded. "We can do that. You have a lead steer?"

"No. Do we need one?"

Harp took off his hat. "Captain Greg, I wouldn't move that many cattle a mile without one."

"Emory is my name. I am certain I can find one. Can we move them to grass without one?"

"We can do about anything needed, but we will sure need a lead steer to go all the way to Missouri."

"I will find one. Now about the horses? These were all that I could find."

"They lied to you. My dad could find you some. These ones the boys are using are a sorry bunch."

"I know where your dad lives. He's got a lead steer, too, I bet."

"He does but he might not sell him."

"Can you and these boys move this bunch for me tomorrow?"

"What about Simons?"

"I'm going to fire him. You're the man in charge, Harp."

"So it's okay that we run off that dirty old man that only cooked beans and made watery oatmeal?"

"You done right. I don't blame you, and I am sure I can find a cook somewhere. You will have to handle it until then."

"We can do that. And there's some open country we can graze north of here. I just hope we can move them up there."

"On Liar's Creek?"

"Yes, sir."

"I know you can handle the men, the cooking, and move those steers north."

Harp had another point he needed to make. "Fine. One more thing. The food wagon's okay, but that one other sorry wagon you bought won't even make it to Fort Worth."

"I'll find a wagon to replace it."

"Good. We can handle the rest." Harp folded his arms while Greg walked over and nudged the sleeping Simons with his boot. "Simons! Get your ass up. You're fired."

"Huh?" Blinking and sitting up, he still looked drunk to Harp.

"You're fired," Greg said.

"Why you—"

"Don't say anything. I may kill you. If it hadn't been for these boys here I might have lost my herd."

On his feet, Simons wasn't even steady, but by

then Greg was on his horse. Mounted, he said, "Get the hell out of my camp."

Simons went off grumbling and cursing all of them. Harp ignored him, talked to the men about the night shifts and moving the cattle. His plans included for Long to ride up early to look over the way north to the open country where he wanted to move the herd to starting in mid- morning. Things were set and they were all laughing over their success at shaping up the outfit while they finished off Norm's dessert.

Harp shook his head, thinking about all the things he had to do if this job continued. *Going to be a helluva drive to ever get this shirttail outfit to Missouri.*

CHAPTER 2

Sun rose. Long and Carl Kimes rode out, eating some leftover biscuits, to find some grass north of the site. Harp headed up the crew, making flapjacks and homemade syrup with coffee for the men. The five cowboys who rode out to replace the night guard and keep the cattle in the herd were promised breakfast relief before they had to begin the move. Things were getting done.

Two hours later Long and Carl were back. The first riders sent out were back to eat breakfast and were warned they'd not have lunch due to the day's work ahead. In a quick huddle Harp made the two scouts his point riders and sent them back to get the move started. Two guys in camp were going to wash the dishes, load the wagons, and move to the new location. Harp put a slender boy, Holy Wars, who'd showed lots of horse sense, in charge of the horse herd. He had the draft animals harnessed and would help them get to the new site. Holy Wars would bring along his remuda, too.

Harp saddled Comanche and rode out to the herd. He hoped the crew could move them. Individual steers were butting heads, mixed with others they did not know, deciding what his father called *a pecking order*. Once the cattle decided which steer to follow, all that would pass. But he warned the boys about the cattle that came out of the brush; they were wild as deer and any loud noise might cause the whole group to stampede. He didn't need that to happen.

Harp told the nearby cowboys that Long and Carl would try to start the herd and for them to push the cattle easy moving to the north. The boys agreed with him so he left, rounded the herd, telling the others they were moving and that they needed to hold them as a herd. The bawling cattle were finally on the move.

At this point it looked like they were going north in a mass. They needed a lead steer with a bell that would direct them where the cowboys wanted them to go. He hoped the boss found one before they really moved too far along the way.

At last he set Comanche down and watched the flow. The cattle had improved a lot by not doing so much head butting or breaking for freedom. New feed would help settle them down, but they really needed to get started on the drive to Sedalia.

An hour later the wagons and horses went past him. Harp checked with Doug Pharr who was taking charge of that operation and driving the first wagon. Harp rode alongside him.

"We know a well up there where we can get fit

drinking water. We'll get set up there and have food started. The herd looks like it's moving good."

Harp agreed, reined up, and rode back to the herd. Red Culver caught him. "This is going better than I figured."

"So far. I think we can move them north all right. Greg finds a lead steer and we will get some more things ironed out."

"Hey, a bunch of us are backing you. Firing that cook took nerve. Thanks."

"We'll see."

Red waved and hurried off to catch a few quitters in the herd.

If Red'd had a real horse—*damn this was a mess fixing to blow up.* He chased another back in and things leveled off.

They were moving into an area that opened into a large grassy meadow that had water. The cattle could spread out to graze and drink. Harp went to find his wagon setup and the bawling grew farther away from him. He saw the canvas top and pushed Comanche on up there.

His cooking crew was unloading things to get started. Doug had pulled a bucket out of the well. He used a dipper to draw a drink, tasted it, and nodded. "We have some good water tonight. Plenty of fuel here, too."

"I think the cattle will be fine. How is that worn-out wagon?" Harp asked.

Doug shrugged. "Worn out."

Harp agreed. Before Long rode in to check with

Harp, he told half the boys to go into camp with him and help getting it set up.

"Well, we made it. What, four or five miles?"

"Hmm," Long snuffed at him. "Take three years to ever get to Sea-dalia at that speed."

"Things went pretty smoothly. How could they go better?" Harp asked him.

"If we had a bell steer they'd fall in when they learned what that bell means ringing."

"The boss is trying to find one. I also mentioned better horses. Told him Dad knew where they were. The boys said the old wagon made it. Captain said he'd find a better one."

"This going to be the crew?" Long asked quietly.

"Looks that way. You, me, and him. He never mentioned finding anyone else. I don't know who was at his house and talked to us. I thought he was part of it—must not be."

Long agreed. "Well, I thought he had some war veterans or someone knew the way. He come back from the war after he got wounded didn't he?"

"Yes. I heard the bullet was too close to his heart and they couldn't remove it."

"He looked all right yesterday didn't he?"

"He was fine. But he's been planning this for over a year. He says they're real short on meat to eat both North and South. If we can get these steers on a train and shipped to somewhere they could bring a big price."

"God will have to help us do it." Shaking his head, disgusted, Long went for a drink.

The cooking had begun. The boys had things rolling and it looked good. They made some cinnamon rolls in a Dutch oven to tide them over.

The boss man arrived in mid-afternoon. Harp met him and noticed he looked paler than Harp recalled when he talked to them a week or so earlier.

"Well, a cook is coming. He's army material but seems sensible. His name is Ira Smith. My brother-in-law Ken has another wagon to replace the wobbly one." The captain sat down on a log. "Harp, there is lots to do. I thought I was ready a week ago. You think that most of them boys will stay with us?"

"Rest a minute." Harp settled down on his haunches; he could tell the man had been pushing himself too hard. "Yes. They'll stay with a decent cook and we get the other things ironed out."

"I saw your dad. He's trying to round up two dozen more ranch horses for me. He also says we can use his big blue steer if you boys will bring him back."

"We need to go get him?"

"No. He's bringing him and those horses in two days."

"Good, then I think the boys will be fine. They tell me they'll stay if we get a good cook."

Emory jabbed his thumb in his chest and made a face that showed he was in pain.

"That bullet hurting you?"

"It does from time to time. Guess I've been doing too much to get things going."

Harp agreed. Somehow the man had to take it easier or he'd not make the whole trip.

He asked his boss, "We have not talked to you about the route we will take. Do you have maps?"

"Just hand-drawn ones. We head north. Go west of Fort Worth and swing in on the Butterfield Road up through the Indian Territory around Fort Smith. Then north through Arkansas Boston Mountains; through Fayetteville, Arkansas; to Cassville, Missouri. On the plains above the Missouri line we head east. When we get to Springfield we head north to Sedalia."

"That is the railhead?" Harp asked.

"Yes. They shut down all the railroad building for the war. The other one up there is at Rolla. But it is way over. Lots of mountains and hard to get through that way."

"Missouri was about halfway either side during the war wasn't it?"

"Yes, lots of support for both sides and know we will meet some opposition going up there. I have two dozen forty-caliber new Winchester rifles in the old wagon and the ammo for them. I don't want war, but I don't want to be denied a chance to market those steers."

"My opinion is to get those men familiar with those rifles. So if the day comes to push or shove we are prepared to handle the matter."

"Good idea. I am not going north to pick a fight, but the delivery and sale of those cattle is my business."

"I understand. You have plans to hire anyone else?"

"I think you and Long can handle it. You both are

educated. I spoke to your father earlier. I know he is a leader, and he told me you boys were as good as him at getting things done. He said with the Comanche still on the prowl out there, someone must stay home to defend the ranch and your mother."

Harp agreed with a wary shake of his head. "Long and I know all about that big bell steer. It'll be driving him home that will be the real task."

"I promised we'd get him back."

"Yes, sir. You say he's bringing more horses, too?"

"He says up to twenty or so head. The best I could do."

Harp agreed. "That will help."

"They left that bullet in me, too close to my heart they said, and warned me it could dislodge and then I might be in dire danger of dying. If anything goes wrong on this trip, I want you and Long to finish the job and get the money that is hers back to my wife, Anna. And all the rest involved in this will need to be paid as well. Harp, I want to teach you all I know about dickering over cattle prices if I am not here. I hope I'll be doing that. There is nothing I want more than to come home with money that will provide for my family's future."

"We also want you there and to come back."

"I am a realist. There is a chance I won't and then it lies with you boys. I consider you two men. Secure the money. Folks will know you took cattle up there and received money for them. You will be like an open-door bank and they will rob or try to rob you, make no mistake. These are the most desperate times in this country I have ever seen, and trust me, peace will make them even more desperate."

"Emory, Long and I will do what is necessary. Go sleep for a few hours. I can set that new cook on the right course and then you go home and be with your wife. If we need more food, I can get it from Kerrville—Mr. Yost at the mercantile, right? You explained to him who I am?"

"Yes. He's another man we will have to pay when we return."

"No problem. Just to be sure I got the plan right . . . in two days we start for Fort Worth and swing west around there to get on the Butterfield Stage Road headed north?"

"Exactly right; that is the plan."

"Good. Long and I will do the rest. Now, I ain't got any cooties. Use my bedroll; get some sleep. The O'Malley brothers are here."

"You two aren't really brothers are you?"

"Yes, we are. Long's father got killed buffalo hunting. Mom married my dad, Hiram, up in Arkansas before Long was even born. I came nine months later. We're like twin brothers. Only thing he can do better than me is put a hand ax in a tree at a greater distance than I can. But we can both shoot the eyes out of squirrels and wild turkey on the wing. Not bragging but we are the O'Malley brothers from Camp Verde, Texas. We've been authorized as Texas Rangers since we were fourteen, patrolling for Comanche. Read, write, and been to school. We can handle it."

"I never doubted it a minute. I'll get me a little sleep. You two are the top men."

When Long rode in, Harp told him the entire story. When he finished, his brother shook his head. "Harp, you know how hard it will be to get that damn bell steer home from up there?"

"I know, but Dad may whup our butts if we don't bring him back." Amused by the notion, Harp laughed at their situation.

Long shook his head in disgust. "I wouldn't have agreed to that under any circumstances."

"Well, we've got him anyway. Start training another point man to take your place. You're going to scout ahead for the drive."

Long moved his head in a circle. "I've never been up there."

"You will have when this is over. Trust me, you will have been."

"He sleeping?" Long gave a head toss in that direction.

"Yes, he's kind of done his self in all this getting ready."

With the hard look that was his brother's habit when considering things, he finally nodded. "We can handle it."

"That's what I told him. Dad did, too."

"Hell, then, brother, we better do it."

Three of their cowhands wore the remains of their service in the Confederate Army. Gray forage caps of soldiers and the shirt or someone else's gray uniform shirt. One by one he'd need to redress them. It wasn't he cared one way or the other, but moving north they'd become a point of contention with people who'd fought against that side. Harp had no ideas what friction they'd face over their origin, but he wanted no remains to flaunt at them. Their drawl alone might be enough to start a new war.

One thing he knew damn good and well, even if a peace accord was signed, some folks would never be over fighting that conflict. He had to start on Chaw first. He was one of them that wore that gray brand.

Emory had recovered some. He thanked Harp for recommending the rest and promised to return before they set out.

After supper Harp took Chaw aside. "Chaw," he said to the man's back, busy pissing in the bushes. "Did Long tell you my plans?"

"He mentioned something to me this afternoon." He finished and buttoned his fly.

"We are picking another man to ride point with you. Long is going to be our scout."

"You have anyone you thinking of?"

"You have someone for us to talk to?"

"Let me think on it." He reset the cap on his head.

"That's another thing. We're going right into the heart of Yankee country with these steers. It will be bad enough to be Texans, but I don't want another war. You earned those clothes you have on, but we ain't wanting or having another battle.

I want you and the other boys with uniform parts to find a hat and a plain shirt. Save these to show your kids someday. You earned every thread in them, but it would be like carrying the Confederate flag at the head of the herd to ride up there in those partial uniforms."

"You make sense to me. I'll talk to the other two. The steers will be enough to handle. I'm glad you saw it. I'd worn it till it was threadbare. Like you said, I earned the right but we may have holy hell getting these bawling bastards up there anyway. I looked on a map and that place ain't fur from Iowa is it?"

"If you boys ain't got a change of clothes I will buy some."

"We may have to do that. I bet there ain't twenty cents in any of our pockets."

"Let me know. I thought they'd listen to you more than me."

"I'll be thinking about that guy you want for point rider. Long said your dad had some good horses he was bringing?"

"Yes. You point men will need them."

"That sounds good, too."

Later he told Long about talking to Chaw.

"That was smart. I bet he handles it and no one gets their backs up over it. Bro, you are learning things that we've never been challenged by before. Good going. You get your new cook lined out. I'd say if he'd take the point job, Doug Pharr is smart enough to do that job with Chaw."

"He gets things done quietly."

"And he ain't afraid to work, either."

Harp nodded. "Emory said the cook he hired would be here shortly."

"Good. I'm getting some sleep now. You've got me on the last shift in the night."

Harp nodded. He wanted someone alert with the herd about then.

Two men showed up the next morning after breakfast. They were ranchers from east of San Antonio—Mike Beersley and Stafford Collins. Beersley was a big man and Collins obviously had some money. He was dressed more businesslike.

"We came to talk to Emory. We heard he was going to try and get by the Yankee forces to sell his beef at the railhead. Is that true?"

"He's not up here yet today, but that's our plan. Emory used to be a captain and he says that during the war they ate up all the chickens and hawgs left in the United States. The north has money, so they might as well eat some Texas beef."

"Where do you think they will stop you?"

"Emory told my brother and I the first place may be up around Fort Smith."

"How are you going up there?"

"Drive up west of Fort Worth, then take the Butterfield Stage Road north to Missouri. Then at Springfield, Missouri, go north to Sedalia. He thinks Rolla, the other railhead, is in tougher country to reach at that point."

"Why, you talk like you've been up there," Collins said.

Harp nodded. He wasn't bragging that was the route.

Beersley asked, "He ever tell you what he expects them steer to bring up there?"

"Right now he says from forty to sixty dollars apiece."

Beersley whistled through his teeth. "A thousand steer is sixty thousand bucks."

Harp shook his head. "We expect to deliver around eight hundred head."

Collins nodded slowly. "That means you have to get them there. You look mighty young to be ram-rodding this outfit."

"He tried a drunk in charge."

"I guess that answers our questions. He's a brave man starting out. If you get to the Arkansas border, they confiscate the herd as enemy property."

"They might try that. Most of the guys with us have seen action either fighting Comanche or Yankees, so we don't aim to have that happen. But it might."

"If you make it and can sell them, you will make Texas history," Collins said, sounding like the deal had impressed him. "We need some way to make money in this poor state, and these wild cattle may pave the way. Good luck and nice to meet you. I hope someday I can tell my grandkids that I shook the hand of the first drover to get through."

Harp hoped it turned out that way, too. The two men rode off.

Harp set in to check on how much his employees

knew about the Winchester rifles that Emory had bought. He had all the guys left in camp gathered and he explained to them the gun's features.

"You side-load bullets in it, cock the lever, and it loads the bullets. These are forty-four-caliber rim fire bullets, and when we issue the guns we will give you bullets. I hope to hell we don't ever need them, but if we do you will appreciate having a smooth-action gun that fires bullets until the next day. You boys need to count your bullets, too. Reload at any break. They told me fighting Comanche, if you can't hit a buck, kill his horse. Afoot he'll be easier to kill. Any questions?"

"We going to carry them?" one boy asked.

"I think we will issue them if we have problems. We aren't an army. We ain't going north to fight a war. We're delivering cattle. I don't want to appear like an army save that we need to be looking like one to protect our jobs. Only way we will get paid is deliver steers to a market and collect the money, not fighting a war that's done been lost. We are not going there for revenge. We are selling cattle and that is our only purpose. Everyone savvy?"

No one questioned his words. He noted that all the gray shirts and caps were gone, too.

One of the younger boys came by. "Mr. O'Malley, how soon we leaving?"

"Next day or so. Why?"

"Just wondering. No one acts like they know. I thought you'd have the day."

"Soon. Very soon."

Emory rode up and joined them. Harp told him

he sent two boys after the supplies Doug listed as needed and they would be back the next day. He mentioned the two men coming by asking questions. Then he said, "They haven't got the nerve, themselves."

Harp shook his head, then mentioned Collins's last words. "He said we would make Texas history if we made it."

Emory smiled. "I hope so, too."

"I took the liberty of asking the men who wore Confederate uniforms to change. I didn't want anyone to think we were still fighting. They agreed and that is now all settled."

"That is great thinking. I'd never thought about that. You're right. We aren't war scavengers; we are Texas cattlemen on a mission. What else?"

"I explained about our rifles to half the men. I will tell the rest later today. The rifles will be in the cook's wagon unless we need them. I don't want us to bristle with guns unless we need them."

"You're doing fine. The cook will be here late today. I went his bail. Guess he went on a bender when I gave him a few dollars to settle things so he could leave."

"If we have to, we can dry him out."

"I wish I'd had you in my company in the army. You'd made a helluva non-com."

"Dad, Long, and I were shooting Comanche. We could have used you as well."

"I heard about that, too. Good. I am hopeful we make it and don't have a skirmish, but I am like you . . . be prepared to be challenged."

Late that evening their father and three other neighbors brought the lead steer and twenty head of good horses. Doug fed them and they visited up into the night.

"Boys," Hiram said to the assembled men at the campfire, "I been wishin' I was going along with the likes of you. These boys, I call them, have protected me backside since they were twelve. But their mother needs someone around and me neighbors do, too. You all have a safe trip and find us a market for these longhorns. We all could use some money in our pockets to jingle. God be with you all and see yeah when yeah get back 'cher."

The crewmembers in camp gave him a cheer.

Harp had expected a lecture on them returning his steer. Shame that Long was asleep but he'd tell him. Be different, not having his father to tell them what to do with all his experience he used outsmarting a war party or getting hostages back.

The toughest time Harp could recall was when the three of them were trapped in a buffalo wallow for three days until they shot enough bucks that they finally left them alone. But they had to walk a long ways out since their own horses had been shot. Times out there he didn't expect to ever see the home place or their mom again.

Later on he told Long about their father's speech and him not mentioning that steer's return, either.

"He must've forgot we had him. But he's not about to forget us for not bringing him back I can tell you that now."

They laughed over it.

"The cook is coming. Doug Pharr is interested in the point man position."

"When do we roll?"

"In a day I guess. Why don't you look north tomorrow and find a place we can camp that first night. Note any problems."

"Those boys can watch the herd. I'll take Carl along . . . he's got good eyes."

"Do that."

"I keep thinking, what did we forget?"

Harp nodded. "Me too. But it will slap us in the face on the road I guess."

"Right. I'll be up for the morning shift. Talk more later."

Harp's shoulders felt stitched together. They were tight and made his neck hurt. His mind kept hitting blind corners. Maybe being on the move would ease some of that, but somehow he felt it would pain him all the way to Sedalia. In his bedroll at last he finally fell asleep.

But what did we leave out?

CHAPTER 3

Harp and Emory traced and retraced a route on the maps spread out on the board table, under the flapping canvas shade, of how to come out west of Fort Worth. That would be a month. Then they'd have the stage route to follow to where they crossed the Red River and use it up through the Indian Territory to Fort Smith. On the far side of the Arkansas River at Fort Smith, they'd go north on the Butterfield route to Cassville, then over to Springfield. From there take the main road that went north to Sedalia, Missouri, and the railhead.

It looked easy on paper. But he could imagine all the problems they'd have from weather and people still wanting to resurrect fighting all over again. But they would make it. He had no doubt about that whatsoever.

"Tomorrow we roll out?"

Emory agreed. They had a long road to go. Conditions and people would get no better.

There was something in the air the first morning.

Harp tried to spell it out. Was it the excitement of at last going north? Every hand was excited. Even his buffalo horse was fidgety when he saddled him. The new cook Ira Smith would do. He made a great breakfast. Doug was now set to ride point with Chaw. They were already out there and both knew the way for the next day. The wagons were loaded and rolling. Long had described to Ira the next night's campground. The six-foot-tall cook knew the place.

An hour out, Long left Doug in place as right point rider, and with Chaw on his left set out to find the second night's camp. Harp studied the big blue steer out in front leading, with the ringing bell on the great belt around his neck. He reined up and moved his horse aside to let the long line pass. They were going north.

Cowboys keeping the herd in place—together. Following each other's tails like oxen yoked together for their lives to pull freight wagons and plows. Hard as it was to believe they were finally bound for Missouri with him and Long in charge— *The O'Malley Brothers from Texas.*

CHAPTER 4

On the seventh day they crossed the Colorado River west of Austin. That was their first big crossing. Blue took to the river and swam to the north bank, climbed out, shook off lots of water, and was welcomed by some punchers already over there. The herd followed, swimming over and assembled with little problem. The two wagons went to Web's Ferry to cross. Harp sent Emory on his horse with them, and they all met up a few miles north of the crossing at the day's camp.

Under a shade tree in camp that afternoon Emory was seated in a canvas folding chair. He motioned to the other one for Harp.

"We have had a good week."

"Yes. We lost one horse in the crossing. I told the boys to take the tie downs off them. They will know better at the next one."

"How?" Emory asked.

"The boy that didn't listen is doing double herd night patrol for two weeks."

Emory nodded his approval. "Rank requires decisions. We are moving along well."

"But we are still deep in Texas. Over half this journey will be on the North's land. Those days I dread."

"There is a saying, 'Dread not. It may never come.'"

"Hell, Emory, I've been around long enough to know you have to be prepared. Our father made several trips to trade with the Comanche for a captive prisoner. We rode along. There was always trouble. But we fought and won. He said they were savages. And they were."

"His lessons tell on you and Long."

"I hope they do when we have to face opposition."

"It will."

It did.

A big man in a suit under a fine beaver hat rode into camp the next day. With him were three *pistoleros*, no doubt to back and protect him.

"Who runs this sorry outfit?" he said, looking around like Harp wasn't even there.

"I'm the trail boss."

"Well, gawdamn, boy. You must just be out of grade school."

"Mister, state your business or get your ass out of my camp."

"Hey, young fellar. My name's Hogan Sargent and I own the Three Star Ranch. All the land north of here is mine, and I don't want your scrubby stock passing over it. You understand?"

"Is it fenced?"

"I said it was my land. Detour this herd west five miles."

"That ain't the Texas way, Mr. Hogan Sargent. If it's not fenced I can pass over it."

"Not and live."

"Oh? I will cross that ground north in the morning."

"I said—"

"Mr. Sargent, there are six Winchester rifles loaded and ready to send you to the promised land. All of you, drop your pistols with two fingers. Dismount now."

"You won't get away with this," Sargent blustered, but they obeyed.

Harp pushed him aside and told the *vaqueros* to remove their boots. Again they obeyed. "Now you start walking south. Go back to Mexico. Don't come back to Texas, 'cause I'll kill you next time you get in my way."

"Take the bridles off their horses and shag them back north, boys. They will go home." They did so and the horses rushed away.

"What about me?"

"Rest easy, Mr. Sargent. Tomorrow you are going to lead us across your ranch for our safety. We get off it you can go home—on foot."

"My men will—"

"No. 'Cause you will be the first man to die. Sit down, Mr. Sargent. They may ride along but they won't dare do a thing. Do you understand?"

"You son of—"

"Finishing that will get you killed. My mother is a God-fearing woman who lives near Camp Verde."

"I'll have you arrested for this."

"No jury will find me guilty moving cattle over unfenced land."

"Then I'll kill you with my bare hands."

"I've killed Comanche, Mr. Sargent, and you won't be one damn bit harder to kill."

Harp moved far enough away from Sargent but close enough to watch him. Long came and sat cross-legged on the ground. "What did he do?"

"Came told me I had to drive the cattle five miles around his land. I sent his *pistoleros* back to Mexico on foot. He's going to walk with us tomorrow until we get across his land."

"What then?"

"I guess turn him loose and go on."

"What if his men come to get us?"

"I guess we do like we did the Comanche. Kill them, too."

Long nodded and bound to his feet, looked at Sargent, and motioned to Chaw. "Chaw, select two men to take shifts and guard him. If he tries anything, shoot him. He's paid for."

"You can't—"

Long swung around with a finger as a gun, pointing at him. "You have no voice in this deal, mister. Shut up or we'll gag you."

"Who in the hell do you think you are?"

Long reached over and jerked the big man to his feet. Then he drew back to hit him. Instead he dropped him. "We are the O'Malley brothers of Texas and don't you forget it."

He left him and then walked over and put his arm around Harp's shoulder. "How is Emory doing?"

"They fed him and he went to bed. Said the day wore him out. He may need to ride in the food wagon tomorrow to rest up."

"He won't like that. But we'd better enforce it."

"How's tomorrow night's campsite look?"

"It will do. They say we're two days at our speed from the Brazos."

"We will be there by then. The spring grass is making the cattle fat." Harp poured himself a cup of coffee. "The boys wasted no time getting them guns when we needed them to back us. Things worked like a clock."

"Yeah. We could use some rain. But no storms."

Harp agreed.

"They'll be even quicker next time we get threatened. I took that boy off double guard duty. He's the one organized things with the crew here tonight."

"That's good."

"Good night, bro."

"Same to you."

They fed their prisoner in the morning, loaded him bareback on a sluggish horse, and took him along, grumbling. When they reached their next site, he agreed they were off his place. They gave him his horse and pistol back. He left telling them they had not seen the last of him.

Long shouted after him, "We better have."

That night it rained. Hard. Most of the lightning was north of them and the cattle were held in the herd, but Harp had extra hands circling them. In the morning they wore slickers and went on. The Brazos River was swollen and muddy, but they crossed it all right and made camp north of it. The two wagons took a ferry downstream. Emory rode with the cook and said he got along fine.

Harp told his brother they needed to make him ride the wagon more often. Long agreed. But Emory was back in the saddle the next day when the sun came out. Over the following few days the big news came that Robert E. Lee had signed the treaty at a place no one knew—Apple-Mattox.

Harp told Emory he had been right and that now the damn war was finally over. "I know you fought in it. But there's no telling how the country could ever be like it was before."

Ira had gotten hold of a secondhand newspaper from a man at the ferry crossing, so Emory could read about it while riding with the cook.

A man came with two black men to their camp. His name was Steven Knight and he asked what Harp would sell two fat steers for. The blacks were his ex-slaves and they worked for him. Harp went to find Emory and ask him what he thought.

"I don't think he'd pay it but sell him them for forty bucks apiece. We want silver or gold, not paper money."

Harp was surprised that Knight agreed to the terms and paid him with eight ten-dollar gold pieces. The boys cut out the two steers. Knight asked the cowboys to shoot both, then he and his help went to butchering with a block and tackle and loading the cuts on the wagon they had with them.

Harp asked him what he'd do with that meat. He said he had cash customers and all of it would be sold before dark the next day.

Emory told Harp to keep the money. He'd have some expenses he'd need it for. The money was a novelty. He'd not seen much since the war began. He, Long, and their dad had lots of script. The state of Texas paid them for ranger work in script, and it would pay all taxes due for them and their neighbors. But there were no plans to ever pay anything in cash that he knew about.

They were north of Fort Worth after a few more passing days. They had the cattle set up and someone mentioned they heard about a nearby schoolhouse dance. Could they go see about it?

Harp gave Doug a ten-dollar coin and told him not to spend it all. Six hands rode over there that evening and the rest stayed with the herd. There was lots of grass and a good spring-fed creek to bathe in. So plans were to spend Sunday there, washing and cleaning up. And resting.

Emory wrote his wife and Harp wrote his mother and dad. They were about three weeks along and things had gone well so far. Plus the war was over.

He and Long had stayed with the herd. Both could dance but didn't feel any urge, and besides, they wanted all the rest they could take on their layover. When the boys came in singing, Harp knew one of them had bought some white lightning. No one got in a fight and all that went had a good time.

Pretty peaceful times.

Bathed and shaved, the outfit looked better. Clothes were washed and hung on a bush to dry. They passed the time sleeping and doing herd duty in shifts.

Three days later they faced the tree-filled Red River. First time Harp had seen it since they crossed it as a boy on a ferry coming from Arkansas. He didn't have a herd back then to get across, either. Harp sent two boys with the wagons, by ferry. They were too damn scared of water and he didn't want to tell their mothers he made them swim the Red River and they drowned. They could greet Blue and make sure the wet cattle got up on the north bank safely. All the water coming off them would make that slope slick and cattle would slide back down, so he needed hands to keep them moving.

He said if any steer got swept away—just let him go. They'd gather them later when they came to shore. No better swimmer than most of his hands, the order was to slip off your horse and hang on to his tail when the horse began to swim. Things went smoothly till one rider lost his tail-hold. Long swam after him and got him safely onto shore.

Harp fell down twice in the mud when he and his horse reached the far side. But he made it up, and they all bragged on how good they did at the crossing. Three boys rode downstream to collect the half dozen swept away.

He felt pretty good not losing more than a few. This ford, they told him, would be one of his worst crossings. They moved the herd north to graze and to camp. They were in the Indian Territory and the sign posted said that no alcohol could be carried into this territory. By order of the U.S. marshal from Van Buren, Arkansas. U.S. Federal Judge Story, presiding, would strictly enforce the law.

There would be lots of tribes and many Indian Nations to cross through, so Harp was glad Long was his scout. They'd talk to him, being part Indian, though he didn't know one word of any Indian language and sounded like the rest of the Texans. Harp and his brother knew their origins because their father explained it and he never showed any side to one over the other, unless they were wrong.

Their mother doted on both of them. Harp really missed her great cooking and sweets she made specially for her men. She made them learn schooling and manners. And since he'd left home, he realized how pretty she was and why his father married her on their first date.

That second Texas ranch, at Camp Verde, they'd carved out of the west Texas land below Kerrville; it was a solid place. Someday he and Long would have a place together, or maybe even places of their own—someday. This trip might contribute to getting one if they made it. He had lots to learn about business and law, but he'd find out how. For right now moving these cattle from ten to fifteen miles a day was his job.

Long spoke about what some friendly Indians told him on the road—that there were gangs of outlaws robbing and murdering people along the stage road. That everyone was to go in pairs whenever they left the herd.

The next day six Indians, wrapped in blankets despite the growing heat and with rifles in hand, stopped them in the road. One old man in a headdress of feathers acted like the leader. Long was ahead scouting, so Harp met them before they could stop the herd.

Harp held up his right hand like his dad did when meeting the Comanche in peace. He gave a head toss for them to move aside. They did to allow the stream of steers to go by.

Harp dismounted and the old man did the same. They sat cross-legged on the short grass and faced each other. The old man began telling him how the great white father gave his people this land. For crossing it he owed them many dollars and several steers for his starving people.

"I have no money." He turned his hands up. "I can give you one steer."

"No. No. Six steers."

With one finger held up, Harp showed him what he'd give him. The old man shook his head and went back to talking. He said he had many warriors and they could massacre the invaders and stampede his herd.

About to tell him to go to hell, Harp stopped and asked, "Do you have a shovel?"

"Huh?"

"Do you have a shovel?"

"Why?"

"When you and them warriors come back to kill us, bring a good shovel. My cook broke the handle out of ours this morning. You bring your shovel."

"Why?"

"I am going to need it to bury you."

"We take one *wahoo*."

"I figured you would. I'll cut one out when we stop around noon."

The chief gathered his men and they rode off.

One of the boys came by and asked, "What did you give him?"

"One lame steer when we make camp at noontime." Harp stood up and brushed off his seat. "Plenty enough . . . the government can feed them."

"Didn't he want a lot more?"

"Hell, you can ask for anything. But you aren't getting it all from me."

The Indians came after lunch and Harp had a limper cut out from the tail end of the herd. The Indians chased him off, ran him about a quarter away, speared him like they did buffalos, and a dozen squaws set in to butcher him.

The Froggy Bottoms was a real swampy land to cross. They avoided farms all they could and tried to not let any cattle break into crops. Another three weeks and they'd crossed the Canadian, which was at a summer low Long heard. Next to cross would be the Arkansas River and circle around to go north of the river city and get back on the stagecoach route to go over the mountains.

They'd moved along at a good pace and the grass

had strength, so the steers were getting slick. They had few losses and the cowboys were all well and the horses doing all right.

Long found a place to ford the Arkansas with the herd. He told the wagon drivers and cook to go through Fort Smith, over to Van Buren, and meet them north of there. The cook said the hill going north through that town was tough for wagons.

"Hire an extra team to pull you," Long told him.

"They cost money I don't have." Ira the cook shook his head.

"Harp, give him some money to get out of Van Buren," Long said.

Harp did and now he was down to six coins.

"I'm feeling good. I'll ford with the cattle," Emory said.

"I wish you'd ride in the wagon. We've never crossed this before," Harp told him.

"I am not an invalid. I'll ride."

"I am not convinced it is a good idea, Emory."

"I do own this outfit."

"But Long and I have to answer to your wife if anything happens to you."

Long dropped his head and shook it. That meant he would not argue with Emory about the issue. That left Harp upset but he said, "Watch yourself. River crossings can be bad."

They lined up to cross the shallowest portion of the Arkansas west of Fort Smith in the Indian Territory. There was another spot below Fort Smith but they'd decided this place was better to cross at and go east to Arkansas, then turn north. The camp boys and Ira the cook planned to meet them near Lee's Creek north of Van Buren.

There was some open land for the herd to graze on there. Then they would turn northeast to get on the Butterfield Stage Road over a range of mountains in the north. The plans were to move north into a land they had a map for. The route was situated east of where the O'Malley brothers once lived at Cincinnati before their father moved the family to Texas.

Harp was down at the river edge with Chaw and Doug. The big steer Blue acted ready. Long had told him that this was the shallowest crossing there was for miles.

"Then, let's go," Harp said, and they shooed Blue into the water. Bell ringing, the large steer set out wading headed north in the wide river, crossing toward the far shore with hills behind beach. Harp reined his horse around as the line of steer began entering the Arkansas's water, some stepping in and others taking a run and splashing into the water. They were bawling their heads off. He met Emory on the hillside.

"We get half of them in, then you and I will move in on the upstream side and cross. Keep an eye where they start swimming so you're ready."

"I'll be fine. You two men are very organized and I can't believe how well the pair of you have done to get here. Your father taught you a lot. I guess you know that. I commanded experienced soldiers all during the war that couldn't match you two."

"I am going to be close. I can swim, Emory. You

get away from your horse I'll do all I can to get to you. There's lots of current going by. It's sweeping a few steers downstream but they are gaining the shore and I don't think we will lose many."

"I'll be fine. I'm not wearing a side arm. I could swim."

"Just try to stay with your horse all you can."

The cattle, with few exceptions, were streaming across an almost quarter-mile-wide ford. Some of the cowboys were going down the bank over on the other side to get the cattle that were carried away some by the current. Harp sent Emory ahead, told him to get his horse upstream from the cattle stream, and head north.

His buffalo horse followed Emory's good Kentucky horse into the shallows. Forty feet out in water some steers had a fuss and swarmed around fighting. The big horse shied. Emory was off and in the water in a flash. Harp charged his horse in to aid him.

Those upset cattle blocked his path and he was caught in a flurry of spooked animals. He saw Emory was swimming, but he knew that the man did not have the strength to swim to that north shore. Milling steers blocked his own horse from getting to him to help him before the water deepened. He rose on his horse standing on the seat, then dove over two steers and began swimming to Emory.

He heard the men shouting as he swam through the water to get to the still swimming Emory. Then he was beside him.

"Get on my back. I can get you over there."

His white face shocked Harp who urged him, "Do it now."

"Thanks—"

"Never mind that. We need you on shore. Just hang on."

"I'm sorry, Harp. You said—"

"Save your strength." He began to stroke for the shore. The current was stronger than it looked, but he wanted his employer in shallow water as fast as possible, and they had a long way to go.

Three of his men were in the river out about as far as he figured their horses could stand in the river's force, waiting for him to get close to them. Once, when Emory let go of him, Harp's heart stopped. He swung around and could see him floating away not struggling.

Harp went after him and in minutes he had hold of him. Holding Emory's head up he fought the river, towing him along going farther downstream but shore bound.

Doug swam his horse out, took Emory's collar, and swung the horse back for shore.

"He alive?"

"I think so."

Chaw waited for Harp in the shallower water, tossed him a lariat, and hauled him to shore. "Did you save him?"

Harp climbed to his feet in the shallows. "I hope so. I think he simply passed out and let go of me."

"Man, where did you learn to swim like that?" Chaw asked, impressed.

"A place on the Illinois River north of here. My

father's first wife drowned and so he made us learn how to swim at an early age."

Chaw shook his head. "When he let go, I thought he was drowned."

Harp dropped on his knees beside the man. "Emory, what happened?"

"My heart I guess. I blanked out. Sorry. You sure risked your life for me."

"Never mind that." He looked up for help. "Men, we need a wagon. And find a doctor to check him. The rest of you, gather all the cattle and start them east. That road up there goes to Lee's Creek and that is where the wagons will be this afternoon." He pointed east.

His point rider Chaw said, "We'll send for a wagon and the rest of us will take the herd to Long."

A hand jumped on his horse and rode off, hard, to find a wagon. Chaw and Doug retrieved the last cattle and drove them to the huddled herd. Several herders rode by to voice their concern about Emory.

Harp told them, "He is alive and will be well. We've sent for a wagon to get him to a doctor who will check him out. You guys get those steers to Lee's Creek."

"Sure will, boss. You tell him we are praying for him to get well."

"I will."

In a few minutes they started the herd east. His point riders left him the young puncher Norm Savoy, a boy in his teens, to help him.

He squatted nearby. "Good thing it's hot today. All our blankets are at Lee's Creek huh?"

"I wish we had some. Never can do a good job planning everything all the time." Harp felt satisfied that Emory was sleeping. Damn, why didn't he put his foot down when he was already worried about him taking the river. Emory, before the war, was out of the same mold he and Long were—did it all. But his war wound and that bullet still in his chest had rationed his activities, and there was no way he could have swum across that damn fishy-smelling river.

No telling what would happen next. His father told him Arkansas people could be real hard nosed. Most of the war had been centered up there with both sides fighting back and forth across the same ground. And for him to expect anything to happen.

In an hour cowboy Kevin Doones returned, followed by a wagon and team. The overall-wearing man on the spring seat who drove it was black. He reined up his mules and wrapped off the reins, jumped down, and came over to ask Harp what he could do for them. They shook hands.

"My name's Washington Adams, sir."

"Harp O'Malley's mine. Where is the closest doctor?"

"Roland there's one."

"We need to take him up there in your wagon. One of us will ride with him. The rest will ride their horses."

"I ain't got no blankets."

"He'll understand. We'll be careful loading him. Best we can do is the best we can do, Washington."

"Yes, sah. I's help you move him."

"Thanks."

On his knees, Harp spoke to him. "Emory, we're taking you to the doctor in Mr. Washington's wagon. We don't have a mattress, but we'll get you there and get you checked out."

The four loaded him. Harp told Norm to ride with him. "We'll catch your horse and bring him on." Kevin caught his horse and Emory's and they all started for Roland.

The doctor's house was a two-story affair on the main road. Harp dismounted and went ahead to knock on the door. Emory was awake and they waited to unload him.

A white-haired woman answered the door.

Harp removed his hat. "Is the doctor in?"

"Yes, do you need to see him?"

"No, ma'am. But my boss had an incident happen crossing the river. I think it is his heart."

"Can you bring him inside?"

"Yes."

"The doctor can see him right away."

"I will get him." He turned to go back. "Thanks."

"The doc will see him. We need to get him inside. Mr. Washington, do you have time to wait? I may need him hauled to Lee's Creek where my herd is waiting."

"Mr. Harp, I got all the time you need."

"Thanks."

They moved Emory inside carefully and put him on a table. To Harp he looked terribly white and drained, but he still could manage a smile.

Doctor Mulligan was a man in his forties. A concerned-looking man who listened to Emory's heart with his stethoscope first, and then asked about the scar on his chest.

"He was wounded in the war. They never got the bullet out. He said they told him it was too close to his heart."

Mulligan nodded. "His heartbeat is irregular. What else happened to him?"

"We forded the river about an hour or so ago. His horse got mixed up with some fighting cattle. He almost drowned before I could swim and catch him, then he passed out on me coming to shore."

Mulligan made a face. "He should have been in a boat and rowed across."

Harp nodded. "My supply wagons used the ferries at Fort Smith and Van Buren. I tried to convince him to go with them. He told me he could make it."

"Not much I can do. I have some medicine that will increase his heart rate and if he is not bleeding internally it will help him."

"Would that business in the river have caused him to bleed inside?"

Mulligan shook his head. "I have no idea where the bullet is or if he's bleeding inside. I can't see that part. A small increase in his heartbeat would help him. That is, if he's not bleeding internally."

"He's a pretty strong man."

"I can tell that. I am recommending small doses of laudanum for the pain and this medicine to increase his heartbeat. You could leave him here to recover, but I get the impression it is urgent for you to move on. With him with you."

"Yes, it is. I have eight hundred head of big Texas steers at Lee's Creek to move north."

The doctor nodded. "He will have to lay flat and hope that his condition improves. I will be frank, moving him may be the death of him, but you will have to be the judge."

"Take the medicine along—I'll make it," Emory managed.

"You heard him, Doctor. Tell me how much and when I need to give it."

Doc explained the procedure. "A drop on his tongue once a day. If his heart slows, two more drops. One teaspoon of laudanum morning and night. His pain goes down, stop it."

"What is this drop stuff?"

"A herb called digitalis. It increases the heartbeat. You can find it if you run out."

"How much do I owe you?"

"Two dollars."

"You have change for ten?"

"Yes."

Harp felt grateful for the steer money. And pocketed the change. He went out to see about Washington and found Norm.

"The black man has gone for a mattress and blankets."

"Guess he read my mind," Harp said, looking up and down the street. No sign of Washington. Surely he was coming back.

"He's sure a nice guy."

"We were lucky to find him," Harp agreed.

"What about Emory?"

"The doc gave me some medicine for him. I don't know much about doctoring folks, Norm, but I have the instructions."

"I hear the wagon coming back. Kevin is letting the horses graze. He'll hear him and come back."

"I imagine it will be a good haul to Lee's Creek."

"I do, too."

With Emory carefully loaded on the bed that Washington acquired, they set out east to find the herd. On the river road, he jogged the horses. They'd be out of daylight before they reached the herd, and Harp sure didn't want to miss them.

About sundown one of the cowboys, Eldon Morehouse, waved them down after they crossed a shallow creek. "We're up the road on a burned-out farm. How is he?"

"Alive," Harp said, and thanked him.

Long met them on the road. "How is he?"

"Tough shape. But he's alive. Doc back at Roland wanted him to stay there and recover. Emory won't hear of it."

Long nodded. "This drive is his baby. We have a good place tonight. I think another good place tomorrow. But there's lots of mountains they say ahead, just timber and no grass."

"Well, it hasn't been a joy ride anywhere we've gone."

"Fayetteville is the next big town. Maybe five days or more north."

Harp nodded. "We need to fix him a bed in the smaller wagon. I simply hope he does not die on us."

Long agreed. When they reached camp it was dark. He invited Washington to eat with him and the boys.

"Aw I don't need to do that."

"Yes, you do. You saved his life today and you got that bedding. We want you to eat with us."

"All right, Mr. Harp. I will eat with you."

"Good. What do I owe you?"

"Fifty cents too much?"

"Too little. I'm paying you two dollars. What did the mattress cost?"

"Ten cents."

"Here's three dollars; now come eat. Ira has lots of food. And you'll stay and eat breakfast with us in the morning."

"Aw, Mr. Harp, that be way too much money."

"No, Washington, you were a lifesaver."

"I sure am proud that cowboy stopped me today. Thank all of yous."

They cheered him.

"By the way, where be this place yous be going?"

"Sedalia, Missouri."

"Never heard of it. But good luck."

"Thanks. We will need it." Harp nodded and sat down, with his plate on the ground, beside the big man.

"How long yous been on the road?"

"A month or maybe more."

"How far dis place be you going to?"

"Maybe two months. Maybe less."

Washington nodded. "I pray for you to get there and him to live."

"Thanks. We need all the help we can get."

"No. Yous'll do it. I see in these boys' faces you bunch are real doers. They worried about the boss man being down but they ain't no quitters in the whole lot. Mr. Harp, I say these boys would go straight through hell with you."

"Thanks again. That is a big compliment for me and them."

"That be the truth." Washington went to feeding his face.

Later Harp talked to Emory, who ate some watery oatmeal and said he felt better.

But the boss man was miles away from being well, and Harp knew he would worry about him and the wagon rocking miles ahead.

Damn . . . how did I get in such a jam?

CHAPTER 5

Two days' drive north of Lee's Creek, Harp rode down and looked at the two-foot waterfall called Natural Dam on the same creek. The first day had been a short one and they stayed near the country store at a place known as Union Town. They had no trouble. A few curious men came by and asked him where they were headed. When they learned of their destination, most shook their heads and as much as said Greg's men would not get there with all those damn cattle.

"Tomorrow we have to cross some mountains, but there are some deserted farms we can stop and graze at. It'll be another short day," Long explained. "I know we aren't making many long moves, but with woods, and finding water and grass, is where we need to stop."

"I understand. Emory don't need any more shaking up, either, than he gets in a day."

"He is not getting stronger very fast is he?"

"Braver yes. Better no," said Harp.

"I know you have considered it, but what will we do if he dies?"

"Bury him and go on. Nothing else we can do. He wants the cattle sold and his wife to get his share."

"We have never sold but two steers in our life-time. How do you do that?"

"He's been telling me how. I think you and I can handle it."

"I hope you're listening good."

"I am. So far so good. The rest of the way like this?"

"Yes. Woods, farms, and water."

"Keep finding us places like that is all I can say."

So far, Harp bet a hundred curious men had come by and asked where they were going. Then they left, shaking their heads about the notion of going to Sedalia.

The cowboys came to a closed stage stop, and a farmer told them Fayetteville was about ten miles north. No stages were running yet since the opera-tion had been closed because of the war efforts.

One passerby said, "I bet the Union Army stops you up there. They have gotten to be real damn bossy since Lee signed that damn armistice. They don't want Rebs to make a dime and he wants us all to starve to death."

Hearing that, Harp told the boys to secure all their rifles, hiding them in the wagon. They might need them and he didn't want to lose them to some zealous Union guards.

No telling what they'd face on up the road.

Some armed men came by that night after dark. The leader called himself Smith and they asked lots of questions. Too many for Harp's comfort.

Harp finally asked if the men were resisting the Union forces.

"You're damn right. Lee might have surrendered, but by gawd we ain't."

"Listen. I am in charge of these cattle for a man and more people back in Texas. My job is to take them to market. I am not fighting the Union Army. I am going to deliver them to the railhead in Missouri and that is all."

"You just going to let them take this land and your rights from you?"

"I know nothing about taking land and rights. I told you what I am doing. Now clear out of my camp."

Smith drew a pistol and threatened to fire it.

"Put down the damn gun. It could stampede our cattle."

"You yellowbellied carp-sucking fish. I ought to kill all of you."

Doug knocked him out from behind with a club, while six guns drawn immediately backed Harp. He ordered the intruders to take their leader out of the camp and be gone.

"You are not welcome here."

They picked up their groggy leader and left the camp.

When they were gone, Harp told the boys, "We didn't come up here to fight the damn war all over again. We have steers to deliver and that's the job. I know many of you fought during the war, but it is over and we have to make the best of it. We have to get these bawling cattle to Missouri and sell them to get a dime for our time. That's my goal. I hope to hell it's yours."

A chorus of amens supported him.

The next day, following the same river that they had learned to swim in, they headed for the town called Fayetteville. Long thought they could go around the town.

A small company of Union soldiers stopped them on the main road.

Harp rode around the stopped cattle to see why.

"What's wrong?" he asked Chaw.

He gave a head toss toward the mounted soldiers and said, "He says we need papers to prove these cattle were not stolen and to enter the town ahead."

Harp booted his horse over to the lieutenant.

"Sir, these cattle come from Kerrville, Texas. The man who owns them is in that wagon. They bear his brand, which in Texas is legal ownership."

"Where are the papers from the newly reformed government of Texas showing you have the right to remove these animals from that state?"

"When I left Texas six weeks ago there was no new government formed."

"Then you will have to stop here and wait until such papers can arrive."

"Sir. There are eight hundred large steers here.

They will eat you out of house and home staying here."

"Then they may have to be destroyed. They are illegal contraband today."

"Sir. You don't have the bullets to shoot them. Second, the smell would drive people crazy and bring along every buzzard and wild hog to eat them."

"I am demanding you stop here until my commander decides what to do."

"May I go along and speak to him?"

"Without a side arm, yes. I consider you a rebel spy."

"I'm sorry. The war is over. I never served in the Confederate Army. I was a Texas Ranger and patrolled against the Comanche." He unbuckled his gun belt and handed it to Chaw. "Let's go see him."

"I will leave some men here to see they obey my orders."

"Chaw, you and Doug spread the cattle out to graze. I'll go find us a way to go on."

"We can do that. I'll send word for the cook to come back here and make camp."

Harp agreed. The officer left three of his men to guard the herd from moving and two more enlisted men rode with them. He could tell they thought he was Jefferson Davis's right arm.

The army's office was in a brick house with armed troops posted outside. They hitched their horses. He'd learned the officer was Lieutenant Craig Johnston.

Johnston told him to wait in the living room.

The commander came out and looked him up and down. "The lieutenant tells me you are moving contraband cattle without papers."

"Sir, the cattle belonged to my boss who had a heart attack a few days ago and was unable to ride up here to talk to you himself. He is back in one of our wagons. We left Texas to bring these cattle to Sedalia, Missouri, so there would be beef available to the empty meat markets in the North. At that time there was no occupying forces in Texas or no new government to issue permits. But I understand there are food shortages in the north and east parts of the United States. So I feel I am doing my public duty bringing these cattle to the railhead to offset that shortage. These cattle all bear the owner's brand, which is proof of ownership in Texas."

"Where did you go to school?"

"The first two grades in Cincinnati, Arkansas, and five more in Texas. My mother was very well educated as well."

"I can tell that. Will you swear you are not part of the Confederate government or that army?"

"I never have been, sir."

"Lieutenant, I think you did an excellent job of stopping him. Food is short in the North. We will give him a pass to go on if he signs the non-enemy agreement."

The lieutenant saluted him. "I will go back with him after that and release his herd."

"Bring me that form," the commander said. "Have you had much opposition coming up here?"

"Some Indians stopped us and we gave them a steer."

"If you sign this we will give you a pass to continue. Perhaps two steers could be left to feed my soldiers. Meat is short here as well."

"When we get up here, have some men meet us and we can provide that, sir."

"Give him a pen."

Harp bent over the desk and skimmed the words and signed it.

"We were thinking about going around your town, sir."

"Oh, no. I want to show the people of the town we are concerned about the food shortage and are allowing you to pass through here."

"Yes, sir."

"When will you drive through?"

"Day after tomorrow, sir."

"I will meet you, and the quartermaster will accept those two head of cows."

"They are steers, sir."

"I meant steers, and thank you, Mr. O'Malley."

Harp rode back with his escort and the soldiers went home.

Every hand in camp could hardly wait for him to tell them what happened.

He took his copy out of his saddlebags and held them up. "This is a pass from the Union Army to take our cattle all the way to Sedalia. I can't tell you what a relief this paper is. After all that damn book reading Lieutenant gave us, the officer in charge gave me a pass to deliver these cattle. It is the best thing could've happened to us guys. That shavetail wanted to slaughter the whole herd and make us go back to Texas with our tail between our legs."

Harp was still overwhelmed by what had happened. "I can't believe it happened, but we really do have a pass from the Union Army to go forth."

He went by to tell Emory and show him the papers. The news revived him and he sat up smiling.

"You damn sure are a hero. How come?"

"All I said was we were doing our duty feeding the people starving in the North. I did, however, promise him two steers for his quartermaster."

"I swear some day you need to run for office in Texas."

"This herding cattle is teaching me that I don't want to do that."

Long came back later and Harp filled him in on what happened.

"Right through town?"

"Yes. He wants credit for us doing such a great job of helping feed the starving people in the North."

With his plate in his lap, Long leaned back and laughed. "You serious?"

"I am."

"You need to be a lawyer."

"Why is everyone looking for work for me? Emory wants me to be in the legislature, you want me being a lawyer. I want to herd cattle in Texas."

"Well, brother, you did it again. Whew. I am glad you are handling all the bull they have been passing out."

The next day they camped south of town on the

West Fork of the White River. The site was on a deserted farm grown up in grass and weeds in a valley surrounded by forest-covered hills. Long said the town was over the hill.

Several individuals came out to see and talk to them. They were mostly farmers curious about the longhorn cattle, and they talked about the war in the area.

One man told them that before the war this was the finest country to live in, but the back and forth fighting had ruined it and most folks had moved away.

"We lived over at Cincinnati," Harp told him. "Dad moved us to Texas before they even talked about war."

"What you think those steers are worth up at that railhead?"

"Oh fifty to sixty dollars a head."

"That is lots of money."

"It has cost lots to get them here," Harp said.

"Oh, you guys are crazy. Why Lee hadn't even surrendered when you left home."

Harp agreed. "We aren't choosing sides. This is a job to me and my brother. There are cattle in Texas. There are hungry people in the North. We are simply the go-between."

"I hope you make it, but I figure these damn Yankees won't let you make a dime if they can help it."

"We have a pass."

"Good luck. You guys look mighty young to be running it to me."

"We've been handling it."

"Oh, you'd not got here, otherwise, without being smart. See yah again I hope."

"So do I."

With the man gone, Harp went to see Emory.

His boss was sitting up under a canvas shade. "I see you're getting some attention."

"We're kinda like a circus came to town. They come to see the wild animals."

Emory laughed. "We must be halfway by now."

"I think so, too. I'm glad you're doing better. These empty farms sure have helped us. There is no other stock I see, so we have graze. But I have no idea what Missouri will be like when we get there."

"In a couple of days we will be at a place called Pea Ridge. I have been this far north during the war. General Benjamin McCullough, early on in the battle, was killed up there by a sniper. After his demise it was a very mismanaged battle. I was there and his death led to bedlam. The Confederate forces fell apart. McCullough was the leader and with him gone, the rest of the officers thought it was over and ran way. We should never have run but we retreated to Fort Smith.

"Before being killed, McCullough had wiped out the whole Yankee Army up at Springfield. They even killed a Yankee general and sent the rest of them all running back to Saint Louis. Folks asked why didn't he run them down? He told me, those poor dedicated farmers didn't have any more ammo or anything else."

"Well, we have the ammo and the rifles still, and God I hope we don't need them."

"Your oral defense saved the soldier from searching for them. They could have said you planned to revolt and those rifles were the proof. That was very smart."

"Aw that shavetail didn't know what to do with that many dead steers."

"They said you warned him he didn't have the bullets to shoot them all."

"I did. I am simply glad tomorrow we will be north of there."

Emory nodded. "Do you know what you will do in Sedalia?"

"Look for buyers?"

"Maybe hold up the herd before getting there, and you go in and advertise in the paper that you have mature Texas beef coming in on the hoof in about ten days, and where to see you about them."

"Ads and hotels cost money. I have maybe forty dollars."

"No," Emory said. "You have two hundred. I am going to give you that money to handle the deal. I kept it for me doing this, but you will have to do that now. It is in gold, so the money will be good anywhere. I knew Confederate paper was worthless, so I made sure to have some real coins."

"What price do you think they will bring per head?"

"Eighty would be wonderful. That's a head. Sixty would be powerful, and less than that is probably what we will get. But secure the money. Don't carry it on you. That will be even a greater job than driving the cattle up here—how to get the money back to Texas. Especially when word is out that you have thousands of dollars on you. It will make you a marker for every outlaw in the five states and the Indian Territory."

"How long can I bluff and not sell them until we get the money we want?"

"That gets dangerous, too. That many cattle being around and not sold won't be appreciated. You better cut and run when you think you've topped the market. Where are you putting this money?" Emory asked as he tossed him a heavy leather sack.

Harp hefted it in one hand. "I'll find a place."

"Good. I'm counting on it."

"No matter what happens, Long and I will see your wife and children are taken care of and all the debts paid."

"You two, and the men need paid as well. Don't leave yourselves out."

"We won't," Harp promised him.

"I remember the Butterfield Hotel is on the side of the hill in Fayetteville. I slept there going and coming back from the Elkhorn Tavern at Pea Ridge. They say he built it there on his stage line saying it would someday be in the heart of a big metropolis. But that was before the war wasn't it?"

Harp agreed. The town had suffered some war damage and there were not many people around there.

The next morning herding the steers north on

the main street going up a steep hill, Harp saw the hotel beside the road and several other buildings, all looking empty. The town square, they said, was west of there. Two army-uniformed men took the two sore-footed steers pointed out to them.

They thanked his men and moved the cattle off without them bawling at the separation. Payment made, he rode back to help his men keep the cattle off the boardwalks as many men, women, and children stood back and watched.

A few brassy women holding up their dresses walked along with the herd and talked to his cowboys about doing business with them. He heard Eldon Morehouse shout, "I'd love to, ma'am, but I ain't got a wooden nickel to pay you."

The herd and his men went on to camp on a creek north of town on more unused pastureland. Dawn they went north by some small community and the Fitzgerald stage stop. It had not been used in some years but this country would wake up—with the war over and ready to open up again.

In a few days they drove past the Elkhorn Tavern, which was off the road, and they took Emory by there in the wagon to simply see it. After looking at the still intact two-story building, he lay back down on his bed and Harp wondered if he was slipping again. If only he lived to see Sedalia. No telling about the man's life span, but it was narrowing. Harp knew that much for certain.

They took the stage route north a few miles east of there. The country they were on was some high rolling plains, and many farms here, too, were empty.

They went through Seligman and camped beyond it on another unnamed creek.

The road turned east at Cassville, and they avoided the town moving toward Springfield. Long thought in three to five days they would be there.

In a few places some farmers, armed with shotguns and on mules, blocked the road, demanding that they not bring the herd through their country.

Hamp was short with them. "Our cattle are healthy. We won't do anything but pass by and won't hurt a thing. Now get the hell out of the road."

"Mister, after the damn war we ain't got much. Our stock dies our families will starve."

"Stand aside," he ordered. "We're only passing through. If we don't sell our cattle our families will starve. Now get back or I'll be forced to shoot you."

Harp could not understand their problem. They had not lost a half dozen steers to any disease. What made these people so hardheaded? Superstition? He had no idea.

When they turned north of Springfield a sheriff came to their camp to serve papers on them.

The lawman said, "You can't go on with these Texas cattle. I have a warrant here to stop you."

"Why? We aren't planning to start the war over. I have heard this bullshit for a week coming from Cassville. Those steers out there are healthy. What are you talking about?"

"They are carriers of Texas tick fever. Those cattle are immune to it and our cattle are not."

"How can one catch it and another can't?"

"I am not a scientist, but the University of Missouri

asked the legislature to ban Texas cattle from coming here."

"Mister, the sooner we go on the better your cattle will be. The longer you impound my cattle here, if they know so much, then the more disease you will get. Let me get out of your county. I will be out of here tomorrow."

"You promise to never come back here again?"

"You won't see me ever again."

"You do I'll lock you in jail and throw away the key."

"Deal."

Texas tick fever . . . he never even heard about that. Never mind, they had to get to Sedalia quickly, sell the steers, and get home.

He paced the ground and Long came back into camp, talking about more trouble for them brewing right up the road.

Huh? What did he mean? They had escaped one lawman only a week before and in duck soup with another wanting to kill them. Hell, they were within days of their goal and the end of the railroad tracks—why couldn't these people simply let them sell their beef and go home?

Long shook his head. "There's some law up there going to kill every rebel soldier in the outfit if you try to go north on this road. It's not a threat. They're saying every Texan is an ex-soldier for the Confederacy."

"Gather the men in camp. Are those idiots on their way to stop us?"

"Supposed to be. That's why I came back so fast."

"Ira, we need to unload rifles and ammo. Tell the men to form a line and stand ten to twelve feet apart. If the shooting starts, mow them down but wait for my word."

Ira agreed.

Long went to gather the men that were in camp. When they were assembled Harp called them to order. "Men we have posse coming to kill us I'm told. If they are coming we need to be prepared. I need you to each get a rifle and ammo. Be sure it is loaded to the gate and come and line up ten to twelve feet apart. Don't shoot until I say so. I think we can stare them down. Remember, don't shoot no matter how much they taunt you. But if pushed I will give the word. One of you get half the herders back here and explain carefully. I'm going up the road to meet them."

Ira handed him a rifle. "It's loaded."

"I want to stop them on the hill," he shouted to Long.

"I'll be there. Kevin's gone to get half the herders."

Harp nodded and, taking long strides, loped for the top of the hill and the road. The steers were pretty well road broke. He doubted they would stampede. But anything could happen. Why kill rebels? In his mind he had no idea—the damn war was over.

When he reached the hilltop and road, he heard the drum of horses in the distance. Their dust rose above the hardwoods that lined the roadway. From the looks of things, Long barely had time to warn them that they were on their way. What a mess.

Next to Harp, Long slid his big horse to a halt and bailed off with his rifle in his hands.

"They're coming for sure," Harp said.

He nodded. "I hope you can stop them."

"Our men are making a line that should impress the comers. You ever meet the head guy?"

Long shook his head. "But I heard that he is a hot head. I'm saying fifty-fifty we are going to have a shoot-out."

"Surely he is not that dumb."

"The folks I talked to say he is."

Harp shook his head. The posse was coming up the road. The men were mostly riding mules and carrying shotguns. Many he could see were single shot, too.

The big man with a badge pinned onto his suit and big hat on a flashy black horse reined up and set his men behind him. Harp noted that mules didn't rein up like horses, and there was some confusion and lots of honking. The man with the silver badge on his chest rode his horse closer.

"I am the sheriff of this county. My name is Sherlock Harris and I am placing all of you and your men under arrest. Throw down your guns."

A mule or two broke rank and had to be jerked back in place.

"My name is Harper O'Malley. I am a rancher from Bexar County, Texas. My friends and neighbors entrusted me to bring their cattle up here to help the food shortage in the North. Since Sedalia is the railhead, we drove these cattle here so people could eat beef."

"You're a bunch of sap-sucking rebel soldiers."

"My men are cowhands who came a thousand miles or more to feed folks who don't have food. Harris, we will not surrender. Move aside so we can do our things and go home peacefully."

"I said throw down your guns or we will start shooting."

"Harris, don't you be stupid. Your men are on mules. When the first shot is fired they are going to buck and kick. Your men have one shot. My men have ten shots apiece in their Winchesters. Who is going to die on this road?"

"I said—"

"Harris, think real hard. Lots of folks are going to die here. There are fathers and brothers with you. You going to tell their wives and mothers you had them slayed?"

Harp knew the man's temper was controlling him. But he also could see Long had his horse for shield and the .44 was pointed at the big man's heart.

"Don't let him bluff you, Sheriff. We can whip their southern asses." Verbal advice came from his posse.

Harp had enough. "Tell that mouthy one to come out here. I'll fistfight him myself. None of my men will do a thing if I lose, but don't let my defeat signal you to move. They will gun you down—"

A shot went off among the posse. Harris's horse whirled around and several mules and their riders were bucked off into the woods. Obviously it was an accidental discharge, but Harp was glad Harris could see what the mules' responses were to only one shot being fired—pure bedlam.

"Does he want to fight me bare fisted?" Harp asked him.

Harris never looked over his shoulder. "Jonathan Carter, get out here."

Another big man, about twenty, took the single shot off over his head by the strap. He handed the shotgun off and someone else took the mule's reins. Harp stepped off his horse, unbuckled his gun belt, re-buckled it, and hung it on his saddle horn.

He put his felt hat over it and turned back to the big-chested man.

"My name's Harp O'Malley. What's yours?"

They had begun circling each other. "Jonathan Carter, the third. I'm going to teach you a lesson here, Reb. One you won't forget for the rest of your short life."

"I've had enough lessons. But thanks . . ."

Head down like a bull, Carter came screaming. Harp threw himself on the ground and made a pair of scissors out of his legs, and that threw Carter ass over teakettle on the ground. He was dazzled some by the tumble, but he came right back at Harp again.

Harp pounded his head with his fists and then tripped him. He had the man dazed and he didn't want him back to full strength. He jumped on his back before he could flip over and pulled his head back with all his strength until Carter screamed, "I quit."

"You had enough?"

"Yah."

Harp let him go and moved off, keeping his attention focused on him.

Carter's face was bleeding and he looked like a wounded bear. He sat up and rubbed his cheeks with his dirty hands.

"Texas, you are the toughest son of a bitch as I ever tackled. When I get up I want to shake your hand. I won't ever pick a fight with you again."

Harp nodded and brushed his hair back with his sore hand. His men still stood in the line, rifles ready. He shook the big man's hand. "Carter, I have a job to do. I am no part of the old or new Confederate Army. I have eight hundred steers to sell so that many folks won't lose their ranches. My boss is dying in a wagon back in our camp from an old war wound. He won't even see his wife again before he dies. I am in charge. Help me get these cattle on a train to market, and I will pay you and all of these men some good wages."

"There's thirty of us," Carter said. "How many do you want?"

"Twenty dollars each when the cattle are on the train going out of here."

"Did you hear him?" Carter asked.

"Hell, yes," someone shouted, and they all agreed.

Harp gave him a sharp nod. "Men, go put up the guns. Let's get the cattle moving. We're going to Sedalia and we have help."

Long rode in and nodded at his brother. "These guys are as hard up as we were for money?"

"Maybe more. Start delegating work. You find a place to graze the herd?"

"The pasture up close to town will cost us a hundred dollars. It has good fences. Best I can do. Has lots of water."

"Show us the way. Men! Long has a place to pasture, close to town."

"John Sutton's farm."

"Okay. Now, one of you take me to the telegraph office," Harp shouted at the mule riders, his new employees.

An older man on a mule rode up. "Follow me, cowboy."

"Harp's my name," he said, and finished buckling on his Colt and then putting on his hat.

"Jedadiah Brant is mine."

"Long, see to things. I'm going to sell these cattle."

"I savvy that, bro. I can handle it."

Jed's mule broke into a trot with Harp's horse single-footing beside him. It was dark when they reached the train depot. He asked the man at the key if he knew any meatpackers in St. Louis.

"I have a directory. Who do you need to contact?"

"All of them."

"Write your message on a pad. I can send them tonight."

He wrote:

Name, Harp O'Malley. 800 fat steers for sale at Sedalia MO Stop Asking eighty dollars apiece Stop Send railcars here at once. Telegraph me at the Sedalia Depot. First one with a letter of credit or cash gets them Stop Harp

"I counted the meatpackers. That many telegrams will cost you twenty-five dollars."

"I can pay you." He dug the money out.

"I will hold any replies you receive."

"I'll be back to check on them."

The clerk, businesslike, nodded. "You from Texas?"

"Yes."

"How the hell did you get that many steers up here?"

"We drove them. Damn hard work."

"Why I thought that posse set out to kill you rebels this morning?"

"I hired them to work instead."

"You did what?"

"I'll need some help loading them when the cars get here and driving them in town so they don't horn anyone."

The telegraph operator was laughing. "Mister, you ever sold fish worms?"

"No."

"I bet they'd take them hook, line, and sinker."

He shook the man's hand. "I'll be back."

"Mister, if you get eighty dollar a head for some old boney steers, I'll give you the money back for the telegrams."

"I'll be back to collect."

"You do that. I damn sure will."

CHAPTER 6

Back in camp that night, two days south of Sedalia, Ira and Long had a candle lamp hanging in the cook's tent. One of the cowboys put Harp's horse up. They poured him some fresh coffee.

"Well, what did you do now?" Long asked.

"I sent a telegram to every packinghouse in Saint Louis. Told them I had eight hundred fleshy steers in Sedalia to the first buyer who had eighty dollars a head for them. Get me a letter of credit from a bank, and sign an agreement to take them all. You will own them."

Long, across the table, shook his head. "Aw hell, no one is going to pay eighty dollars apiece for them damn steers."

"If there aren't any chickens or hawgs left in this country they will and be proud of them."

"That clown hurt your head this morning. Emory was talking about forty or more. By the way, he's not any better tonight. I'm afraid he's slipping away."

"We can't do any more for him. You and I talked

about it. I wanted him to know how much we made—we owed him that."

"Times you shock me, brother. You figure out angles I never dreamed about. Every packing company in Saint Louis got a telegram from you that said we have eighty-dollar steers in Sedalia?"

"I damn sure did. Let's get some sleep. You use part of those men tomorrow to keep kids out of the street while we move the herd to that farm."

"Good idea. I'll arrange the safety. The place isn't real close."

"Jed showed me the shipping pens they have in town."

"We will be glad we have all this help."

"I agree but, guys, that sheriff told us at Springfield that the Missouri legislature had banned them from the state. We need those steers on the butcher rail in Saint Louis and our butts back in Texas."

"You're right about that," Long said. "That sounds smart to me."

"I need some sleep."

"The cattle will be in his pasture tomorrow. Can you pay him?"

"When I sell the cattle. I won't cheat him."

"You better talk to him then. He's worried we are con men out to beat everyone out of their pay."

"I bet they've had lots of those guys here during the war."

Long nodded. "Tomorrow we will go see him."

"Fine. Good night."

Sleep didn't came easy that evening. Harp worried about state officials coming down on him and impounding the cattle. That would be all he needed. So far so good, but the unknown future made his belly cramp.

Next morning he told Emory about his efforts to sell the steers by wire.

"You are thinking. Those packers will have the political push to slaughter those steers regardless under the war act, which is still on. Meat's short enough they can do that. But not Texans, you are right. Long thinks eighty is too high." He broke into deep coughing and lost his voice. His condition stabbed Harp.

When he recovered some, he squeezed Harp's hand. "You have done things ten times better than I could have done them. Do what you can for all of us."

That was the last time he ever talked to Emory. He died that evening.

There were plenty of pallbearers. Harp had the local Methodist minister do the services, and the parson let them bury Emory in the nearby church cemetery. Harp wrote a long letter to his wife and mailed it. Promised her he would be bringing the money back—her share—in a few months when they got home. That they were in Sedalia and her husband was buried with fellow church members.

He also ordered a granite stone for Captain Emory Greg of the Confederate Army.

Born in Texas. Died here after a cattle drive in 1865 from his war wounds. Father. Soldier. Cattleman.

The man said it would cost a hundred dollars. He agreed to pay for it before he left and they would put it up.

Two special train passenger cars full of cattle buyers arrived in Sedalia searching for Harper O'Malley the next afternoon.

Long, in town at the time, told Harp, "I told all of them I talked to that you'd meet them eight o'clock tomorrow morning in that one-room schoolhouse down the road from the pasture. They are letting school out tomorrow so you can use it. You owe them something for the use of that building."

"I can handle that."

"I bet they've looked at the cattle already. One guy asked me how many more herds are coming up and I told him none. That Missouri is blocking them."

Harp nodded. "What did he say?"

"That is pretty damn stupid."

"Did you tell him we thought the same thing?"

"Yes. Hey, they need cattle, but we don't know of any others coming."

Harp went to the meeting and took Doug Pharr who had enough education to write things down; Chaw Michaels to be a peacekeeper; and Long to help keep order.

The schoolhouse was packed. Many taxis and buggies waited for their passengers to take them back into town. Businessmen in suits and derby hats; drovers hitched their horses and went inside. Harp and Long went up front and both took off their hats.

Harper quieted the room down. "I am Harp O'Malley. This is my brother, Long. We started up here even before the war had ended. We knew you needed butcher cattle and we brought some. We didn't come to fight the war, but we almost had to. I know of no one else, nor did we see anyone else, on the old Butterfield Stage Road bringing cattle up here.

"Now I am in charge. My boss, Emory Greg, died two days ago from old war wounds. He knew you butchers needed beef. I can sell them as one lot or several. We are here to sell those cattle to one buyer or all of you. Is there anyone in here wants them all?"

A man in a fancy lacy shirt and tie stood up. The crowd booed him.

"Sir, my name is Horace Williams. I am prepared to buy all these steers of yours."

The crowd booed him some more.

"Mr. Williams, are you prepared to pay my price?"

"No, it is way too high." He sat down.

That bothered Harp. Was he too high? Or was that fancy Dan just spouting off? "Then you won't buy my cattle. Is there any other buyer here wants all my cattle?"

"Mr. O'Malley sir, my name's Aaron Kennedy. I have six buyers that can buy from fifty to a hundred head."

"At my price?"

"Yes, sir."

"All right, if you want cattle at eighty dollars a head form a line over here. I will not sell you any steers crippled or in poor condition, but you will get them at random, since they are range cattle. Any animal not fit can and will be culled."

The number of buyers lining up on the north side of the schoolhouse was impressive. Horace

Williams stood up again. "You, obviously, with these small lot buyers have not sold the entire herd."

"What do you suggest, sir?"

"I will take the remaining cattle—at your price."

"Thank you, sir." He wanted to take his old felt hat and throw it at the clouds outside. But he never cracked a smile. *Emory, old boy, wish you were here. We've done it.*

"Gentlemen. Thank you. We lost a few and there could be some culls. But we left Texas with a long count of eight hundred head. You will only pay for what you get. I have spoken to Ralph Edmonson at the Corner Stone Bank here. Be sure to have your money–letter of credit into him today.

"Has anyone talked to the railroad about getting cattle cars here?"

"They are sending all they have now," Williams said as he waved his hat to tell the room. "They plan to have more here shortly."

Williams walked up to the teacher platform. "You two guys are mighty young to have pulled off a sale the size of this one."

"Our late boss never thought so. We left Texas before Lee surrendered. We were in Fort Worth, I think, when that news came. That's several hundred miles from our home near San Antonio. We have bribed Indians, swum rivers, dealt with thugs, and run into the law in Missouri."

"How could you get more cattle like these up here?"

"Long, what do you think?" Harp asked his brother.

"We damn sure aren't coming up here again.

Maybe when the railroad gets built to the west we can deliver more."

"If you two ever need financing, contact me. I'll partner up here with you when you find a delivery point." He handed Harp his business card.

"Thank you, sir. Long and I may do that."

Williams turned to Doug who was adding up the list of takers. "Less the ones we lost and sold, you will have two hundred and sixty head, sir."

"I can handle that. Well, thanks, my rich cowboy friends, and good luck to you."

A man in a blood-stained apron came up. "I can buy the culls if we can settle on a price."

"There may be a few, sir. I can discount them. What is your name?"

"Adam Swartz, I am a small butcher shop man. Thanks."

"Have a representative ready to take them at the pens when we load the rest?"

"Oh, yes. Thank you, sir."

"Doug, you have the list of buyers. We'll take it to the bank and they can collect from these men. We have plenty of help to load them."

Long clapped Harp on the back. "I can't wait to tell Father what we've done."

"Hell, yes. He won't believe us anyhow."

"No he won't."

The three rode back to the bank together and they left the list with Edmonson who just stared at the paper, then at them, and softly asked, "Eighty dollars apiece?"

"That's what they will bring."

"I can't imagine that much money for cattle."

"They will all be by with a letter of credit. You will furnish clerks to handle the money transactions at the depot?"

"Oh, yes; when will it start?"

"They say cattle cars are coming now."

"We will be ready; I am sure proud you boys did so well here."

"So are we. Thanks for furnishing your help, sir."

The cowboys were equally excited in camp. Chaw said, "I never believed we'd make it, but I am damn sure happy I came and we did it. Thanks to you two guys. What do you have planned for next year?"

"We told them we aren't coming back to Missouri, but if there are places out west of here where we can meet the trains, we may bring a herd up to there."

"Sign us boys up," Chaw said. "I'll damn sure come back. Hot digitty dog I am going to find me some sweet Missouri *puta* who'll love me, and then I can ride home happy as a pig in sunshine."

Harp laughed. "We still have to load the cattle first. That will be a chore."

"Naw, we've made it here. Loading will be just another piece of cake, boss man."

Harp wished he felt that way. He still had cramps in his belly expecting trouble to break out at any time. No way would he feel safe until the last door slid shut on the last steers and they were in the saddle going home. It couldn't be fast enough.

CHAPTER 7

The first train pulled out for St. Louis three days later. More cars were coming, Williams said. The trains weren't very busy yet because of the slow war recovery and, besides, you could only fit so many longhorns in a cattle car. But they were busy each day filling cars and sending them east. With all the men he had hired to drive them downtown, the operation went smoothly as another engine puffing smoke went on out to St. Louie.

In ten days they'd be gone—maybe less.

The next morning Sheriff Harris showed up at the depot and Harp wondered what he wanted. He was seated at a desk the tellers used.

"Something wrong?" Harp asked.

"The governor is sending state police to stop you from loading the trains."

Harp blinked at him. "When will they get here?"

"Two days I figure."

"Do what you can to stop them. I will pay for your protection."

"What if I can't? They overrule me."

"I will go see Williams. He must have some pull to stop it."

"I never thought about him."

"He's staying at the Grand Hotel. I'll go do that now."

"I will, meanwhile, do what I can."

"Thanks, Harris. I will pay you for your troubles." He realized Harris was the only one not getting bucks for helping. Oh, hell, he had warned him.

He found Williams in the restaurant having a late breakfast.

He looked up at Harp. "Sit down, Texas." Between bites of eggs he asked, "What's on your mind?"

"They say the governor has sent some police down here to stop our sale of cattle."

"How?"

"The legislature passed a law no Texas cattle are allowed in Missouri."

"I will wire him to stop them. He will do that. He does not understand the problems we have getting meat. I will wire him when I get through with breakfast. Now if I can get river barges moving, is there some place I can get boats close to your cattle?"

"I had not considered it, sir."

"Start your brain working on a port down where you could get cattle to."

"I will do that."

"Meantime don't worry. Keep loading cattle."

"Thank you." Relieved, he left the man and headed for the depot where they were loading cars. The crew was penning the next shipment when he rode up. Chaw was in charge, and between mules and horse riders things looked under control.

Long came riding in a few minutes later and dismounted. "What's wrong?"

"Oh, the governor is sending the state police to stop us from loading steers."

"Hell. What did you do?"

"I sicced the biggest meatpacker in Missouri, Williams, on him. He told me not to worry he would stop him."

"Well thank God for him. We'll be through in a week if the cattle cars keep coming."

"I am ready to be done now."

"It has been a hell of an adventure. What are we going to do next?"

"Williams wants us to think of ways to deliver cattle to him at a boat port." Harp shook his head on the notion.

"Oh, you'd have to go through the damn swamps in Louisiana."

"Not me. But we need to figure out a way to sell more cattle. There damn sure is no money in Texas like what we did here. Railroads will be building more tracks now the war is over. Maybe somewhere west we can find a new shipping point. I don't aim to buck this route again."

"But we learned a lot."

"Oh, hell, lots and lots about trailing cattle."

"Harp, you are the money man. How much do you see this deal making?"

"Before all our expenses, we'll take in over sixty thousand dollars."

"That was my count. They sell steers like that for ten bucks or less in Texas."

"They won't for long, after word gets out, but they haven't drove them north yet, either."

Long rested his butt against the depot fence and shook his head. "And there's still thousands of un-branded stock left down there to round up."

About then an angry steer blowing snot butted the fence with his head right beside him. Long jumped away and looked back. "Easy, guy, you will be roast beef in a short while."

Everyone in the area laughed.

The two walked into the depot and the banker's men were at the desk.

"Morning. Whose cattle go today?" Harp asked them.

"John Paterson. He bought two carloads. Then four others and we start tomorrow loading Mr. Williams's cattle."

"Money is coming through?"

"No hitches so far, sir."

"You men do good work."

"Thanks; we try. Will you bring any more cattle up here?"

Harp shook his head. "Missouri doesn't want me to."

The older of the two young men, Oren Spalding, shook his head. "Pretty dumb. Besides the men you've hired and the things you've bought and the railroad business, they are going to miss out on lots of money."

"That's the way they want it. That empty farmland we crossed and grazed getting up here, now the war is over, will fill in fast. Be too many people in the land to bring herds of cattle through."

"What's it like in Texas?"

"No jobs. No money. We hear from our letters that they set up an occupational government and disbanded the people saving folks' lives— the rangers—out on the western fringe from the Comanche."

"Well, we do appreciate you twos' efforts. A little cow shit on our shoes is not hurting anyone."

"Good."

They left the depot and agreed to meet in camp later. Harp said he'd stay around town to see if they turned the governor's enforcer away.

Long went and mounted his horse. "See you, bro."

"You bet."

In his mail was a letter addressed to them from Emory's wife, Anna.

Dear Men,

You two have done a wonderful job. I am of course saddened by his death. He was a generous father to our children and a grand husband to me. To be taken so young from us is a tragedy. But you two have done a wonderful job and thank God. Be careful coming home. Even Texas has turned into a lawless place and people are being robbed and killed every day. I shall pray for your safe return.

Sincerely yours,
Anna Greg

Harp thought about Emory's wife. Anna was an attractive woman with three children. He didn't need a wife and family. But she would be well to do until she found someone and chose a suitable husband. He knew Long would not be interested in her, either.

Women were simply not his thing. Well, he'd been sweet on Sally Graham, but she told him she couldn't wait for him to decide and married Clarence Ward. A widower fifteen years older than her who had a ranch and a short leg, so he never was drafted.

Harp felt he had plenty of time to find a wife. Now he needed to make more money to build a ranch and make a place in Texas for himself and Long. He wished he knew a gypsy who could tell him his future fortune. Otherwise he'd have to make it up as he went along.

Two days later the head of the Missouri State Police arrived with a telegram in hand that ordered the police to suspend all operations against Harp and the Texas cattle. Due to the food shortages caused by the war, the public needed the beef.

The man was not happy about his new instructions and openly told Long O'Malley that if they ever again brought Texas beef to Missouri he'd personally shoot them.

Long thanked him for the warning, then went about his business and later reported the comments to his brother.

"Nice guy," Harp commented.

The last Texas steer was poked onto the car on Thursday and the door slid shut on him. Williams was there and thanked them. He reminded Harp about his promise to find him a way to ship cattle by barge. They shook hands.

"I will look into it. I promise."

Harp and the banker Edmonson went over his figures:

> 780 steers @ $80 = $62,400
> Cattle partners' owed half value, 390 head,
>   after expenses
> Emory's bank debt at home, $1,500
> Sedalia hired crew, $750 at 30 bucks a head
> Pasture, $100
> Sheriff fee, $50
> Schoolhouse rent, $30
> Banking fee, $300
> Misc. expenses, $50
> Supplies for trip home, $800
> Owed Hiram O'Malley for 25 horses and use
>   of his steer, $1,000
> Crew of nine paid $100 apiece
>
> Amount left $56,920
> Half to partners = $28,460

Harp looked up hard under the lamplight at his brother. "If we split it in half with her, our part is just over fourteen thousand dollars."

Long simply shook his head in dismay. "I knew we

were in for some big bucks, but I had no idea it would be that much money."

"I didn't include his tombstone. I'll pay for it out of our share."

"How do we get that much cash home to Texas and not get robbed?" Long asked.

"Edmonson, at the bank, says they have this outfit who will transfer the money to a bank at home with no danger of losing any."

"Are they sure it will get there?"

"He says people do it all the time and they are bonded."

"If they can't steal it, then let's do that."

Harp made a face about the expense. "The service costs money. Two fifty for that much money."

"Ha. Better to let them get it there than us have to worry about it and get killed carrying it ourselves going home."

"I'll do it tomorrow."

"You'll keep out our expenses to go home on?"

Harp nodded. "I charged that as our food going home from the settlement."

Long reached over and clapped him on the shoulder. "Bro, we've done won the first war didn't we?"

"I'll say yes when we get home alive. We've had a pretty interesting trip up here."

"Oh, we'll make the trip home easy. Them boys are all in town tonight raising hell and chasing wild women. Just hope they're going to be sober enough to drive home tomorrow."

"They will moan and groan a lot."

"Long, when you and I signed on as Greg's cowboys, we were still kids going on a big adventure. I think we both grew up and both of us did a man-size job for Missus Greg."

His brother nodded. "We did. You settle that bank thing. Let them boys have their fun and we go home tomorrow as planned."

"Damn good idea."

They left Sedalia for Texas with red paint on both wagons that said O'MALLEY BROTHERS LAND AND CATTLE COMPANY, CAMP VERDE, TEXAS.

Scratching his new haircut riding next to Harp, Chaw asked, "Where's the damn land part at?"

"We are going to buy some when we get home," Harp told him.

Chaw was not the last man to ask about the land part. A storekeeper in a white apron, leaning on a broom handle on his porch in Cassville, asked them the same question.

Harp climbed the steps and looked back at the wagons. "Oh, near Camp Verde. Come by. I'll feed you if I am at home."

"I'll bet you would, cowboy. What do you need?"

"Salt pork if you have any. A short barrel of flour and brown beans."

"Got navy beans, no brown ones, sorry."

"Hey we aren't sailors, we're cowboys. Cowboys eat *frijoles*. I'll try farther south."

"There's less down there than is up here."

"Maybe so. I guess I'll find out along the way. How much do I owe you?"

"Five bucks."

"Put a dollar's worth of hard candy in that order. I bet you don't have any good coffee, either?"

The man shook his head, finishing his sweeping. "I have some tea bricks. I ain't had any coffee, good or bad, in eighteen months. Where you coming from?"

"Sedalia. We sold the herd we drug up here."

"I won't tell anyone about that. Folks been losing cows to Texas tick fever ever since then."

"Sorry about that. I'll keep it to myself." He paid the man, got his goods, and left.

He later told Long and the crew not to talk about their drive anymore until they got home. A few days later they stopped to shoe some sore-footed horses at Fayetteville, Arkansas, camping below the city square. The local blacksmith named Handy Jones and the men all pitched in and shod the horses. Jones was grateful for the cash business and asked them how it went going up there since he had heard about the drive.

Long told him privately that it went well but they didn't want it out that they broke the law going there. Jones agreed to keep it quiet.

Harp met a pretty girl in a woman's dress shop when he went in looking for a present for their mother. Something she could wear. The girl's name was Heidi Holstein and she showed him many things. In the end the blue-eyed girl told him to check back with her again.

He said he would but doubted he'd ever see her again the next time. Her face stayed in his mind, and he had dreams of dancing the polka with her at a schoolhouse dance in Van Buren near the army's Fort Smith.

He did buy a sack of good brown beans in a store there. Two different doves also accosted him before he made it back to his horse, packing the load on his shoulder.

One would not give up. "Oh, my, a big man like you sure needs to love me."

"No, ma'am, I need to take these up the hill to my crew so they can eat."

"I can feed you love, mister, and for only two dollars."

"No thanks."

"Step in the alley and I'll show you my body. You will love it."

"No thanks, ma'am."

"Gawdamn it. Then I will do it for a dollar."

He shook his head, not impressed by her. "Not today at any price."

"I hope that sheep you use gives you the clap." She stomped off.

At least she wouldn't give him any of her diseases. He waved down a black man with mules and a wagon who for fifty cents was willing to deliver the sack of beans to their camp on the hill.

He loaded them in his rickety-rick and then paid him. The man thanked him. Then he promised to deliver them and went on up the hill.

"This your horse, mister?"

Damn there was another of them women untying his horse.

"Yes and thank you, ma'am. I'll take those reins."

This one wasn't wearing a dress; she wore men's britches and a man's shirt. "I wasn't going to steal him. You leaving town?"

"I planned to shortly. Why?"

"Why don't you buy us two cans of peaches and some forks?"

"What are we going to do with them?"

"Go over to Lee's Creek on your horse and eat them in private."

"What's your name?"

"Kate Martin. What's yours?"

"Harper O'Malley."

"Well, since you aren't doing anything important, why don't we do that, Harper O'Malley?"

"Where do you live?"

"Around here."

"Where are your folks?"

"Dead."

"Where do you live then?"

"Where I can. I just thought we'd go somewhere and talk and eat peaches. You are a nice-looking man and I just thought—"

"If I buy those peaches, let's be straight, I am under no obligation to you except to eat them with you."

"Honest, mister. That's all."

"Stay here. I'll be back."

"Hey, guy."

"Yes."

"Thanks."

She sure was not the typical tramp he'd ever met. What the hell. She intrigued him. That was a word his mother taught him. First chance he had to ever use the word that he could recall. He purchased two large cans of peaches. He had utensils in his saddlebags.

When he returned she was sitting there cross-legged on the ground, and she bound up like she was on springs, brushed her small butt off, and laughed. "I picked a winner."

"Put your can in that side. I'll put mine over here."

"This horse pack double?" she asked as she put her can away.

"He will if I want him to."

"You must live in Texas?" she asked as he pulled her up behind him.

"I do when I am home. West of San Antonio at Camp Verde. Dad had a ranch west of Fort Worth originally; we moved south later on."

"Why are you up here then?"

"I took a big herd of cattle to Sedalia, Missouri. Going home."

She scooted up behind him and put her hands around his waist, hugging him tightly. "He don't act like he will buck."

"I think he'll be fine. He's been rode a million miles. Can I ask how you exist? Being a young female with no family?"

"I do the best I can. I am not some angel, but I think you knew that. I try to find a man to put up with me so that I am not like today when I am without one."

"Where did the last one go?"

"Prison."

"Why?"

"He shot a man and they found him guilty."

"You love him."

"He provided for me. I spent the last dime he gave me for breakfast this morning."

"They're going to hang him?"

"Yes, in three weeks. Listen . . . Jimmy Groves, for my part, is already dead. Let's talk about you."

"Not much to say. My brother Long and I own the O'Malley Brothers Land and Cattle Company. We're headed home. Taking a break down here and tomorrow we go on to Texas."

"You have a crew with you?"

"Ten others besides ourselves. Two wagons and a remuda."

"What is that?"

"Fifty horses to switch out and one big bell steer."

"What's he for anyway?"

"He led the cattle to Sedalia for us."

"Take this road west. Were they big longhorns?"

"Yes. And I'm going back for more."

"You do this all the time? Drive cattle up and down the country?"

"I guess after this we do. No one ever dreamed you could take cattle to Missouri and sell them. Emory, the man who hired us, believed we could do it, and we started north before Lee signed the surrender."

"It was a wonder you didn't get killed. Where's he now?"

"He died after we got there. He's got a family back in Texas."

She waved for him to turn. "Take this side road up the creek. There are places to be alone up there."

"You come over here often?"

"When Jimmy was with me . . . yes."

"It bring bad memories to you coming back?"

"Honest no. I told you, he's as good as dead. He can't ever come back here. I need a new life. I saw you today, carrying that sack like it was a pillow, and I told myself I needed to meet you. I want to turn a new corner in my life, and I hoped you might want to be the man to help me do it."

"I simply wondered why you stopped me."

"You ain't married are you?"

"No."

"Some men would lie about it. You ain't a liar, either, are you?"

"No. I don't lie to anyone."

She hugged him tightly from behind in the saddle. "I am not obligating you to anything."

"Okay, I am listening."

"What I mean . . . whoa, turn in here. Ain't a soul around here."

Kate slipped off the horse. He dismounted and led the animal into the glen she pointed him to, and then she showed the way onto the short grassy beach above the stream surrounded by bamboo.

"You ready for peaches?"

"I guess. I can open them with my big knife."

"Good. Open yours, then mine."

"Why not yours first."

"Because I am beholden to you for buying them and bringing me up here today."

He opened her can and gave her a fork. Then he opened his and bent the lid back. She was already smiling and licking her lips when he looked up.

"What would you have done today if you hadn't invited me down here?"

"Harper, I have to admit I was concerned. But I don't know—I'd done something. Might not been what I liked. I am a survivor. My step-people been dead since I was fourteen. I'll be eighteen this winter. I don't look back much. I try to steer ahead, but I must say with him in jail my life has been rocky. Today is much better and I have you to thank."

He savored the first bite. That sweet peachy taste filled his mouth and he felt wonderful eating it. What a good treat. She set her can down and came over to him.

"You want to kiss a sweet mouth?"

Hell, yes. Words were not necessary. He kissed her, and he liked it so well he kissed her some more. Heady business in a hot afternoon. He never noticed the heat before now, and now here he was sprawled over this wisp of a girl and kissing the fire out of her.

"Should we finish the peaches?" she asked, looking dreamy-eyed up at him.

"I guess we better."

They ate and looked what he called moon-eyed at each other the whole time. He didn't want to lose her. Peaches and loving her—they all went together.

By the time the peaches were eaten, the sun was

setting. She suggested they unsaddle his horse and then go take a bath in the river. Then, if they wanted to, they could dry off sitting on his horse blanket rather than on the grass.

"I have soap and a towel in my saddlebags." As he unsaddled Comanche she laid out the saddle blanket.

That done she began to undress. He did the same. Then, hand in hand, they ran off into the creek and splashed—kissed—splashed some more. The moon was rising in the east hours later when the two weary lovers finally rode into the cow camp.

He threw his leg over the horn to dismount and caught her in his arms to set her down.

"Long, I want you to meet someone I met today."

"Howdy," Long said, realizing it was a girl and taking off his hat.

"Long O'Malley, this is Kate Martin, and she's going to Texas with us."

"Well, come over here. We have some fresh real coffee and your beans made it to camp, too," he said to Harp.

"Good. She and I got detoured. We ate a couple of cans of peaches and took a bath in Lee's Creek."

Harp would've sworn she blushed at his tale. But he hugged her and that made her smile. "I guess we can go by and get her few things tomorrow before we ride out of here."

"I don't know how he found you, little lady, but welcome. Just so you know, Harp and I are brothers, nine months apart, and I'm the elder one. I will tell the crew you are here. This has been a boys' camp up until now. But they all have manners and will treat you nicely. They don't, I'll teach them better."

"Thank you, Long. How'd you both get those names?"

"Dad said that when I came in the world, Mom said, 'He's Long.'"

"I came along and Dad said we can't have two Longs, so I'm Harper."

They had her laughing. "I can see," she said behind tears of laughter. "This is going to be a great ride to your home."

Harp learned one thing that night—two lovers could both sleep on a single cot.

At breakfast the crew met her, and they all told her that she chose the wrong one. Every one of them wanted her. She enjoyed the attention and told them sorry, she picked him and was tickled to have him.

Harp and Kate went with a packhorse to get her things. Told the crew they'd catch up with them.

The shack she took him to had a low roof. Obviously the man she lived with before was not as tall as he was. She brought him the blankets and bedding she wanted to keep. She had a few dresses. It wasn't much. An older man came around saying she owed rent and was she going to pay it.

She told him to get it from the man in jail. He got red faced and before he started in on her, Harp spun him around. "How much?"

"Five dollars."

"Here." He stuck it in the man's shirt pocket,

spun him back around, and told him to get his ass out of there.

A short while later she closed the door, mounted her own horse, and they went to the free ferry, loaded up on it, and went over to Fort Smith. They kept moving cross-country to the brick army barracks and then took the pay-for-paddlewheel ferry to the west bank. It cost a quarter an animal.

"I am going to break you from paying ferry fees," she said on the far side, mounting up again.

"No, it beats swimming across the river with steers."

She laughed. That girl laughed a whole lot. He was getting prouder and prouder by the day, having her along. They caught up with the crew in camp south of the Canadian River.

It was suppertime and his belly button was gnawing at his backbone by then. Ira found a man that sold him beef for five bucks, and he had cooked a loin. It was damn good and there was lots of it.

The drive home went faster than going up, and they crossed the Red River on a ferry into Texas in five days. In Fort Worth, Harp took Kate to a hotel. She put on a dress to eat out in and they slept in a bed that night. The men camped and some came into town while they took a day to reassemble things before forging on. He bought her two good dresses that really made her feel like a lady, and two new pairs of boy's pants to wear when she rode.

She told him she felt like a queen, never had that many clothes in all her life. In San Antonio, he went by the Texas National Bank and showed them his receipt. They showed him his deposit and took him back to the number two man in the large bank, Fred Newman. Fred told Harp how proud he was to meet him and asked how could he help him.

He got checks to pay everyone, and Newman showed him how to make out the checks and sign them. Next he and Kate rode onto Kerrville and stayed at the Grand Hotel.

If there was one thing he dreaded, it was taking Kate to the ranch to meet his mom. He'd faced some mean men in fistfights but never before faced his mother with a woman he lived with who was not his wife. He'd never even had a wife.

He rented a buckboard. Kate wore a good dress and had clothes to change into so she could see the family ranch. If, of course, he was still alive to show it to her.

When they came up the quarter-mile drive to the ranch house, he warned her. "If this turns into hell raising we will leave, Katy darling."

"Your folks will be that bad after you've been gone for six months?"

"No. But Mom may be so upset that you and I aren't married that we can't stay here."

"Harper O'Malley, I never asked for you to marry me."

"Don't be upset. That is her way."

"Well if it gets bad we can leave, but I will cry."

"Darling, I hope it won't happen, but you've been warned."

He reined up, got down, then tied the horses to the hitch rail and went back to take her off the buckboard. Besides the stock dogs barking, he heard his mother say, "You must be Kate Martin. Welcome to the O'Malley Ranch. I am so glad to meet you." Then she hugged her like a daughter-in-law should be hugged.

That damn Long had informed her all about Katy. Bless his soul. He never expected that from his half-Cherokee brother—but he owed him one that was for sure.

Those two women were so engaged in talking, he waited patiently for them to go into the house. Then his father came around the corner, hugged her, then whirled her around in a circle like he did his wife many times and told her how happy he was Harp had found her.

What a helluva welcome home.

Thank you, Lord, one more time for helping this sinner out.

CHAPTER 8

Harp, Long, and his family set up a party for everyone that was owed money from the cattle drive. It was a celebration to come to the ranch, eat, and get paid. Other neighbors were invited as well. It was planned for Saturday starting at three in the afternoon. A nearby German had plenty of home-made beer capped to sell to Long, and, submerged in the springhouse tank, it would be cool enough to drink.

They'd planned to barbecue goats and one hog. Everyone lent a hand. Harp saw how his Katy and mom made a powerful team, cooking and baking for three days. The cook, Ira, was still around and he did the meat, at which he was a mesquite marvel at cooking.

Harp had Long bring Emory's widow, Anna, and kids over early, since the celebration was in her honor. By midday, lots of others were coming up the driveway. They had plenty to snack on, meat, and every kind of pie ever made in Texas, plus cakes and something sweet the Czechs made called Danish.

Emory's widow looked very nice in the black dress, and big brother had her arm. She was a nice lady and he wondered what Long was feeling about her since he was staying close.

He pulled Katy aside, and out of sight, kissed her.

She was breathless. "You were so worried huh? You devil. This is wild and your mom is wonderful. I have learned so damn much my head is about to crack open. Buddy, I sure made a good grab getting you."

"Maybe."

"No maybe about it. Kissing is over. I have to fix some more things. They're drinking more lemonade than beer."

He let her go. The envelopes were all ready to pay each person with a check inside. She'd helped him fix each one. To say the amounts had amazed her was an understatement.

"You two are tycoons," she'd mentioned the night before. "And you plan to go back?"

"Yes, but not through Missouri."

"Oh, Harp, this is unbelievable."

"The trip was that way to me six months ago."

They had the Baptist preacher give the grace. Harper welcomed them all to the party.

"We want you to know, for you people missed it, and who's selling any cattle this year, Long and I are going north, destination unknown at this time, but we plan to have a market next year and are taking consignments of big steers for delivery north in 1866.

"From this trip just finished, the first check is for a great lady. I am so sad that her husband, Emory, who advised Long and I and made the plans for the trip, is not here to do this. Here is your check, Anna."

Long had her elbow. Harper decided if he had not held her up, her knees would have caved.

"This—ah—is my share, and everyone else has been paid?" she asked him.

Harp looked her in the eye. "Your husband told us we should share the proceeds with you. All the money he owed at the bank is paid and any bills I know of are paid. That amount is yours."

"But it is way too much money, Harper O'Malley."

"How much did you pay her?" someone asked.

"No one need know amounts."

A hush fell over the crowd.

"She has her share after everyone will be paid."

Long escorted her to the side. His mother and Katy were there to calm her.

"John Haycox. Here is your amount for a hundred steers."

"Oh, my God, John. We are out of debt," his wife screamed, hugging his neck.

"Walter Scott, a hundred steers, same amount."

"I'm coming, Harp. My get-along isn't that fast anymore. You boys need hugging and kissed, but I ain't doing no part of that." The crowd laughed. "You sure you got all your expenses out of here."

"Yes, sir. Mike Howard, a hundred head."

Long said, "His daughter, Emily, is coming. Mike is under the weather."

A big, buxom, red-faced gal about thirty came grinning. "That'll make Pappy well I bet you."

The list went on and on. Harp knew the check for forty head went to Baldy Sorenson was as big to him as any handed out that evening. He came crying. "I'd never believed you boys could have done that for me."

The last check was for a widow woman for eight head. Natty Coins was in her forties, gray headed, and sharp talking. When Harp told her the amount she stopped and blinked her eyes. "I only drove eight head to you boys' house. How could this be my check?"

"I recall you started out with ten, Natty. You told me that two got away from you on foot."

"That's right. I couldn't catch them two rascals. Oh, mercy, I called them lots worse than that."

"Long and I paid you for the two that got away."

The crowd gave them more applause.

"Now you see we do what we say. Could have been worse or maybe better. But our first drive turned out all right. Thank you all for believing and trusting us."

That night, he and Katy went to bed in the attic where they'd slept each evening since coming home. Lying on his back he was still feeling high from the payoffs.

She was, too. "Your mother told me a story, since I have been here, that I think kind of explains things. About how you were so worried she wouldn't accept me and why she acted like she did when I got here. I bet she never told you this story."

"What did she tell you?"

"She loved a Cherokee and he lied to her before he went off hunting in the Cherokee Outlet. He got killed out there and she had Long in her when your father, whose wife who had drowned, came by and took her away and married her."

"I heard a shorter version. But you don't have a baby in you do you?"

"Oh, damn you, Harp O'Malley—she understood me and my way since she had been there. No I swear I have no baby in me that I know about."

"Good, let's try for one."

She sighed, exasperated. "You are the neatest guy I ever knew. Why, those people talked all night about sending cattle north with you two next year."

Uh-huh.

CHAPTER 9

Harp and Long talked all the next morning about buying a ranch of their own. They discussed all the places they knew might be for sale or they knew were for sale.

Then the brothers and Kate jumped on a two-seat buckboard and drove it to town.

They split up and Harp and Katy went to see the local banker, Jim Yale. Long went to find the lawyer, Tommy Snyder, who sold places. The three were to meet at Kelly's Diner for more talk later when they were through.

Jim Yale had five places for sale. Three were repossessions and Harp knew them all—they were dumps. The place on Lavender Mountain was not much of a ranch, but the one in Grass Valley might be.

"Two sections, nice house. Has sixty acres hay meadow, forty cropland. More could be developed in the creek bottom. Some windmills and several watering tanks. Run a hundred and twenty mother cows."

"How much?"

"Ten thousand with the cows on it."

"How many cow calf pairs?"

"They say a hundred. I expect eighty."

"Less than eighty you'd replace them?"

"No, I can't do that. This place has not been run right."

"I still have a crew of guys. Let me count the cows and I'll look at the place and be back in five days. You hold it for me until then. We will see what it has and doesn't by then."

"Word is out you guys killed the golden calf in Missouri?"

"We did all right. Just don't finance anyone going up there. They don't like Texas cattle and have a law against bringing them into the state. We barely got in and out alive."

"Folks say you sold sixty thousand dollars' worth of cattle up there."

"I am not lying to you if I say that if they weren't so starved for meat we'd never have made it."

"More will try now they have the word."

"Well, I am not ever going back to Missouri. If you loan money to anyone going up there you are a damn fool, and don't say I didn't warn you."

Katy wanted him to sit down. He did.

"Back to the RXB Ranch. Will you hold it that long?"

"For you, ten days."

"Good.

Long had two places the lawyer found, but he agreed he wanted to look over the RXB place first. They hurried home and gathered the crew. Ira was going to get supplies in town on his way out there with the big supply wagon. The hands were riding over there in the morning to start counting cattle and recording them. Two hands were bringing half the remuda over and helping the cook set up.

Hiram said the boys helping him had his place working fine so he wanted to go along and see it, too. That made Harp feel good. His dad knew lots about cattle ranches. His mother sent a wall tent over in the wagon for Katy to sleep in if the house wasn't fit.

Katy wore a used pair of chaps to bust through brush with. Despite Harp telling her she wasn't a *vaquero* and the men could do that, he knew she'd do anything those boys did. And had her hat on a cord so she wouldn't have to get off her horse to recover it. They got to the RXB and split up into four bunches.

Chaw took two men. Doug Pharr two. Chadron three. Red Culver went with Katy, Harp, Long, and Hiram.

They left in four directions and were to meet back by five at the headquarters.

Harp and his bunch rode west. In the next few hours they found forty pair and fifteen yearlings. Harp booked the cows with Katy's help, scribbling what he hoped he could read later. Going in they found twenty more head of yearlings.

Chadron found thirty cow calves and twenty

yearlings. Doug found thirty cows and twenty-five yearlings. Chaw brought back the number forty-five pairs with a hundred yearlings.

That evening the men talked about the bulls and realized that no one had counted them. To the men, most were pure shorthorn and looked in very good shape. They were ready for chuck when the triangle was rung.

"I see, Miss Katy, you didn't get your britches tore up today wearing them chaps."

"No problem, boys," she said. "These chaps are not easy to walk around in, but on horseback they are great."

Things went well at supper. The men talked about the range and how good the grass looked to them.

After supper Kate and Harp rode the fenced hay and farm ground. The cropland had grown up in goose grass since no crop was planted. There also was no hay in the stacks except for a few old ones. They'd need to buy forage to get through winter.

"Too late to plant oats for next year?" he asked his father when he and Kate got back.

"No, but who will plow it and plant it?"

"I bet we can get some Mexicans to come do that," one of the hands suggested.

Hiram agreed. "I guess there isn't much you two can't do once you set your mind to it."

Long grinned big. "We think there are a hundred sixty cows and a hundred fifty calves. That isn't a bad calf crop with no help. We counted over two hundred yearlings, some younger and about half heifers. We'll need to cull old cows, sell some big cattle, and pasture about a hundred to sell next year. Then we should have a hundred to one fifty head to sell each year if we can trail them." It was one of Long's longest speeches in years—Harp liked it.

Hiram spoke up next. "There is no money in Texas, boys. The owner wants ten. He don't have any cash buyers. If it was me I'd offer him five and you can always pay him more. Boys, you have the cash and spent right you might end up in taller cotton, huh? Missouri is out. You boys learned that this year. Where they going to find markets?"

"You really think we have that much advantage?"

"As I said, Texas has not got a thing to pay their debts with. You mind my thinking."

"You never got those gray hairs sitting around, Dad."

"This is a damn good place. One of us needs this place to raise their family. Harp, you thinking like I am?" Long asked.

"Oh, I'd buy it in a minute for five."

"Hell, offer it to him. He might take it."

"It could be good. I'll do it."

Long said, "Good. We've got two more to look at—one tomorrow and one the next day."

Harp agreed. After supper, he and Katy crawled into his blankets off by themselves and discussed the place.

"If you are going off trailing steers somewhere next year, unless I'm big as a bear with a baby, I'm going along."

He drew back. "You in a family way now?"

"No. But we keep working at it I will be. I still ain't staying down here by myself."

"Okay."

"I like this ranch, but it is too isolated."

"Ranches won't be in towns."

"I know. If your husband is on the ranch that's fine, but if he's off to hell knows where anyone can come by."

"We can make it work."

"We will. Your father is a smart man isn't he?"

"He always has been. He never had a chance to make any big money like we did with Emory. Things turned out good for us, but we took care of Emory's wife. Originally he was paying us fifteen dollars a month, which we'd been pleased with since there were no jobs anywhere."

He hugged and kissed her. This ranch would be a solid one if they could get it for the price.

The next place they looked at, that Long wanted to see, was a decent range ranch. However, the headquarters looked like a Mexican *bandito*'s hideout. They had some scrubby yearling stock grazing it. In two days they found fifty head valued at five dollars apiece. Long said they owned two sections of mostly cedar–live oak hills.

The two women who were there smoked cob pipes, chewed snuff, and went barefoot. No one ate with them, and the women could not allure even the cowboys, though Harp heard the younger girls propositioning the men. Their own men folks were gone somewhere.

In conference before they left Harp asked his brother what they wanted for it.

"Too much. I'd only pay them six hundred for a clear title."

"Or five," Hiram piped in, and everyone laughed.

The next place was in some creek bottoms. This land was not fenced and there was only half a section. The adobe house was in bad shape and the corral might only hold a crippled horse. Harp liked the soil and said most of it could be turned into farmland.

Hiram agreed.

Long said he had no idea about the price but wondered what they could pay for it.

"A dollar an acre?"

Long said he'd see the owner about it.

Back in town, Harp and Kate went by the bank. They offered five thousand for RXB and Jim Yale took it under advisement. He had to ask the bank board, and he sounded certain they would turn it down.

On the way riding home together, she said, "So we did not get the ranch?"

"Not yet. We are dickering for a lower price."

"I don't understand."

"Darling, it is like horse trading. He wants one price, but we want a lower one. So we counter offer. I think Dad is right. Our money is more valuable since there is no other money around."

"Harp, I have never had any money. I appreciate your explaining things to me."

"Hey, it is my pleasure."

At home, they planned to go find some maverick cattle they could catch and sell while they still had a crew. That suited the men, and plans were to check out the rough country north and west of them.

The cook's wagon was to go through town and to restock, so Harp and Katy rode with him. A remuda was to be chosen by Holy Wars, who was going to go cross-country to meet them at a creek crossing where they would set up. Some of the hands would go with him in case of trouble. Things in Texas were upset. Federal officials were pouring in to run the state government. U.S. marshals were arriving by trainloads looking for anyone ready to cause unrest in the population.

Chaw, Darvon, and Red accompanied them to town. Before going into the mercantile, Ira told the boys to drink two beers, not start any fights, and be ready to ride. Harp and Kate went to a saddle maker shop to look for a saddle for her. She'd been using an old hull they took from her old home place, and Harp realized, riding to the new ranch, she needed a better one.

Newell Kent had a nice used one that fit her. He wanted thirty dollars, and after arguing a while Harp bought it for twenty-one. Packing it on his shoulders with her beside him, he came down the boardwalk, when he saw a fight spill out of the Red Bull Saloon.

Red Culver, bareheaded, stood exchanging blows with some other hatless puncher among the horses. Darvon threw another one by his shirt collar out through the parted swinging door into the street.

Harp set the saddle down on its nose and hurried down to stop the fighting.

Hands on his hips, he shouted, "Red, Darvon, quit it. What the hell are you fighting over?"

Red's head bobbed up over a horse's saddle. "They called us Yankee sympathizers. Hell, you tell them we didn't do a damn things for them Yankees."

One of the town marshals was coming on the run. Harp called him down. "I can settle this for you."

"Hi, Harp. I heard you guys sold cattle in Missouri."

"Yes, we did, and now my boys were being accused of supporting the Yankees in that drive. Hell, we're just trying to survive. I'll settle the damages."

Two of his men came out dusting off with their hats and cussing under their breaths. Red had his hat and was reshaping it.

Harp told Red where Kate's new saddle was and to put it on her horse and set the old one in the wagon.

He walked by the other two and went inside.

Going by him, Chaw said, "We didn't start it."

The bartender shook his head. "Them other boys had it coming, Harp. Your boys tried to ignore them."

"What's broke?"

"Oh, two chairs."

"What did they cost?"

"A dollar."

"Here's two." He told him to take it, and he ran out to join his men.

The store workers were loading the wagon. Kate was smiling, sitting in her new saddle, and ready to start the wild cattle hunt.

They set up at a spring in some rough brush country. Harp had trapped mavericks with his father in this brushy area. They'd built traps around water holes; wild cattle came in and could not get out of the spear-loaded gates.

The chute-like trap had spear points shaved on the end of the gates. The gates closed by weights, which could be sprung open by squeezing through the spears to go back out. But that system was way too slow to use to get the whole job done.

The project, instead, was going to be to flush them out and then with many riders, force them into corrals to be branded using a squeeze chute. Roped, branded, ear marked, bulls would then be castrated and turned out.

Harp heard some old outfit had left a big corral in good shape nearby. They had gathered cattle for their hides and tallow, hauled two hundred miles or more down to the gulf, and put on a ship. Those cattle hides and tallow were maybe worth fifty cents each one, so in the end they couldn't make any money at it.

The setup was built on unclaimed state land. There was lots of such land unused and unclaimed. Harp and his brother wanted the cattle still on four hooves to drive to a yet undesignated market the next spring. They might not be worth eighty dollars a head like in Sedalia, but whatever it was, it would beat the market at home in a *cashless* Texas. Folks could burn all their Confederate money for heat in the winter. All of it was worthless.

The cowboys found plenty of droppings and began to make short trips to get an idea how far around they needed to ride to flush the cattle out and down into the pens they had repaired. Harp and Katy were in some open country when he discovered some scattered horse droppings. He reined up and dropped off his horse and handed her the reins.

"What's wrong?" she asked.

"We aren't the only ones here." He swung into the saddle, anxious to get everyone together before hell broke loose.

"Who else?"

He sat and gripped the horn. "We're going back to camp, now."

"Who's here besides us?" she insisted.

"There are Comanche in the area."

She paled.

"We still have the good guns. They come we can whip them, but I want to do it up there."

Woodenly she nodded. He tossed his head toward the camp, and they charged off for the headquarters. They went hard, others joining him when they saw them in a hurry.

"What's wrong?" Doug asked, riding along beside him in a fast lope.

Harp said one word. "Comanche."

"Damn." Doug passed the word to others, telling them to spread out and go find the rest of the crew and bring them all back to camp.

Harp and those with him charged on, and in a short while they all slid to a halt at the wagon.

Ira came running. "What's wrong?"

"I saw fresh Comanche sign."

"Oh, hell. Break out the rifles, boys. We got some bad company out here."

Everyone made it back to camp. Long came in with his party and frowned.

"Why in the hell is everyone armed?"

"I cut some real fresh Comanche tracks over south. They are around here."

"Oh, hell." Long dropped his head. "How many do you figure are out there?"

"Looked to me like a war party that might be scouting us out."

"Boy, bro, that is going to mess up our stock roundup."

"I damn sure didn't invite them."

"Good thing you were the one that saw it. Anyone else had seen the sign might not thought anything. You and I have done enough to recognize and know them. I think we need to grab some saws and axes, make a ring of cedar trees we can ignite to better see those red devils if they come at us in the night."

"Yes, and I'll get that canvas off the cook's wagon or they may use fire arrows to burn it up. A few arrows won't ignite it, but the canvas burning on the ribs will burn it down."

"What about the horses?" Doug asked.

"Unsaddle them. The saddles will make good barriers to be behind and shoot from at the raiders. We need to put the horses in the corral and be certain they can't bust them out. They'd like us out here on foot. Assign two men to guard them. It will be a dangerous job, but we will need horses to ride for help when this is over."

Harp caught Long by the arm. "I think we need some trenches dug. There is no house here and that corral won't stop bullets."

"Lay it out and we can dig them. I am going to check the rifles, be sure they're all in working condition, and see how much ammo we have."

"Chaw, get some shovels and picks out. We are going to dig some trenches to get into." Harp took off at a trot to look how an Indian racing in on a horse would see them. That would tell him where they needed to dig to face their enemy.

By felling a few big trees he could funnel the Indians in close enough for the men to shoot and stop them. They needed that funnel. He recalled the first time as a young boy when all the families took shelter in a log fort. The so-called fort became a nasty place fast. Babies crying, bad water to drink. Hysterical women screaming they'd all be killed.

But they weren't all killed. A few years later Hiram sold out, left that country, and settled at Camp Verde. The first few years at the new ranch the Comanche gave them hell, but there were a greater number of people around, which was why their father sold the first place and bought the

Camp Verde one. As boys they'd spend weeks camped out on the west side of civilization to watch for scattered horse poop and barefoot horses, which meant the red man was in the area.

He and Long had some close calls, but they managed to get away unharmed and shot a few of them every time they could score and get away. He could smell them on a soft wind from over a quarter mile away. His brother could do the same.

If they could force the Comanche to charge in from the north and were ready, they'd be able to cut them down. That was his plan. The largest thing he faced was where to put Katy. He didn't let her come out here to lose her or have her hurt. He didn't consider that the enemy would be this far east or she could have stayed with his parents. That regret stabbed him hard. She had to be the greatest thing to come in his life. Their successful cattle drive had been a super thing they'd pulled off, a good realization about people and their needs and his bargaining from a place of strength when he had it. The next twenty-four to thirty-six hours would prove their ability to stop the enemy, or his handful of great guys would be left for buzzards to angrily fight over their mutilated carcasses.

He took off his hat and wiped the sweat from his forehead. It was a hot fall day, and the anxiety building inside him from the impending trouble only added to his body heat. They needed two big live oaks felled to make the tunnel to herd them closer to his soldiers—ah, rangers would be a better name for them. People were so damn tired of war, the name *soldier* brought that back to him.

Chadron Turner could use a crosscut saw better than anyone, or an ax. He was with Chaw waiting for the trench design. Harp crossed the dusty open dirt churned up by all the horse traffic. Some of it was in all their noses and there would be lots more of it.

"Chaw, face the northwest. See that break in the trees. They will come down through to here, and our shooting at them will push them away. But the fallen trees, placed that way, will stop them. They will be stymied and we can cut them down. If you were in a trench to shoot at them do you see how we need it dug? Pile your dirt on the Indian side."

"I got you." Chaw spoke to the two others what to do.

"Chadron, let me show you a couple of trees I need felled to make it so they can't turn away from us when they realize the firepower we have."

"I'll get a saw and get Eldon to help me. He's a good timber man."

"Good."

When Chadron left him he saw Kate standing, hugging her arms and shifting her feet. He went to her. "I'm sorry I let you come, but I promise I will protect you from any harm."

"Harp, I'd like to do anything I can to help you. I understand if we try to run they'd overtake us. Long told me you two knew Indian ways. I can shoot a gun, and being with you I am not afraid. I will stay low."

"I don't want anything to happen to you." He

hugged and kissed her, then ran off to see about his tree choppers. The big trees fell perfectly, and the attackers couldn't turn away once they were channeled into the area in front of the crew. The day was slipping away fast. The trenches were being dug at a fast pace. Long had made two trips beyond the perimeter of the meadow to try to see where the Comanche were located.

He returned, shaking his head at Harp. "I didn't locate them."

Harp thanked him. They were out there. Indians could be well hidden and then burst out and strike. His experience with them was that they were as elusive as anything.

He had some blasting sticks made up that could, at close range, really help. It depended on the arm of the one tossing them. Long could toss them the farthest of anyone he knew. "Sit down," Ira said to him sharply. "This defense will work. I know you've got all of this warfare on your mind, but these boys will fight. Ease off. You're the best damn leader I ever been with in war or on the trail. We will mow them down."

Harp dropped his head. "I hate Kate's here."

"She don't. We all get into corners. We will fight our way out of it. There isn't one more thing you can do but face them."

"Thanks." He accepted the tin cup of hot coffee. "I guess when you've done it all, then you sit back and pray that it works."

Busy making dough on his table, Ira nodded. "I was in some bad situations in the war. Never figured

I'd live to see the next sunrise. But things worked out. I didn't have half the leadership of you two brothers. They should have gave you a parade when we slipped by Austin coming home. Hell, you took longhorn cattle to the heart of Yankee land at a profit. And some handful of nasty Comanche ain't going to turn us aside are they? Hell, no."

Harp finished his coffee and set the cup down. "Thanks for the talk."

Darkness began and cooler weather came with the curtain of night. He found Kate seated under a blanket beneath the wagon with a small candlelight to eat by. His plate loaded, he set his hat aside and settled into a place with her close by.

"These men that work for you are special, aren't they?"

He nodded. "They all grew up going north. Some even fought in the war, so they were no longer kids. River crossings, the challenges we met, they had a part in getting us through."

"You ever regret eating peaches with me?"

"You know better than that."

"Well, things happen that a person thinks are good and they can turn bad. I have no regrets. You exceeded my expectations. In fact it took me a while to realize how big a man I'd joined up with."

"You suit me fine."

"I know you were concerned driving me up to meet your family that day. I even feared they'd stone me."

"Stone you?"

She nodded.

"My mother raised us boys to do the right things.

I knew some things about her past—Long's and my story. As boys she'd feed us some homemade soap for using bad words handling work mules, and she pointed out people who were not living good lives. I didn't know how she would take our partnership."

"She opened her arms so wide I could not believe it. There are classes of people in this country. I had lived on the lower shelf and she was three or four higher. It made me proud. But you are—I can't believe you haven't left me—you are, well, a damn neat guy."

"Just another cowboy."

She laughed. "No. No. Harper O'Malley, you are much more than that."

He put down his plate and kissed her. "We're an outfit together."

Later with her in a bedroll back under the wagon and behind some upright saddles as shields from stray bullets, he told her to sleep. She had a loaded Paterson pistol and said she could use it. He kissed and left her.

Long and Chaw were out scouting in the night. There would be no moon until after midnight and it would be near full when it did come up. The big moon at that time of year, in Harp's experience, led the Comanche to come east to raid.

His sentries were listening for any sound in the night to tip them off. Others napped, expecting the guard to be switched and up all night. The way they were set up, the Comanche could not attack coming from the east. A steep hill and the large corral was where they'd have to maneuver to have the sun in the camp's face. Two hands guarded the corral, but it was not a Comanche way to charge in and strike. They would sneak.

Harp slept some and they awoke him when the moon began to rise. Long had not come back. Getting to his feet he wondered where his partner was. No doubt scouting the enemy. Still, filled with concern, he hoped his brother was not taking any chances.

Running low, two cowboy hats came across the open area carrying rifles in their right hands. Harp met them.

"You find them?" he hissed.

Long nodded. He caught his breath when his brother stopped Chaw, too. "They are out there."

"How many?"

"Maybe two dozen."

"They'll be here at dawn?"

Long nodded. "I think so. They were waking so we started back here."

"Get some food. I will pass your information on to the others."

The news clutched his heart for a second. He hoped the red men had gone back west, but an isolated camp like theirs with horses and guns that could be taken would be a coup. The Comanche were like all armies, they needed blood to keep them on edge, and a success would reconfirm they could attack and win over the white eyes.

He told the others at the various stations what to expect. Then he dropped back to his scouts and asked if they were that close.

"Yes. I could have hurled blasting sticks among their horses and killed half of them."

"No way to stamp them and get away?"

"No, we were too vulnerable."

"I was getting concerned."

"They'll be here—and soon."

"We are ready. We have some sticks. Ira can fuse them up."

Standing nearby, Ira said, "You'll have them."

"Whew, it's been a night. Thanks. We'll stop them."

Harp left and made sure his men were ready. There were sounds in the night. Some flushed birds out there upset by the Comanche passing; hammers being clicked back followed the birds' flight.

Then the shill screams of the attackers filled the night. The rumble of many horse hooves rolled out the charge. A wall of bullets met them coming through the gap, and in the increasing moonlight horses and riders went down making for more wrecks, colliding on the fallen. Some made it past the mess and were hanging low, shooting over their horses at the corral.

Constant ear-shattering rifle shots from his men cut down horses forced to stay on the track left by the fallen trees and made them more like duck targets in a carnival tent. The shooters took them down. Finally some Comanche broke to the left and fled into the live oak and cedar brush.

Moaning horses thrashed and dying Comanche chanted final songs. Harp told his men to stay put until daylight. They would end all the misery when they could see the ones who might threaten them. The battle had been won. Aside from some scratches, no one on their team was wounded or hurt.

Kate joined him, excited and hugging his arm. "I knew you two would stop them, but I never thought it would be this big a defeat."

"We planned on stopping them. A couple of our saddle horses is all we lost. We will drag the dead away and have a funeral pyre for them."

Three men came to get them.

"Ira has breakfast."

Harp nodded. "Two of you with loaded guns watch the Indians. We'll eat in shifts."

At the meal, he stopped before his brother with his plate in his lap. "You, Chaw, and I will finish off those that are not dead."

Both men nodded.

"Thanks."

"You won't save any?" she asked in a low voice.

"No. They would have killed us. I don't want to face them again."

"I guess a leader has to do those things."

He sat down with his plate of food and strained against the tightness between his shoulder blades.

"Later. I can work that out," she said, noticing his stiffness.

"It may take blasting powder."

"No. Trust me. I can get it out of you."

After the meal, Harp, Long, and Chaw, armed with rifles, walked the death field. One by one each man checked a body. Long shot a buck lying on his back. Obviously still alive, Long sent him to the good Indian place for an eternity.

"His eyes blinked."

Carefully Harp turned another over onto his back. He had the rifle ready in his other hand to shoot if he was still alive. He was dead. This job was no fun, and the grotesque death scene made it hard for him to keep his food down.

Long silenced a pained horse.

Chaw shot another buck lying on his side. Then on the fringe he shot one crawling away. Shaking his head, he hooked the dead Indian's foot to the lariat to be drug away by a cowboy on horseback.

The rest were dead. Then they began to shoot the hurt and crippled horses. It was a day Harp knew he'd not easily forget.

His crew began to double up and haul the dead Indians and horses a good distance away from the corral and their camp as the buzzards, by the hundreds, began to congregate in the air overhead for the feast.

The last body and horse corpse hauled away, Harp seated himself on a bench and she was kneading his stiff back with both hands. Something began to lighten in Harp's head and brighten his mind while swallowing the sourness that kept rising in his throat.

"Your back is really tight," she leaned in to tell him.

"It is getting better."

"Ma'am, you ain't got a sister do you?" Doug asked, going by with his lunch plate full of food.

She laughed. "I don't know. I've been an orphan all my life."

"Really. What a shame."

Harp agreed.

With the sides of her hands she pounded his back. "Can you eat or do you want me to pound more?"

He smiled up at her. "Thanks. That's much better."

"We starting to round up unbranded cattle today or tomorrow?" Long asked, squatting down beside him.

"Yes. And we need to burn the bodies today."

"We will do that after lunch. Then I want to take three hands with me and see what cattle we can shake out of the brush."

"Sure; sooner we get done up here, the better I will feel."

Long agreed. "The funeral burn is in Doug's hands. I'll get my three when we get through eating and see what we can find."

"Good job."

Long said, "Oh, and on Saturday I am going to a dance with Anna. So I'm quitting about noon."

"Why not ride out after breakfast Saturday?"

"And leave you with all this to do?"

"Yes, do that."

By then Katy was laughing at the two men's conversation.

"Don't laugh. This is a new side to my brother," Harp said.

Long shot back, "Hell, Kate, he ain't the only O'Malley who dates women."

She winked at him. "I wish you luck. She's a lovely lady."

"Thanks. Keep him straight while I am gone. Someone has to do that all the time." Long smiled at her and went to find a place to sit and eat his lunch.

"He sounds serious."

"You never can tell. I found you."

"Well, I invited you to eat peaches."

"Yeah, I liked that. You caught me on a day I wasn't vexed by any of the problems I had all the way there."

"No. God helped me with that."

"Oh, Katy, God don't help sinners."

"I think he did. But those peaches and you were both sweet. I felt blessed."

"I might take you and my bedroll out of sight and take a nap after we eat."

"Everyone will see us hightailing it and know what we are doing."

He was laughing. "You think they believe all I have you for is rubbing my back?"

"Eat lunch first. You'll need your strength."

With some effort he rose and followed her to the food line—he was lucky he found her. Their life, so far, was fun.

CHAPTER 10

On his circle, Long found mavericks of all shapes and sizes, and wild as deer. Squatted on his haunches back in camp he told Harp they could get lots of free cattle out of this country they were in. "Remember, I'll be back Sunday—late."

"Don't rush back; they'll be here."

Long looked around to be sure no one was close. "You're lucky, bro. Anna ain't Kate."

Harp nodded. The words slipped off his lips. "They only made one of her."

"You know I believe that. You're lucky. Kate has no rules. Anna has strict ones."

"You can win if you want to—bad enough."

"I'll tell you Sunday."

"Maybe Monday."

"I doubt it."

"I want to make a run tomorrow and see how many we can get without my best man."

"Half your world. Build to it. Good night."

Katy joined Harp. "You two through for the night?"

"You bet. Is Chaw up at the wagon?" Harp said.

"He was a minute ago."

"I need a word with him." He left them to find him. At the wagon he caught his point man. "Tomorrow, saddle up at dawn. I want a hundred head in these pens at sundown."

"Long's going—"

"Hey, I want to show him we can do this while he courts the lady."

"I'm game. We will all be in the saddle at sunup."

"See you at breakfast."

"Harp. I know we can do it."

"That's why I want to do it." Then he took Katy off to their tent.

"What were you and Long talking so serious about?"

"I think Anna is keeping him at arm's length."

"Really?"

"And I think Long's jealous of us."

"He's as neat a guy as you are. Why would she do that?"

"Strict upbringing."

"I had none of that in my life. Folks did things and no one looked."

Harp laughed, undressing. "Darling, if and when you get pregnant, I want to get married."

"Really?"

"What's wrong? Are you crying?"

She was up kissing him. Her wet tears spilling on

him as they kissed. "I never thought I was worth being anyone's real wife."

He hugged her. "We don't have to have a baby to get married."

"Harper, no one in my life ever asked me to marry them."

"I just did."

"I don't know what to say."

"Yes, if you want to put up with me. No, if you have plans to see France, because I ain't going there."

"Silly. I would be proud as anything to be your wife."

"You are now."

"Do it in a church?"

"Hell, wherever. Do it on the moon coming up if that's what you want."

She threw her arms around his neck. "Let's go back to bed."

"Anything you want."

"I want you."

"When we get back home, you and Mother set it up. She'll know what to do."

"She means a lot to you doesn't she?"

"Yes, she's been great."

"I hope if I ever have kids they love me like that."

"No problem. I know they will."

He meant every word of it. Maybe tomorrow they'd set a record on wild cattle gathered. Who knew anything?

CHAPTER 11

Sun was cracking the eastern sky when every hand that worked for the O'Malley Brothers Land and Cattle Company was on deck, save half owner Long O'Malley who had gone off to see the widow Greg. They rode out singing and swinging their ropes like the day would be a Sunday picnic and dance mixed in.

He recalled how his dad would drop them off, like he did his cowboys, in a wide circle. One by one he set them off until the circle was complete. He'd told each one to listen for the shot and charge. When Katy and he reached the other side, he drew the Colt .44 and smiled. "Ready, Mrs. O'Malley?"

"Yes, Mr. O'Malley."

"Ee-ha!" The busted cap shocked his eardrums, and the men's wild war cries must have sent every longhorn in that part of Texas into a stampede. The brush was tough to dodge through, but every horseman charged off the surrounding ridges and the dust from their flight boiled in the air. He caught glimpses of hysterical cattle jumping barriers and running to escape this new threat. The riders on the south forced them to thicken their ranks, and the north flank riders kept them moving.

Harp led the riders on the north side. He wanted them headed for the great meadow and then turned into the chute-like structure that boxed the Comanche, and into the stout pens. Kate wasn't far away, paralleling his course after promising to take no chances if things went sour. The brush swept by them, and he saw a rider and horse go down. God protect him.

Harp spurred the buffalo horse on to the drum of a thousand hooves, cattle brawling and things crashing down. The leaders were approaching the open land and began to slow. His riders began to start the circle that would line them up with the corrals.

How long had they been running? He had no idea, and riding as hard as his hard-breathing horse could go he didn't intend to check his pocket watch. Once in the great meadow he began to slack back.

The front steers took the lead and were heading north like a pretty picture. Harp shouted a war cry, and, as his line eased back, the cattle were making a beeline for the opening. Forty-eight hours before the Comanche took the same route. Now cattle were filing in through the open gates of the huge round pen. Hundreds of cattle and calves all went into the five-acre pen swirling around in a cloud of dust.

He reined up his horse and opened the gold watch. Twelve o'clock.

"What time is it?" she asked him, sitting her horse beside him as the cattle passed them flowing into the pens.

Red Culver took off his hat and wiped his sweaty face on his sleeve. Then taking a look at the sun, said, "A little after twelve, ma'am."

"You got it pegged, Red," Harp said.

Katy laughed. "Nice job, and, Red, you don't have to wind yours."

"How many did we catch?" Red asked him.

"Guessing, maybe three hundred? I don't know. We've got our work cut out for us."

"Hey, won't Long be shocked when he sees 'em?" Chaw asked.

"Naw. He'll want more."

The others laughed.

"What now, boss man?" Katy asked, brushing the dust off her shirt.

"Ira will be serving lunch. Chaw, round up the boys. Was that rider who went down all right?"

"Yeah, he's riding in double with Darvon. They had to shoot the horse and are going back for his saddle."

When he and Katy got to camp, one of the men took both their horses. Harp saw the buckboard and team hitched nearby. Who was that?

Then he saw his banker, Jim Yale, hatless with a coffee cup in his hand. Ira pointed Harp out to the man.

"Well, let me wash up and then you can tell me what brings you out here," Harp said.

"Miss Katy, good to see you. Harper, I came to talk some business if you have time. I thought it was an earthquake coming. How many head did you bring in?"

"Couple hundred, maybe. We ain't counted them yet."

"Wow." Jim walked along to where they washed up. "You taking them back to Missouri?"

"At eighty dollars a head I damn sure would . . . if I could." He dried his hands and face on a flour sack towel.

"I came to let you know the bank will accept your cash offer on that place with the cattle thrown in. Come in next week and sign the papers. We'd like to be your bank, too."

"We can shift an account over to your bank; however, I need to talk to Long before I say for sure."

"I understand," Jim said. "Where is he? With the men coming in?"

"No. We gave him the day off to take the widow Greg to dinner and dance."

Jim shot him a questioning look.

"Don't ask me. He's showing her around. I have no idea. Katy and I like her."

"I just wondered."

"Let's eat. We can talk more then."

"Ira has a table for us he said."

Katy laughed. "He knew you were important."

Jim looked a little embarrassed by her words. "Nice of him."

The poor man was not used to being teased Harp noticed. The bashful guy would have a lot to learn, especially that some folks could and would gouge him.

Katy told them to sit and she'd get their food.

When she was out of hearing he asked Harp where he met her.

"Lee's Creek, Arkansas."

"You found her?"

"More like she found me. Her previous man was going to be hung and she asked if we could get acquainted."

"He did what?"

"Killed a man."

"Was she married to him?"

"No, but we now have plans."

"She's an unusual neat lady. Good luck."

Katy brought them each a plate. "Ira said this is a special treat. He found some real good beef in town and bought it for all the crew to feast on and celebrate."

Jim said, "Heavens, Miss Kate, you've put half a cow on my plate."

She wrinkled her nose at him. "Ain't that much."

Harp laughed. She'd got the banker again.

They ate well, and Jim even had room for apple cobbler.

There was enough water in the corral from a spring-fed stream for the cattle. They'd need to work them quickly because there was no feed for them when they ate up the grass. His crew'd get it done, but they'd be tired by sundown next day, if they even had all of them done by then.

One ranch bought and things going on. They had lots of cattle to work and he even wondered how Long got along with his widow.

They had one squeeze chute. One of the men restrung a new pull rope on the squeeze portion. The head catch was in good shape, and the long-horns had lots of clearance to fit their rack in it before it was locked shut. Experienced hands told him it would work well and they'd not have to head-and heel-rope the cattle.

The men looked sleepy eyed at breakfast, but a few rode horseback to fill the pen that fed the cattle into the chute. Lots of jackknifes were re-sharpened to put the Hiram's ear notch on the right ear, the H Bar H brand on the left. One cowboy had started the fire to heat the irons red-hot.

Harp finished his coffee standing.

"You can stay and help us today," he said to his banker.

"I would but I hardly came dressed for it."

"I understand. Long and I will be in and close that ranch deal next week."

"I want to thank Ira for the great food and you, too, missy."

"Come back any time. These two will find some-thing for you to do."

All three laughed.

There was a sharp smell in the smoke from a brand-ing iron burning through the hair of a cow's hide.

The men knew that branders had to have that iron red-hot and to press hard to get that right effect. The animal needed to be held down or held tight for the brand not to be smeared from the iron moving.

Keeping the irons red-hot was a full-time job for one of the men, while the man working as head catcher had to jerk the stanchion-like holder shut at a precise moment so it caught the neck and not farther back on the animal to be worked on. If they missed the head catch the animal had to be manually caught, laid on the ground, and tied for it to be worked. The strength to do that on mature stock was demandingly tough and even got arms and legs broken in the struggle. All the men were aware, and watchful.

Don't miss was the advice given the head gate man.

They castrated all the bulls standing. The mountain oysters were a treasured product recovered during the surgery and kept in clean buckets for Ira to fry at the next meal. Harp remembered, at smaller roundups, them being thrown in the iron fire. When they popped out from the heat, they were chased down, speared on a pocketknife, brushed off, and eaten right there. That was manna from heaven to a real cowboy.

They worked on bulls, yearlings to five years old in that chute. With young calves, they opened the chute, flanked them on the ground, and two men stretched them out and did the same thing to them. It was nonstop work.

By mid-afternoon, Harp's clerk and lady had recorded over three hundred head in the pocket-size logbook and made a duplicate on a Chief tablet to back up the count.

Harp hugged her after the last old cow came out of the chute.

"Men, I appreciate the job we did here. Help load up the wagons before you leave. You wranglers can pen the horses overnight here since we don't need the pens. But I want them driven back to the place where we're staying tomorrow. I am issuing a check to Chaw to cash in town. You'll each get ten bucks of your wages for the month there. Be ready Monday morning; we'll have another site to do this at next week."

He took the tablet she handed him and continued, "We rounded up three hundred forty-two head that belong to us now. That might be a Texas record for great cowboys in that short a time. Thank you."

Excited she squeezed and kissed him. "What will Long say?"

"Aw hell, I bet you missed a hundred head."

Kate and Chaw laughed at the statement.

Ira served them mountain oysters, fresh-baked bread, and brown beans. He had the largest Dutch oven full of peach cobbler. Harp wasn't certain the cowboys would even be back to celebrate later on. He knew, somehow, they'd be renewed enough to raise hell and help the town's economy before sundown.

"I bet if you do this kind of catching cattle very

often, that you are going to make some people mad," she said, riding beside him.

He looked at her riding beside him. "Free country. They can do it as well as we can."

"No. I bet there is not another outfit in this part of Texas that has the number of good hands as you two have to do this work. I am just warning you there will be some hotheads after it comes out what you did here today."

"You can't build a ranch catching a half dozen cattle a day."

"I know that. But you watch my words."

"Ah hell. Let's find a water hole and swim some. It's warm today. I know some secret ones."

"Teach me how?"

"If I can find a deep enough one."

They set their ponies into a trot. He was so damn lucky to have Kate. He doubted Anna Greg would even consider skinny-dipping with his brother. But that was his business. Harp and Kate were going to have some fun.

CHAPTER 12

The water was too cold to stay in, but the sun's heat warmed them quickly as they sat on the blanket.

"I thought it would be warmer, but I guess it didn't have time enough to warm. I'm sorry."

She sighed. "You are so neat, Harp. I really can't believe how nice you treat me. Most guys would say, 'Hurry up; I ain't got no time for you now.'"

"I guess I was so wound up about having all those cattle worked and branded; now it's done, I wanted to show you a good time."

"I understand. Let's go back to our camp and while everyone is gone we can do what we do—at night."

"I love you."

"Oh, you saved my life." She kissed him and they dressed, rode to the camp, and entertained each other until someone outside shouted, "You two dressed?"

"No."

"I'll wait."

They scrambled into their clothes. When Harp was sure that she was covered he untied the flap and invited Long inside.

Hatless, he ducked in and sat on a cot.

Harp and Kate sat across from his brother in the shady light of their tent.

"Well, are you and Anna still talking?" Kate asked him.

"It is hard to tell you, but Katy, you are my sister. Don't spread this around, but she is concerned about her children accepting me as their father. She said she is not ready to marry anyone or even become involved with anyone. She apologized if she let me believe anything else. I respect her. I understand her situation, but I am not happy about this."

"If we were up near Fort Smith I could find you a good woman, but I don't know any down here."

"Thanks, Katy. I will find someone. I just pinned too much on getting her."

Kate jumped up, went over, and hugged him. "There are thousands of good women would give their eye teeth to have you, Long O'Malley."

"Katy, that damn brother of mine is just so damn lucky to have you."

She put a finger on his nose. "He saved my life. The man I lived with was sentenced to hang. When I went down to the store to get something to eat, I found this tall cowboy leaving the store. The notion that I wanted to know him struck me like lightning from a cloudless sky.

"I said let's go eat some canned peaches, I want

to meet you. He frowned at me. I guess some doves had propositioned him before that. I really simply wanted to meet him—that was all."

Harp laughed. "If she was struck I soon got that way. We went off by ourselves up on Lee's Creek, sat on a blanket, ate some and then kissed some, ate some more and kissed some more. She said we needed to bathe next. We were naked in a flash and splashing in the water. I never thought about it. She didn't, either. I later decided that was the way it should be for lovers. Clothes were nothing.

"Then like we had made love forever, we did so on the blanket. Afterward I took her to the camp and you know we have not been apart since. She promised me earlier she would marry me before we have children."

Shaking his head, Long chuckled. "Mom will like that part."

"I told her that, too. Jim Yale came by. We have that ranch and cattle we looked at for five thousand. He wants our banking business."

"Is that what you want to do? Bank with him?"

"Only if we can borrow enough money from him for two herds of steers to drive somewhere north where we can unload them."

"Good idea. We might need two banks. I saw that you have about three hundred head of branded cattle."

She said, "Three hundred and forty-two to be exact."

Harp shrugged. "Those were the first. We need to build another corral like that one on Ivy Mountain and have two squeeze chutes to work them through over there."

"When are we building it?"

"Next week."

Long elbowed her. "Damn. He is a task maker ain't he?"

She gave him a sure nod. "But because he is, you two own three hundred and forty-two head of branded cattle now."

"Not only is she cute but accurate, huh?"

Harp agreed. "She thinks we will soon be in a pushing and shoving match with the big ranchers for catching these unbranded cattle now that we put a price on them."

"Katy, do you believe that?" Long asked.

"It makes sense. You two did the impossible. Taking all those steers to Missouri and selling them for such a high price. Over here you caught all those cattle and branded them before they even got out of bed. Yes, at this rate, I can see you two will be, in their opinion, keeping them from getting rich. That to them will be stealing."

"Then we better do a lot more before they really catch on," Long said.

"Christmas is around the corner. And we'll have some cold weather and I hope rain. We need that corral built over on Ivy Mountain in a hurry."

"You think that is better than rounding them up and roping them?" Long asked.

"We took the whole crew, surrounded them in a circle, and charged them off the mountain and into that pen. Then we worked them all in six hours.

If we'd had another squeeze chute we could've done it in four hours."

"We have a great crew, but we'll need more good horses for next year. Those boys aren't going to quit us if we pay them all winter."

Harp agreed. "We will keep them working. They are too experienced to lose."

"First, why not buy a hundred and sixty acres where there is water, and build the chutes and corrals on our own land? Then they can't use it and they will have to build their own facilities to work cattle or do it in the open."

"That might be a better idea. I bet that you and a hand can find some deeded land and get us a place to do that," Harp said.

"What is that other lawyer's name who sells land in Kerrville?"

"Sandy Van Hook."

Long nodded his head. "I will be in his office bright and early Monday."

"Obviously money talks, so use it," Harp said.

"Boy, don't it? Seven months ago they considered us boys. Today, hell, we're businessmen."

"And going to be bigger."

"I'm going to get some sleep. Harp, you did something real neat, sending them boys to town with a little money. They were having a helluva time. And, little lady, thanks to you for making a place for my brother in your life. I'd never have thought about buying two cans of peaches and sharing them with some gal. I bet that was a neat deal. I'd rather eat a can of sweet peaches than drink whiskey."

"It was a ball. You see Van Hook. The men can grease the wagons, look over the harnesses, and check the horses. They'll have work. We'll need about three hands up there at the new place in the future."

"What will we call that place?" Long asked.

"Not Kate's place. I like it for a ranch but not for me. I don't want to dry up over there."

"Well, scratch that name." Long laughed. Then with a *see yeah*, he took his hat and went off.

When he was gone, Katy tackled him onto the cot and more tickling, kissing, and wrestling went on between them. Damn, he was glad he found such a fun-loving girl. Shame that Long and Anna didn't make it together. His brother would find someone.

Morning came and Harp had his list of things for the men to do, and he and Kate took the buckboard and team to the Mexican village St. Frances on the south banks of the Portales River.

He found some men on the bench in front of the *cantina* while she went off to look at the handmade goods some women had for sale under the cotton-wood trees.

He asked them about who he could hire to plow some ground on his new ranch purchase at Grass Valley. Among the men he found three takers. They would plow with their own oxen for two dollars a day. He acted pained at the price, so they agreed to do it for one dollar a day and he would buy the *frijoles* they would eat. He knew they would take their wives and children, so it would cost a little more.

They asked when they could start.

"Oh, move up there after church on Sunday?"

"*Sí*. What will you sow, *señor*?"

"Oats. I will meet you up there and show you the field."

They agreed they could plow, and for the same money per day broadcast and harrow in the seed. He shook hands with them over the deal and advanced them three dollars apiece. Next he must order the seed from Frank Skyler at the mercantile. His dad told him it wasn't too late to get oats up and ready for a spring hay crop. That was good.

He also got names of two men who could cut posts on his land and build corrals. They needed work, too. Van Hook better find that place for Long fast. Ranch building would be expensive, but some day they'd be large area ranchers.

Among the women, Kate found a leather vest that fit him and he liked it. The sun was warm but not warm enough to go swimming. Back in town, he had his first face-to-face with Katy's forewarned opposition. He tied the team off and started up the stairs to the porch. A man of medium height with gray temples stopped him.

"You one of those two damn O'Malleys?"

His wife, standing next to him with two armloads of groceries, tried to stop him. "Now, Earl, that boy—"

"Shut up, woman. I can handle this. If you are, you better stay out of that country—sneaking in on a Saturday, working all those maverick cattle is damn close to stealing them from the ranchers around there like me. You ain't got no claim on those critters."

"What's your name?" Harp demanded.

"Earl Carson, and I can tell you right now you do that trick again, I'll blow your head off."

"Mine's Harper O'Malley, and you have any cattle aren't branded up there I will brand them, because under Texas law I have that right."

"No you don't."

"Then try to stop me."

"Earl Carson, get your hand off that gun," his wife demanded, and pushed at him, with both sacks of grocery, enough to move him.

"I'll get your ass, boy."

But she had him herded a little farther away by then.

"Try and you better wear a nice suit, 'cause they will be burying you in it."

"Quit, Harp. He's going away. She's driving him away, telling him to stop threatening you."

Carson, loud enough to hear, said, "Shit, Lea. He ain't no more than a snotty-nosed kid, and I ain't going to be run over by him in my own country." But his wife forced him across the street and made him take the purchases and load them in the farm wagon parked there.

Harper stopped on the covered porch, watching. Katy moved him toward the door, shaking her head. Quietly, so only he would hear, she said, "He's just blowing smoke about what he will do, Harper O'Malley. I told you this would happen."

"Hey, O'Malley," one of the bench sitters whittling and gossiping on the porch said. "He was sure glad to see you, wasn't he?"

Harper stopped in the door and nodded. "He won't be seeing much longer if he tries me again."

Katy made him go inside. "Forget him."

"Katy, you can't simply forget a man who threatens your life like that."

"You are going to have to, or shoot it out with a lot more of these folks. I told you things would blow up."

Still upset, he agreed and they went on shopping. She got the small items that Ira wanted and he ordered the oat seed, so they'd have them up at the ranch in two weeks.

He vowed he'd not forget Earl Carson for threatening him in public, which made it worse. On the road he might have sloughed it off, but in town where everyone could hear—that made him damn sure sizzling mad. And no one was pushing him or his brother around.

No one.

CHAPTER 13

That evening in camp, he and Long discussed the day's happening. Katy refilled their coffee cups as they sat facing each other.

"Van Hook has two places in the Ivy Mountain area. One is a hundred-and-twenty-acre strip on Swain Creek. It has some farmland. The other is on the west side of that country and it might be more liable to be Comanche country. It is a hundred sixty square, supposed to have water and a dug-out house on it.

"How much is he asking for them?"

"The Swaine Creek one, two hundred. The west one, three hundred."

"Could we offer him four for both if we can use them?"

"I never offered him a thing; just wrote it down. We know money talks. I want you to look. He says there are lots of wild cattle in that country. But we know the Comanche still come through there a lot."

"I know the next time we meet them we may have more damage to our men."

"I agree. We were lucky no one was even scratched."

"You tell him about Earl Carson today?" Kate asked, taking a seat beside him on the bench.

"Not yet."

"Who's he?"

"A rancher. He warned us about showing up. He has a place up near the corrals where we worked those cattle this past weekend. Katy had warned us that someone would come and threaten us—well, he did that today coming out of the mercantile as we were going in. He made loud threats saying we snuck in there on a weekend and claimed we took cattle we had no rights to."

"What was he going to do about it?"

Kate said, "His poor wife with her arms full of groceries forced him across the street, telling him to get his hand off his gun."

"It was a damn open threat, and he called me a snotty-nosed kid. It made me mad. Katy tried to cool me off."

Long laughed. "And you just back from Missouri driving cattle up there and selling them for more, apiece, than they'd get out of a herd down here."

"Katy can tell you I was mad."

"We better watch that peckerwood. He might jump our men."

"No telling. But we did step on his toes. I want a place to corral them out there. Can we go look at those places tomorrow?"

"Probably need a pack outfit in case we get caught

out there overnight," Long said. "What about the bank deal?"

Harp shook his head. "It won't be ready until later in the week. I hired three men to plow and sow oats on the new ranch, and I already ordered the oat seed."

"Good. I better get us some packhorses and things from Ira," Long said.

"I'll get the food, you get the horses," Katy said.

Long got up, stopped, and leaned on the table, looking hard at Harp. "You think Carson will give us trouble?"

"Yes, I do."

"Well, he better have burial insurance. I ain't digging no hole for him."

Harp agreed.

As the sun was going down, Katy asked in a small voice, "You want me along?"

"I expected you to come along." He kissed her cheek and she left, smiling, to arrange for food. Poor girl, her past men must have treated her terribly.

This building of their land and cattle company would sure take lots of work and planning. He had plenty on his plate. It all started when Simons dumped the night guard job in his lap and it hadn't let up since. So far he had made some good decisions. He simply needed to keep that habit going.

Long was a great guy, but he left things to his brother that he didn't want to mess with. He'd never have taken the job of running the cattle drive in the first place, but he sure backed him. Planting oats was another job he didn't want, but his brother could work men and they'd follow him to hell and back. This Earl Carson better never get in Long's face—he'd not walk away from that discussion.

They left Chaw in charge before the sun came up. Mid-afternoon they found the creek place. It had been farmed, but the fences were split rail and not good. It would require a smooth wire fence with several stays between posts. Harp had seen some barbed wire made by blacksmith shops, but with screwworms, a scratched-up cow or calf would be dead in a week in the summertime. The cost was high for that kind of wire but taut telegraph wire fence with stays could hold even goats in.

It would cost more than the land was worth. Oh, well. They camped there. He'd pay two hundred bucks for it but no more. Long agreed. Riding out there they saw lots of maverick cattle popping up in the brush.

Harp wondered who out there would be mad about them rounding up these cattle. He felt sure that Carson wouldn't be the last one. His partner, Katy, he realized knew a lot about how people resented things than he did. Another reason to have her around.

Harp and Long built her a fire and she cooked supper in the ranch bottoms under cottonwoods. The people that had settled this place must have lived in a wagon. They found no signs of a house or cabin. The previous owners had not dug a well, either, so the three used creek water. Strange. Harp bet there was no history on how this place got homesteaded. And the folks who done it were not to be found.

It wasn't going to rain or be too cold, so they never set up a tent. Harp and Kate shared a bedroll. Up before dawn, Long had a fire going in the near frosty bottoms.

She cooked them oatmeal with bugs and brown sugar. Her coffee was delicious, and afterward they rolled their bedrolls up and left. Mid-day they rode toward the second place west of Ivy Mountain. Plenty of deer. Some hardly lifted their heads from grazing at their passing. They cut some north-south older Comanche sign.

Long could read a map Van Hook gave him, and a little past noon they found the dug-out house. The shakes needed fixing. Inside, the narrow windows meant the floor was five feet deep. Outside, there was a dug well and it had water. No bucket but Kate had some canvas they weighted to sink and drew up sweet water.

That was real good news since many such wells gave chalky water. The fields were split rail fencing and would be of little help. There were even two haystacks the wild game couldn't reach. But it was old. Before the war there had been lots of expansion, but with the Comanche threat and no markets or neighbors the owners must have moved back to civilization.

"I think this place has lots of potential," Harp said, eating some jerky on the rise next to the house.

"I brought some peaches for dessert," Kate announced, and they laughed.

"Bring them on, sister. I can't share mine but I think that story was so damn neat. Can I pry about your past?" Long asked.

"Sure. What do you need to know about me?"

"This guy that was with you before my brother. Why were they hanging him?"

"Be kinda hard to explain. Neither of you drink. But all kinds of folks make whiskey—moonshine they call it up there. You can't legally sell it in the Indian Territory, but they do. They do it in Arkansas and don't pay the revenue tax.

"Jimmy Groves bought some good stuff, or so the guy told him. See he drank all the time and was really spinning away his life and wouldn't listen to me. Well, some wild whiskey can make you blind. What he bought made him blind and he stumbled around drunk in a rage, cussing he'd been poisoned. He was still only seeing outlines the second day, and the third day he took a shotgun and went to Van Buren to find the bootlegger. I begged and pleaded with him not to go.

"Jimmy found him and ran him out of a saloon and into the street. He shot him twice, reloaded the gun, and shot him in the head twice more at close range. If he'd shot him once a jury might've let him off. Twice was not good. But blowing his face away with the last two shells was a hanging offense."

Long nodded at her story. "I see that as bad, too. But why did you live with him in the first place?"

"He saved me from a much worse man. Jimmy never hit me. Oh, he threatened to a time or two when he was too drunk. But the man who bought me before Jimmy—he took me and hauled me off Shannon Mountain—was Bill Staley. I had lived with Granny Schultz and her husband Horace Schultz for as long as I could remember. They told me they had raised me since I was five, maybe four, no one was sure—I am not. There was a house fire and everyone in my family perished but me. I recall little about that. Granny never had any kids so they took me on. She read the Bible and books. They never went to church.

"See, hill folks were real superstitious in them days. Granny told me they all wondered why I lived and the rest died. I couldn't tell them. So a rumor went around I was spawned by the Devil. No one wanted me. Granny didn't believe that, and she took me by the hand to her house. I was fourteen when they both took pneumonia and died.

"The neighbors all decided I was not any real kin to them and so I had no rights to their farm. They felt they could sell the farm and the money would go to a good cause—to the local church that Granny and Horace never attended. Said that would pay back the tithe they never paid and they should have. I was locked in a shed to protect the God Fearing people from me harming them.

"Late one night one of those church sisters secretly sold me for forty bucks. I can recall her name well.

Theresa Stone. That whisker-faced bad-smelling man who bought me, Bill Staley, was filthy dirty." She held up her hands to keep them back. "I ain't proud, but after that first horrible night as his wife, I cleaned him up. But he whipped me all the time. I guess I didn't suit him about anything I did.

"He got mad at me about some infraction of his rules he never told me about. I think he made it up to whip me. Had my hands tied to a rafter, and me on my toes buck-naked he whipped me with his belt until I passed out.

"Jimmy Groves broke in after hearing my screams, and they had a bad knife fight. Both got cut up. I never saw my first husband ever again. I think he died but it was self-defense. Jimmy healed me and I owed him my life. We lived hand-to-mouth doing odd jobs. But Jimmy never offered me to anyone else like the first one had done, so I felt safe. You know what I mean. But I sure couldn't stop him from murdering that bootlegger.

"His trial was over. I had no money, nothing, and I met this cowboy who came along, liked peaches, and I liked him right off."

"Long, thanks, I'm glad you asked her. I knew she had big problems in her past, but I feared she wanted them buried."

Long said, "Katy, there were worse things in your life that happened. If those church women thought you were evil they wouldn't let their daughters play with you would they?"

"No. Two boys were nice to me, but I bet they never said at home 'I helped Katy today.' I got spanked by the teacher for what other girls did. Don't ever let your house burn down and have a daughter survive. You see why I am so happy with this one. I have escaped hell. He doesn't need to marry me. I never pleased anyone but Granny before in my life."

"I feel the same way about him. I'm half Cherokee and growing up some people thought Indians were less than real people. We had some of it in Arkansas in school, but back-to-back we settled it. Fourth grade in Texas we had another war and they found the two of us could whip the hell out of Indian haters. I try not to dwell on that. I don't know much about the Cherokees. I don't speak it. I kinda had a thought in my mind that maybe Anna thought that way, but she cleared that up fast and I believed her.

"She love— she simply still loved Emory. He'd gave her the position of being an officer's wife. I did not believe it but she is nine years older than I am. I am not blaming my ancestry for my problems there. It simply didn't work out."

Katy agreed. "I feel free. Those years are behind me. But I guess since I was always in that spot."

"I agree. Harp, we need to decide what to do about these two places."

"I would buy and build a large corral here. Buy the other place really cheap."

"I know if these cattle sale deals continue these places will be gobbled up."

"But this is not a Kate ranch," Harp teased.

"You know I get feelings about this place today. Let's not camp here tonight. There may not be a Comanche within five hundred miles of us, but I don't think we should stay. We can push all night and tomorrow sleep in a safer place."

A little past mid-day they headed east in a long trot. They kept their eyes peeled for any sign and wasted no time hustling the packhorses. Dim wagon tracks were washed out in places. It would be hard to get a wagon over this way and would require some work. But there was no shortage of mustangs or maverick cattle out there.

They reached a spread near sundown and decided they might be far enough away to consider stopping. It was a rambling-looking outfit and it looked like the residents were gathering wild horses.

When they first rode up, an old man with a mustache, his hand down in his overalls scratching his privates, must have been bad sighted. He quit when he heard Harp say, "This is my wife, Kate."

"Tom McIvor. You're at the Lonely River Ranch."

"I don't see no river around here," Long said.

The old man slapped his knees. "That's why we named it that. We were lonely for one. Me and my boys catch mustangs. Break a bunch and take them back east and sell them."

"How far east?" Long asked.

"Not a mile farther than where we can sell them." He slapped his knees again and laughed some more. "Get down and have supper. Tell me where you been—oh, you too, nice lady. I meant you and them."

"We've been to Sedalia, Missouri."

"Why?"

"We sold over near eight hundred steers to some packers in Saint Louis."

"Ain't they still fighting up there?"

"War's been over since last April."

"I'll tell the boys they don't need soldiers anymore."

The three looked at each other. Under his breath Long asked, "Where have they been?"

They spent the night with McIvor and his two sons. Before they left, Long asked the sons, who were in their twenties, if the Comanche ever bothered them.

The oldest son, John, said, "They come around but not often. We poison them."

They thanked the McIvors and rode on, Harp thinking they were tetched in the head from staying alone so long.

"They were sort of crazy," Katy said, confirming Harp's thoughts.

"Long, Dad, and I were rangers during the war. We were the patrol that kept the Comanche away or met them head on. We never avoided the draft. It would have been better to have gone and fought than be the way they are."

"Takes all kinds of folks to make up the world population. Those kind back there make me shiver," Long said.

Katy laughed. "There are some worse in the Arkansas Mountains. Brothers marry sisters and they have monkeys."

"Really?"

"Yes, I can't even describe them."

"Guess we are lucky then. Long and I only turned out to be cowboys."

"You and him may dress like cowboys but, soon, both of you are going to be businessmen."

"Why thanks, Katy," Long said. "See there, Harp, all Mother's learning has not been to no avail. That's how she said it?"

"Something like that. We'd do something funny and she'd toss her hands in the air, and say, 'I taught you better than that.'"

"You watch her some time when she gets mad; she throws her hands up like she's feeding chickens. Dad told us the first time he asked her out and he wouldn't take no for an answer, she did that. He still laughs about it."

"What happened to your father, Long?"

"She only knew he was killed out in the Cherokee Outlet. She had found it out a short time before Dad asked her to go out. She protested she was with child and Dad said he had lost his wife in a swimming accident, so they were both alone and should go out."

"I'd say meeting women is a funny business for you menfolk."

"Mine may fall off a cloud. Huh?" Long asked her.

"Chances are—" Katy was laughing too hard to say any more.

That was how the rest of the ride back to their cow camp went. One funny thing after the other until they rode in. Everyone was there to meet them, looking upset.

Chaw stepped forward. "Some guy named Fallen was here and told us you owed him money for using his pens. Four more come by and told us if we didn't load up in twenty-four hours they'd string us up for cattle rustling."

"That is Texas state land that those corrals are setting on. No one else owns that land," Harp said, recalling checking the ownership out a year earlier when they discovered it.

"Was there a short mouthy guy named Carson in the bunch that ordered you away?"

"He never gave his name, but he wasn't tall," Doug said.

"Boys, you did well," Long said. "That guy nearly got shot in town threatening Harp. Walk easy and always in pairs from now on. We found some new ranches we are going to buy west of here. Because of Carson, I guess they think all these unbranded cattle are theirs. They're not. You boys showed how to work 'em, and they are jealous and mad. Roping and tying them down takes all day. We are having two of those squeeze chutes made to take along. They have not seen the O'Malley Brothers Land and Cattle Company in action, but I promise you that H Bar H brand will be stamped on more than you can count in the next six months."

Harp felt damn proud of his brother's speech. Katy winked at him when it was over. It was universal with them cowboys. Like it or lump it—the O'Malley brothers were to be reckoned with in that part of Texas.

CHAPTER 14

They bought what they called New Ranch for five thousand. Jim Yale arranged for them to get the maximum loans they'd probably need for the coming year and approval to use two banks. He shook his head in amazement at the new cattle count.

"That is amazing. What next?"

"We are going to work on lots more," Harp said. "We'd like lots of the cattle we take north to be ours, but after the first of the year we will advertise for other folk's cattle. Long and I plan to take two herds of two thousand head apiece."

"I have small ranchers, all the time, wanting to ship cattle. Can I send them to you?"

"Big two-year-old steers, prefer three. No cows or heifers."

"I will keep that in mind. Thanks. You now have one ranch of your own to put that sign that says O'MALLEY BROTHERS LAND AND CATTLE COMPANY on the cross bar over the gate. And I can say I knew those guys back when."

The three of them laughed. They bought the other two parcels for three hundred dollars cash from Van Hook an hour later. Then they went and had a meal at Sam's Place.

The café was near the river and lots of local rancher folks ate there when they were in town. Two guys they went to school with had heard their cattle drive story. Jeb Ransum and Orrie Carpenter both were taken aback by all the things they had to get around to get there.

"You going back?" Orrie asked.

"Yes, but farther west."

"There's this guy has a trail up through Kansas to Abilene, Joe McCoy. He says he has lots of markets for our cattle." Orrie handed him the paper.

"Where's Abilene, Long?" Harp studied the information.

"I don't know."

"He wants us to cross the Red River at Doane's Store, go across the Indian Territory on wagon tracks left from the federal retreat to the Chouteau's trading post, then take the tracks on to Jesse Chisholm's Trading Post on the Salt Fork of the Arkansas. It says this winter McCoy's men are plowing sod furrows and making sod markers the next seventy-five miles to Abilene, Kansas."

"Anyone in here know McCoy?"

"All we've heard is good things."

"What do you think, Harp?"

"Long, I think he designed that highway for us. But we better get more cattle branded."

Katy's blues eyes were following their conversation. She bent his head down to whisper in Harp's ears. "Now you really are going to piss them ranchers off, branding mavericks."

"They damn sure won't be happy."

"What's that?" Long asked.

"For us branding mavericks."

"The hell with them. What are you going to do next?" Long asked.

"I want to ride up to Camp Verde and get Mom and Katy together. My plowing people will be out there next Sunday at New Ranch, and I should have the oat seed to take out there and some of the foodstuff I promised them. We need three of our people out there. You got a foreman idea?"

"What about Hoot Crane?" Long asked.

"Him and three good boys can get the new ranch straight this winter. Damn, he will need some saddle stock and hay for them. Who's going to cook?"

"Hoot usually has some Mexican *wife*. She can do that," Long said.

"He don't have one, he can find one." Harp and Long laughed.

"Right. Get him a team and a light wagon. Ten horses. A couple of tons of hay, and hell only knows what he will need besides that." Harp's head was spinning with costs and needs for all this.

"Those three boys need to be able to sit a horse real good."

"Yes, and the boys will cost twenty a month, Hoot

thirty-five, and twenty for her cooking. That's a hundred and fifty a month counting food and needs. That will cost us eighteen hundred a year plus hay—I bet we need to take thirty steers to Kansas a year to pay our wages and them sell at sixty dollars apiece."

Long kept on nodding. "I bet there are that many steers out there now. Maybe more."

"You have to spend money to make money."

"Yes you do. I'll go find Hoot and probably have to sober him up."

"I am going to take Katy out to the home place and let her talk to Mom about our wedding. I want that under way."

"Amen." Long shook his head at Katy. "Darling, you must get tired of all this business talk."

"Long, after all the places I have been and put up with—this is like heaven. Don't ever worry about me being bored. I do know four thousand steers won't be enough for your and Harp's plans," she said.

Harp set in. "We may never get eighty dollars a head ever again, either, but at forty bucks that is eighty thousand dollars for one herd, and if we make twenty dollars a head on the other herd that's forty thousand. Ranch expenses won't be any problem."

"The crew is fine at camp. I'll swing up there today and take them to the far-away ranch and they can get it all set up. Then I'll go find Hoot tonight, get him ready to be set up for New Ranch," Long said. "Chaw can meet you in town at the mercantile with the wagon on Friday, get the supplies and the oat seed you will need, and take it up there and come back and get ready to move Hoot and his crew to New Ranch on Sunday."

"Good plan. Fence builders next week up at the Ivy Mountain. Put up a corral. Have the blacksmith shop build us two squeeze chutes for that place that we can assemble and break down to move from place to place."

"Go home and tell Mom I love her, Katy. You keep him out of gunfights," Long said.

"I'll sure try. You be careful, too."

That night they got to his folk's place late. Lights came on when the stock dogs barked. His folks got up all excited. What was it in the Bible? The prodigal son had come home. Lord.

His mom went to making coffee, scrambling eggs, hashing potatoes, and Katy sliced bacon. Then biscuits went in the oven and Easter asked a hundred questions all at one time.

But when Katy mentioned to his mom she needed help planning their wedding—you could've heard a pin drop.

Easter cried out. "See there, Hiram O'Malley, that boy of yours does have some of the bringing up in him I planted. Come here, Kate darling. God bless you—when?"

"I never had a big Christmas in my life. I figure this could be a big one."

"You will, my dear. You certainly will."

Hiram got up and fixed a plate of food and Harp followed.

"We bought that ranch," Harp said.

"Get a good buy?"

"Cattle and all, five thousand."

Hiram nodded. "That sounds really good."

"We branded three hundred forty-two head at those big pens last Saturday."

"Aw shit. How did you do that?"

"A squeeze chute."

"I heard they're neat."

"You recall those guys back a few years ago who were going to get rich turning free cattle into tallow and hides?"

"Yeah. Lost their backsides."

"Well, we made a real big roundup and drove them into their corral and the next day we worked and branded them all in six hours."

"That was a fast deal."

"And you won't believe the chewing out I took from a guy named Earl Carson in town over catching that many head. He said those cattle did not belong to us."

His dad gave him a smug smile. "Aye, my laddie, you're learning lots about the likes of people."

"I am. Real quickly. He has had those cattle around him for years and never got off his chair to catch them."

"They weren't worth eighty dollars a head back then." Hiram laughed. "Ignore those people."

"I'll try."

"I take it you are happy with your Katy gal."

"Yes. Very much so."

"I felt like that the day I married your mother, and I am still happy. What're your plans?"

"Brand more mavericks. We bought two more ranches out on Ivy Mountain. Lots of wild cattle out there. That's why we bought them. I'm still not over that Comanche attack we had last week."

"They don't go away easy."

"No."

Harp didn't sleep that night, either.

CHAPTER 15

He took Kate and his mother to the dress shop the next day. The lady who ran it said they'd be one hour measuring his wife-to-be and for him to go find something to do.

For the hour, he spoke to the man Newell Kent at the Saddle and Harness Shop, told him he wanted to buy a matched team and a good buckboard. Kent asked what color.

"Bays, blood bays, unless someone's got a sharp team of buckskins, but they'd probably want a fortune for them."

"I think I know a man with such a pair. Would yah pay three hundred dollars for them and the rig?"

"No, but I'd pay two if they suited me."

"Of course you're talking federal money?"

"Of course."

"If I kin buy 'em for that, would yah pay me twenty for the fee?"

"Yes. You know where they are?" Harp asked him.

"Yeah. Around town. They're matched. Full brothers. When will you be needing them?"

"Christmas Eve at my father's house. I am getting married and they are for her."

Kent stuck his hand over and they shook on it, and he paid the man the money. Smugly he went back to the dress shop just as the two women walked out. He went around and helped them both onto the seats of his father's rig.

"You ladies need anything else?" he asked, gathering the reins.

"Look, Katy. That's that team of buckskins I told you about," his mother said.

"Wow. They are pretty."

He set his hat on his head and clucked to the team, with a small ripple in the lines to wake them. "Nice outfit. Someday I'll have some like that."

"No," his mother said. "You are too much like your father. Plain ones work well, too. Oh, he once borrowed this fancy buggy and two high-stepping horses. It was that wild night we got married. I was so afraid he'd wreck it and spend all his life paying for it."

"That must have been fun," Katy said.

"Not really. I was showing Long by then. I knew his father had been killed and this huge Irishman, who would not take no for answer, was taking me to a dance. His wife drowned back that spring while on a picnic. He said we both lost our mates and we should be married. By the time we got to the dance, I agreed to marry him. After that we went back to my folks' house, told them what we'd done, loaded some of my things in that coach, and went to his house. And we have never stopped since. I love him so much."

"What would you have done if he had not come along?"

"I guess become an old maid with one boy."

"No," Kate said. "Someone would have found you, as pretty as you are."

"If you say so, my dear. I hope you'll tell me how this boy of mine swept you up."

"Easter, my story is not as pretty as yours. When I was five years old my family's house burned to the ground. I lost everyone and yet I survived and was not able to tell them how. That marked me as the Devil's own. An older couple with no kids took me in and loved me in a neighborhood where I was not welcome. One winter they both died from pneumonia and the people in town said I was not their heir. They sold the estate and gave the money to a better cause, they said, their local church. A woman, and I know her name, Theresa Stone, sold me to a man for forty dollars. She probably kept the money. I was fourteen. He was a grimy, whiskered, fat old man. I became his wife and slave."

Easter reached up and put her hand on Kate's shoulder. "You were just fourteen?"

Katy nodded.

"Dear God, you have certainly saved this young woman for my son. Thank you, sir, amen."

Not many things shocked his mother, but Kate's story did that day. She was really taken aback hearing it. Harp knew that later his dad would hear the story. Everything about it bothered him. How badly she was treated growing up, about a fire she innocently escaped and her family didn't, selling her into slavery. It was a bad deal, but that night in the attic, wanting her to forget and feel better, he showed her how much he loved her.

Wouldn't that team of horses shock her? He could hardly hold the secret to himself.

Next morning they rode to New Ranch. On the way, they passed two heaping loads of hay he'd bought for horse fodder. Everyone was there. They were cleaning up everything, even had sickles to mow down weeds; axes and saws to trim trees and cut down excess brush. Dead oaks were being sawn down and split into firewood.

Two hands were running the pack rats off and cleaning the house. They had the wall tents and wagon fly up for shade. The corrals were being repaired. One guy was on a tall ladder, with flattened tin cans, replacing shingles on the barn roof to stop the leaks.

Long came up from checking something in the hollow.

"Well?" he asked Harper.

"They are making Katy a dress. Best man, you can pack the ring and Dad said he wanted to give her away since she's an orphan. She cried about that. She's up talking to Ira about how she can help him on meals here."

"Glad she's back. She makes better desserts than

he does. Oh, they had a springhouse to keep milk and butter cool down in that holler I just came from. We need to build a stock tank below it to catch the water for stock. It is a real strong spring.

"Windmill works, too, but we need to replace the main bearings. They must not have turned it off when they left, so it ran all the time and not having grease hurt them. It works, jacking water upstairs into a big copper tank, but not great."

"How is Hoot?"

"He's excited. His latest wife, Bonita, wants to be the cook. He can't believe all we've done since he knew us as boys from Dad's ranch. We have two wagons moving them. They should be here any time now."

"You ever see that buckskin team and buckboard in town?"

"Yeah. Nice rig. Belongs to the Peabody Ranch."

"Not after Christmas Eve. I bought it for her for our wedding."

Long frowned at him. "What did that cost?"

"Two hundred dollars."

He shook his head, smiling. "Money does talks doesn't it?"

"Yes. We plan to get married on Christmas Day."

"Good. Your plow people are coming. Some are set up already. I see we need a bunkhouse for cowboys and maybe two *jacales* for farm hands and their families."

"At least one horse-drawn mower, rake, hayracks, and a couple of draft teams." Harp was adding them all up in his head.

"I think we can make them *jacales* from adobe. Find some suitable clay and make our own bricks here. Then the windows, roof, and doors will be the only cash outlay. We can make our own cedar shingles."

"I hope Hoot can manage all that. We will be off, branding cattle."

"He will." Long said it like he had no doubts about the older man.

"We need everyone armed here, though. Comanche will find this place. Those Winchesters we have for the crew proved vital even going north. This ranch business would be a hell of a lot easier if we were rich."

Long gave him a hard look. "Next fall I plan to be that rich."

"I bet we both are. That's Hoot leading the parade coming in."

Under the widest brim black felt hat they made, smoking a quirley, a starched long-sleeve white shirt buttoned to his Adam's apple, an expensive blue silk neckerchief around his chicken neck, came their new foreman. A very pregnant young Mexican woman sat on the spring seat driving one of the wagons. She was wearing a loud red rose–patterned dress and a wide straw hat. That was his wife.

What did his father say? Snow on the mountain but still fire in the chimney. Hoot reined up. His clear blue eyes looked dark staring at Harp.

"By damn, Hiram does have two—men. Howdy, Long. Harper, Hiram said you were around, glad you could make it."

He stepped off the Mexican big wooden-horned saddle like a kid, hitched his holster, and strode over to shake Harp's hand. Instead, he threw down the small cigarette butt, ground it under his pointed toed boots, and hugged him and then Long.

"Why you boys have got a helluva reputation since going to Missouri with them cattle. I tell everyone I helped raise you both. No one believes me, but I know the truth. Come meet my woman, Bonita. She's a little big in the family way"—he stopped and looked around—"he said."

"Katy is helping Ira, the crew cook. She's up there."

"Good. Come down, darling. I'll help you. Thanks, boys, for letting me bring her here. I don't know what I'd do without her."

Coming off the wagon seat backward and using a spoke for a step, Bonita's dark eyes flashed at him. "Oh, you know. Find another one."

"That is not fair, Bonita. I love you and that baby."

On the ground and out of wind, she tossed her luxurious curly head of hair back and hugged Harp as close to her belly as it would let him. "You are as handsome as your father." She then turned to Long and did the same.

"Thanks. Welcome to New Ranch and your *casa*."

"It looks a damn sight better than the last *ranchero* we were on."

"It has running water in the house."

"And I hear a creaking windmill, too." She gave him a smile. "As long as I do not have to carry water and the roof does not leak I will be pleased."

"When is the baby due?"

She turned up her small palms. "Someday I guess—soon I hope."

"Come along. Katy is up at that big tent helping my cook."

"That is your wife?"

"Yes."

She looked at him affronted. "Why does she work? You are a *patron*."

"When you meet her you will understand."

Bonita shrugged and matched his steps. Kate must have seen her and ran to hug her.

"This is my wife, Katy. She is Bonita. Take care of her. I'm going to join Hoot and Long."

"I will." She waved him away busy talking to the girl.

He hurried to catch the other two headed toward the house.

Hoot had stopped for him. "Thanks for introducing her. Long says wedding bells are coming Christmas."

"Yes, they are."

"You met her in Arkansas?"

"Yes, coming home."

"She expecting?"

"Not yet."

Hoot gave him a big wide smile. "Get busy."

"I am." They laughed.

"When we get time I want the whole story about that trip. I knew that Captain Greg was not crazy, but when they said you two were in charge on that drive, it blew my mind. Then I said hell, no. Hiram

O'Malley raised them boys for that job, and I went to placing bets you two could do it."

"I wouldn't have bet on it until after they slid the last car shut."

"You had to worry about it until then, but not me. By damn, boys, you've got a spread here."

"We even branded three hundred and forty more head over at the corrals last Saturday for you."

"That makes over five hundred head?"

"More than that, Hoot. There are a hundred and eighty pairs plus yearlings here now."

He took off his hat and wiped his forehead on his sleeve. "I've got a helluva big job ain't I?"

"These cattle, here, have a B Slash F brand. We own it but in time we want the H Bar H on them all. No rush."

"Say, this is a nice house. You are going to spoil her for me. She's used to sprinkling down dirt floors every day to keep the dust down."

Harp nodded. "I've seen women do it. Part of their ritual."

"How do you find all these pretty women?" Long asked Hoot.

"Aw, they're out there. I found this one down on the border. Her man, before I got her, sold her body for beer money. It was not hard to get her away from him. She lost two babies while his wife. She said he poisoned them."

"Tell him about Kate," Long said.

"Sold at fourteen as a wife to a grubby drunk that beat her. A guy rescued her and treated her better.

Then he shot a bootlegger over some bad liquor and they were fixing to hang him."

Hoot nodded. "See, Long, you aren't looking hard enough."

They both laughed at his expense.

"Now what are your plans for the coming year?" Hoot asked.

"Take two herds of two thousand steers to a rail-head. Right now we are considering Abilene, Kansas."

"I've seen McCoy's ads. I bet it would be better than Missouri."

Harp nodded. "Anything would be better than that route."

"Boys, you have a bull by the tail and you are sure swinging him 'round and 'round. How old are you?"

"I'll be nineteen in February and Long twenty next May."

"Wow. Did Greg know how old you were when he hired you?"

"We never lied to him. We took charge. We fired his cook first, then he fired his drunk foreman and we demanded better horses and a lead steer."

"Old Blue, huh? Boys, there aren't any boys your age that could have done that job. Grown men would have failed. God cut you two out of a stamp of a big man, Hiram O'Malley, to do that for Greg. I would have turned him down. Figured I'd get my head blown by some damn Yankee cannon for simply going up there."

"Thanks," Long said. "But we don't need any glory. We did a job and we have another to do. Build us a big ranch while this cattle business goes for broke."

"No. I see it continuing. Who wants to eat stringy chickens and fat pork when they can have beef? They will get addicted to it while they grow more chickens and hogs."

"I never thought about it that deeply," Harp said.

"They damn sure will."

Long laughed. "The O'Malley brothers of Texas want to feed it to them."

Hoot saw Bonita and another gal headed their way.

"Ah, this must be your lovely wife—Kathy, Kate?" He swung off his hat and crossed the room to kiss her forehead. "You are an angel to put up with that boy."

"Kate. You must be Hoot. Nice to meet you. And don't underestimate those men, they are the most envied men in Texas today."

"They cut the real track didn't they?"

"Hoot, Texas has not seen it all yet."

"I don't doubt it. Bonita, now you have a house. What do you say?"

She sniffed and began crying. "I love it."

Katy said, "You men. Out. I am going to heat water. Bonita wants a bath before her baby comes."

"Coming today?"

"I think so."

Before leaving, the men fired up the kitchen range and brought in three pails of water. Then they left. When the dinner triangle rang, Katy came out.

"She is soaking and fine. Harp, send us two plates of food on trays. We will eat here."

"I can do that."

Hand on her hips she said, "Have a boy do it. You're the boss now."

"Yes, ma'am."

The long wait for Bonita's delivery had begun. After supper, the men set up Hoot and Bonita's new double bed that they had brought in the living room.

Hoot said, "She won't know how to sleep in it. She's always slept on a pallet on the floor. I bought that bed and mattress special for her in town."

Everyone laughed. They only made one Hoot Crane. The baby's cries didn't come until dawn the next day. Salvador Crane was that boy's name. Harp went off to bed once he saw him and slept till supper when Kate awoke him.

He had that same experience to look forward to. *Someday.*

CHAPTER 16

They would have two weeks before his wedding to build corrals and get things ready. Harp felt there was no way they'd get it all done in time for roundup, but he didn't know how many helpers Long hired. The smell of fresh-cut cedar posts and rails filled his nose, and he never saw the fervor in men building the huge pen just west of the New Ranch headquarters.

Post contractors had hauled in a thousand posts and the slit rails. Then they went to work digging, blasting in places that needed the three-foot depth down into the rocks. The chutes arrived and were being assembled on site. The loading chute behind the squeeze was built in a V shape to allow the longhorns entrance down into it. Harp saw they built it stoutly.

Two men from the blacksmith shop came and did some cutting and fitting. When they finished, the new chutes worked well and Harp thanked them. With a bill for three hundred dollars in his hand, someone elbowed him.

"I think trouble just rode in."

Six hardcase-looking riders came in the gate opening. Coming across the pen, the tough look on their faces showed they came with a purpose to their visit.

Suddenly, every worker on Harp's payroll vanished.

"Howdy. Can I help you? My name is Harper O'Malley."

"We know who you are. We're here on business, kid."

"First, I am not a kid. I own this land and you are on it. There are several children and women here, including my wife, so clean up your language or leave. Now what do you want?"

"I want this corral burned down and your ass out of here by sundown. We know what you did over at the other corral, and you aren't doing it over here."

"You six boys came here to tell me to leave my own property?" Harp asked.

"Go now or go feet first."

"Rest of you agree with him?"

Straight-backed in the saddle, hands on their gun butts, they nodded.

"What was your name? I never heard it?"

"Jack Mills."

"You, the tall one. What's your name?"

"Jasper Graham."

Harp pulled out his tally book and scribbled down the names.

"Red?"

"Rufus Lemons."

"Next guy?"

"Navel Thomas."

"Cody Brandon."

"Next?"

"Screw you."

Harp frowned at the man. "Your mother call you that?"

"Those names won't do you no good when you are on your ass full of bullet holes."

"Jack Mills. How many parties like this you had?"

"A dozen. Maybe more."

"Well." Harp paused. "This may be thirteen then?"

"Listen—"

"No, Mills, you listen to me. You and your men, with two fingers drop your guns in the dust or this will be the most unluckiest party you have ever attended."

As Harp said it, a dozen Winchester actions clacked. The six went for their guns and twelve rifles cracked. Harp had to jump away or get run over by some of their spooked horses. Short screams as the invaders went down like cut stalks. Through the gun smoke five horses raced around the large pen, rider-less. Then there was silence.

One wounded horse had to be destroyed. Three mortally wounded raiders were put out of their misery by bullets. Harp saw Kate coming, holstered his gun, and ran to cut her off.

Short of the corral he caught her. "They are dead. It's all over."

She clung to him and cried. "You are all right? Thank God. Who hired them?"

"They never said. Told me I had to burn the corral and leave or die. Word will get out."

"The bodies?"

"Like the Comanche. We will burn them."

"Will it ever stop?"

"Yes. Eventually they will learn not to mess with us."

"Did you know any of them?"

"No. But money buys their kind."

"Katy?" Long was there. "I am so sorry, but those men would have killed us. We had no choice."

Squeezing her wet eyes, she pulled Long down and kissed his cheek. "I will thank God that both of you are safe."

The hired guns were stripped to their underwear, their spoils divided and carried off. Saddles taken to the tack room and the horses were driven away to wander home or join a wild band. Some land was cleared, and cedar boughs had been piled into a mountain and the bodies tossed atop them and burned.

Supper was a silent meal. Even in bed later, Harper could not sleep for a long time. He heard the new baby cry over at the New Ranch house, and a coyote answered him.

CHAPTER 17

Christmas moved closer. The corral was done. Harp gave the men their pay and a week off. Mexican people really celebrated the holiday. Half the oats sowed and harrowed in and another quarter of the land plowed. Hiram, the farmer, drove over and approved it. He told Harp to have them plow the other field to plant corn in March before he left for Kansas. He agreed to do it.

"Brother. You're going on your honeymoon, and while you are gone I am going to break your record on working cattle," Long said.

"You have two new chutes," said Harp.

"That will make it easier to break it."

Amused by Long's challenge, Harp threw in, "Just so you keep an eye out for Comanche. They may try you again."

With Hoot in charge of the ranch, and a few hands to back him, they rode for Camp Verde and the big party planned. On the afternoon of Christmas Eve two boys arrived with the buckskins and shiny buckboard. They went to the door of the house and one stepped forward and asked for Kathy O'Malley.

"I'm Katy."

"That must be who he meant." The boy almost stammered. "Your horses and carriage await you."

She ran to the door and then held her hands over her heart, staring at the team. "You say those are mine?"

"You are Mrs. Harper O'Malley?"

"I am, I am. No one ever bought me anything that fine. Oh, wait until I get my hands on him, I'll kill him."

The boy said, "Oh, ma'am, don't do that. This is one helluva gift and only a millionaire could afford them."

She was running, dress in hand, for the yard gate. "That is why I am going to kill him. I am not worth that much money."

Harp jumped up from hiding behind the gate and hugged her. "Let me be the judge of that."

So she couldn't talk him down, he kissed the fire out of her.

After they were done she jumped into the buckboard and drove the team around, hardly able to keep from crying. Neither ate a thing for supper and she cried herself to sleep. When she woke, Harp flat out asked her if marrying him was that bad they shouldn't get married.

Shaking her head, she explained, "You don't understand. I am pregnant and I am happy now we have conceived.

He hugged and rocked her. "I am sorry for what you went through till you found me, but all that is over now. When will it be here?"

"When you are in Kansas, next summer. Your mother said I will stay with them and have him there and so I will be safe, while worrying about you being safe."

"You sure it will be a him?"

"Trust me I know what I am doing."

Trust her or not, he knew that no one knew the sex of a baby before it arrived.

CHAPTER 18

They spent their honeymoon in downtown San Antonio, seeing the Alamo ruins across from the hotel every day. They went to *fiestas* and Mexican markets, art shows and *fandangos*. He found her two nice dresses to grow into. They looked at furniture for the house to be built. She said God knew where that would be, and he was keeping it a secret.

Harp met two interesting men. One was a northern investor who wanted to promote the O'Malley brothers' next cattle drive when he learned about their Missouri sojourn the past year. James McVeigh didn't know anything about bovines except the front end had horns and the back end possessed a tail. Harp decided he must have had lots of money, since he threw two lavish parties in the five days they were in town. McVeigh could not believe that Harper did not drink and he rather openly flirted with Kate.

She wasn't, in any way, moved by him, and she told Harper she would bet he never ate peaches with a girl on a creek bank and then seduced her. They both laughed about it.

The second man he met was Arthur Shea, a land agent. He had a drink or two with him. Actually Harp had tea and the agent had hard Kentucky whiskey. Collins had some large tracts of land in west Texas listed that Harp would've loved to have, but they were way too pricey to even consider.

In their last meeting, Collins asked if he found a buyer, what would be considered a fair price to pay for a big ranch manager job.

"More than anyone would ever pay me. Fifty thousand a year."

"Oh, you would be way too high."

"My dad said there were two kinds of oats in the world. Ones before the horse ate, and the ones after he ate them. Those after he ate them are cheaper."

"Oh, I never heard that one before, but you struck the nail on the head, me boy, and can I use it?"

"Of course. I have no claim on it."

"You are nearly nineteen years old, and in the coming year you say you will earn that much money in this pathetic economy?"

"Maybe more."

"My heavens. How much do you charge to show people what you do?"

"Arthur. You need to be born in a Texas saddle, understand longhorn thinking, and be able to swim across an ice-cold river a half-mile wide. Also stop stampedes of two thousand cattle running wide open in the dark and shoot any sum bitch that gets in your way."

"I decline the offer. I am not that tough."

They shook hands and parted friends.

Later his bride laughed at his stories. "You tell full-grown men these stories don't you?"

"They couldn't do those things like drive cattle to market if their life depended on it. That is very unique."

"Unique?"

"Different or a strange way. Also means specialized to someone how they make it work."

"You will face the test when we go home. Will people trust you?"

"Long and I have a track record."

"But now the road is to Kansas."

"It can't be that bad. I am talking about holding them together."

"You had eight hundred. Now two thousand in each herd?"

"We will deliver them. Oh, why are we talking anyway?" He wrestled her down on the bed. "We can't hurt the baby can we?"

"No, not unless we get violent. Your mom told me to have fun. She did to the last day. She even said you were conceived in less than twenty-four hours of Long's birth."

"And she never had another."

"No one can explain that, either. She wanted a daughter."

He laughed. "You want a boy."

"That is what he is." She patted her belly.

How did he get so lucky to find her on the last day she aimed to be around there—him showing up and accepting the peach challenge?

They drove back in a drizzle. It fell on his oats in good measure.

CHAPTER 19

They celebrated the New Year's coming in at his folk's house. Long had not been back from the Underground Ranch. He must be really working cattle hard. A state policeman came by earlier and asked if his father knew anything about a Jack Mills who had disappeared in that part of Texas. State Police were the carpetbagger's answer to the rangers. His father wouldn't have told them a damn thing if he even knew Jack Mills was dead.

"What did he say this Mills did?"

"Oh, the officer was acting tough. Never told me much of anything. Said folks were missing and no one had seen them. Strange I said, and he got angry. Hell with guys like that Mills, he might've gone somewhere else and never told anyone."

"If I can get Katy to stay here I want to go check on Long tomorrow."

"I'll go with you."

"Thanks. Then she won't have to worry about me being alone going there."

"No problem."

Kate agreed to stay if he was coming back shortly.

Hiram and Harp rode their horses hard and made camp among the cattle bawling at the Underground Ranch, Long's name for it. The men were eating supper and waved them over to the cook's wagon.

Long sent two boys to put up their horses, so they washed up and filled their plates.

"Well, Long, did you beat my record?" Harp asked, sitting down on the bench with his plate.

"We got close. But we have steadily worked as many as two hundred fifty head each day and we have over nine hundred fifty head branded. It is getting harder not to bring in worked cattle, and sorting the worked ones off takes time."

"Wow, we are close to fifteen hundred head counting them all. That is wonderful."

"We have over two hundred fifty steers we can go north with, and I am trying to hold them in a herd. Where should we move them?"

"The Diamond Ranch has some large well-fenced pasture," Hiram said.

Hamp started wondering how he could rent some of that pasture.

Long asked, "Dad, you think those old maids that own that ranch would rent us some fenced grass?"

Hiram grinned at Long's words. "I'd send your brother over to dicker with them. He did all right as your mouthpiece in Missouri."

Harper shook his head. *Why me?* "All right, I agree we need a place to gather these steers to go north and the Diamond has those pastures goat fenced. It would cost lots of labor to re-gather them. We can bring probably a hundred and fifty head from New Ranch up there as well as the ones you branded here."

"Hoot's a good man. He knows longhorns and how to handle them. I think he is as good as any man. I would put him up against you boys day in and day out," Hiram said.

"Hell, Dad, that's why we hired him," Long said. "Well, it is up to you, brother."

"Dad, could those sisters need money?"

"Depends how much Confederate money they have. I'd bet they have silver and gold, but try, say, a thousand steers at five dollars is five thousand dollars. I think you could afford that to have a gathering place."

"That would be half our own herd huh?" Harp looked for his brother's nod.

"That might not get it done. You understand that better than I do. But try."

"I'm going back, get my wife, put her in a dress, and go see Edna and Josie Cranford."

"Yes, with Kate in a dress. How old are the sisters?" Long asked.

Hiram shrugged. "Seventies. I am not sure. I always wondered why they never married."

Long said, "I heard that their father said they both had to find a man and have a double wedding the same day. He refused to pay for two of them. They never could both get a man at the same time."

"That's what I heard, too," Harp said, laughing. "Katy and I will go see them."

"Dad, stay a day. I want to show you how we get things done over here."

"You ever come across a man named Jack Mills?" Hiram asked.

"No, why?" Long asked, avoiding eye contact.

"The state police say he vanished around here."

"They have any leads?"

Hiram shook his head. "I'm not sure that police guy could find his way back to Austin without a map."

"Did he say what Mills did or was doing?"

"No, and I didn't worry about him, either. You get home by yourself all right, Harp?"

"Sure, no problem. I'll cut out early so I can get home, get Katy, and go see the Cranford sisters."

"Hope you can do some good with them old ladies," Long said.

"All I can do is try."

Long spoke sharply to him. "Hey, old married man, those damn Comanche are still down here. Be careful going home."

Harp cut out from the Underground Ranch before the sun came up on the short January day. He probably had forty to fifty miles to get back to Camp Verde, but, pushing his buffalo horse, he'd be in his wife's arms by seven o'clock. It was cold, but he had enough clothes on not to mind it, and when the sun came up he'd have to shed some. They could use some rain if God could spare them some. That last drizzle wasn't much and things dried up fast.

He was crossing some open meadowland when the skin on the back of his neck went to crawling. The sun was trying to peek up on the land, in that half-pink light, before it showed its face. He turned to look over his shoulder and caught sight of a spear coming over the rise.

Damn. No time to count them and it was over a half mile away to cover. He set spurs to the buffalo horse and tore out for the cover. They took the challenge, yapping like a pack of coyotes, and when he glanced back, a half dozen bucks who'd shed their blankets were pursuing him.

Man it was too cold to do that, but he wasn't their mother. Harp thought that they decided it would be a short chase and threw caution to the wind, determined to bring this single white-eyes down and then go back to warm up. He hoped to hell they froze to death first.

The roan was giving it his all; being grain fed he had an advantage over their grass-fed mounts, but it wasn't like he had wings, either. By Harp's estimation, he was not leaving those yapping red bastards fast enough to escape them. It was still a good distance to the cedars and his mount was taking in lots of air, still giving his best effort. The horse must've shared his fear of those painted faces.

He counted that he had nine shots from the Winchester under his right leg and five in his .45 Colt strapped on his hip. The older .30-caliber pistol in his saddlebags had five as well. He'd switched to wearing the larger gun, but he was a better shot with the smaller one.

At the moment he needed to shed these half dozen lodge brothers on his horse's tail. They were not overtaking him, but they were maintaining a steady distance back there when he twisted in the saddle to check on them.

He'd been all the way to Sedalia, Missouri, crossed mighty rivers, met lawmen and turned them aside, and now a half dozen illiterate savages had him running for his life. This dead grass would not hide him. He could only hope to get to the cedar cover and pick them off.

Katy, if I don't manage to get free, you and that boy enjoy what I started for us.

Those yapping redskins had not slacked off one bit; he went splashing through a small creek, and the roan gained the next rise. While pushing the animal harder, he undid the right saddlebags and shook the .30-caliber out of the holster. He rose and stuck it in his waistband. The barrel gouged him but also gave him those five more bullets.

The hillside of cedar and live oak was closer when he left the wagon tracks and took for the cover. He hoped the roan wouldn't step in any badger holes. He looked back in time to see one of the Comanche fly off his horse doing just that. He went end over end and smacked hard onto the ground. The other five kept coming.

At last he slid the horse to a stop, jerked the Winchester out, and saw the shock on their faces while the Winchester, with the butt slammed against his shoulder, smoked fire and bullets. Three were shot. Two horses screamed—hit by the bullets—and two bucks were running away.

He took aim and shot the one running on his right, right in the middle of his back. In the cloud of gun smoke he saw him go facedown. He levered a fresh round in the chamber and made a head shot at the last one still fleeing.

The ear-shattering shot cut the buck's screaming off, and he, also, went facedown. The injured horses made tough sounds and somewhere a killdeer shrieked.

He used his .45 to finish off the dying horses. One buck had not been accounted for—the one that spilled in the horse wreck about a hundred yards back. Harp searched in that direction and saw nothing moving.

His own pony was standing ground-tied. He caught him and carefully reloaded his rifle with ammo from the saddlebags. The sharp smell of gun smoke burned the inside of his nose along with the bear-grease perfume the Comanche wore. Rifle loaded, he still watched to the east where the horse went down.

Were there any more in the area to come to their aid? He mounted up with the rifle in his hand. When he found the last one, he'd put the .30-caliber back in the side pocket of his saddlebags.

The five had gone to Indian heaven or hell. Mounted on his faithful horse, Harp began to ride out through the knee-high dead grass looking for a survivor. He found the savage's mount struggling on his side. His front leg was shattered. Harp rode in close and shot the pained animal. When he reached the rise, he saw the last Comanche running away down the swale the small stream had made in the meadow.

The Indian glanced back over his shoulder and apparently saw Harp because he began to run faster. Harp spurred the roan after him. He was closing in when the short buck in a loincloth whirled to face him with a homemade butcher knife. Why, he was a boy. Maybe ten or twelve years old.

He shot him in the chest with the .45 and the boy staggered. Shot hard, he still raised the knife and made a screaming death charge that was stopped by a second shot to his face. The roan reined in; Harp knew that boy's angry face would haunt him for a long time.

It was over.

He rode all day and it was after nightfall when the stock dogs heralded his welcome at the Camp Verde Ranch of his parents.

"That you, Harp?" a warm voice called out holding a candle lamp up high enough to see him.

"I'm unsaddling the roan. I'll be right there."

"You all right?" she asked, running down the steps.

"I will be now I am here."

"Where is your dad?"

"Up with Long. My brother has near a thousand head of cattle branded."

She hugged and kissed him. "You feeling all right?"

"I'll be fine. I had a brush with some Comanche coming home."

"What happened?"

"There's six dead ones back about twenty miles I guess."

"No one with you?"

He shook his head. "I wasn't looking for trouble. Just to come home."

She hit him in the chest with the side of her fist. "Harper O'Malley, I don't want to be a widow with a boy to raise by myself. Where's your dad?" she demanded.

"They're fooling around up there branding two fifty head of cattle a day. They sent me home on a mission."

She laughed at his remarks. "Sounds busy enough for me. What's your mission?"

"Go over to the Diamond Ranch and rent some fenced pasture."

Katy shook her head. "You two guys have more going on than a one-armed cow milker. I'll heat you some food," she said while he washed up.

"Fine." He drank two dippers of water from the well bucket on the dry sink.

"Tell us the truth about today," his mother said, coming up to them.

"I deprived six Comanche bucks of breathing."

"No one with you?"

"I never imagined I'd get stopped."

"No wonder your wife is upset. Didn't we all talk about riding two bodies at a time?"

"They needed all the hands over there. Dad stayed to help for a day or so."

"That does not surprise me. He can't believe his boys are doing all this, and he's busting buttons he's so proud of you two."

"Well, we have several large steers to be headed for Kansas among the new cattle. But we don't have hands hired to herd them until next spring. One of the Diamond Ranch fenced sections would hold a lot of them."

"They sent you huh?" his mom asked.

"I am their talking piece."

"Who are these women?" Katy asked.

"Two old maids—who never married and have more money than the U.S. mint."

"When will you go see them?"

"Tomorrow. I want you along to help me."

Katy frowned at him. "I am not the talker."

"Long said to take my wife. You might convince them if I can't."

"I will come but don't expect to be much help. I don't even know those ladies."

"You will after tomorrow won't she, Ma?"

"I am afraid so." She smiled and shook her head.

Katy slapped her forehead and laughed. "I said I will go along."

They had a nice reunion in bed later. He asked her how she felt.

"Like I have a baby in my belly. I am glad I have you, and your mother is here to help me this time."

"I may be in Kansas when it comes, but I will worry less knowing you're safe and sound with Mom."

"I will be."

Next morning after breakfast, he curried and harnessed the buckskins and they went to see the sisters. The trip was not long, and by noontime they pulled up the long drive to the pillared southern-style mansion. It showed a little wear and tear but it was still a majestic dwelling.

Smiling, she said, "I'd live here."

"So would the king of France."

They laughed and he lifted her off the buck-board. The yard had been mowed, and an elderly black butler answered the door.

"Good day, sir. My name is Able. How may I help you?"

"Would you tell the ladies that Harper O'Malley is here and would like to speak to them? This is my wife, Katy."

"I will announce you, sir."

"Very good, Able. They know me."

Able tossed his head, indicating they follow him down the hallway.

"Everyone knows about those O'Malley brothers who sold Texas steers for a fortune in Missouri," the butler said over his shoulder.

Katy elbowed Harp and gave him a big smile.

"Thank you, Able."

"Ladies, may I introduce Katy and Harper O'Malley."

The two sisters stood up, standing side by side wearing their white lace dresses. Edna the tall straight-backed sister nodded. Her shorter and fatter sister showed them the faded flowered couch to sit on. The elderly ladies took opposing high-back chairs.

"To what do we owe this visit?" Josie asked.

Her sister interrupted her. "Sister, first tell them how pleased we are he brought his new wife to introduce to us."

"Oh, yes. She is very lovely isn't she?"

"Thank you for the compliment. Ladies, I came because I need a favor from you. I would like to rent a fenced section that you are not using, to keep my for-sale steers on until March when we go on our drive."

"Will you be going back to Missouri with them?" Edna asked.

"No. I am taking them up into Kansas to Abilene where they have a market, and there will be less problems getting the cattle there."

"My heavens, will they pay you that much per head as they did in Missouri?"

"I am not sure, Miss Edna, but Missouri sure did not want us to cross them again."

"Katy, I don't imagine you are involved in this cattle business?"

"No. I am going to stay here with Easter to have our firstborn next July while he is gone."

"She is such a lovely lady, Harper. We both wish you the best of good fortunes."

"Back to business. How much is the pasture worth?" Edna asked.

"Five thousand dollars for the next three months," he said.

"My, Edna. That is a nice sum of money, don't you think?"

"I think, my dear, we have some other business to speak to him about now. Harper, we have not sold any cattle at all during the war years. What size herds will you take north this spring?"

"They must be three years old and full-grown steers. Our two herds will be two thousand head apiece."

"I am certain they won't be worth as much as those you took up there."

"Miss Edna, if they only bring sixty dollars a head that's a hundred and twenty thousand dollars gross for each herd."

"Sixty thousand each here to the owners?"

"Yes, ma'am."

"Josie, let's rent him a section for a dollar and let him add a herd of our own steers to take with him to Kansas."

"What a good idea, Edna."

"Ladies, you have yourself a deal."

"You can have the southwest pasture we call number four. When do we need our cattle gathered up for you to take to Kansas?"

"Early March. We will road-brand them here. But I will be in touch and bring papers for you to sign your steers over to us."

"There is no stock in pasture number four now, so you can start using it as soon as you are ready."

"Ladies, thanks to you, I have lots to do now, so if you'll excuse us. Thanks for the pasture and my brother Long and I welcome your business."

"No way. You are not leaving yet. Your wife needs to eat lunch," Josie said, shaking her head in disapproval. "It is ready in the dining room."

So they ate with Harper in a near panic to get back and talk to Long. Now they had three herds to go north. He had one. Long had another. And they would need a head drover for this new one—would their dad take on that job?

That was something he'd have to sort out. Roughly speaking they could make over three hundred thousand dollars considering one herd now looked like it would be all their own cattle. That was more money than he could count. Long would think he had gone completely crazy.

Thank heavens that Katy talked to the women over the meal while he sorted the whole plan out in his mind. Three supply wagons, three remudas, three crews, three cooks, three scouts. More rifles—hell, he had lots to do in ninety days or less.

After lunch he thanked the sisters and told them he'd be back to work out the details.

Going home Kate asked him, "Where will you get enough help for all this? How will you manage three herds on the trail?"

He set in to explain his plan.

When he finished, she asked, "Those girls have no family heirs, do they?"

"No. They were never married nor had any children."

"They won't, now, for sure. I think listening to them today, they may ask you to be their heir," Katy said.

He turned and blinked at her. "Katy, you warned me about people getting jealous about our branding the mavericks. That happened. Are you a mind reader?"

"No, but I get things in my mind that might happen. That just did in there. Like my mind told me on that day when you and I met for me to stay close to the store—that you were coming."

"You never told me that before."

"I didn't want you to think I was a gypsy. All my younger life they scorned me for the fire they thought I set or something. Did my mind say *Get out of the house, little girl*? I don't know if it did or not. As for these sisters, I have a feeling those two are considering it. Our baby in my belly may have made them think that this is the way they might have heirs."

"Let's keep it a secret," he said, thinking deeply about what she said. "If it comes true at least you will live in that house."

She poked him. "Try for ninety dollars a head in Abilene."

"If you say so. Don't tell me much more or I'll have brain overload and it will spill out of my head in pink matter."

She shook her head and laughed.

At Camp Verde that evening they told Easter about parts of their adventure. The crystal ball things he left out.

He used lots of paper and pencil lead that night listing his necessities and the money he must borrow to cover those needs. Katy finally dragged him off to bed knowing that this night might be their last time to share sleeping together—for days.

On a fresh grain-fed horse, the next day, he made a fast trip to the Underground Ranch. Arriving in the camp after lunch, he sent the horse wrangler after Long and his dad.

They arrived in a short time, all dust coated from branding and grinning.

"What's up, bro?"

"I have pasture number four from the sisters, rented for one dollar."

"For one dollar? How'd you manage that? And that pasture . . . there hasn't been anything in there in years I bet," Long said while his dad poured coffee.

Hiram agreed. "Cattle should do good. But you didn't say how you managed it for a dollar."

"On the condition we take a herd of their steers to Kansas with us. Fifty-fifty."

"Three herds?" Long asked.

"Three herds. Dad, will you take one?"

"I better ask my wife first."

"Fine; we have time. Start thinking, guys. We need two more crews, two more remudas, two more wagons, two more cooks."

"We will have over fifteen hundred head branded here by today," Long said.

"Several steers among them?"

"Yes. Lots of big steers we can move to number four," their dad said.

"We have lots of work to do."

"One of us needs to go to hiring help," Long said.

"Borrowing money and finding things," Harp added. It would be March in no time. And he knew most of the business rested on his shoulders.

Hiram laughed. "Why you two, even a year ago, had no worries in this world. Now you are overloaded. Isn't it nice?"

Harp shook his head "I guess. I can recall as kids how busy you got when we moved to Fort Worth and then the place west of there."

"That was a long move from Arkansas."

"Well, I'll go back to town, borrow money, hire help, and try to get ready for Kansas."

"We will shut down here temporarily, get the big cattle rounded up, and move them to pasture number four," Long said. "Then we will know how many more we need."

"Be careful. My trip back home the last time, I had six Comanche after me."

"Aw hell. Take a hand along back with you. Doug could make a good interviewer and he writes good reports."

"That short you?"

"Hell, no. Just find more good ones to help us."

Harp rounded up Doug, who got his things, and they rode back to Camp Verde, arriving in the night. Katy met them with a lamp. "What's next, guys?"

She sounded happy. Harp explained, "We need to hire more drovers. Doug rode with me so I didn't fall out of the saddle. He's going to help us find more help."

She kissed him. "You are doing much better. Thanks, Doug. Anything else happen?"

"Dad, Long, and the crew are going to move all our big steers to pasture four next. Long thinks, at this rate, we will have enough steers for our own herd. We are getting more consignments for herd number two and the Diamond Ranch will provide the third herd. I asked dad if he'd take the job—he wants to talk with Mom about it."

She nodded. "You guys get unsaddled. I will have some food ready for you."

When she went back inside, Doug held the lamp up for Harp to finish putting up his saddle. "You've got to be the luckiest guy I know. That gal is as sweet as she was when you brought her along up there in Arkansas. I can't believe it. She ever get mad? Complain?"

"She told me the day she saw it that New Ranch did not suit her."

"Wow, hell, half the women in this world would turn down that place."

"I am lucky, Doug, damn lucky I found her that day, 'cause she was moving away."

CHAPTER 20

Katy had some sewing to do with Easter, so she stayed at the ranch while Harp and Doug rode into Kerrville, arriving about mid-morning. Harp went straight to the bank where he saw his banker in his private office. They talked about his money needs, Harp explaining to Jim all that was happening and how he figured twenty thousand would get them there. He also told him he'd have enough steers not to have to buy any for the first herd; the second herd would be on consignment, and number three would be from the Diamond Ranch herd on shares.

Jim whistled a wow. Then he said he would run everything by his board, but he felt they would approve. Satisfied, Harp went to meet Doug at the diner.

"I have some news that might help us. The soldiers they recently moved to Texas found a large Comanche bunch, charged the camp, had a big fight, and their huge horse herd got scattered from hell to breakfast. A man said they were some great buffalo horses like you and Long ride among those loose horses."

"Where did it happen?"

"They said west of here, forty miles on Pearl Creek."

"We need to grab some hands, bedrolls, and packhorses, then run out there and find them. We've got time enough to break them."

"How many hands?"

"Five."

"I can get them. They are all afoot. They've got tack. We get them out to the ranch today, we can leave in the morning to find them."

"How many horses did they scatter?" Harp asked, excited about the opportunity he needed.

"They said over a thousand."

"Get those boys hired. Hire a wagon and meet me at the mercantile. I'll get the supplies and we'll load them and the boys and take it all to the ranch."

"They're all real good guys."

"Sounds great. Once the banker gets the nod on the loan, we will be all right."

Doug frowned at the notion of denial. "Hell, you ain't no risk."

"Money is very tight. In fact there is none in Texas at this moment, I bet."

"You might be right. I'll get the wagon rented, tell the boys we're going to the ranch, and meet you at the store."

"I'll wait for you there."

The young clerk waiting on him made a list of

his wants and needs and said he'd have it in boxes on the porch in no time. Harp thanked him, then went for the mail at the post office across the street. He had several letters from ranch hands wanting work, plus the San Antonio newspaper that he subscribed to.

He had a cloth sack for it all. The wagon arrived and the ranch hands Doug hired shook his hand one by one and thanked him for the job. Next they loaded the supplies the clerk had placed on the front porch as promised. Harp got a teenage boy to help.

Before they left, Harp stopped the boy and gave him three silver dollars.

The youngster looked at them. "That's a dollar more than I said I'd do it for."

"I know it, but for you being so polite I added one."

"Thanks a lot, Mr. O'Malley. Next year Maw says I kin go to Kansas with you all."

"I'll hire you then, son."

"Whoopee. I've got a job."

He ran off with Doug laughing. "Hell, they all want to be a part of us."

"And that ain't bad."

"How long do you think it will take all of us to get to Pearl Creek?" Doug asked.

"A day, day and a half."

"You think we might get some good horses huh?"

"Oh, yes. If we can catch them."

At the ranch Harp had one problem. When he told Kate that evening, she wanted to go along.

"I am sorry, but no. I can't leave you in camp while we chase horses. I want to have a wife when I get back. Those damn Comanche will sure want those horses back. We may have a fight on our hands when we get out there."

"I can—" He put his finger on her lips.

"This time trust me. Mother, do you have any rifles I can borrow?"

"Two of those tube-feeding Spencers. Dad's got his Winchester."

"I better borrow them. Is there ammo for them?"

"Of course. I'll get it."

"You going to war out there?" his wife asked, looking concerned.

"Only if they want one."

"You just remember there is more than me waiting here now."

"Oh, I hope not, but if they try me I will fight."

She hugged him. "I just dread ever losing you, big man."

"You won't."

They inventoried the guns they had. Five rifles—his; Doug had his Winchester; one of the men had a Winchester, too; plus the two Spencer models. They all had .45-caliber cap-and-ball ammunition for their side arms. Plus Harp had his extra .30-caliber in his saddlebag. With plenty of ammo for the guns, he felt they should be fine.

The sun still had not crested the eastern rim

when they were trotting their saddle horses and pack ones westward in the cool winter west Texas morning.

Not one horse bucked, which was a new record for Hiram O'Malley's ranch horses.

His dad lived by the verse, *There had never been a horse couldn't be rode nor a cowboy hadn't been throwed.* He went by the rule that a horse that didn't buck a little was not worth the salt you fed him. Harp held them to a hard trot all morning. Mid-afternoon the solar heat was up and they began to find loose Comanche horses. They roped several and found a brush corral to hold them in. These horses were broke. They let the mares and colts go, the tough stallions, too. The Comanche gelded the horses they usually rode—he had seen some hard-nosed bucks ride stallions but most rode the neutered horses.

They had several horses in the pen when they shut down for the evening and had coffee and jerky for supper. Before dawn they made coffee and oat-meal, and when the short day dawned they went after more. By late afternoon he felt they had the good ones in the area caught. There might be more, farther west, but Harp and his crew had stayed out there long enough to suit him. There was an itching under the shirt material on his back between his shoulder blades—some of those bucks might be coming back to look for those good horses they had lost.

In the morning, one of the riders caught a broke

mare. The horses they'd penned followed her and they headed home. There was lots of color in the herd: paints, piebalds, buckskins, and two snow-white horses. Not albino, either. With forty horses, he considered the men had sure earned their keep.

It took a day and a half to get back, driving them right through Kerrville and arriving at the home ranch about dark. He'd be glad when the days grew longer.

He signed up the five hands. Then he set them to breaking those new horses to ride under a saddle. Also to swap sides, mounting from the right to the left. They'd learn fast and make super cattle drive horses. All he needed was another seventy or so. Whew he had lots to do to make it work, and not much time.

The next morning three men stopped by the ranch—Amos Thornton and his sons Wade and Corley. Harp had never met them before, and Thornton said he heard that Harp needed some more using horses.

"How many do you have?"

"How many horses do you need?" Thornton asked, dismounting and hitching up his pants.

"About seventy-five."

"Whew. I can probably get them. Can you pay thirty a head for sound ones?"

"Round it off. Seventy-five head for two thousand dollars."

"I can do that. I won't bring you junk, but some will be green-broke."

"March first? Will we have them by then?"

"Can we do that, boys?" the older man asked his sons.

They both nodded. Harp shook hands with the man.

"The women will feed you breakfast."

"We'd take it. I pushed pretty hard to get here to catch you."

"I appreciate it. That makes one less thing to worry about."

"You won't need to. We can get you those horses."

His wife came out on the porch. "Katy, please fix breakfast for these horse traders. They've just solved one of my problems. His name is Thornton and these are his sons."

"Come on inside. Easter and I can sure do that," Katy said.

"Their names are Wade and Corley. Ma'am, that man of yours ever treats you wrong, me and them boys will court you."

She laughed. "I doubt he'll ever do that."

"I do, too. But I had to offer. You two been together long?"

"Oh, six months I'd say. But I am very happy with him."

"My, my, he sure is busy."

"Yes, he is, and he will be more so heading north."

"We heard the story how he went to Missouri last year and sold them high-priced cattle."

"He can tell you all about it."

"It wasn't a story? He did sell the cattle?"

Harper had heard the conversation. "Yes, we sold them high, but it was hell. After taking those cattle up there I was glad to even be alive. I am looking forward to be headed for Kansas this spring."

"You think that is the way?"

"Yes. Missouri has laws against coming there to start with, and there are folks up there don't like Rebs."

"You expect them to be like that in Kansas?"

"I hope not. I get real anxious about folks stopping me."

"Thanks for doing business with us. We'll go home and get those horses gathered. There isn't much money in Texas these days."

"You'll get my money, but you won't get my wife."

They agreed, laughing.

With a smile for her, Harper was off to check on more things he needed to get done. He had a list and was going over it when Doug came in from checking on the horse-breaking crew.

"We, maybe, can find some boys in San Antonio," Harper said to him.

Doug shrugged. "I think we hired all that're worth a damn in Kerrville."

"Let's take the stage to San Antonio tomorrow and take a few days at the stockyards and around. We need several more hands."

"I think these guys we have will make good hands. They are working those horses hard and doing it right."

"The three men here this morning promised me seventy-five more horses in a month. Those, with the Comanche ones, will solve the horse problem. Now it will be cowhands we need to hire."

"Our crew is down three guys," Doug pointed out, "so we need three there."

"And I say two dozen more to make up the other two crews. But Doug, we need to share those experienced men on all three crews. You be thinking who's who so we don't have all new men on any herd."

"I can do that. You said we're going tomorrow to San Antonio?"

"Yes, and my wife will want to go along."

"Fine with me."

"I'll talk to her. We will need two camp wagons, too, and that might be the place to buy them."

"I bet the good ones will be in short supply the closer we get to leaving. If everyone in Texas is going north this spring with a herd, it might be good to buy them now. As for the men, I know several guys that have job promises. We could hire them, because a bunch going north won't want to pay until right before they leave and most won't pay to go back. We can use them now and pay them. They'll want to work a sure thing with us."

Harp quickly agreed. "Good idea, I can stand the expense if they're good."

The next morning, Katy, Harp, and Doug bundled up against the cool spell and rain, to take the stage to San Antonio. A-day-and-a-half hassle to get there but it beat riding horses in the wet weather. They made it and got hotel rooms, then met for dinner and had a nice meal. The rain swept in and out, but it was a good soaking moisture and the kind his dad called a kick in the ass for spring/winter oats.

They found a dealer of farm machinery, and he told them the cost of a horse-drawn mower and rake would be around two hundred dollars. Delivery was suspect, but he could order one set for him and try to get it up to Kerrville soon as possible.

Harp ordered it to be delivered to Hiram O'Malley at Camp Verde, Texas. Harp paid the man, who was grateful, and gave the receipt to his wife. Kate would be there and she could arrange for Hoot to get it.

"Mr. O'Malley, are you the man who sold those cattle in Missouri last summer?" the dealer asked.

"Yes, my brother and I drove eight hundred head to Sedalia last fall."

"Mr. O'Malley, I am sure proud to meet you, and every need of any kind of farm machinery, I would sure like to sell it to you."

"Your name's Earl Burns?"

"Yes, wait till I tell my friends."

"Well, Earl Burns, what can you find me two ambulances for? Price wise?"

"I know where they be two like-new ones in a shed. I can get them for two hundred dollars apiece. Two teams of real stout mules to pull them for a hundred fifty dollars."

"Harness?"

"Both pair for eighty dollars. New harness, the best made."

"That's 630 dollars?"

"Exactly, sir."

"Can they have bows and a canvas top on each wagon?"

"Make it seven hundred and they will have that, too."

"Spring seats?"

"Two of them as well. When you need them?"

"Four days. The two of us will drive them home."

"No, siree," Earl said. "Why, that pretty lady don't have to ride home in no stiff wagon. I will pay some boys to take both of them to your Camp Verde Ranch."

Harp shook his hand. "I thank you and I know Kate does, too. We have some boys coming for try-outs to be on our payroll this spring, so we need to run right now. I will look for the wagons in a week. Better get me a receipt for them, too."

"Yes, sir. And I mean it, Mr. O'Malley. I sure want to be your implement dealer."

"Harp is my handle. I appreciate you and will be in touch."

They took the receipts, climbed into the buckboard, and drove at a trot—in the livery surrey—for the stockyards. For the tryouts, Harp had rented two horses, saddles, and ropes from the livery. He also had two nail kegs for each cowboy to try to rope from off the horse.

They were all set up in a large pen. There was a canvas shade put up over the setup with a board desk and a chair for Kate to record each man's name and how they did at the job trials.

The large crowd of teenage boys wanting jobs

impressed Harper, and several fence watchers were perched on the top rail.

"Everyone, listen. You report in your turn to the lady at the desk; be polite to her and tell her your name and hometown. A horse will be hitched. You untie him, mount him, and short-lope him around the pen. Then set him down where the white lime is on the ground. Undo the rope and rope the barrel from the saddle. You have three tries to rope it. Then coil the rope and ride the horse back and hitch him for the next man.

"First man to show you how is Clarence Fowler." Harp had talked to the young man before it started. He said he could do that to show them how.

"Ma'am my name is Clarence Fowler. My town is Berne."

"Thanks, Clarence," she said.

He put his worn felt cowboy hat back on, went to the bay horse, and unhitched him. Then without stirrups he handily flipped up into the saddle, sat the horse down, found his stirrups, and charged him off in a lope around the pen. Slid him to a stop, undid the lariat on the spot, uncoiled his lariat, made a loop, and tossed it neatly over the barrel and jerked up the slack.

A young boy Harp hired ran out, took his loop off of it, reset the barrel, and ran for the fence. Clarence coiled it going back, dismounted, and hitched the horse back to the fence.

Harp looked at Doug, who nodded his approval. "Clarence, you're hired to go to Kansas with the O'Malley brothers. See Miss Kate later."

Everyone gave Clarence a round of applause.

"Johnny Marks," Doug called off his list.

Some had trouble getting on the horse. Others were too round bottomed to even ride. But there were many good ones. A Mexican boy came with his own *reata* and asked to use it instead of the rope.

"Sure, Carlos Rey, use it," Harp said.

When he roped the barrel he dallied his rope around the horn and backed the horse up, too. He got the hired call.

Two boys could damn sure ride but could not rope. But Harp and Doug both liked them and hired them. The afternoon wore on. It was obvious that the trial would not finish before sundown. Besides he figured Katy must be getting tired. Harp told the ones left to be back there at eight thirty in the morning and bring along anyone else who wanted to work.

Katy whispered, "Call Billy McCall up here. I know he failed, but he's an orphan. Could he help in camp?"

"Billy McCall, come over here," Harp shouted.

A boy in oversized bib overalls came on the run—bare footed.

"You got a job for me, sir?"

"You an orphan?"

"Yes, sir, but I don't beg."

"I don't need a beggar, either. I need an assistant cook. We want you back here for the trials tomorrow. So find a place to sleep and eat, and tomorrow you will be on our payroll." He gave him fifty cents, plenty enough money to eat on in the *barrio*.

Billy thanked Harp and left.

After he was gone, Kate stood up on her toes and kissed him. "You won't regret doing that."

"I didn't figure I would. Doug, Katy, let's go eat supper. We've found some good boys and I am convinced we will have enough hired by tomorrow to go to Kansas. Plus we have those two more supply wagons and the farm machinery."

They ate supper in the hotel dining room. Plans were to eat breakfast at seven and then go back for the rest of the trials.

First thing Harp noticed in the morning at the pens was that the number of boys and onlookers had really increased. Two were black teens and sure enough cowboys, riding and roping both.

"You Trent boys brothers?" Harp asked them.

Sly said, "We really cousins, but we been raised by *dee* same woman, sah."

Jimbo agreed. "Sir, we will do our damndest to make hands for you outfit. Ain't no jobs 'chere, so we really need the work."

"I pay the same wage to all my hands. You understand me?"

"That be fine, sah."

"My biggest rule is no fighting with crew members. This is serious business. All of you remember that. There will be no fighting or you will be afoot in no man's land. If you can't get along you walk around that other one. No stealing. You can't live by the rules, don't leave San Antonio. No one is any better than the other. If you are told to help the cook, you help him. We all have to pull together. We may have to shoot people who get in our way, but by damn, if you don't give me your all, I will leave you out in the prairie.

"A man named Earl Burns is taking two wagons up to Kerrville and on to my family ranch. He will bring you out to our ranch. It will take over two days to get up there. Bring a blanket and clothes. If you don't have a bedroll, we will supply you one when you get up there. We will have a rubber slicker and a hat for you to wear. If you have a saddle bring it. We can get some saddles for those don't have one. If you don't want the job don't come, we won't be back until sometime in the fall.

"There is hardly a way to get mail. But you can send notes home. We will have paper, pen, stamps, and envelopes. At the ranch I need to know who to notify as your next of kin in the case of your death. You can get mail to you at General Delivery, Abilene, Kansas. You will get it there in four months from our leaving here.

"Any questions?"

He arranged with Earl to take the boys, who didn't ride their own horses out there, in the wagons. He paid him twenty dollars to feed them.

Everyone was informed. He went by and saw his banker Fred Newman.

Fred asked him if he needed any money.

"If I do need some I can wire you, can't I?"

"Yes, and we can have it delivered to you."

"So far we have enough. But it will get more expensive."

"How many head are you taking?"

"We have two thousand head that we rounded up. That's one herd. The number two herd belongs to our neighbors, small ranchers with a few hundred or less, with up to two thousand head in that herd. Herd three is ours on the shares with two older women who needed some help."

"Seven thousand head?"

"Yes. We've been hiring cowboys and we have some good ones picked out."

"Oh, my, Harp. That will be a feat even larger than the Sedalia one."

"Bigger, yes, but we know more now."

"Harp and Mrs. O'Malley, you have my prayers. You need money, just wire me. Be careful . . . you are too good a man to lose."

"Thanks. We are headed home tomorrow. In a month we go north."

"God bless you and your family."

He left the man still in shock thinking about their huge undertaking.

Katy asked him, riding in the rented surrey back to the hotel, if he thought it was that scary.

He clucked to the team that was laying back a little. "Darling, we will do what we have to do, and no, I think with the crew we are assembling we can do it."

Back at the hotel they joined up with Doug for supper, and Doug asked how they met.

Kate answered, "Doug, I found me a man, one day, to buy me some canned peaches."

"I know the guy."

"He acted like he was foot loose and fancy free. Boy, did he ever fool me. He's a tycoon turned loose."

Doug agreed with her. "I'm jealous as hell of him. My mind don't move as fast as him, but I am learning. He fired a terrible cook one day, and the next he was running the whole damn outfit and did a wonderful job at it, so I don't think this cattle-moving business is new. While it is bigger, it is not anything to be scared of. And I am also jealous as how you picked him out up there at Lee's Creek and not me."

"Doug, you have to keep your eyes open. There is a lady out there looking for you that you will be proud of."

"I will be a-looking then."

"Doug, you better listen to her. She knows a lot about the future that I can't figure how she knows it, but she does."

"This has been a great experience. Where did you get the tryout deal for the boys?" Doug asked Harp.

"He gets things like that so easy," she said, shaking her head and laughing.

"I decided if they could ride and rope we'd take them and make cowboys out of them. It was just a way to see them in action."

"I won't forget it. Now I know what to look at and for."

"Now we need to eat and some sleep. We take the eight-o'clock stage back home. Remember we still need to hire more cooks."

Damn he was closing in getting things done, but now he knew how Emory felt back then getting ready. Whew there was still a lot to do.

CHAPTER 21

In the cool of morning the threesome left for home on the rocking stagecoach. Three miles west of Berne, three men wearing flour-sack masks stopped the driver and told everyone to get out. They were being held up.

Harp sharply told Katy to do as they asked. He had his .30-caliber Colt in his waistband and kept the presence of it under the brown suit coat he wore. He helped her down under the gun barrels of two of the outlaws on horseback, rifles pointed at them on that side of the coach.

"Get your hands up, mister," said one of them, who, he figured, was only a boy.

The outlaws' horses acted ready to spook, and two of them were shaky-handed pointing their guns. One of them dismounted and stepped up close to Doug, then demanded he unbuckle his gun belt and drop it.

Doug, instead, forced the robber's gun hand up

in the air and shot the man at close range with his own pistol. Gun smoke boiled.

Harp had his Colt out, cocked, and fired it in the other boy's face. The third rider's horse shied to the right and Doug's next shot took him out and off his horse after the bullet from the robber's rifle went off overhead.

Harp caught his wife when her knees buckled. He dropped his pistol to hold her. He was satisfied Doug was checking on the downed outlaws and seeing if there was any fight left in them.

The driver had the spooked teams held down. "You three all right?"

Doug told Harp to turn Katy around and then he shot each of the still living in their heads.

"Come help me get them off the road. The law can collect them," he said to the driver.

"By gawd they sure won't ever try to rob another stage. Mister, is your wife all right?"

"She will be shortly. Things got rather tight here for a minute or two."

Kate was pale but getting her breath back. "Sorry. I just knew we'd all get killed."

Set on her feet, she leaned her forehead on his chest.

"It is going to be all right. Walk around a little. This matter is over."

Harp walked his wife in the short grass back and forth away from the corpses, while Doug hitched the would-be robbers' horses to a farmer's fence nearby. He checked their saddlebags.

Doug shook his head at him. "No loot in them."

The driver said, "I'll have the agent report this to the law at the next stage stop. The sheriff can handle it. Let's load up and go."

"I'm putting her back in the coach," Harp said, then he retrieved his gun off the ground.

"Ma'am, I sure am so sorry about this happening," the driver said as he closed the coach door after them.

"Don't worry about me. I am fine. It's over."

"Still it is a bad thing every time someone tries that."

In her seat she asked Harp, "Did he hear me?"

"Yes. I think it shook him badly, too."

"Well, it was damn exciting. Doug, thank you, too."

"Next stop, I need to reload my gun."

"Yes, so do I. Let's hope that does our robberies for now."

They were off again and Harp started thinking about the drive. Doug was definitely the man to take one of the herds. Long needed to scout. He was damn good at appraising sites and knowing what was ahead. Their dad never said if he would take a herd. He was getting near fifty years old. He had no physical things wrong that Harp knew about—but he didn't like to leave their mom alone that long.

He still needed another man to head the third herd if his dad didn't. Chaw Michaels might be the one. Long would have some ideas by this time and they'd need to nail down that third herd leader.

When they got back to his parents' place, Katy became sick. His mother told him not to worry, that it was part of her pregnancy, but he looked back on the violent scene they had with the stage robbers as bringing it on and regretted her being there. He stayed busy making plans and learned that Long was still branding cattle in the same location. Hiram had not come home, either.

His mother sounded concerned about Hiram working too hard since he had eased back a lot on doing physical things in the past two years. His brother had lots of things going on up there at that ranch they owned, and since his mom was well behind the line from the Comanche raids, Hiram was probably enjoying himself being in on the scheme of things.

Harp did all he could on his books, and, the next morning, when Kate felt somewhat better, he and Doug rode for the cow camp. They made a quick trip and found everyone busy branding. The whole outfit looked worn out except his dad, who was laughing and enjoying himself over the whole situation.

Long looked gaunt to him; he must have lost twenty pounds in the past ten days. When finally dragged back into camp, Harp asked him how many cattle they had gathered.

Long took off his hat and wiped his forehead on his sleeve. "I can tell you now we'll have three thousand steers in our own herd going north."

"That's one helluva herd."

His brother slumped down on the bench and nodded his head. "And we will have them all in the pasture you rented."

"Sounds great. I found enough cowboys for our old plan. I bought two good supply wagons and mules to pull them. A mowing machine and rake for Hoot. I have it coming."

"You will never guess what I bought?" Long smiled over his secret.

"What is that?"

"Two bell steers. They are coming from Mexico."

"Great. How much?"

"Two fifty for the pair."

"That's not bad. So when we get things all lined up we can road-brand all the cattle going north, but we will still need two cooks."

"Ira has a good buddy. He knows this guy well and there also is a Chinese man in Kerrville that wants to be the other one."

"If Dad can buy us twenty-five more saddle horses around the country, we'll soon be set."

"That may be hard, but he's a hand at finding things. How else did it go in San Antonio?"

"Our banker there says if we need money wire him. Doug and I had a run-in with some stage robbers west of Berne."

"I take it they didn't rob you."

"They won't rob anyone again."

"More people need to use that policy."

Harp agreed. "Who's taking the third herd? I figure Doug to take number two."

"Good choice. Dad said he'd pass on it. I think Chaw can handle it. He ain't Doug, but he has lots of savvy about men and isn't afraid to work."

Harp agreed with the choice. He had thought that all along. "I want him dressed up more. He needs to look like a leader. He don't need a suit coat, but dress him up so he looks like the boss."

"I had not thought about that, but yes, he needs to make an impression on people and his own men."

"Horse wranglers?"

"We can pick them. I know you want Holy Wars wrangling for your bunch."

"Yes, and we'll need some camp boys to help the cooks. I found one in San Antonio. Say one or two per outfit? Whatever the cooks say they'll need."

"Yes, we can find them. I know we'll be stretched thin, but I think spreading out the good men that we took north last year, who have some experience, throughout all three groups will help us get there. My lands, Harp, they have worked their butts off rounding up these cattle."

"I know. And we will have a great drive. Let's get them back to the home place and organize them into three teams."

"I promised them two days off."

"That's good. They need it. Mom is concerned that Dad is working too hard."

"He won't take a desk job."

"Long, we both knew that."

The two started chuckling at the thought.

When he got back he could have called the home place "Tent City." In no time, they had sidewall tents up for the men to sleep in in case of rain. One large tent for a mess hall and meetings was set up down near the large barn. A deep ditch was dug for their latrine and two sheepherder showers. Ira's buddy's name was Hopalong Sessions. He had a stiff right leg from the war, but he was a friendly guy and knew lots about minor doctor things. This was a good thing, since the cook was usually the acting physician on these trips. The third cook was Wing Chong. He cooked things more like what the boys would eat. He talked *velly* fast, but he came with good recommendations on how serious he was about his work.

One of the boys in the groups breaking Comanche horses was Holy Wars Brown who was the wrangler on the Greg drive and now took the position with the number one herd.

Harp had to know how he got that handle, but he had not had the chance to ask earlier.

"Well, sir, when I was born my real dad named me that and it stuck. I learned later that my mother and dad did not get along very good together. I never knew my real dad. Mom remarried two other men after that."

"Thanks for sharing. Now, you will need to know every horse in your remuda. Each hand will be assigned five or six horses. They will give you the horse's name that they want to ride; you rope it for them. They might not be a hand at doing it, but if you see some boy is a hand at roping horses, use him to help you. These horses, if used properly, won't need grain. I mean them being rode on an every-five-day schedule. We only shoe the tender-footed ones. They get gaunt we can probably buy some grain—but that is expensive on the road. You are in charge . . . if we get a new hand, you will tell him what horses he will ride. Don't give someone green a green bunch of horses. Let the bronc twisters have them. Savvy?"

"I think I'll enjoy that. Say, Harper, I have learned

a lot the last few weeks. When we caught them I said, why is he messing with this wild-colored bunch of plugs? I learned quick that they are powerful horses and will be great on the drive."

"Holy, I know you are a great wrangler from the Sedalia drive. Thanks for staying on with us."

Ira took the orphan boy Billy McCall for his helper.

Chaw was wearing his new Boss of the Plains Stetson hat. He also sported a tailored, blue denim shirt, as well as a leather vest and tan pants. He told Harp not to worry, he'd find someone to wrangle his horses.

Then he laughingly said, "I feel like a city dude in these clothes, but I know they make a man look like he's a boss man. A year ago I wore a Confederate uniform and I agreed with you that none of us should wear them going north. I know that helped some in Missouri. I understand all what Long told me—you need to look like you're the boss if you are the boss."

Doug took his crew and went from ranch to ranch, road-branding the cattle he would take on the consignment phase. Chaw and his men went to the Diamond Ranch to do the same with the sisters' herd. They had plenty of *vaqueros* there who helped them. Long took Harp's bunch to work their own cattle already in pasture number four.

Long told him to take Katy, who was feeling much better, over and visit the old maids. They needed to be the team to satisfy those sisters, so they could do other drives for them over the years.

Harp hated to spend the time drinking tea and eating dry cookies, but he went over there a little dressed up. His boot shined, hair trimmed by his wife, and he wore his suit coat with a white shirt.

The two ladies were friendly and wanted to know how well the horse-drawn mowing machine that he ordered for Hoot would work.

"The man I bought it from said that if you have a good team of horses, twenty acres a day can get it done."

"Is it hard to learn how to fix it?"

"No. If you hire a boy knows a little about them, he could run it."

"Could you find us one?"

"The war just being over, those mowers are scarce. But I will write my dealer in San Antonio on how to contact you. He also sells dump rakes."

"Thank you. Sister and I don't know how you have done all this. Assembling three herds, and you find the nicest people—like Chaw, is it?—to do everything that is needed."

"Yes, ma'am. He's a top-notch drover."

"Is that his real name?"

"I bet it is. My horse wrangler's name is Holy Wars."

"Oh, my, people name their children anything I guess nowadays."

"Katy and I are learning that signing up hands for the drive."

"Thank you so much for coming by and visiting

with us. We appreciate you taking our cattle to Kansas."

"Well, ladies, we will be in the same business next year, so I hope you are satisfied with our work this year and allow us to work the same next year."

"Don't worry, we are, and yes, we will continue next year. Katy, how have you been feeling, dear?"

"Full. He is getting big and he kicks a lot."

"You don't know how lucky you are to have him," one of the sisters said.

"Oh yes, I do, and I thank God every day for Harp finding me."

"Dear, were you living at home when he found you?"

Katy shook her head. "I was orphaned at five and raised by an older couple. They died and I was on my own, but Harp found me and here I am expecting my first in a few months."

"Oh, what a nice story. Good luck with the baby. Bring him by to show him to us one day when you are well."

"I can do that this summer."

"We will look forward to your visit."

In the buckboard and heading home, he hugged her close. "Thanks for the short life story."

"They didn't need the rest of it. That happened and is done. I still say some day you will be their heir."

"Whatever. They make good customers now."

"Oh my, yes. I will be praying a lot for your safe return."

It wouldn't hurt to pray for their ranch, too.

CHAPTER 22

Their dad came back to his own ranch and took *siestas* when he wasn't helping to get some things ready. He took the wagons, one at a time, into town and had the blacksmith in Kerrville mount water barrels—one on each side of the wagons. A shovel rack for the side and two ax holders, some towing chains with hooks on the ends in case they got stuck in the mud. He went over every inch of the new sets of harnesses and bragged on the mules. Best he ever drove were his words about the long ears. He was not a mule man so that meant a lot to Harp coming from him.

Amos Thornton and his boys drove in the promised horse herd, much to Harp's relief. He ordered three wagonloads of hay for them, from some farmers, to feed them until they left.

The two head men, Doug and Chaw, plus Long and Harp met in the mess tent each morning. All the horses were divided between them. Each man had five horses to ride. Herd one had fourteen hands due to the herd size.

Days warmed, rain fell generously, grass broke its dormancy, and the elms leaved out. Harp found sixty more horses and he bought them. The daylight hours lengthened.

Chadron Turner was to be Doug's scout. Chaw chose Eldon Morehouse to be his. Red Culver was to be Harp's number two man. Harp wanted the herds to stay a day or two apart and not to get their herds mixed in with any other. Such a mess would take days to sort the many cattle from each other, out in the open country without corrals.

Every supply wagon carried enough new Winchester rifles and ammo for each hand, plus .45 lead bullets, gunpowder, and caps. The gunpowder and caps fit other calibers. The bullets were good for the .30- or .44-caliber side arms. His used saddles, and for those cowboys that did not own one, their mounts were gone over with new girths and latigo leathers. Things were as right as they could be or at least how Harp could make them.

On the final day he took his pregnant wife to an isolated creek and they played in the water, picnicked, and made love on a blanket capped off with a can of peaches for each of them. It was a very sweet yet sad day since they had not been apart for long since Lee's Creek, and the few times he was gone he always missed her. This would be a tough period of time, not to have her with him.

Their time to go back was closing. They were

lying on their backs watching fluffy clouds pass over. She sat up and shook her hair, caressing her expanded stomach. "I never dreamed about this happening to me."

"I wouldn't know. My dreams are all about horse wrecks that never happen and me falling off cliffs I'd never climb."

"Did you ever dream about getting ready for this drive?"

"No. And I never dreamed of you before you came into my life. But there was some powerful force that showed me you should be mine. I wasn't finding someone new—you were mine already. We made love on that beach like we had done it many times before. It was wonderful but not shockingly new."

"More reason to take care of yourself on this long trip. I agree it was like we were overcome by some spirit, and it has been like that every day since then. Let's pray together."

He sat up and got on his knees.

"You say the words," Kate said in a soft voice.

"Our dear heavenly father, tomorrow we part for a short while. Help her get through this pregnancy into motherhood. Be with me as I ride north on business . . ." His prayer went on, hands clasped, eyes shut tightly talking about facing the big undertaking and a long sentence of time away from his lovely wife.

CHAPTER 23

Cattle bawling woke him up. Harp gently kissed Kate and quietly dressed to not disturb her. Those incisive eternal cattle sounds would be with him until he loaded the last one onto the stock car in Abilene, Kansas. He finally no longer heard it after the last drive, but it took many hundreds of miles on the return trip for it to stop. His crew ate first that morning. Long joined him at the table and asked him if he had any regrets.

"Only leaving her."

"You know you're a lucky man. But I can see down the long road at our lives, well, yours, hers, and the kids. Katy is a special person. She bears few scars of her horrible past because she is so strong. God gave you a gift. I see you and her waltzing at governors' balls someday in D.C., when the bad taste of the war is over and Texans are accepted again in those halls. You will come back to her this fall dancing a jig, and people will say those damn two O'Malley brothers have done it again."

"Amen, brother. Amen."

"What have they done again?" Katy asked, slipping onto the bench beside him.

"That's next fall," Long whispered to her. "When you and Harp dance in the street and those O'Malley brothers have done it again."

"You bet and I'll dance with you, too."

Long rose up, leaned over, and kissed her cheek. "I'll watch out for him, little lady."

Hiram joined them. "I will help the others get out the gate after you're gone."

"Thanks. The men we have are capable enough, but any help is appreciated," Harp told him.

"I knew Doug was a good candidate for the job. I was not around him ten minutes and I knew. But Chaw Michaels is the man impressed me the most. He not only wears that Boss of the Plains Stetson hat, he has become a boss of the plains leader since he got that job."

"Brother here got him out of a Reb uniform, and Chaw got the rest out of theirs to save any fights on the trip last year. First thing Long told him down here, about the job, was he had to dress to be the boss on this drive and he did, didn't he?"

"A radical change. It worked. He will be all right."

Harp told his leader, Red Culver, to have the two black point riders to get Old Blue up and take the rag off his clapper. The two black cousins had won the point rider's jobs competing for it. They were horseback riders deluxe. The outfit was Kansas bound.

They rode after Red, smiling. "Going to be a great day, Captain, sir."

Harp agreed they had to be formal toward Red so they called him Captain all the time.

"We came to wish you well and we'll see you at the end. Horses, equipment, and men all better than when we left last year," Doug said. "I also have to thank you. Not only for firing that cook before you got to be boss last year, but the jobs you have provided us. Every one of us is damn proud to be part of the flagship of this cattle-driving business."

"Thanks, guys. Good luck to us all."

Cold chills ran up his cheeks as he waved to his wife standing back out of the way, then he short-loped his horse to check on his point men, leaders of the biggest herd they knew about going north.

Long planned a twelve-mile trip that day. Ira and his new camp boy, Billy, had the same team of stout horses used on the Missouri trip, pulling his completely rebuilt supply wagon with a bright new canvas top, their names on it in red.

The steers were doing some butting heads but nothing like a fresh mixed bunch. The bawling continued and a few tried for liberty but were turned back by much better horses than the last time. The worst three days lay ahead. After that, the herding business would ease a whole lot.

Noontime they reached their goal and they spread the cattle out to graze. It was an uneventful day for all. Harp liked Red's efficiency. The boys took his commands well and he encouraged them a lot, helped the new boys, and had a settling effect on everything. From here on it would be day-by-day, head-to-tail monotony. He hoped. Harp and Red visited privately before the evening meal.

"Those cousins have good control as point riders. They damn sure can ride and they get lots out of their horses."

"You ever hear where they learned all that?" Harp asked.

"No. But I bet they'll tell us some day."

"That blond boy—"

"Harold Nelson."

"Someone said he had brought a guitar. Maybe he'd make some music after supper."

"I'll ask him."

"It might build a little fellowship in the crew."

"I'll check it out."

Harp went to make notes in his diary about their first day. As the shadows grew long, he put his pencil down and closed the leather-bound book. With care, he placed it back in the wooden secretary box Kate had bought him in San Antonio on their last trip. *"Make a record, Harp, for your son to read some-day about these days of yours on the cattle drive. When he is old enough these days will all be over. Our world is changing so fast. Tell him the inside thinking of an emerg-ing cattle baron."*

How did an orphan learn to talk like she did? Maybe the old people who raised her instilled that in her. He and Long had read many books, Shake-speare even, but he never imagined such things like someday there would be no more cattle drives . . .

Those people will be mad you branded their cattle.

And he could not ask her a single question until he came back in the fall. He should start a list of them. He had to get to the bottom of her source of all the things she knew, he didn't, and why. Bless her pea-picking soul—he sure loved her.

He heard the guitar and the crew singing what they knew about "leaving this valley." Good. That might pass the time faster. At the moment the trip, looked to him, like a woodpecker trying to peck down a big oak.

Time to go to bed. "Katy, I already miss you."

CHAPTER 24

Day two started out with a bang. One of those Comanche buffalo ponies gave a hand named Hank Dryer a wild ride and bucked his damndest. He covered a lot of ground and finally quit and blew the snot out of his nose. The crew shouted and tossed hats at him to make him buck some more. Instead he went off single-footing like he'd never done anything, and Hank acted like it simply was another day to top a bronc.

He'd jot that down in his diary when he got to camp that evening. His son could laugh about it someday. They had the herd moving out. Blue's bell was clacking and the steers followed the next tail ahead of them—going north.

Somewhere over that northern horizon on this side of the Arctic Circle was a dusty cattle-shipping town called Abilene—probably at the end of the tracks like Sedalia. Harp jobbed the buffalo horse with his spur to get back to work, and the gelding ducked his head and went to bucking, grunting like a fat hog on legs of steel springs, landing hard and going for another leap into the sky with Harp sawing his jaw off with the bridle.

He never quit bucking until they were near a quarter mile from the herd. Red came whipping and driving his pony hard across the flat to come to his aid, but by then Harp was loping him in a circle, the fit over. Red slid to a halt.

"You all right, boss?"

Harp reined up his horse and shook his head. "My dad said a horse that won't buck ain't worth his salt. I've rode that horse two thousand miles or more, and he never bucked before today."

They both laughed about it. In three hours they were spreading the cattle out to graze. The cousins rode in. Sly shouted, "Hey, boss man, that Comanche can really buck."

"You see my ride?"

"Damn good one."

"Naw, I was damn lucky he quit."

"No, sir, he's not gonna be the first one or the last one you rode like that."

"Thanks."

Long had rode in, heard the laughter, and asked what it was about.

"My horse was dinking along and I spurred him. He broke and bucked all the way across the flat, having a fit. I wasn't the only one. Hank had one break earlier this morning and he had a helluva ride on him. All is good now. How does tomorrow look?"

"No problem," Long said. "I'll give Ira and Holy

Wars Brown, your wrangler, good directions. I guess we were just green when we left with Emory. This drive is too smooth compared to then."

"Well, we do know more about how to handle cattle, we're mounted better, and we're having good weather. There's already been some herds ahead of us. I hear a different rumor each day. The price for cattle is sky high in some place named Springs in south Kansas, but I think we better stick with this road and go all the way."

"I am with you. I guess tomorrow the last herd starts out?"

"Yes, that was the plan."

"Chaw should do okay," Long said. "The Arkansas will be just inside Kansas where we cross it on this route. Day after tomorrow we cross the Colorado River. That shouldn't be too high with no more rain than we have received."

"Where you figure we'll have the first trouble?" Harp asked him.

"Right now I can't say but I bet them carpetbaggers, like they call them damn Yankees in Austin, are going to realize that tax dollars are going out of state and try to tax us on exporting the cattle. You know the grass isn't as good this year as it was last." Long shook his head.

"Not enough rain this winter. We started later, too, last year."

"Bro, if this drive works, we're going to be big ranchers."

"My wife's word for us is emerging cattle barons."

Long laughed. "You are the luckiest man on this earth getting that woman, and you two are as natural together as Mom and Dad are."

"You will find someone."

"I know."

Holy Wars took Long's horse.

"Thanks," Long said after him. "But my leg ain't broke, I can do it."

"Long, you've been many miles today. Glad to have you back."

Ira rang the triangle. And everyone sleeping woke up and went for grub. Red handled the cowhands, all doing one three-hour shift a night riding herd. That interrupted their sleeping. They could read time on the big dipper. Red used a wind-up alarm clock like Harp used going north to get the next shift up.

Harp wrote about the two bronc rides in his diary and started a letter to Katy.

In the morning big dark ominous clouds began to gather. Everyone tied a slicker behind their cantles before they rode out. It was cooler and rain looked imminent. Once on the move, Harp pulled his hat down low when he got on board his saddle, like most men that wore felt hats. When there were thirty-mile-per-hour gusts, he'd pull some leather strings out of his saddlebags. He would thread them through the holes punched about his ears so the leather strings would hold the hat down, or catch it on his back. All to keep it from blowing away.

Harp rode up to the point riders and told them

close the gap if the weather got rough. Sly made some signals, pointed at the sky, and closed his hands, so across the herd, Jimbo nodded and waved. Everyone knew that if you wanted the cattle to go faster you narrowed the space between them and they'd begin to trot. By trotting they were less liable to stampede even in a bad thunderstorm.

That herd speed set, Harp rode back keeping an eye on the moving flow. He spoke to the boy on the right flank and they both agreed the incoming weather was going to be rowdy. The curtain swept in and hail arrived on the first wave, thumbnail-sized ice that his horse did not appreciate and danced around in under him. About then, Harp recalled seeing a green-looking curtain under the coming storm clouds, and realized they'd get a lot of hail out of it.

The downpours were blinding walls of water and ice. The face of the running cattle herd faded in and out beside him, but they were trotting. The thunder roared. Bolts of lightning pounded the ground, and the smell of the nitrogen they produced filled his nose. The surface turned slick and he worried that someone would get hurt. He had Comanche gallop hard north to be close to the front of the herd in case they needed to be turned back or aside to avoid a collision.

Nothing let up. The rain, the blinding flashes of lightning, or the roar of the angry weather. Water ran off the brim of his hat in buckets, but the surging powerful horse never faltered or stumbled. He swam through it all, racing into the unknown night like it was daytime. Hail pounded them relentlessly, stingingly hard at times. Then he saw Sly and knew he was at the front of the herd, but had no idea what was ahead—if they faced a bluff or a river. The earth tilted down, so he eased up on his horse and, in the next flash of lightning, saw Sly and his horse were in the water. They had crossed a raging wash like it was only a step off and quickly ran up the other side to a new flat.

Then his God made the storm rise like a curtain and he shouted to Jimbo, "Circle left."

Somehow the cousin on the far side heard the command. The huge line of cattle began to slow into a circle as if in a great doughnut and brought them to a halt. The sun was still not out, and the chill of the wetness made him quake sitting in the saddle. Off to the side, he watched as the circle slowed and wound larger.

Red joined him. "One helluva storm. I bet there was a tornado somewhere with it. I have no idea the losses, but I will count riders first."

"Yes, there was a tornado, I bet. Red, you check on the riders and I'll search for the camp bunch."

"If a man never had any religion, surviving a storm like this would bring him around, wouldn't it?"

"You want the two of us to pray?" Harp asked his man.

"Harp—yes, please. You have words I don't." He bowed his head and waited.

"Our dear heavenly father, thanks for preserving our lives, sir, so we may continue our journey. Protect all our crews on the trail and accept any part of our departed crew in your arms now, sir. Forgive our sins and help us lead a better life and be safe. Lord, care for our families at home as well. Amen."

Red put his wet hat back on. "Thanks . . . I needed that."

"We both did."

Sly had ridden over. "I didn't interrupt your praying did I?"

"No. Help Red find all the crew. The cattle will settle and I am going to try to find our camp crew."

"We can do that, sah."

"I trust you two can." He smiled at them in the dim light.

They parted. Harp rode east feeling they'd deviated a lot to the left in the rain. This part of Texas was fairly flat, broken here and there by woods. In an hour he found a road he decided was the route. He looked south, saw nothing, and decided to go north for a while. He took a good look at the surroundings where he had merged on this north-south road to know the route back and set it in his memory.

Short-loping his horse, he crossed a high horizon. Then in the growing light of the broken sky he saw the canvas wagon top way off in the distance. They'd stopped there and he was grateful. One of his horses, with Holy Wars on him, showed up on the panorama bringing in the horses behind the bell mare that kept the geldings with her. The scene warmed Harp under the canvas coat he'd chosen over a rubber slicker.

"How is the herd?" Ira asked when he reached him.

"Intact in the west. Red is checking on the men. I came to find you. Everything all right?"

"Me and the boys are fine. Helluva storm. Holy Wars is bringing in the remuda." He gave a head toss toward them.

"I am glad to see you're not hurt. Follow me."

The outfit was going to take two hours at wagon speed getting back. He rode his mount back around to Ira and the wagon. "I need to get back. I'll tie a rag on a stick where you have to turn west."

"We're coming. Ride careful; we sure need you."

He waved to the pair on the seat and set the horse in lope southward, taking a shortcut to get back to the herd. The rest of the day was going to be a pick-up-the-pieces day; so much for things going so smoothly. His bighearted horse ate up the miles and past noontime he heard bawling and topped the rise to see cattle spread out everywhere. He gave a sigh of relief at the sight of them settled. He noticed some saddled horses in a group and swung Comanche left to join them.

Coming closer, he saw they had a body on the ground covered under a blanket.

Harp slid his horse to a stop and dismounted. A hand caught him by the reins. "I've got him." Red came to meet him. "New hand, Johnny Green. Must have broken his neck when his horse went down. We destroyed his horse. Everyone else is okay."

"I hate we lost him. He was single?"

"He has a widow mother, the boys said."

"We can't give him back to her, but we can help her."

"Is the wagon coming?"

"Yes. They are fine and the horses are good."

"That's wonderful. Of course we don't have a shovel," Red said.

"Fellows, I am sorry about Johnny. When Ira gets here, he has a shovel and we will bury him with services. Get some rest . . . the worst is over for now."

They all nodded.

"All the benches and our things are in the wagon. Too wet to sit on the ground and not a tree trunk close by. Boys, they say it is miles between trees north of here. Guess we will get used to it."

"What was Missouri like?" the cowhand holding his horse asked.

"Big hardwoods, steep mountains but not high ones. Lots of farms burned out and abandoned. They fought hard over in that part of the country, back and forth. I figure many folks have moved back in there by now. Small farms in pockets in the woods . . . nice rivers. No money there, either."

"They said you had a tough time getting there?"

"Reb haters. They even had a law barring Texas cattle coming in."

"Did you really hire the posse who came to kill you?"

"Yes. It was a lot cheaper than killing them."

They laughed.

Mid-afternoon Ira and the horse herd arrived.

Long rode up, gave his reins to a hand, and headed for Harp.

"We lost a new hand, Johnny Green," Harp said. "His horse went down in the rush. He has a widowed mother we need to help when we get home."

Long agreed. The men had shovels and were digging the grave. Harp had lots to put in his diary. He hoped his pregnant wife was safe. He figured they weren't much over sixty miles north of home— maybe not that far. No matter—

CHAPTER 25

On day six of the drive Harp and the herd reached the Colorado River. The floodwater had receded some, but it still made for a full enough river bank to bank. Camped west of Austin, Harp listened to Long's explanation of where Ira's supply wagon could cross on a ferry and rejoin them north of there.

Harp gathered his riders and went over the river-crossing plans. "Put your clothes and boots in the wagon and hold on to your horses and the saddle horn. Stay out of the way of any cattle fighting in the river. Keep an eye out for anyone who can't swim, loses his hold, and point him out to the swimmers. We need to help each other, but if you can't swim don't try it. Go with Ira and the wagon."

Four men, who felt they couldn't swim, went with the supply wagon. They would be at the other end to receive the herd and move them away from the landing as fast as possible to avoid a pileup.

Things were set. This would be, so far, the wildest

crossing for them. He didn't want to lose another man. They'd made it to Missouri with no casualties. He hoped he'd lost his last man for this trip. When the welcome party was assembled across from them, Sly put Blue in the river and the crossing of three thousand steers began.

Things went smoothly. A few steers floated downstream, but they crossed and could be gathered. Harp watched them closely, from a high point, and noted the cattle had settled a lot since the spooky bunch they were when they first combined them into the larger herd.

When the large part of the herd had crossed, dressed in his underwear, Harp slipped the horse into the river and headed for Abilene. The water was cold. Reminded him of the day he took Katy swimming and it was too cold to swim. A shiver went up his spine as he clung to his saddle horn and the veteran pony took to swimming. Shortly, Comanche was shaking off water on the far bank. They headed up the wet slope past the steers, reached the top, swung around them, and headed for the wagon.

Shivering, he dismounted. Long threw a blanket over him. "Get over to the fire and warm up."

"I will. Boy that was cold. Thanks."

"It looks like it went smoothly."

Harp nodded. "We were later last year weren't we?"

"Yes. It was a bit warmer then."

Harp agreed, shivered again, as the trash underfoot hurt his bare soles as he headed for the fire. Once with the others, he nodded his head at his men huddled around the fire also trying to warm up.

"I never wanted to be a sailor."

They laughed.

It was a good sign that they had some humor left in them after a cold crossing.

Long came over and told him they were all across with no losses.

"We will get reassembled and move out in the morning," Harp promised him.

The sun warmed some as the day advanced. In his diary he wrote down the uneventful cold crossing and laughed. Remembering how he thought the cold crossing reminded him of his previous cold swim with Kate, he added that along with his enchantment and his missing her.

In the following days they rode on, finally reaching the Brazos, and knew Fort Worth wasn't far away. The crossing of the Red would be farther west this time, and they'd be west of the Indian Territory wet bottoms that they mucked through the first trip. His plans were to resupply the wagon at Fort Worth and give the men a two-day holiday. Actually only a one-day off for half the crew to go to town and the other half going the next day. Each with five dollars in their pants. Beer was ten cents and the more common ladies of the night cost a dollar or less for a toss in the hay.

What more could a young drover want than that . . . ? Oh, maybe eat a big meal in a café. Ira would drive the supply wagon in and replenish the food supplies. Long was careful not to get their cattle close to any other herd also parked for the same reason.

While they lay over Harp rode south and found Doug's herd. They spoke about the storm and two of his boys hurt—one with a broken arm and the other a broken leg. All else had gone well. Doug said Chaw, who was two days behind him, had no problems.

The Indian Territory came next. With a head-aching bunch of moaners and groaners they left the area west of Fort Worth and in a few days made the crossing over the Red River. There was a carpet of wild flowers covering the land they crossed.

The wagon went over first with some of the hands on the ferry with their mounts. The far bank was steep and wet and they didn't need stalled cattle on the slope blocking those in the river trying to get out. He warned Red several would be swept downstream but instinct would deliver them on the north side. But if they tried to come onto land separated by large log floats they'd probably drown trying.

Some of the large dislodged trees were coming downstream and split some of the herd, but they managed to miss most of them, so the stream of cattle recovered. It was a hair-raising crossing with that many steers and took hours to get all of them over. More time was spent to drive the ones back that went downstream. But losses projected, they'd lost less than a dozen head. This satisfied Harper, on the north bank, warming at the big bonfire under a blanket. The Red River was a tough one at any time to cross. He thanked his maker, and when dry, killed the fire, dressed, and rode on into camp.

Somehow, he had a feeling his brother was not nearly as excited about this journey as he had been the year before. It was more of a job to do than the adventure they had going to Sedalia. But this one held even greater rewards for them if they succeeded. Maybe, too, they had simply become more grown up in the time span, branding mavericks, wheeling and dealing in ranches, and getting ready to go north.

Kate had promised him a son. He damn sure missed her, but the sex of the baby was not earth shaking for him. Healthy, the both of them, is what he wished for, and then there would be more. He hoped. His mother never had another one after he was born nine months after Long, but this was the future and he'd have lots of time for that later.

The Indians came for beef. Not the same ones, but these three demanded beef by the handfuls. In broken English, he let them talk on, forever, about how ferocious their warriors were.

Finally Harp had enough jabbering and he held up two fingers and said to come for them in the morning after they started. The hands would cut out two limpers from the back of the herd for them.

The Indians ranted some more, but Harper was unshaken and they finally agreed and rode off.

Red laughed. "I think you argued more last time."

"We aren't through here yet. There will be more beggars, so get ready for them."

Two days farther up the road, with the herd on the road a few hours, Holy Wars came back and told Harp there was a woman they'd found delirious beside the road and Ira wanted him to come look at her. She had nothing but the clothes on her body.

"I better tell Red where I'm going. Only take a minute . . . he's not too far away."

He swung back on his horse and galloped off.

Catching up to Red, Harp explained, "Holy Wars found a woman on the road this morning. Says she's delirious. I am going to try to help her."

"Be careful. Things are smooth with this bunch."

"See you later." He and his wrangler rode off in a lope.

He spotted the supply wagon and they rode to it.

"How is she, Ira?"

"She's under the wagon's shade on a ground cloth. Don't make a lot of sense to me, but maybe you can understand her."

He hitched Comanche to the nearest wheel and went around to see her.

Someone had beaten her up—badly. Her right cheek was purple and her other eye was black. He guessed her to be in her teens. The wash-worn dress needed replacing. No shoes and by her splayed toes he figured she'd not worn many shoes, if ever.

How old was she? Sixteen, seventeen? Her hair needed brushing and she was dirty.

"Miss, can you hear me?"

"Uh-huh."

"What's your name?" He was on his hands and knees bending down so she could see him.

"I really don't kno— Is he gone?"

"No one was with you when my men found you, unconscious."

When she tried to sit up, she hit her head on the trailer beam and fell back down.

"Sorry. Be careful. You are lying under a wagon. So, you don't know your name?"

She ran her hand over the new bump. "I-I ain't sure."

"What was his name?"

"Who?"

"The guy that beat you up?"

"Is he the one standing there behind you?"

"No. His name is Holy Wars. He found you."

She snickered. "That wasn't his name?"

"Where do you live?"

"I guess here? Mister, I don't know nothing. You got any food?"

"Lady, come out from under there. These men don't have all day. They have to get set up in their new camp."

She came out from under the wagon. "I can't help. I don't know nothing more. My head is spinning." And she fainted.

"Ira, can you make a space for her in the wagon? We haven't got all day. I think she's weak from not eating. Hell, I am not sure of anything." He scooped her up easily. She didn't weigh anything. Between him and Holy they handed her up to Ira and Billy, the boy who helped him. Somehow they managed to find a place to lay her on a palette.

"Good. You can feed her when you make camp."

Ira agreed, undid his reins, and Harp got off the wheel so he could drive on.

"What'cha figure she is?" Holy asked.

"Besides a badly beaten up girl, hungry and delirious, I have no idea."

Holy handed him his reins. "I didn't know, either. Kinda strange finding her out here with no one. Why, if a wolf had found her, he'd ate her."

"He might have if he was hungry enough, though she don't have much meat on her."

In the saddle they rode out to his grazing horses. Holy raised the end of his lariat and went to slapping his chaps with it making a popping sound. The horses took off after the wagon like they knew where they were going.

The bell mare was Holy's secret. She knew she'd get a handful of oats for following the wagon. The geldings were all pledged to her and followed her wherever she went. Holy made a real good horse wrangler, all without a lot of shouting and cussing. Most outfits would need three guys to hold them, herd them everywhere, and still cuss them as stupid. He had a notion about the youth. Now he knew how one man held sixty plus horses, drove them, and kept them ready to ride.

Sweet deal.

When they stopped for the night at the place Long had marked with a flag on a stick, Holy drove the horses to water in the creek. Harp, Ira, and Billy got the girl down and laid her on a ground cloth in the shade. The temperature was rising.

"We can make her some oatmeal when you get started," Harp said to Ira.

Some of the hands came by to look at her. None had ever seen her before, and they left shaking their heads. Harp wondered if his brother had seen her before, but he was not back yet. That was just about his last hope of learning where she came from and where to take her.

When Long came in, Harp took him to look at her. She was still groggy, making little sense lying on her pallet.

"I saw her with a man on the road," Long said. "I can't put two and two together of what I know about 'em. He was leading a small horse she rode. He had a white beard and acted kinda gruff when I asked about her. He said she was none of my gawdamn business. Got my back up. She looked groggy then, but she was not as beat up then like she is now."

"She's out of her mind. There's nowhere to dump her off at. I am not going to let her die if we can help it, but I'd like to know more about what happened, and she is the only one can tell us anything . . . if she could talk."

Long agreed and shook his head. "I see that old man again, I'll get the reason for her problems out of him."

"Guess that's all we can do." Harp knew his brother well enough. He'd do what he said he would and that old man better be ready to spill the beans or he'd have a tough time getting away from Long.

Ira came over. "Billy and me'll feed her. No one

will touch her. Pitiful as all get out that someone beat her senseless. I ever learn who done it, I'll clean his plow."

"I want part of his hide, too," Harp said. "Thanks, Ira. I bet we find them."

"She seems a little better."

"You are closer than we are, so you'd know. And we appreciate how hard you've worked to keep us fed."

Ira smiled. "Harper, I told you once before, I really respect you and the way you run things. I get up every morning and tell Billy to look around, that he is part of a great outfit and that beats the hell out of most places he'll ever work."

Long nodded. "O'Malley brothers are tough, too."

"No shortage of that," Harp said. "Long, how are things up ahead?"

"Fine. Lots of grass and water." Long looked back toward the supply wagon, then turned back. "Do you think she was doped some way or is only half here and they used her until they tired of her?"

"I have no idea. I am pleased we have gotten this far without any more troubles. I hope the others coming behind us are doing this well."

"This rolling grass country beats mountains and woods for moving cattle." Long laughed. "People will never believe the hell we had east of here last year."

"I don't miss it," Harp said. "This open unpopulated country is ideal for moving them."

The days and nights warmed as it was moving

toward summer on the calendar. They had been making between twelve and sixteen miles a day. The new grass became strong and each passing day meant the steers added pounds and condition. Those were his concern—having them ready for buyers. The whole purpose of taking them north was sell the best cattle they could deliver.

Ira reported the next morning that the girl was improving.

At the evening meal she helped Ira and Billy prepare it. Harp could tell her mind was not any better when he tried to converse with her. So he left them, satisfied the two were taking care of her.

Holy checked on two of the horses the boys told him were showing they had a limp. One had a rock in his frog that Holy removed and said to skip his use for two rounds. The other must have bruised his hoof. Skip his usage for two turns also and he'd watch him.

The cowboy Harold Nelson, who played the guitar, was strumming it again after the meal. This was a relaxing time for his crew and they enjoyed it. Ira quit what he was doing, dried his hands, and came over to listen, standing close to Harp.

"I learned a little about her today. She said her name was Candy. And the last guy who beat her up was Howard somebody."

"Long saw the two of them on this road before someone beat her up. Said he was white headed and whiskered."

"She comes and goes in and out of her mind. We may never know the truth."

"Right. You good on your supplies?"

"Oh, we should make it to Abilene on what I have on hand."

"If you run out we may be up a bad creek. We have seen little civilization out here."

"It sure isn't populated."

The next day Harp saw his first herd of buffalo moving west of his cattle. Not a large group but cows, calves, and some bulls. An impressive enough sight. He knew Comanche knew them. The way his horse stiffened his gait, tensed up, and laid his ears back like he expected Harp to chase them. But instead, he swung him back to the herd. He'd put that sighting in his diary and also write Katy that he saw them when they made camp.

She'd sure get lots of mail when he found a post office to mail all his letters from. He wondered about his son's arrival. Simply thinking about her was enough to upset him. Not that he didn't trust her waiting for him, but their first long separation was not easy for him to take. He'd make it up to her.

That evening, Long told him there was a store on the way north they'd pass the next day, and it had a post office. Harp told the men, and some accepted paper, envelopes, and pencils to share, and wrote notes for him to mail. He had all his mail ready as well. A touch of civilization but being still in the Indian Territory there would be no alcohol. Not that he used it, but while Kansas frowned on it, they'd find some above that line.

Pikesville I. T. was the address there. The store was a soddy and smelled like sour unbathed humans. The place was dark and lighted with candle lamps, and the other smell inside was from the stacks of dried buffalo hides. He bought two sacks of hard candy to hand out to the men from time to time.

The crotchety clerk said Harp's cook had bought some girl a dress and other things, and the cook said Harp'd pay for them when he got there. That didn't count all the three-cent postage stamps he owed the man for mailing all the letters. It all cost seven dollars. Harp paid him and left the place with some Bull Durham tobacco, paper to roll the cigarettes with, and strike-anywhere torpedo matches. There were boys on his crew that would be extremely grateful for those smoking supplies.

Lots to do and many more miles to go.

In a week they forded the wide, shallow Arkansas River, and on the far side a sign said, "*Follow the piles of sod to Abilene—Joe McCoy.*"

He damn sure intended to. The crossing was not nearly as wild as the one that put Emory out of commission.

In two weeks or so he knew they would be in Abilene—selling steers.

God's blessed them all.

CHAPTER 26

They were in and out of rain the next week. Long heard some rumors that the cattle herds ahead had not yet sold because the herd owners thought the buyers were not offering enough money for them.

"How much will they pay?" Harp asked Long.

"They said ninety dollars a head."

Harp laughed. "They will damn sure buy all I've got here for that."

"I'm with you."

"What do the owners expect?" Harp asked.

"One hundred and twenty-five dollars a head."

"Do they think no one else will bring cattle up here?" Harp shook his head.

"Something like that."

"We get closer, I am going to ride in and sell all three herds."

"Right on, brother. That should satisfy the trains for a while, too, if they are as slow as Sedalia was."

"We will do that."

"I ain't really figured it out to the penny, but we have over a half million dollars' worth of cattle in these three herds."

"Mother never showed us how to count that high in our lives."

"It is something. We will be all right if things keep going on like they have. Cross your fingers, brother, the O'Malley outfit is coming on strong."

The next five days passed, confirmed by gossip. The cattlemen and the buyers were still at an impasse over the price. Not one livestock car had left Abilene and they had a string of them waiting, according to the men who were coming back from there.

Everyone he stopped on the road told him that the Abilene dream had blown up. There would be no sales that summer unless they found some other better buyers.

Three fancy surreys were headed south full of high-priced women of the night.

A fancy dressed man with them riding a Kentucky horse asked Harp how far south would he have to go to find customers.

Harper said he didn't know. All his cowboys were too broke until they sold their cattle. The man scowled back in the direction of Abilene. "They won't ever make it work back there."

"If they have the money they say they have, I will sell them seven thousand head."

The man looked at him in disbelief. "You'd take ninety dollars a head for them?"

"Damn right, and I bet a hundred more behind me will, too."

"Thanks. Albert, turn the buggies around we are going back to get set up. Abilene will soon blossom."

His first driver took off his derby and stuck his head out to look at his boss. "Boss, you sure you want to do that?"

"Hell, yes, this man is betting a half a million dollars on Abilene."

"Whatever you say." The driver did as ordered.

"How many men are in your outfit?"

"Three crews . . . over three dozen men."

He reached and tossed him three small cloth bags to catch.

"There's twenty tokens for services in each of those bags at the new establishment I will set up in Abilene. May your men have at least one great time there in Abilene on me."

He tipped his hat and galloped after his carriages.

"What did he give you?" Red asked him.

"Enough tokens for every hand we have to make a free trip to his house of ill repute in Abilene."

"Why did he do that?"

"I told him not to worry, that we were selling our cattle when we got there."

"Open one up. I want to see them."

The others in his lap, Harp opened one. The brass coin had a crowing rooster on one side and two bucks on the other side.

"Here, you hand yours out. I'll do the same to the other foremen for their crews."

"You need one?"

"Not no, but hell, no. Thanks anyway, Red."

"I can use yours then?"

"You bet your life you can."

"Keep giving out that good information. Why, that bunch of ours will be tickled pink to get one of these."

Harp rode off laughing and dreaming he sold all those steers for that much per head. Wouldn't that be great?

That evening, Long came in late.

Harp met him short of camp. "Anything wrong?"

"I made a wide loop today. By my figures this herd is three days out of Abilene. You can ride in, get a room tomorrow, and the next day sell all three herds. How's that?"

"Ninety a head is enough isn't it?"

"Hell, yes. They won't bring five bucks a head at home."

Then he told Long about the whorehouse tokens while Ira fixed his plate of food.

Long chuckled about the story, and with a biscuit in one hand and a fork in the other he looked at Harp. "Ma said stay out of those places. I've never been in one in my life, have you?"

"No."

"Then it ain't no time to start."

They both laughed.

Next morning, Harp shaved and cleaned up, then put on a new white shirt, his suit coat, and clean pants. He mounted Comanche and rode off to *war*. Red knew where he was headed and said he could handle things. Harp wore his .45 on his hip and figured it would be near dark when he got to town.

Comanche stabled at the livery, and his room for the night secured, Harp went into a restaurant. The waiter seated him, and he knew he drew some looks from the crowd in the room. Soon a big man with a whiskey bottle in his left hand came over and introduced himself as Claude Clower from Texas.

"You bring a herd up here, sonny boy, or did your daddy?" he asked, standing over Harp like he was a king or something.

"My father is home in Texas. I brought three herds with me," Harp answered.

"Three? Oh, my, and the market at this stalemate that we are in? That is a shame."

"No, it is not a shame. I sold cattle a year ago at Sedalia for eighty bucks a head."

"Yes, but the meat market shortage conditions are twice as bad now as they were then, so we expect a much better price."

"Well, tell me where it is that good?" Harper asked Clower, then nodded his approval as a waiter set his supper on the table.

"They can pay it if we all hold their feet to the fire and none of us don't undersell the rest."

Clower set the liquor bottle on Harp's table and took the opposing chair. "You drink whiskey?"

"No, sir, I don't. But help yourself."

"You look a little young to be heading an outfit."

"Mister, my name's O'Malley. I drove that herd to Sedalia last year. I have three herds coming here.

Don't worry about my years old. I can and will sell them."

Clower poured half a glass of the brown liquor. "If you step over our deadline to sell cattle for less than what we want, you may not live much longer."

Harp threw down his napkin. "I have had all the threats I am going to take. Get your damn whiskey and get the hell out of my way."

"Listen—"

"I will not. So get away before I shoot your head off. And believe me I have shot Comanche and out-laws alike, so you wouldn't be any different if you threaten me again."

"Well, the organization can stop you if you aim to ruin our strike."

"Load your guns, Clower. If I can make a deal, you won't stop me. But they can preserve your body in alcohol and lead casket to haul back to Texas."

"Boy, just try it and you will be buried here." The man rose and started to leave.

"Wear your best damn suit . . . I will bury you in it."

Clower stopped by a table and picked up his two hard-looking hands and left the restaurant. Still boiling mad, Harp threw down money for the meal that would go uneaten, went to the stables, and rode back to their camp. It was near sundown, and his ar-rival drew many of the crew around to see what went wrong.

"What happened?" Long said, putting on his shirt while coming out of the tent.

Still near shaking mad, Harp dismounted and

gave the reins to the closest man. "Some old man threatened me if I sold our cattle for less than they are demanding. He acted like he was in charge and that I better listen. I told him I'd already killed Comanche and outlaws and he better not get in my way or I'd kill him."

"Whew, brother, you are as mad as I have ever seen you. He really pulled your chain."

"Long, tomorrow I want four men armed with rifles with me, and I am going back and selling seven thousand steers for ninety dollars a head."

"I'll go along."

"No. If they kill us both no one wins. We have many people's wealth here. Someone needs to finish this job if I can't."

"All right, but you be careful. I ain't saying run from a fight, but you and the men you take are important to us all. I don't want telling Mom or their moms I let you go without me."

"I am handling Clower. He thinks I am some boy, and I know damn well and good I'm more than that. He will find that out tomorrow."

"Bro, settle down. He's a damn fool if he tries."

"He is that, too."

He chose Red Culver, who picked the guitar man, Harold Nelson, and his two black point men, Sly and Jimbo Trent, when the two cousins volunteered to back him. Harp felt they were some of the toughest men in the outfit. Others would fight but since Nelson began playing—he showed himself to be a stronger guy than Harp first imagined.

The two cousins, he had no doubt they'd surely do in a clutch.

Breakfast was ready before sunup. Harp noticed the girl was proving to be good help, but Ira said she still didn't have her mind back.

Harp noticed, too, that everyone kind of walked around him since he came back. Obviously Clower had made him fighting mad. Today he'd show him and any others who he was and they better stand clear or die.

They rode in a long lope most of the way and reached the sight of the growing community on sweaty horses. At the edge of town, just in case, each man jerked out and carried a loaded Winchester across his lap. They all had Colt pistols to back their long guns.

"Watch the roofs of buildings; they may be lying in wait for us. I don't want to cause a fight. But I don't aim to die here, either," Harp told his men.

He could see the depot building, which, he understood, the cattle buyers used as their office. Next he noticed four men step out of some batwing doors on a saloon porch and move into the street. No one that he knew.

"I've seed the two on the right," Sly said under his breath. "They be wanted in Texas. Them other two be kids who think they're tough. It will be the two on the right give us *dee* most hell here, boss man."

"I agree," Red said.

Harp and his men never stopped walking their head-bobbing, hard-breathing horses toward this new threat spreading apart to face Harp and his force.

"You fellows blocking the street or just resting?" Harp asked them as he and the others reined up.

The second one from the right nodded. "What business you got past here?"

"What if I said it was none of your business?"

"Then I am making it my business, mister. Turn around and go back to herding your cattle. There won't be any cattle sold here today."

"Wait a minute." A big man in a suit stepped off the porch. He showed his badge. "I am U.S. Marshal Sam Ryder. Interfering in another man's business isn't allowed in any state or territory. I say you four step aside and let these gentlemen pass."

"What if I don't?" their leader asked.

"Then I will deputize those five men as U.S. deputy marshals and we will arrest you and the men with you as interfering with commerce."

"You've got some big damn words, mister."

"Sorry, sir, what is your name?" Ryder asked Harp.

"Harper O'Malley of Kerrville, Texas, sir. Red Culver, my foreman. Harold Nelson, one of my hands, and Sly and Jimbo Trent, my point men."

"Nice to meet the five of you. Gentlemen, move aside," Ryder said to the others.

"I don't believe—"

Ryder had the leader by a fistful of his shirt and his six-gun jammed in his belly faster than a wasp could sting. "Now you've made me mad. You and your men are under arrest."

Four Winchesters were cocked beside Harp as he

leaned forward on his horn. "Marshal, you need any help throwing them in jail."

"I don't think so," he said, holstering his gun and handcuffing the lead man.

Ryder disarmed the others and handcuffed them into a chain of four.

"Thanks for the aid and assistance, gentlemen. Good day to you. Now you four head up the street to the jail."

"Yes, thank you, Marshal. We have some business to do."

"You won't ever bring one head of stock in here to load," the leader promised him.

"I want your name," Harp said, reining beside him.

"Huh?"

"Tell him your names," Ryder ordered.

"Luke Kincaid."

Harp felt the muscles in his jaw tighten. "Kincaid, you've got mine and I've got a forty-five bullet with your name on it if you ever try to stop me."

A little later in the day, Harp met Joe McCoy who had convinced the railroad to lay siding tracks at Abilene to load cattle. He also met the men buying cattle. They had drawn cards to buy the first, second, and third herd, then it was business on their own. Cally Claxton, of Orica Packing Company, offered Harp ninety dollars a head for every good steer in herd one. Harp agreed and they shook hands on the deal.

Oscar Roma, a swarthy Italian with a huge smile, bought the two thousand head of consigned cattle in the second herd, and Rex Laken of Laken and Grimes Packing Company bought the sisters' herd.

The secretaries scribbled down the parties' names and the amounts. When both parties signed the documents, Joe McCoy shook Harp's hand.

"I heard about your sale at Sedalia and wondered if you would come up here this year. I am so glad you made it. You are a tough young man. We asked for some federal assistance and they sent one man, but he is a tough law man."

"Quite frankly, Mr. McCoy, that marshal saved some men their lives. We'd have left them dead in the street to get this done. My family and the sellers at home thank all of you. I had five months of hell getting up to Sedalia, but aside from a couple of Indians, who I fed, we had only small problems getting here.

"But, back to the cattle. How many cars are here to load?" Harp asked.

"We plan to load four hundred head a day."

"Give me two days and I can have the cattle here for that many cars."

"Hurrah," went up from the room of buyers and their employees.

A reporter followed them out, asking questions and scribbling at a hundred words a minute.

"Sir, did you expect to be the first man to sell here."

"No, but I expected to sell those cattle here. In Missouri I was never sure if I'd live that long."

"What will you do now you have sold over six hundred thousand dollars' worth of cattle here today?"

"Go home and pay all the people who helped me get them together and get here. Excuse me, I have been so upset, I forgot to go and see about the mail."

Harold Nelson said, "Red's gone to get it."

"He take two sacks?"

"Ira gave him two large washed hundred-pound flour sacks to get it in."

"Can I buy you and these men a drink?" Joe McCoy interrupted, and asked him.

"I don't drink, sir. But thanks. We have a herd that needs to be moved closer, so we need to get to work."

"I think you have broken the strike. I hated that it happened, but these men, like you, have jobs and they can't pay more than what they think will make money."

"Joe, I came here to sell my cattle at a fair price and get my butt back to Texas."

"I heard what Clower told you last night. You had every right to be mad, but thanks for carrying through. I have spent a fortune to get all this going. It had to work for me, too."

"I can imagine. As much as it cost to get cattle up to Sedalia, here a man could live for years on that sum."

Joe smiled. "But that quiet life wouldn't be half as much fun as yours and mine are. Would it?"

"You know I think you are right, sir."

Before he left town he wired his father and the Cranford sisters.

WE ARE HERE STOP SOLD THEM NINETY
DOLLARS A HEAD LOCK STOCK AND
BARREL STOP THE O MALLEY
BROTHERS HARP AND LONG

They rode for the herd, and the news he was
looking for he finally found in the fifth letter from
Katy that he opened riding back.

Congratulations. Your son, Lee O'Malley, was
born July 2nd. Big boy, blond hair, and louder
than you. Your mom says you looked like him.
I had to name him Lee for our meeting place.
Creek was not a good middle name so I left it off.
Someday I'll tell him that all this was caused by us
eating peaches at Lee's Creek. Hurry home.

> *I miss you badly,*
> *Katy*

"Well, did someone die?" one of his fellow riders
asked.

"Hell, no. I have a son, Lee O'Malley, a big blond
boy."

His team riding with him shouted and congratu-
lated him.

At camp Long danced a jig and everyone was
excited. Harp told them about Marshal Ryder and
his help. The cattle were sold, but all the men were
to wear their guns, go in pairs, and to expect trouble.

It might not be over until they slid the last cattle car door shut.

That night he dreamed that someone kept ringing a cash register that conveyed six hundred and thirty thousand dollars in the glass window, showing it to him like he was the customer.

Long had a place picked out for them north of town, but they had trouble with the cattle. The animals had never seen ties or iron rails in their lifetime. Some would not cross the tracks, some jumped them, but finally all were driven across. Harp did have to ask the engineers not to toot any horns until they got the cattle farther away, because they spooked every time one went off.

Ira had camp set up and the men were relaxing. There would be cars to load the next day, and everyone wanted this business to start. They knew they had to stay to load, but they'd have more help and the suspense was over—the O'Malley bothers had won another war.

Harp wrote Katy giving her details to share with everyone. Under the night lamp he wrote and told her he could hardly wait to get home. And he'd see her and Lee this fall. He signed it, *Amen, Harp O'Malley, your homesick husband.*

CHAPTER 27

Harp never thought the whole situation would end by Ryder simply arresting four hired guns. But he wasn't going to let anyone prohibit the sale of his cattle. Everyone had to make a living, and he wasn't going to let anyone deprive him of settling the business he came to do in Abilene, and then going home as soon as he could to be with his wife.

He became acquainted with the buyers, and he listened to their advice on how British-crossed cattle were the future for Texas cattlemen. The word was out that Durham-Shorthorns, Herefords, and other such breeds needed to be blended into the long-horn herds and those would, someday, be the way to get top prices for cattle.

It put him to pondering on how these breeds would do in the more arid land of west Texas where the longhorn thrived, and if these other breeds could survive the droughts and climate. Time would tell.

He knew the cattle of Texas had centuries to

evolve, like deer in the brush country, after escaping their Spanish owners. But he listened and made notes for their own ranch's future programs.

There was still no real money back in Texas and the supply of common goods like coffee and cloth had not yet arrived on store shelves, according to his wife's letters. Many ranchers had stopped her and his mother when on their way to town, or in the stores, asking if they could send cattle north with the O'Malley outfit next year? How were they doing? Was it going to work like they planned?

He tried to answer those questions for her in his letters. They were surely going back next year. Despite the hardships of the drives, they were profitable.

By the third week, they were loading Doug's herd. Doug had his own stories to tell about a cowboy's death while cleaning his pistol and another took pneumonia after a river crossing. Both had died and were buried on the trail. They were local boys and Harp would have to tell their folks about their loss and give the families the boys' pay. He felt they were owed that. That would be a hard job.

Ira took Candy to a doctor and told both Harp and Long about it that night.

"Well, Doc Gripewater says she had some *try-matic* things happen to her and she lost her mind. Either they poisoned her or drugged her so much they damaged her brain and she probably won't ever recover."

"That wasn't the answer you wanted," Harp said.

"No, sir. That girl's become a daughter to me, boss. The men all respect her and I wanted a cure for her so badly. I may try someone else at home. I am not leaving her here for the buzzards or the bastards that did that to her to get her back."

"You kind of wonder about some folks. Who would do that to another human being?" Harp asked.

"Would your wife or your mom look after her, when I'm busy with you?"

"Ira, I believe they would. I appreciate all you do for the crew and me. You feeding them and looking out for each man have made this the best cattle drive I could have hoped for. So we can thank you by having Katy and Mom look after her when you are not around."

"I told you in Sedalia that you were a real leader of men, and I've said it on this trip. I've enjoyed my part in supporting you and Long. You two are the empire builders of Texas, and Candy's recovery lies with you and the others that plunge on when the going gets tough.

"And I still can't believe that guy back in Texas told you those maverick cattle were not yours that we branded."

"Yeah, he's one of those sore losers. Why Dad, Long, and I have branded cattle for years. Of course the three of us never got done what this outfit can do in a day, but we built a herd with dreams that someday there would be a market for them."

"You planning to do it again when we get home?"

"As long as we can. These boys need work and so

do you. The O'Malleys will be in the cattle business from here on, the good Lord willing."

"Kate called your son Lee?"

"You recall Lee's Creek flowed into the Arkansas north of Van Buren?"

"Oh, yes. You shocked the hell out of us all bringing her back to camp. You sure were lucky. That was the best move of your life."

"Amen. Long is back. I need to talk to him some."

"Go ahead. Hopalong is helping me now that Doug is up here, so I have plenty of help."

"Those boys had some losses. I hate when things go wrong on any drive. Chaw is coming in here himself tonight. So we will hear about his trip then. Hopefully no losses."

Ira agreed, shook his hand, and said, "May God go with you my friend."

"Thanks." Harp hurried to catch Long. "How's Chaw?"

"Mad as hell. I guess some of Clower's bunch told him to stay where he was, that there was no place for his herd up here and that you'd send him word when you needed him."

"I never thought of that. We'll get him up here. He lose many boys or cattle?"

"One boy drowned. Had a few broken bones, usual things that happen on a roundup. I was thinking about the money. You have a way to transport that back to Texas?"

"Yes. The buyers tell me there is a transfer company that is really respected called Wells Fargo. All the money will go into a special account in the San

Antonio bank and this Wells Fargo will guarantee delivery."

"Never heard of them before but I bet I do from here on. Did you hear back from those old maids?"

"I have a wire in my pocket that says they are very pleased and cannot wait to congratulate both of us."

"You think any more about what Katy said they'd eventually do?"

"Not much, Long. I didn't want to be disappointed if they do something else."

His brother laughed. "Well, hell, we'll make it now. Get us some more new places huh?"

"We can sure build them while the money is so short."

"What did Dad always say—strike that horseshoe while it was still hot?"

"That was his statement. You have plans?"

"If you can get this bunch home and not get in any trouble I think I'll make a swing west on my own and look at a lot of country I'm just itching to see."

"Not take anyone along with you?"

"I'll be fine alone. I think I'll enjoy the solitude of there being just me for a while. That's the word isn't it?"

"One of our mother's words, yes. You be damn careful, you may be half Indian but there's lots of tribes on the warpath out there."

"I will be and I ain't staying out there forever."

"You are my right-hand, brother. Remember that."

"Oh, I do and I appreciate your handling of this

deal so well. I can't even believe the money we've made here. Sedalia was great but this is wonderful."

"A dead brother in a prairie grave won't help me, either."

"I will keep that in mind. I met that trader down on the Salt Fork, John Chisholm, and spoke to him. He's sat in as a translator on most all the government peace treaties they've had. Real nice fellow. You'd like him. He has an aura about him. Mom explained that to us."

"Kind of like a cloud to cover him, but a good one?" Harp asked.

"Exactly."

"Well, the train cars are coming faster. Ten days we'll be heading home. Most men I talked to want to go back and work for us down there."

Long nodded. "I won't leave until things are all settled here."

"Good. I am sending a pay-off break down with the money in case neither of us make it back."

"Good idea. You tell me to be careful, but you be careful, too."

"I will. You can count on it."

Harp and Red rode back into Abilene that afternoon to check on things. They met Doug at the loading pens.

"Things are going fine. All my cattle should be shipped in the next three days," Doug said from behind the shaggy beard he grew coming up. "Then I can bathe, shave, and spend a token or two. The boys say he takes them and smiles. None of our men have been paid yet, but he knows you broke the strike and he said thanks again for you helping him."

"Any trouble over anything?"

"Oh, there are some people pissed off about you selling at their price, and they knowing they will be coming behind Chaw's herd makes them even madder."

Harp had heard all that, too. "I really don't care."

"Me either. That's a helluva price when long-horns aren't worth a nickel in Texas."

"You explained to your men that wages going back to Texas go down to twenty bucks a month? Most outfits will pay their men off here and they'll get no money to go home on. You and I need them at home and coming back next year, so we are paying them something."

"Wages go up when we get back?"

"Right. We will have lots of work for them at home."

"The men will appreciate the pay going home and having a job in these times. Can I cull some horses that ain't worth driving home?" Doug asked.

"Yes. Red, you tell Chaw to do that, too."

"Harp, I am damn sure ready to head home."

"Not one drop more than I am to see Katy and my son. Long wants to see some new country and go home by himself. He's doing that."

"Only country I want to see is Texas. I keep getting word there are lots of cattle coming this way."

"Yes, I imagine so, and travel up here will get more crowded over the coming years."

"Aw hell. There is lots of open land to use," Doug

said, and laughed. "Plus it beats all the crap we had in Missouri last year."

"Amen. No way we'd have got this many cattle through all that, and I bet people are returning now that the war is over. All those abandoned farms we used to graze have probably been reclaimed."

"Oh, yeah, that would make it tougher than ever. Well, things to do. I'll see you later," Doug said, and left him.

Harp went by the post office and got the mail. He stopped and read Katy's latest letter. She said:

I can't hardly wait for you to get home. The mowing machines arrived and the men are using them. They put up the oat hay with hand scythes. These will mow so much grass acreage your dad can't believe it. I went down and saw the one work at the Diamond Ranch. Those two women were real excited and you got the blame. You watch my words will come true and they've nearly worn the hide off Lee.

> *Be careful my love I so miss you,*
> *Katy*

Thinking about Katy, he crossed the busy street and started on the boardwalk for the W. W. Clineflet Merchantable to get some things off a list that Ira gave him earlier.

Two drovers blocked his way. He felt a cold wave of fear run up his spine. They were blocking the way on purpose.

Some women saw it, and they hurried to cross the

busy street to escape what looked like an explosion about to occur. Both men were drunk. They didn't scare him; it was his slow discovery and his lack of being ready for opposition that concerned him.

He stuffed her letter in his shirt pocket, feeling the skin on his face tighten.

"You blocking my way here on purpose?"

"Yeah, you yellowbelly son of a bitch. You breaking the strike is causing us to ride home unpaid. They were going to give us a bonus to go home, and you caused us to lose it and now we've got to stay around up here weeks longer."

Harp flexed his hands at his side. "All I can say is you work for a damn cheap outfit. I pay my men to go home."

"We think you belong in hell for selling us out."

"I am not standing here listening to you two drunks for much longer. Stand aside or go for your guns."

"Yeah. We've shot enough polecats you won't last two seconds—"

While they were talking, Harp had drawn his gun, and now they were looking down the muzzle. "Who of you dies first? I ain't got all day. Tell me and tell me now."

They both paled.

"No? Then use two fingers and drop your guns carefully on the boardwalk. Get them out now."

They did as he said.

"Now step aside of them. Move," he said, waving them aside with the gun barrel. They about fell over each other to get off the boardwalk. "You have ten seconds to get out of my sight. Run."

They obeyed. The shorter one ran into a team coming up the street and was knocked down. His buddy didn't wait for him. The wagon driver cussed him out for upsetting his horses as he scrambled to get away. Harp holstered his own six-gun.

He retrieved both weapons and stood up. Marshal Ryder came from across the street. "You the new town marshal?"

Holding the second pistol, the first was already in his waistband. Harp smiled. "Just keeping the peace."

"I saw most of it. Busy as the town was I figured someone would've got hurt if shooting started."

"Yes, sir. But I didn't aim to be gunned down, either."

"Old man booze brings out the worst in men at times."

"I don't know. I don't drink."

"Good thing."

"I was going into the store to order some things we need at camp."

"Do that later. Let's go have a cup of coffee in that café since you don't drink."

"I can go in the saloon. You don't have to drink in those places."

"No, the café is better."

They went inside and the girl brought them coffee.

"How old are you, Harp?"

"I'll be twenty next February."

"Boy general, aren't you?"

"Marshal, I do what I have to do."

"No, you are what I said you were. Lots of people had to grow up fast because of the war. You can do whatever you are called on for. I heard lots about the Sedalia drive you made. One man said you were about thirty years old when I asked."

"Long and I never had much time to be boys. I was fifteen when five of us were attacked by Comanche trying to recover a young girl they kidnapped."

"Did you get her back?"

Harp shook his head. "Dad later thought she was already dead at the time. But we recovered several others and shot plenty Comanche."

"Your dad must have been a tough man."

"He still is. My mother is, too. She was alone one day when some outlaw busted down her door, and she shot him twice with a Paterson Colt in her doorway. Then hitched a mule and drug his body out of her doorway and out of the yard."

Ryder laughed.

"Dad taught Long and I to do what we have to do."

"He was not along on the Missouri drive?"

"No. Long and I hired on as cowboys to the man making the drive."

"How did you get to be in charge?"

"The man he had in charge was a drunk. I fired the sorry cook and sent him packing. Emory came and when he learned I was running the outfit, he fired the drunk. Emory had been discharged from the war because he had a bullet close to his heart.

His health was poor but he wouldn't quit. He lived to learn we sold the herd for eighty bucks a head."

"That is close to the story I heard. Looks like Joe McCoy will have big successes here."

"I'd say he will. I am grateful for all he's got done. I knew I'd drive cattle up here somewhere but not up the Butterfield Road."

"What will you and Long do in Texas?"

"We are building a large ranch in Kerrville County. That's west of San Antonio."

"I imagine, by the time you two get through, it will be a large one."

Harp agreed. The coffee was good and he wondered what the big man had in mind—it wasn't all talk about the O'Malley brothers' future.

"If you ever tire of ranching let me know. We are looking for U.S. marshals all the time."

"Thank you, sir. That is flattering, but my plans are to ranch full time and not do these long drives forever. They make a good return and I probably will do it for several more years."

"Good luck, General O'Malley. I am proud I met you."

At the mercantile he ordered the things needed, and was promised the supply wagon would deliver them in the next three days. Riding back to camp, it began to rain, so he put on his canvas coat. Lightning streaked the sky and thunder rolled across the land. He pushed Comanche hard for camp. At least they only had a handful of cattle at Chaw's camp. Heavy rain beat on his hat. This was going to be a stem-winder of a storm.

A cowboy in a slicker took his horse's bridle while he stripped off the saddle, thanking him for seeing about his horse as he took the saddle and pad into the tent. The lamps were up and the tent struts obviously screwed down against the wind.

"Helluva storm, bro," Long said, standing up to greet him.

"Yeah a real one. But if it was home I'd be grateful for the moisture."

Everyone laughed above the roar and drumming going on outside. Someone brought him a tin cup of hot coffee; he nodded thanks and sat down with the crew.

"Well, two drunk cowboys tried to stop me on the sidewalk and accused me of costing them money. Seems if I hadn't sold our cattle they'd been paid for riding home, but since their boss sold them for less than the holdout price he wasn't paying them trip-back money. I got the drop on them and they fled."

"All right." Long stood up. "You don't go back to town without one of us with you. Hear me, men. That is an order."

"Yes, sir."

"That is not necessary."

"The hell it isn't, brother. We need you alive and kicking and since I am going scouting. All of you remember, he goes, then one of you goes along. We have been betting, ever since we left Texas, with seven thousand head of steers. We lost a few along the way. The bet is how many of them will be in the final count sold?"

"There were twenty short of five thousand after we sold Doug's herd."

"Then my bet we are twenty-five short is good," Long said.

"I got thirty short," Ira said.

Red said, "I say thirty-two short."

"Well, if the town didn't blow away in this storm noon tomorrow, we will have that count," Harp said.

"How long will it take us to get home?" one of the cowboys asked.

"Four to six weeks, graining those three bell steers and the horses along the way."

"Can we do that?"

"Damn right we can," Harp said. "I plan to be home as quick as I can."

One cowboy laughing said, "And we all know why."

"Amen, buddy. Amen."

The rain finally let up, but everyone slept in the tent. Thanks to Ira's trenching he had them do, the tents stayed dry inside.

Dawn came and Harp rode back to Abilene with Red and Long. Chaw and his bunch were camped north of town, and Harp hoped they were able to keep the last of the steers together. When they arrived at the depot they learned he had corralled them in the loading pens before the rain struck, so all were there and good.

The last steer loaded they were thirty-two head short of seven thousand head. That meant the total amount came to near $627,000. He had held back $700 to meet expenses going home. The crew voted that afternoon they were going to go on a toot, and they asked for their ten-dollar raise to give 'em hell.

Back home he'd owe each of the hands three hundred bucks, and he didn't intend to hold out the ten, but they didn't know that. His headmen would get six hundred for their efforts, the three cooks five hundred apiece.

After he paid each their ten bucks it got real loud as they cut out to shoot holes in the moon—but they'd earned it.

The following morning, Ira and the cooks got everything ready to leave as the men slept off their hell raising. No one landed in jail and that was good. Holy Wars and the other wranglers had their horses culled down to only the good ones going back in one herd.

Long had two packhorses loaded and his own best buffalo horse to ride. He shook everyone's hand and told them how much he appreciated them all, and his plans were to be back to give them hell before Christmas.

He had plenty of money, he told Harp. The two men were parting, after so long having been each other's backs. It kind of kicked Harp in the guts to part with him after all the years of having him right there, but Long had this wish to see more country. They shook hands, short on words to say to each other.

Standing on a high place, Harp watched Long ride off leading those packhorses in a good jog.

God, watch after him. He's a strong man but he will need your help, and bring him home to all of us. He slapped his leg with his hat and went back to camp. He'd miss him. And he knew that all too well.

On the way home Harp made the men a deal. They would push south as hard as they could until they crossed the Red River. Then a skeleton crew made up of the cooks driving their wagons, two wranglers with the horses, and three cowboys would bring everything home. The rest would ride hard, find their own meals, and get home in half the time of the bunch bringing the wagons and horses.

The system worked fine. At the Red River he left Ira a hundred dollars for expenses. The rest going home fast got five dollars each and they left for Kerrville riding hard. Doug, Chaw, and Red rode with Harp. They pushed, grained their horses, and in eight days Harp and his party rode up the lane to his father's house.

His mother saw them coming first and shouted, "Harp's here! Oh, my God, he's back, Katy."

With the baby in her arms Kate ran down the steps to greet him. "Oh, thank God you're home and safe—where's Long?"

"He's gone off on an adventure, he called it."

"Where? Why?" his mother asked.

"To see the white elephant. He told me he wanted

to see more country and left us in Kansas. He promised to be back here by Christmas."

His mother shook her head in a scowl. "That boy doesn't ever write."

"Mother, you know your eldest son."

She frowned, concerned. "No one went with him?"

"That was the way he wanted it." He held his son up in his hands. "Damn, cowboy, you have lots of growing to do before you can go back to Kansas with me."

"One is enough going that far away. I am so glad you're finally back," Katy said, hugging him.

Harp handed the baby to his mother and kissed Kate. He was sure glad to be back home, holding his lovely wife in his arms at long last. What a bright warm day to be home with Katy. How wonderful this was.

"Have you men eaten?" his mother asked.

"Not a whole lot lately, ma'am," Chaw said, laughing and slapping his leg with his once fine, now dusty, Boss of the Plains hat. "We've been riding hard to get back here, and that reunion right there was worth it all to see."

"I am simply glad to see Harp in one piece. Come on, I can whip up some food for all of us."

"We are coming and happy as all get out to be here. Where is Hiram at?"

"Oh, checking on things. I expect him back by dark. We had no idea you were coming in this soon."

Chaw explained how they left the supply wagons,

horses, and bells steers to come along behind them, and they rode like they were on fire from the Red River crossing. Harp heard her familiar laughter taking the men inside. Damn it was great to be home with them, his wife, and son.

He closed his eyes. There was still lots to do. He hoped Long was all right wherever he was, this sunny day, him home with Katy and his boy, Lee, in Texas.

CHAPTER 28

Hiram O'Malley rode in that evening and shouted at Harp when he saw only him. "Well, where is your brother?"

"Dad, you know Long. He gets an idea and you can't shake him off it. He told me not to worry that he wanted to look at some new country and didn't need anyone. He promised me to be back here by Christmas."

"Yes. He's hardheaded enough when he makes up his mind; we both know that."

"Dad, he's as tough as any guy but numbers can over-swarm you."

"Well, I know you tried. I heard from your letters, and I can't believe those drovers were holding out for that much for cattle worth ten cents in Texas. You did great. I am so proud of you and what you accomplished for our friends and our family."

"Any problem here?"

"Nothing recent. Of course fall is the season the Indians leave the plains to raid us. There are no rangers. They abolished them. The state police are not that effective, and I fear there'll be lots of trouble out here on the frontier."

"I am taking some time to be here with Katy and Lee. I sent my men out in pairs to check on things and to see what we need to do to get back into gathering cattle."

"There is more activity by several outfits to hire men and go after the wild cattle like you did, but no one has taken on big herds like you gathered. It will be harder to get the numbers you need as we get further into this game."

"It was bound to happen," Harp said.

"Were there lots of herds on the road going when you were coming home?"

"Yes, and there will be lots more."

"What are your plans?" his father asked.

"Find mavericks, gather and brand them, and take them north. Also, sign up more people who have cattle they need moved."

"The sisters?"

"I will go see them in the next two days. Bless them. I think they have at least that many more steers for next year's drive."

"Well, I know you're glad to be home. And we can hope your brother survives his searching."

His dad slung his arm over Harp's shoulder. "The O'Malley brothers did it again."

"By damn we did."

CHAPTER 29

Doug and Red went to investigate the number of wild cattle left up at the Underground Ranch. Harp told them to take a quick look at things and then they could decide if it was worth their time to set up and brand the wild cattle there or go elsewhere.

Katy, with baby Lee and Harp, rode over in the buckboard and buckskin team to see the sisters. They were excited about everything.

"This is a miracle," Josie said.

"More than that, we need to talk very seriously to you about the state of this ranch. You have met our foreman Estevan Montoya. He is having lots of pain in his joints and he would like to retire, but he won't do that until we find someone," Edna said. Her sister nodded.

"Would you consider running our ranch and hiring a foreman? Josie and I are getting older. We have a sizable fortune and more than we will ever spend. We think this ranch is well run, but times change, like what the mower did for us. We'd never seen a mower before the one you ordered came. That clacking machine is something else."

"I have some men capable of being a ranch foreman. How would this work?"

"You put this check in a bank account. That will be your money to manage this ranch. You give us quarterly reports of your plans, needs, what is happening, how much things will cost, including you."

"I will let you be the judge of our pay. When Long gets back he will share this job with me and we will have a foreman here. I see some things, already, like the house needing painting, and other repairs. We can get it done," Harp said, looking toward Kate, then back at the sisters.

"I would like to talk more about the cattle. I have been told that British bulls to cross with longhorns will be the future of the cattle business. I know you have some. They have more beef on them, so a greater value on the market."

"See what I said," Josie said to her sister. "Our new superintendent is already shaping this place up."

"Let me talk to my foremen prospects. Then the three of us will ride with Estevan or his man and see what else needs attention. I will be sure that Estevan will have a say in who replaces him."

"Now, painting the house we will pay for," Edna said, and her sister agreed. "But you understand these families have worked here all their life."

"They will have a place here as always."

"Thank you. We can work the rest out."

"Is Long back, too?" Josie asked.

"No, he's off seeing the world, but he says he will be back by Christmas."

"Did he go overseas?"

"No that has no calling for Long. He may have gone far enough west to see the Rocky Mountains, but nothing over the waters."

"Edna and I always wanted to go to France and see Paris, but all we did was talk about it."

"Long will be back. He and I are very close. He is a really great man. Ladies, I want to tell you I appreciate being asked to be your superintendent. I will do my damndest to suit you."

"We know you will," Edna said. "We have fretted about what we should do. She and I decided to ask you to run it. Would you two have a glass of champagne to celebrate with us?"

"Certainly," Kate said.

A little shaken by the request to manage their ranch, he nodded and agreed they would.

When they were on the buckboard seat headed home, Katy asked, "Did the bubbles get in your nose?"

"No. But my head almost exploded thinking about running that whole ranch."

"I almost know who you will put over there." She shifted Lee to her other arm, sitting beside him on the spring seat.

"Tell me, gypsy woman, who will I ask?" he asked.

"Doug."

"How did you guess?"

"He is the second man after your brother for the job. Long is too busy, and I know you want this ranch in top shape when those two ladies give it to you."

"When they gave me that check to run this ranch, I really began to believe you were right." He shook his head. It all was too much to conceive. "Darling, I love you and our little cowboy, but we are going to build our own big ranch, too."

She bumped him with her shoulder. "Lee and I believe that, and we will help you."

He felt damn lucky to have her and the boy. He and Long would be at the top of the pile at this rate. He hoped his brother was getting his fill of the western frontier safely. He missed him not being there, but no matter what, they'd make it.

CHAPTER 30

He and Doug talked into the night about him taking the foreman job at the Diamond Ranch.

"I'll really have to polish up my Spanish," Doug said, sounding concerned. "Those workers are all Hispanic."

"They do things Hispanic, but they need to be brought up into this century. They're hardworking, loyal, and they will support you. You can do it. You took some green cowboys to Kansas and made it."

"Yeah, I want the job. Say, you said we needed to see those parents of the four men we lost. You dreading that as much as I am?"

"Oh, yes. And Saturday we pay the ranchers who sent their cattle north with us. That will make up, somewhat, for those sad visits to see those parents. Get back to the topic, does the language bother you that much about this new job?"

"Oh, no. Hell, Harp, it's the opportunity of a lifetime. I'm older than you by near ten years, but being a cowboy is not the opportunity for a man having enough of a job to support a wife and family, if I can ever find someone to marry me. I can do that working the foreman job. Have kids and feed them. I can overcome any problems like talking to my help. You and Long have treated me like I was kin since going to Sedalia. Having this job, in these terrible economic times people are having in Texas, is a thank-God-every-day issue for me. After Sedalia I wondered, but what you did in Abilene shocked all of us. Every guy on that team saw in Abilene that the O'Malley brothers' deal was going to bring all of us working for you two out of these depressing times."

"Well, the Diamond Ranch is a good start for you."

"And I am truly grateful."

"Now, ride with me tomorrow. We have four families to see. I will need some help along, to have the courage for the job."

The following morning, Harp and Doug began the sad task of visiting the families who had lost their loved ones. The first one they went to see was the widow. She lived on a small place outside of Kerrville. They drove the team into town and got the boy's money in twenty-dollar bills. He and Long had decided to pay each family who lost a son or husband, four hundred dollars.

"Mrs. Green, I wrote you a letter from Kansas about Johnny's death. I know money won't replace your son, but my brother and I want you to have four hundred dollars, for his pay. He was a gallant, brave young man and it hurt us all he was killed in a horse wreck doing his job keeping the cattle moving. So thank you very much, and if I can ever help you, feel free to call on me." He gave her the money in a cloth sack.

"Thank you, Mr. O'Malley; he was so proud you chose him. I know he worked hard. That was his way."

He hugged her and excused himself. It would be a damn tough day. Doug drove the buckboard and he sat beside him on the spring seat.

The two boys that worked for Doug that got killed were the next two stops. Pete Yates shot himself cleaning a pistol. This father was on the porch when they drove up. Doug climbed down and introduced himself. "Pete was a good man and we are sad he didn't come home. The men gave him a Christian funeral, and we want you to have the money he earned for the trip."

The man swallowed hard. "My wife couldn't face you. We don't blame you or Mr. O'Malley, but when you raise a boy to that age and his life is snuffed out miles away from here it is real damn hard—thanks for the money. I'm sorry—" He walked off crying.

A teenage girl answered the door at the next place. Said she was A. J. Henry's sister and she accepted the money politely. Just stood there sad faced and nodded. She had no words. There was nothing to say.

Harp was beside himself by then. The last hand died of pneumonia. Clarence Fowler's heir was an older brother and his wife who accepted the money gratefully. She ended up head down weeping. "My man can use the money but he could have used

Rupert more. They were close and he hasn't been himself since we got the kind letter you wrote us." *Sniff.* "Thank you is all I can manage."

Then she ran into the house.

Harper climbed back onto the buckboard seat. "Let's go home, Doug. I see why folks drink. If I drank I'd go drown in it. Better get home. My Katy will cheer me up. Thanks for coming along. This must have been the worst day of my life. *Son of a bitch.*"

CHAPTER 31

Wild cattle were spotted, and holding pens were close by on state-owned land. If anyone built such structures on state land, the facilities were free for the public to use. Of course it was first come, first to have possession and use. Doug had told him where they were located, and they sat right in the vicinity that would work well while gathering cattle over there.

Harp then sent Doug over to learn all about the Diamond Ranch from the retiring foreman Estevan Montoya. Red went along to back him since he spoke lots of border Spanish. Languages got murdered in isolated places by the users there. The Texas border lingo was bad, the real Hispanics said, having words no one else understood. But they made do and so could his men who were going to work it.

Some of the boys were left cleaning up the home place, plus repairing fences and even building some more for Hiram. Harp had wanted to hold the teams intact for the following year, so everyone had a job to do. The other two cooks fed them.

Chaw headed the roundup crew and all the top hands went with him along with the supply wagon headed by Ira, his helper Billy, and Candy who had become part of that team.

Until Chaw was comfortable enough with the job, Harp felt he needed to be with them. Harp and Chaw rode at the head of the line of over two dozen hands and two wagons behind bringing food, tents, bedrolls and gear they'd need including one of the squeeze chutes. They were coming through some short timber and cedars on a narrow set of tracks that resembled a road when Harp saw four armed men blocking their way.

He rode up and stopped a small distance from their roadblock.

"Morning, gentlemen, but we'd like to pass here. Any reason we can't?"

"Gawdamn right. This is our range, and that brush-busting crew behind you ain't clearing up our rangeland of the free cattle. Those are our cattle and we intend to brand them for ourselves."

"Have you been trying to brand them?"

"Not yet."

"Then that is now my business. If you are just trying to stop us and you have not been running them in and working them, then I say you aren't interested enough in them to own them. We are."

"No you ain't. We ain't going to let you come an inch farther."

Harp was nodding his head. *The hell you say.* "Then

who's going to die here today? Those men back
there have fought off Yankee veterans and tribes of
Plains Indian. They won't mind killing you like the
snap of your finger. Men, if you have families and
children to think about being orphaned, then think
hard. Those men have been to Sedalia and Abilene
and they fight to kill. So put your guns up and go
home."

They talked among themselves. Finally their
spokesman said, "You better not rebrand any of our
cattle while you are over here."

Harp nodded. "I promise you we won't do that.
We are not thieves."

And the men rode off. Harp sat for a long time
on his horse not saying anything, letting his anger
slowly slip away. Comanche stomped a hind foot at
biting flies.

When the men were finally gone from sight, he
turned to his men and said, "That was better than
dying. Everyone goes out goes out in pairs. There
may be more out there upset. Let's go round up
cattle."

A loud cheer went up. No doubt in his mind his
bunch would have won, but the price was too high
to risk it.

By evening the camp was set up. Sweet wood
smoke hung in the air. Good Arbuckle's coffee was
being shared and the guitar music with songs was
resounding off the nearby hills. Chaw showed
everyone the map on the tabletop they had, and
how it was quartered to make the drives to bring the
cattle into the pens. He appointed men as leaders

with four or five riders each and what course they must take to bring the wild ones into the five-acre pen.

Harp thought about the face-off they had earlier. These damn cattle were not worth more than fifty cents when he and the outfit left for Sedalia eighteen months ago. Now that they were worth something, everyone claimed them. Well, he and the crew were rounding these up, branding them, and driving the big steers out to lock up on one of the Diamond Ranch–fenced sections to get fat before springtime.

And they could like it or lump it.

Before dawn the following morning, they ate breakfast and had saddled their mounts. Each group left in the early pink of day for their place to start bringing in the cattle. An hour later Chaw fired a pistol in the air. Another west of him went off, farther on one more, then Harp shot his gun off on the far western point.

Cattle were on the move, stampeding through brush timber and open meadows to escape the shots. Cowboys on horseback cut off any retreat and drove them toward the pen. The cattle ran to join others as they fled for the pens. Bawling in protest, they soon made a large herd. Those trying to escape joined others, all heading right where Harp wanted them. Cows, bulls, calves, and steers all with tails above their backs charging for where they didn't want to go, but the force they were caught up in would eventually put them through the gates and locked up in the pen to be worked.

Harp was pleased, riding hard, sweeping through the cedar boughs and live oak to send them for the open gates. From here on there would be no breaking back, just running in the direction the bosses wanted them to go.

On a great horse, this was the place that Harp wanted to be the most on these drives. They would have branded cattle to sort off, but there must be hundreds here that would soon wear the H Bar H brand on their hide.

Hell, Long, you are missing all the fun.

The herd swept into the huge pen and soon settled while the crew ate lunch. The squeeze chute unit was set up. Maverick cows and calves plus yearlings would be returned to the open after being worked and branded. Steers and castrated bulls would be held to drive to the Diamond Ranch.

They worked cattle that day until dark, and there still were more head to work in the morning. Everyone ate hearty on the good tender roast beef Ira cooked along with potatoes and carrots, biscuits and peach cobbler.

By end of next day, Chaw had his weathered hat on the back of his head, counting numbers. "The men have three hundred head of cows and calves worked, and a hundred and twenty big steers ready to go to pasture."

"Guys," Harp shouted over their roaring about it. "That's a great record and we ain't half done here."

In the next four days they branded about every

head of stock they could find in a large radius of the pens. It moved the cow count on this drive to 600 and 520 calves. Big steers to go to Diamond numbered 240, near a quarter of the herd they needed for Abilene.

Two of the better hands went south to look for more pockets of cattle. The job there done, half the main crew went back to the ranch for a two-day break. Others took the big steers to pasture and planned to be back at the home ranch that night.

They were all worn out when they reached home. The pasture bunch never got in until after midnight. Only a handful of them were up the next morning with Harp to have breakfast in the tent with his wife. Her nanny had Lee and Kate was giving Ira a hard time.

"You know what to do about that girl, Candy?"

"No. I don't want her hurt again."

"You know as big and tough as you are, you have a softer than peach fuzz heart."

"I can't help it. She has no one she remembers to care for her."

"I am seriously afraid of her getting hurt out there. Leave her with me for a short while. Maybe I can help her find herself."

"Kate, I'd do anything I can for her. I will ask her if that's all right."

"Ira, you are the man. But maybe I can do something."

Candy told Ira she feared being away from him. He told Katy her wishes and he accepted them.

Later Harp thanked her for trying. Katy was a

little upset but nodded. "You can't be helped if you don't want help."

The two men who had left to go looking for stock rode in and said there were several head in the region they called Hard Rocks. The boys said they could rent some pens and work them nearby. Harp decided he would send Chaw and two men to make the deal after they had some time off to relax.

He paid the returning men their needed ten bucks and sent them into town for some rest and rowdy time.

Things were going well. Harp and Hiram sat out in the sun and talked about needed deals. "You sure are making lots of progress on all this business. Why I know men been back damn near as long as you have been home and have not turned a tap; yet they were so worn out."

"That won't get it done. If Long was here we'd got twice this much done already."

"Hey, hey, ye already have a good wife and a son. He's only got himself, and going looking isn't a bad thing for him."

"Do you think he's maybe looking for a woman?"

"It bothered him you just rode up and found Katy. It worked out as smooth as silk. You were lucky to find her. I lost me first wife on a picnic. A very good woman. The river stole her and I couldn't swim fast enough to save her. One minute the woman I liked and appreciated was on a shelf wading in the river, the next she was shouting for help and was swept away under the water.

"I didn't really want another woman. I wanted

her back and I must have cursed God many times for letting her drown. A few months later I met your mother working in a big fine garden. I knew nothing about her except she was the first woman I saw since burying me last one that I really wanted to know better.

"She'd lost the man she was pledged to. I guess she had just found it out the second time I crossed paths with her in Cincinnati. She said he was dead, and I said like me, that I lost me wife three months ago so come and we will dance at the Cane Hill social Saturday night. Then she started talking about being pregnant. I didn't care. She was a beautiful woman and a kinder soul as I had never met.

"Her mother said for her to answer my request. She said she may as well since I would not take no for me answer.

"We got engaged going to the social and a preacher married us when we got there. Then we turned around and I took her home and told her parents we were married. As you can see, we have lived happily ever after."

Harp was laughing. "You believe in things being planned?"

"I guess. Why?"

"Katy was going to leave Lee's Creek area but some voice said, no, stay at the store a while longer. So she stayed until I got there. And like you saw Mom, this nice lady told me to buy two cans of peaches and we'd go somewhere and eat them. We did and have been together ever since except for this last cattle drive. What do you call that?"

"Ah, Harp, me boy, they call that fate in Ireland. It was intended that you would be coming there, and that force held her there no matter how silly she considered it. Either some witch, or God, plans for things to happen to us all."

"In all your years you haven't found out which force does it?"

"Why worry about who does it? You'll sure not change it anyway. We were surely having really wild times up there, when I courted your mother. There were raiders and they hurt people. I was the head of the safety unit. We were over a long day's ride from the county seat and any real help."

"She told you she was with child?"

"She said to her mother that I would not listen or take no for an answer. My heavens, her man was dead and my wife had drowned. I told her that life was left to the two of us and it might be short, too, so why not celebrate it together? Oh, Harp, it was one of the most glorious days in me life when she said she'd marry me."

"You were on the way to a dance?"

"I was with her. The preacher must have thought I was drunk when I said hurry up and marry us before she changes her bloody mind. I was but not on any spirits. Still he married us. They threw rice at us driving back north in that fancy coach I had borrowed to impress her. It was like we had wings."

"I hate to dig, but was your first marriage that wild?"

"Her husband died coming down from Iowa. A nice chap but obviously too fragile for the hardships we had on the road. She had two children and a wagon—her things. I only had a good saddle horse and was helping protect the train that was going to western Arkansas from Iowa. The captain said she needed a man after we buried him that afternoon. Three of us drew straws and she married me in the campfire light.

"The children both died shortly after. She was a kind, generous woman. But those losses had shocked her into what I called a numb stage. She wasn't really all there, and the day of the picnic she wandered away from the crowd like she intended to do it. Then I discovered she'd gone wading out in the swift stream and that water swept her away. I never said it was suicide, but losses piled on more losses were more than her mind could stand, I always believed.

"It was never love between us, like me and your mother found. She was like a sewn rag doll, just there. I wanted her to spring up and be the woman I saw before her husband died, but that never happened. Your mother was the biggest blessing in me life from the first minute right up to today.

"I am glad Katy came along and waited that extra time for you to come. She did what I wanted me first wife to do—forget the past and live for tomorrow. And, Harper, I pray that God will find Long a woman as great as the ones we have."

"Oh, yes. Emory's woman wasn't ready. But there are lots more out there—good ones, too."

His dad agreed.

* * *

About to be off to another cattle chasing, Harp kissed Katy and Lee good-bye. He greeted his buffalo horse Comanche and soon was leading the gang to another roundup. It was getting to be a regular thing for him to saddle up and go find the elusive unbranded livestock with his men, then come home like Roman soldiers with a tally book full of newly claimed cattle. But as their circle widened, he knew his competition also was doing the same thing and they would soon have every damn stray longhorn in west Texas wearing someone's brand.

The place the men rented from one of the landowners, for a small fee, had some large corrals and looked suited to buy. The elderly man who owned the land had no teeth and looked like he'd been put away wet.

Harp stepped off his Comanche horse. "Mr. Erickson, how much land have you got here?"

"Ten sections."

"You have a price for it?"

"Yeah, I want a nice little house paid for near a town to live in. Nothing fancy but where I can walk to and fish for bullheads and pan fish and forty dollar a month income until I die."

Harp nodded his head maybe ten times. "How many head of cows you got?"

"About a hundred and there are calves, too."

Harp nodded. "You and I are going to town and find that house tomorrow, and you will have that income. I will buy your land and cows."

"Good."

"Mr. Erickson, thank you, sir. Chaw, you better ask him where the corners are on this land."

Chaw looked hard at him. "Why?"

"Mr. Erickson, what brand do you have?"

"CHX."

"Chaw, you are going to be the foreman of the CHX Ranch. I just bought it from Mr. Erickson. He says there are a hundred cows and calves. You better learn all about it."

Chaw took off his weather-beaten hat and slapped his chap-clad leg with it. "I can damn sure handle that. Harp, you ever met Calamity Morton?"

"No." The name didn't strike a bell for him.

"She's Watson Morton's daughter up at Mason. We're engaged. Now I can marry her. Boss man, that is just dandy."

He hugged Harp.

"Boss man, you made my day. My whole day. That little gal will holler so loud you will hear, at the home ranch, when she learns we will have our own place and can afford to be married."

Harp was laughing too hard to speak. Finally he managed, "Damn you, Chaw. You are the biggest mess in Texas, but I am pleased she will be that happy being your missus. You know Katy will want to help you two get married, buy her a wedding dress if her folks can't afford one."

"Oh, that girl would be pleased. I expect her folks are like the rest of Texas, penniless."

"Tell her not to worry. Who is next in command behind you to lead the cattle drive?"

"Chadron Turner. The boys will listen to him. Could I run up there to tell her and then meet you in Kerrville? I'd really like to do that."

"Get a fresh horse. Mr. Erickson can wait a couple of days to show you what is what. You go take care of business. And then report back here."

"Oh, sure."

The old man was really amused, listening to it all, and told Chaw, "Just don't break your neck doing it. I'm plumb tickled I won't have to worry about a thing thanks to Mr. O'Malley's deal."

The crew was congratulating poor Chaw, and Harp could see he was shaken by the entire situation.

Harp was now owner of another rough ranch— ten sections. He hoped his brother liked it. Hell, Long liked Texas; he wouldn't be hard to please with his name on ten more sections.

Chadron sauntered over leading his horse, while they all watched Chaw saddle a fresh horse. "Chaw said you wanted me."

"I am surprised he did anything, as excited as he is. Yes. He said you should be the one to lead the cattle drive in his place."

"Well, thanks. I won't go plumb crazy, but thanks, I believe I can handle it."

"I do, too. You lay out the plan with the men. I am taking Mr. Erickson to town tomorrow to find him a house and make out some plans for him to move closer to a fishing hole."

"I can handle it." They both watched Chaw on his fresh horse barreling north.

"He's going to get his life with her, boss man."

"No doubt about that."

At times he could not believe all that happened over two cattle drives. Two dumb boys taking eight hundred head to the railhead in Missouri with a dying boss and enough opposition to turn back an army. Then the Abilene trip.

Wherever you are, bro, I hope you're being careful.

CHAPTER 32

Harper left Chadron Turner in charge. The men saddled up in the cool predawn and under his new man's orders divided up forces to make the first roundup while he rode off to handle the land deal. He and the old man used his buckboard and team to head into town and find him a house.

When they reached town he bought the old man lunch in a café and sent word to his land man, by a boy, to tell him where he was. Clare's Café was busy, and Tommy Snyder, lawyer and land man, soon joined them. Tommy ordered lunch while Harp explained, between eating his chicken-fried steak, what he needed.

"I have one house close to the river we can go look at."

"Can you guarantee him he will catch fish?" Harp asked when the man said the house sounded like it would suit him fine.

"If he can't catch any, we can always use a blasting stick for it," Tommy said.

Erickson closed his eyes, laughing.

Between looking at the house, and the lawyer drawing up the papers, the business ate up the entire day. He fed the old man, put him in a hotel room, and drove out to the ranch in the dark. When the dogs barked, lights came on and his dad came out on the porch.

"Just me unharnessing," Harp told him. "I will be up there in a few minutes."

"Naw, boss let me put them up," a hand said, taking over the job.

"Thanks. Please grain and water them. They've been harnessed all day."

Katy tackled him on the porch. "What is wrong?"

"Oh not much—" He kissed her. "I bought another ranch, made Chaw foreman. He got so excited he ran off to Mason to tell some girl they could get married. I told him you'd buy her a dress."

"Of course. What else?"

"I left Mr. Erickson, who is selling us his ranch, to sleep in a hotel and decided I would drive out here and sleep with my wife."

"Wonderful. You hungry?"

"Don't go to any trouble."

"It won't be."

"What ranch?" his father asked as he and his mother joined them.

"Erickson's ten sections south of town." Lord sakes, by then everyone was up. All he wanted was to sleep with his wife.

Up at dawn, he drove the rig back to town, met the old rancher, and they had breakfast. They went to see the snug house and ten acres again. The cost was fifteen hundred dollars and later at the lawyer's office, the papers completed, he drove Erickson back to the ranch.

He saw the dust. His bunch was bringing in the first drive of cattle and it looked big. Once at the ranch, he was amazed at the numbers being pushed into the corrals. He let the old man off at his house—a typical shotgun Texas ranch home—and asked if he'd be all right.

"Fine. Fine. My lands. Them boys must ah went to Mexico to find that many cattle."

"There's no telling."

Holy Wars told him that he'd put the team up and gave him a saddled horse to ride.

"Those boys got a bunch didn't they?"

Holy was laughing. "I bet Chadron wants the next foreman's job is my thought."

"He's gaining on it."

The two men parted laughing.

He found his headman, wearing a kerchief for a mask against the dust. When they met he pulled it down and the Texas dust rolled off it.

"Lots of cattle," Harp said to compliment the man.

"Ah, some of them are branded. We can cut them out and drive them off."

"No problem. We aren't cattle rustlers."

"Right. I met two angry ranchers about daybreak. They threatened me. I told them we only wanted the mavericks. Nothing come of it but they were mad as hell about us being down here."

"Not the first or the last."

"Oh, I knew that."

"We better get to sorting huh?"

Chadron looked around. "Yeah. I've been expecting Chaw to be back."

"He will. I can help meantime."

"I guess so." Chadron shrugged and they joined the crew.

He made the two cousins Sly and Jimbo as the cutting riders. Things were moving along.

When Ira rang the triangle for lunch, they had most of the branded ones outside and the holding team split to take turns eating lunch. The plans were to drive the branded ones off the ranch.

The remaining wild cattle needed to be worked. They quit branding at dark that evening. Ira had lanterns hung for light on the meal. One man drew night watch. He was to wake another in two hours and so on. Harp's eyes felt sunburned. Dust scratched and he was anxious to finish the meal and find his bedroll.

Chaw arrived and slid onto the bench beside him, his plate full. "Lucky you guys worked late or I'd have starved."

"No. Ira would have fed you. We worked late and still have some two hundred head to work tomorrow. Excuse me, how's Calamity?"

He put down his fork. "She is excited. She is real excited that we can be married. I told her you would buy her a wedding dress—"

"My wife Katy will."

"Oh, okay. No problem. What do I need to do with Erickson?"

"When we finish working cattle tomorrow, move him to the house I bought him in town. Take a few boys, hire a wagon, and get him settled. Get your gal to Katy, and we will take them to town to find a dress."

"Good. I am really grateful for this opportunity."

"Let's get these cattle worked first."

"Yes, sir. Get some sleep; you look tired."

"I am."

Harp fell asleep when his head hit the saddle seat he used for a pillow. It was a groggy wake-up call. He could sure use his brother there to spread some of this load off on to. No telling about him or what he was up to; he simply hoped he was breathing and taking nourishment somewhere.

He ate breakfast and drank the good coffee. They worked cattle till noon. Chadron had the tally book and read off his numbers. They had found 100 cows and 70 calves with Erickson's brand. Then they branded another 150 maverick cows and 25 springing heifers. They turned 180 bulls into steers, and there were 85 yearling steers and 75 yearling heifers.

Chadron said there were a lot more in the region they were working. They took the afternoon off. Most everyone was so damn tired they slept. Erickson said he was in no hurry so the next day they made another drive and brought in a lot more— sorted the branded ones, drove them off the ranch, and worked the rest that day and another half day. Mother cows and springing heifers made another

110. There were 150 steers and 120 mixed-sex yearlings. The number of mother cows impressed him the most.

Chaw and Darvon Studdy thought a regular crew there on that ranch could get the rest. So it was set up that some would go home, some were assigned to move Erickson, and Harp and Kate would help Chaw get some furniture and his bride find a wedding dress. A regular crew was left to keep an eye on the place and still work cattle, but two men were to stay on the place at all times. Harp had a notion if anyone knew the O'Malleys had bought it, they might burn it down to get even.

Erickson's things were loaded in two farm wagons Harp hired. Some of the crew and Ira's supply wagon followed. The old man drove his buckboard at the rear. When they got close, four men went with the old man to help unload his stuff. The rest rode into Kerrville.

It was at the Keystone livery, where they were hitching their horses near mid-day, when hell broke loose. Someone in the loft doorway was firing a Winchester at them. Horses, in panic mode, broke reins, reared, and ran. Shots were exchanged and some of Harp's men, he knew, were shot. Harp had emptied his pistol, got knocked down by his horse breaking away, and managed, after he scrambled up, to get a rifle out of another scabbard. He shot it at someone firing a pistol across the pen of horses;

the animals were stamping up dust, charging around, trying to escape the shooting.

Then silence rang in his ears. Two of the ranch's downed horses broke the silence with screams of pain from bullet wounds. The dust raised up by the penned horses clouded the air.

"Who's shot?" Harp asked, his guts roiling, him wondering who had done this.

Sly came to him, holding his bloody left arm. "Scratched is all."

Two boys were on their knees. "Frank Wayne's dead, boss."

Holy Wars was hatless and shook his head, stumbling out of the dust. "Them worthless bastards have shot Candy."

Hatless, Ira carried her limp form in his arms.

"She dead?"

Ira was so angry, his jaw was set tight. "Why in the hell did them sons of bitches shoot her for? She's dead, Harper. Dead. And she never did a damn thing to any of them."

"Some of you boys, help him."

"No. I am going to carry her to Neal's Funeral Home."

"Holy, go along and you boys reload your pistols."

"Boss, come here." Chaw waved him to the big open doors of the livery.

The owner, Kelsey Hale, and two of his men were tied to wooden kitchen chairs and had been gagged. Chaw began cutting them loose.

"Who did this?"

"They were five of them. Rode in an hour ago,

I knew one. Phil Holland. He was a hired gun, but from the blood leaking out of my loft, I figure he's well on his way out of here."

"They tell you why?"

"I heard him tell the others to kill both of them O'Malley boys."

"Who hired them?" He'd cut Hale free.

"I never heard."

The other two workers, rubbing their wrists from rope burns, shook their heads.

"I'll go see about the one in the loft," Chaw said.

About then two town marshals arrived, carrying sawed-off shotguns.

"Harp, what's happened here?"

"Hale just told us. Some men came, tied him and his men up, and ambushed my bunch when we rode up. I have at least one dead cowboy and a dead girl."

"Dead girl?"

"They shot an orphan girl that helped my cook Ira. He took her body to the undertaker."

"We missed him hurrying down here. Why did they do this?"

"Flat out I'd say to stop us from catching any more mavericks."

"You know who's behind it?"

"I don't. But I promise you if you don't learn it, I will."

"Where is your brother?"

Harp shook his head. "He might be climbing the Rocky Mountains. He split off to see some new country when we left Abilene."

"I hadn't heard that," the lawman said.

"I think there's more dead guys lying around."

"Herb, go out back and see what you can find," John Tyler said to the other man.

Two of Harp's cowboys were dragging someone by the arms, coming from behind the barn.

"Who's he?" Tyler asked.

"He says he's Allen Capps," Virgil, one of the new boys, said. "But he says Phil Holland hired him to catch some rustlers named O'Malley."

"Watch out. This one's dead," Chaw said from up in the loft, and rolled that shooter's body out to plunk on the ground in front.

"Who's this one?" Tyler asked.

The liveryman Hale said, "Phil Holland. I knew him from years ago."

"There's two more dead out back," Virgil said.

"Damn. How many of your men are wounded?"

"Sly, one of my point riders, was scratched. Candy and one of my boys, Frank Wayne, dead. Lost some damn good horses. You need us?"

"I guess not. What next?"

"A couple of boys can help Holy get his remuda gathered. Chaw, go see what you can do for Ira at the funeral home. Tell him I'll take care of expenses. I am taking Sly to the doctor. He's black but he is vital to us as a point rider. I want to be sure and have him fixed him up right."

Tyler nodded.

"Chadron, go check on Erickson and those boys we sent to help set him up. This is a damn mess, and I want to get to the bottom of it after the doc's.

They even shot one of my best working horses. Damn. This all really makes me mad."

"I damn sure want this ended, too, Harp."

"Thanks. Now I need to get my man to the doc."

Sly didn't want to go see a doctor; said his cousin Jimbo had already bandaged it.

Harp wouldn't listen and the three set out on foot for the doc's house a block away. A grumpy attendant told Jimbo to stay outside since he wasn't shot.

Harp caught the man by the sleeve. "That man works for me. He'll be in here or you will be on your ass out on the lawn."

"Yes, sir. I just—"

"I know. They both stay in here."

An older woman showed them into a side room. Sly shook his head. "I knowed they wouldn't—"

Harp cut him off. "We talked a long time ago. You are my men and color don't count."

"Not if you work for the O'Malley brothers it don't." Jimbo laughed.

Doc Randolph cleaned the wound, stitched it, and bandaged it. "He will be fine."

While Harp paid the doctor, Tyler's men brought in the wounded outlaw.

Tyler said the other two had died. He didn't know their names, but promised to send word if he learned any more. Harp thanked him.

Holy had left three saddled horses at the hitch rail out front of the doc's office for the men to ride back to the ranch. That boy thought of everything.

They rode back and a worried Katy ran out to hug her husband.

"They tried to kill you?"

"Yes. But they failed. Sorry it worried you."

"You sure you are not hurt?"

"No. Sly was scratched. A young cowboy, Frank Wayne, was killed. They got my good horse, Comanche, too. Marshal Tyler is trying to find out who hired them, but their leader is dead and two more with him."

"They are having Candy's funeral tomorrow," Katy said.

"We will all be there."

"How is Ira?"

"I imagine not very well. She was like a daughter to him."

"She never recovered mentally did she?"

Harp shook his head. "But she didn't deserve to die, either."

He hugged his wife and tried not to, but some tears escaped his eyes. "Damn, Katy, all of our successes and this had to happen."

He recalled the time, as a boy, when his welch pony Briar died of colic. Oh, he'd been heartbroken and his dad had hugged him and said in his brogue, "And into every man's life there shall be a tragedy and it will cause a tear to fall maybe two. But the living must go on."

How true on this sunny late fall day.

CHAPTER 33

God cried for Candy. A soft rain with only distant thunder fell on the shoulders of Harp's canvas coat as he held the umbrella over his wife. The Methodist preacher sent Candy and the young cowboy to be with God. Solemn times for everyone after a good drive, branding work done, and a new ranch added to the list of successes.

Chaw brought Calamity over. Katy bonded with the dark-eyed girl immediately, and she planned to stay at the big house while they found the dress and prepared for the wedding. She was younger than Katy but intelligent and happy. Harp hoped for the best. That she was one of the good ones he wanted for all his men.

Doug told him all was well over at the Diamond Ranch.

Hoot had come to the ranch to catch Harp up on things, and promised to be at the wedding, which, he understood, would be soon.

"They say you bought another nice spread," Hoot said.

"It looks good. His name is Erickson. Up in years and he wanted out and to fish away the rest of his life on the river.

"He fought with Sam Houston and got part of that ranch as a veteran. Bought the rest for pennies back then. Tough old man. Comanche killed his wife and four kids. He killed that old chief before it was all over and cut his man parts all the way off. Someone asked him why he did it when the Indian was already dead.

"Erickson said, 'He won't have any pleasure up there or down below this way.' It explains why he wanted to sell that place. Too many bad memories was why."

It was raining when they went and everyone had lunch under the large tent. Ranchers never complained about rain—it might stop. Many folks in the community were there, and they spoke to him about the shoot-out. Asked why.

He turned up his hands. In his book they were cowards who hired gun hands to do their bad deeds, themselves afraid to face them. Tyler dropped by with the undersheriff, Jack Freeman from San Antonio, who was in charge until they formed a new county.

Freeman had no idea who hired them but said he had feelers out. Someone knew who had hired them, but to get them to step forward might be hard. They promised to keep working on it.

Harp wished he had the names of the different

men who halted him on the road the few times. But they were gone, like smoke. Still, folks talked and someone had to know them.

Chaw and Calamity were going to be married at the home place. A dress secured. In the midst of these preparations Harp worked on books to get his entire ranch accounts straight. It was getting to be headache work for him until his mother said there was a young man who lived on Loller's Creek who had worked in a bank before the war. He was wheelchair bound because of damage a war injury had done to his legs. He needed an accounting job because the bank laid him off when he returned not able to walk around. Yes, his mother said, she'd house him at her home if he wanted him.

He went to see Reg Hoffman the next day. His mother showed him in and told Reg he had company, then left the room. Reg put down a book.

"You are one of the O'Malley brothers?"

"Yes, Reg. My mother told me you were looking for an accounting job."

"Such a job I would like; however"—he drew in his breath—"I worked for a bank but they required me to move a lot and a wheelchair is not easily moved."

"We were thinking you could do our ranch books. My parents have a large house, and my mother said she'd see you were cared for."

"Oh, I'd be too big a bother."

"You don't know my mother. It would give you

something to do. We have no customers you'd have to serve. Just keep things like payroll, taking care of our banking business from the house. My brother and I are pretty solvent. I think that is the word, but he's not a bookkeeping guy and it sure isn't my game. If you desired to go somewhere, we have conveyances and people to take you."

"What does the job pay?"

"What did you make at the bank?"

"A dollar a workday."

"Like five or six dollars a week?"

"That was it."

"If you can keep my books and the bank accounts up to date, I'd pay you fifty dollars a month."

"When could I start?"

"I'll find a big cowboy and send him for you next Monday. He is big enough to put you on the buckboard seat and get you down, then wheelchair you to the house. Have your personal things in a trunk to take along, and if you don't like it he can bring you back. Or you can try handling things for five days, and when that time is over we can talk more about it."

"That's why you come here?"

"Yes. My mother told me about you and we need an accountant."

"I know her. She's a nice lady. Mother, come in here. This is Harper O'Malley. Monday I will go to his house and do his accounting."

"Oh, yes," the lady in her forties said, drying her hands on a tea towel. "Easter told me last week she'd find you a job. Thanks so much, Mr. O'Malley."

"That's my dad. I'm Harp or Harper."

"Oh, I won't forget that, Harp. Does he need anything to bring?"

"Just his personals. When we get him over to the house, we can modify things to fit his chair and ease of movement. I know he can go through the house and get onto the front porch from inside. My cowboys can fix anything else that needs doing."

"We heard you got attacked. Did you learn any more about the attackers?"

"No one has come forth with an answer so far."

"I hope this gets solved. Your mother is worried some. Said she has not heard from your brother. He went out west?"

"Long is not much of a letter writer. I did that for him, but I am certain he's all right and seeing lots of new country."

"I knew you boys were quite close."

"I sure miss him but he'll drop in some time, I figure."

Standing up to leave, Harp said, "Reg and Mrs. Hoffman, I am glad to have met both of you. Reg, look for my cowboys coming to get you next Monday."

"Thanks, Harp."

Harp figured to be nearly halfway home, where the road dropped off to cross a deep cut made by a small creek, when a high-powered bullet struck the exposed banks and sent dirt all over him and his horse. The pony shied and he shed the saddle, jerking the Winchester out of the scabbard as he went. The gulch he was in might offer some shelter. To survive he needed to keep low. Was the shooter in a tree or on higher ground?

He tried to imagine the bullet's path and where it came from to barely miss him and plow into the bank. The shooter was south of him, and probably in a higher position, either bellied down or using a tripod to hold that big gun.

If he dared to look up over the bank he might get a bullet in his face. What did he tell the men that worked for him? Go in pairs. Here he was miles from the home place and Reg's, alone. They weren't trying to make him quit any longer. They wanted him dead. Downstream he saw some brush growing on the bank. He might be able to get behind it and not be seen before he saw them.

Rifle in his right hand, bent over, he hurried downstream. The brush still had leaves so he used it. He saw a reflection when a gun barrel turned and heard someone ask, "Is he dead or wounded in the crick?"

"Let the sumbitch bleed some before we try to find out," Harp heard as the shooter stood up and stretched, bareheaded, with the rifle barrel in his hand.

That was the same position the man held two seconds later when the 44/40 hunk of lead went through his chest, heart, and lungs and ended his sorry life.

"Donny!" the other man shouted, and whirled to shoot in the direction of the gun smoke. By then Harper levered out the brass casing, reloaded, and shot through the smoke surrounding him at the second person in the ambush. The bullet also caught the outlaw square in the chest and sent him flying backward, as his own gun discharged in the air.

Who was left? He held his position carefully eyeing, through the wavering smoke, his ears still ringing from the shots. Was that all? No. He heard some rustling around with horses. He needed to get up top of the bank and try to stop whomever.

A horse brand might tell him who hired them. Fleet footed, he ran up the hill hard as he could, past the two downed men. He saw a rider with two horses in tow. They were holding him back. His actions looked impatient, even at that distance, and he finally let the reins go, turning in the saddle to see what was happening.

Harp stopped in his tracks, took aim, and fired. The rider went head first off the horse and the animal tore away. That made three of them down. He levered another shell in the rifle and started in that direction. *Three against one sure ain't no fun.* He said that over and over to himself until he came in sight of the stilled rider lying on the ground looking like he had broken his neck.

The downed rider never moved a muscle. He was dead. Even from thirty feet away he knew the dead one on the ground was the son of a rancher by the name of Holder. A damned teenage boy. What the hell was he doing out there with those two killers?

His luck got worse and worse. No witnesses. His word against the three dead men's silence. Oh, hell. *Long, where are you when I need your help?*

With a lot of effort he finally loaded their bodies across the horses he caught. And when he got them into town he'd give his story. How could he have done anything else; it simply happened that way.

It was dark when Harp reached town. First place he stopped was at the marshal's office, and a deputy came to the door leaning on the frame. He took the toothpick out of his mouth and threw it down to stare at the bodies slung, facedown, over the saddles.

"Who are they, Harp?"

"One is Cal Holder's boy. He rode with these two. They tried to ambush me at the crossing on Loller's Crick."

"How did that teenager get in with those tough men?" The deputy lifted one by the hair, dropped him, and shook his head. Harp was certain he didn't know either of them.

"If I knew that I'd sure be a lot richer than I am now. Those two were waiting for me to ride through there. He was with them. I had no way to know it was the kid. I'd been shot at and I was mad."

The deputy agreed. "I'd have been mad, too, if they'd shot at me. There will probably be a coroner's hearing. That's a formality."

"I will be available."

Harp remounted his horse and rode for the home place.

Katy came out on the porch while he started to unsaddle, but a ranch hand took the job away from him.

"Thanks, Keith."

"That's all right, sir."

"Reg is coming. I mean we're going to send someone for him Monday morning. He is an accountant. He's wheelchair bound but he gets around well and is independent. On the way home, I had to shoot three men that tried to ambush me."

She gasped. "No backup. When will you learn, Harper O'Malley? Who was it this time?"

"Two men I never saw before and that teenage Holder boy who was holding their horses."

"Roger Holder?"

"I guess. One guy shot at me. I moved and was able to shoot the two of them. Then someone took all three horses and ran. I considered him to be one of the killers and shot him, too. I never knew it was a boy. They're all dead."

She hugged him tightly. "I am so sorry. What can we do?"

"I don't know. I can't give the man his boy back. I almost took the boy's body home, but I figured they'd kill me for sure no matter how respectful I did it."

"That was smart."

"Let's go inside so I can tell everyone else."

She agreed and hugged him as he led her into the house.

"Did you hire the young man?" Easter asked.

"Yes, Mom, I think he will do swell, but you will have to help him some."

"I can do that. I bet he makes a good bookkeeper for you and Long."

"Tell them the rest of this shooting business," Katy said.

"Coming home I rode off into Loller's Crick, and you know it is a real deep cut. Someone shot at me, and the bullet was so close I swear I felt it as it crashed into the bank near my face. I got the rifle and ran low downstream until I could use a bush for cover. I saw the number one man thinking he had hit me because they had not seen me since that shot was fired at me. They were talking about killing me, and he was standing up when I cut down one. Then I shot the second. Someone was fooling with the horses over on the hill. I broke and ran to catch sight of him. The horses he led were being stubborn and he was arguing with them, so I was able to take him out, too. I never knew it was a boy—I was mad and not going to let any one of them get away."

"What a terrible thing to have happen," his mother said.

His dad agreed. He shook his head. "And of course he was out there innocently trapping flying squirrels?"

After eating a little, with no appetite, Harp took his wife off to bed. He was pleased Reg was coming to be their bookman, and Long would give him an A for doing it. Just as long as he didn't have to do them himself.

But the mess was not over. Not by a long shot.

CHAPTER 34

He met his men at breakfast and started off by apologizing for going alone to find an accountant. He said Chadron Turner was in charge of the home operations until Red came back from helping Doug at Diamond. Chaw was going to move over and be the new foreman at the Erickson Ranch.

After Harp outlined the new bosses, he said, "I bet some of you saw that dark-eyed pretty girl who's been staying at the main house."

Most of them nodded and grinned.

"Well, our old buddy Chaw never introduced her to any of you until after she said she'd marry him. Can you believe that?"

"Good thing he's leaving," one of the punchers said.

Another piped up. "He ain't so damn far away we can shiveree him, either."

"Yeah!"

"Men, all kidding aside now, I think we will have trouble over this last try at killing me. I really hated the results, but that won't bring the boy back, and his family will be angry. Ride in pairs and keep your eyes peeled for trouble."

Later in the day the head deputy Kent Roberts came out and spoke to him. "I know you're a busy man. I want you to ride over with me and show me the details about yesterday."

"I will be glad to do that. They picked the fight. I only survived it."

"Let's reenact it for the Justice of the Peace's court."

"You had lunch?"

"I had some jerky; I'll be fine."

He told Katy his plans and the two rode out.

The first thing he showed was where the bullet barely missed him and how he came off his horse and armed himself. Then how, when he was out of sight of them, he changed positions. Harp showed how the one with the single-shot target rifle had stood up and he shot the man. Then, when his partner was in sight, Harper explained how he shot the second one.

Roberts picked up the casings in the dirt and then Harp showed him where he ran up the hill to stop number three from escaping. He explained that the horses were fighting the rider or he'd been gone. Harp showed him where he stopped, couldn't see the person's face, and then shot him.

They searched until Roberts found the last empty casing, where he made the long shot from, and he agreed that it all read like Harp said.

"A helluva shot with your rifle."

"I knew I only had one chance and he'd be gone. When I got over there and saw it was a kid I got sick to my stomach. But what was he up here for, if he hadn't showed the others where I'd cross?"

"I agree. He was running with wolves in my estimation. That's why I came up here to see the whole thing and to back your story. I can see it perfectly."

"One was concerned that I might be conscious and that they should wait to not risk that. Let me bleed to death he said. At the time I was looking right at those two through some brush."

"Thanks. It may be hell to prove, but they don't have another witness to dispute what happened. To me, it is open and shut."

"We can get back in time for supper if we hurry."

Roberts agreed and they rode for the ranch.

Roberts told Hiram that it all was like Harper had said and he'd picked up the empty cartridges on the spots. Everyone at the family table sighed with relief and thanked him for coming out.

But the next day, when Harp drove his wife to town for a few things she still needed for the up and coming wedding, he was shocked to see hand-painted board signs posted on the way into town, and all over the town.

O'Malley Murdered a fourteen-year-old boy
in cold blood. Why deosn't the law arrest him?
Rich cowboy gets away with murder!!
Help us find <u>Justuce</u>!

The town marshal, Tyler, met him before he got off the buckboard in front of the store. "Harper, I hired two men to take down and burn them signs north and south of town."

"How much did it cost?"

"Couple of dollars. I am so sorry."

"No problem." He repaid the man and clapped him on the shoulder. "Thanks."

He saw other painted boards asking for *justice*. Damn. He might have to use his knuckles to show people what justice was.

Word was out the JP planned to hold hearings about the three deaths. Justice of the Peace, Patrick Cassidy, was the man in that office and he had summoned Harp to testify at the hearing the next day. Harp said he'd be there. His crew, except for a few to guard the ranches, would be there as well. The men took a crow bar with them and removed the remaining high-up signs by standing on saddles and ripping them off the trees and buildings. Harp asked them not to fight unless pressed into it. He wanted the matter resolved, especially any bad feeling with the boy's parents.

Harp knew a lot was astir. But, as Darvon pointed out, Harp had many supporters among the crowd, folks that he had delivered cattle for in Kansas. A few spoke to him and said they were there to support him. Katy revealed, under her breath on the way to the schoolhouse where the case would be heard, that she'd heard the same information.

He and Kate found benches while his men stood around at the wall. There was a crowd inside and outside the schoolhouse. His mother joined them and his dad was at the wall with the men.

JP Cassidy pounded the gavel for silence. "This coroner's hearing concerns the deaths of three individuals. Jonah, read the deceased names."

"Donny Joseph McEntry, age thirty-five, residence unknown; Kilmer Morgan, age thirty-two, residence unknown; and Roger Holder, age sixteen, a county resident."

"Thank you. Now will Doc Combs please step forward and give his information?" The physician was sworn in.

"All three were dead when delivered to the local funeral home. McEntry had been shot from the front, the bullet passing through his chest. The wound was fatal. Morgan also received a fatal bullet in his chest. That bullet was forty-four-forty lead, too. Holder was shot in the back and his heart blown apart by a similar caliber bullet."

"Do you have anything else, Doc?"

"No, Your Honor."

"You are excused. Harper O'Malley, please come forward and tell us your side of this situation."

"That gawdamn coward murdered my son—"

"If I hear one more uncalled for outburst from you, you will be removed," Patrick said to the boy's father.

"I'll leave, Patrick, because you sons of bitches are going to turn my son's killer loose. He's bought you off like he and the other O'Malleys have done a lot of ranchers around here."

Patrick rose. "I am fining you twenty dollars for blowing your filthy mouth off in my courtroom."

"Arrest me. I ain't got twenty dollars to my name."

"Deputy."

"Jack will take him to jail, Your Honor," Kent Roberts said.

"Fine. Any more outbursts will be handled like that one," Justice Patrick warned the crowd.

"Harper O'Malley, you have been sworn in. Have a seat in that chair. Tell us about the incident as you saw it happen, please."

"I was coming home by myself. At Loller's Creek a bullet, which was intended for me, hit the bank. That cut the creek made there at that crossing is a deep one, so I was out of sight to any shooters on the higher ground. I dismounted and armed myself with my rifle from the scabbard and hurried up the creek to where some bushes would give me cover enough to try and locate them. I found cover, and heard this McEntry, who was standing up, talking about my demise to the other bushwhacker. I didn't know him.

"I shot him first—to be certain. Then I shot his partner who I also did not know. The third party was gathering the horses. The horses were resisting him, but I had no way to know it was a boy. He was up the hill a ways. Two men had shot at me and the last one was escaping. I shot him. That is what I told the deputy when I brought their bodies in and also told Deputy Roberts the next day when I showed him everything. I could have let them lie there and gone on home. I didn't like the fact that a boy was shot, but if you ride in bad company you can expect bad things to happen, Your Honor."

"Anything else you have to say, sir?"

"No, Judge. Nothing more."

"You are excused for now, but please remain in case something else turns up today."

"I will, Your Honor."

"Thank you. Deputy Sheriff Roberts is next witness."

The hearing continued. "Roberts, you are sworn in now. Tell us your side of this situation."

"Your Honor, the very next day I rode out to the O'Malley ranch and then rode with Harper O'Malley to the ambush site. We went there and I found the empty shells in all three cases right there as he said in his testimony. He exhibited his regret at the boy's death, but that young man was participating in that ambush."

"You have proof?"

"Your Honor, Harper O'Malley brought those horses, carrying their bodies, into town. All were wearing the Holder brand."

The entire crowd oh'd.

Patrick rapped the gavel on the desktop. "It is in the opinion of this court today that it was justified homicide. Case dismissed."

Everyone on Harp's side reached in to shake his hand and tell him he'd done the right thing. He nodded, and in the case of a woman congratulating him, he removed his hat for her. Still he saw the hate-filled sharp-eyed hawks leaving the building, whose hearts, he had no doubt, were filled with evil feelings toward him since they were on Holder's side.

He stood in the cool sunshine, outside of the schoolhouse, making conversation. His mom and Kate were inviting folks to Chaw's wedding. He spoke with Red and they talked about eating lunch at the hotel restaurant.

He also learned that Holder's friends had scraped up the money to pay for Holder's fine.

They were walking in a group when a shot went off half a block away. Harp and Red had the women behind them and were joined by his dad. A cowboy Harp knew rode by and said, "It's all right now. Town marshal disarmed Mary Holder before she could use it. Went off in the air."

"Thanks," Harper said, even more convinced that the boy's death had not been set aside yet.

Damn you, Long O'Malley, wherever you are at. I could use your backing here, right now. Holder's horses were involved. Someone was footing the bill of those two dead gunmen. Harper knew his outfit couldn't be hurting Holder by branding maverick cattle. Holder was in on the dirty work of someone powerful, and Harp couldn't think who that was—but he'd damn sure find out who, hopefully sooner rather than later.

The hotel meal went well. Red gave the men in town enough money to eat off the sandwich bar at the saloon and have a beer or two before they rode home.

Harp spoke briefly with Roberts before leaving town. They both wondered who hired the shooters. For sure if Holder didn't have the cash money for bail, he wouldn't have it to hire shooters.

Leaving town, he drove the buckskins home smartly, with his wife talking about Chaw's wedding and what a fine foreman he'd make.

Harp recalled the tough rebel veteran at Greg's herd the first day when Chaw sided with him and Long against the drunk boss and bad cook. He'd made a good candidate for being a boss after two cattle drives. His gal had cleaned him up some more and that didn't hurt, either. The O'Malley outfit was shaping into a good one.

He simply needed eyes in the back of his head from there on, especially after the coroner's court decision, which would not stop bad thinking on his opponent's side of the fence.

Long, you rascal, it is near mid-November and no sign of your hide.

CHAPTER 35

In the next two weeks, his well-organized army made two more successful drives. They had over a thousand big steers for the next spring's drive penned over on the Diamond Ranch's fenced section, and a buyer from down on the border sold Harp eight hundred big Mexican steers, well worth the money, to be driven to Kerrville after Christmas.

Things went on fast and furious. Small pockets of reported maverick cattle were being gathered and branded by big and small outfits, so by now Harp knew the free cattle would be harder to find. His son, Lee, was trying to crawl and provided him with lots of entertainment.

Hoot sent word some of his horses had been rustled and his men had lost the tracks. They were gone.

Times were growing real tough. Lots of what were called grub line riders passed by looking for work. Harp fed them and they moved on but more came by, and more would come.

Harp decided he'd never understand economics except he knew Texas was dirt poor and no one was helping to cure it. The government's war debt was blamed. Texans blamed the carpetbaggers for ruining the state's recovery. He knew that he and his brother possessed more money than most people in Texas had.

Money talked and they'd used it to buy ranches. Cattle drives were their business while ranching was their anchor in Texas. He had several teams of men out searching for herds of wild cattle still unbranded. His team at home was inspecting quality of the stock from people who wanted the O'Malleys to sell in Kansas. That market did not buy culls. They were worthless and so no need to drive them to Kansas, as precious as those spaces were. Herders were paid for cattle that met market standards and were accepted by the buyers. Many herders discovered what they had brought up from Texas had zero value in the market. There were even some shootings over it in Abilene. Harper was aware of all that was going on, and he was wary.

His bookkeeper worked hard on his new job, asking for information that Katy and his mother had to find. They made him feel at home, and one day he told them, "I'm really enjoying my work and the cowboys are great to me. I hate to go home on the weekends."

Harp was glad he had hired him. He could see his efforts in doing the books really looked very businesslike. It was getting to be a big business as they moved forward. Reg promised to have a report on all expenses they had going to Kansas on that last trip, so they would have better control over the next one. He promised to show Harp the costs for everything they had done so far.

Doug, as the foreman at the Diamond Ranch, was upgrading it everywhere. When Harp last talked to the two sisters, they were excited at Doug's handling of the job. He assured them they had a good man.

After sundown one evening he and Katy sat on the front porch swing with Lee asleep in his crib. The chains creaked a little with his foot shoving to make it swing.

"The shooting of the Holder boy is not settled yet, is it, despite the judge's saying it wasn't murder but self-defense?" Kate asked, snuggling up to Harp.

"I know how you feel about this situation. I have no idea how to stop all the bad talk. I am almost glad Long isn't here. He'd beat them over the head with those hateful signs. I really thought that when the deputy said they were all riding his father's horses, folks would know that Holder was behind the killers or simply aiding them."

"I worry about your safety."

"Katy, I can't crawl in a hole until the clouds pass. That is not my style. I will go do what I need to do for the ranch, for us, for our future."

"And even his wife having a shotgun and the town marshal disarming her."

"Katy, I have lots of faith in God. Saving Emory in the Arkansas River, he was there. It was a lot more dangerous than Mrs. Holder with a gun. They didn't kill me in Missouri when I faced an army."

"Hey, you are my saver. You made me feel like a real woman and wife that I hope I am."

He hugged her close. "Katy, I am so proud of you I can't say it enough. You filled a big hole in my life. Try not to worry, and I will be double careful for your and Lee's sake. I am going to be here when he grows up, for his wedding, to see my own grand-kids and lots more that this life has to hold for me."

"All right. I won't trouble you anymore." He kissed her and they rocked in each other's arms for a while, then went off to their bedroom.

Next morning at the cowboys' breakfast in the big tent, he went over everyone's plans and finished with, "Men, ride in pairs. The ambush on me has become a call for those people that hate us to take up arms against us. They could try and kill you. If that happens I will find that dog and he won't live long, but please be careful night and day. Be aware of where you are and who is around you. This will pass, though I don't know when. Everyone cover each other's backs. We have a large spread-out ranch operation to run and a couple of herds to gather for our drive to Kansas next spring."

They gave him a loud yeah and stood up to applaud him.

"Thank you. Be careful."

His father walked with him back to the house. "We have lots to keep an eye on don't we?"

"Yes," Harp said with a shudder. "No telling what they will try next. They have threatened us on the road and told us we were rustling their stock. They had not lifted a hand to brand them even before the war like the three of us did."

"I told you boys owning those cattle would be a big asset to us. No one believed me until you and Long brought that money back. I hope he is back here by Christmas. He don't have any idea how bad things are shaping up here, does he?"

"Not unless he is talking to some bald eagle that flew out there to tell him."

Hiram chuckled. "I just saw that screaming eagle circling him, screaming at him. *They need you at home.*"

"Maybe he can ride a cloud in," Harp teased.

"It might be like him to do that."

They both laughed at the idea, while the situation really stabbed Harp in the chest every waking hour of the day. All he wanted to do was to get on with his plans to ranch and have a large enough operation for his family to comfortably ranch the rest of their lives.

"Everyone up and wide eyed?" Katy asked when he got back to the house.

"I told them they better be."

"Are you still going into town today?"

"I need to speak to the two men looking for more places we can buy. This is something we talked about before Long rode off on his own. We need to find and buy all we can, while we have the money."

"Who goes along with you?"

"Red will find someone for me or I won't go."

"Thanks." She kissed his cheek, standing on her toes.

He found some maps showing places he'd studied

that they could buy, carried them out to where two guards, Jim Lawson and Tyrone Clayman, held his saddled horse's reins. He put the maps in his saddlebags and with a kind thanks for them for riding with him to town, they rode off.

He met lawyer Tommy Snyder and sat down at the seat in front of his desk.

Tommy leaned forward. "I have a big map here that includes lots of country in the area of the big corral. Including it. It is all state land and since state land has not been selling, and you have adjoining land, the government says owners can buy the rangeland at a discount. I just learned this two days ago."

"How cheap?"

"Two dollars an acre. That's one thousand two hundred and eighty dollars a section, but don't tell anyone."

"So, the land that we don't have in that region, for us to tie it up, will cost around twenty-seven thousand dollars for twenty sections?"

Snyder made a face. "It has to be designated as rangeland first. To get that stamped on that land may cost five hundred dollars. You see where that goes?"

"I'd pay that but how sure are you we can do that?"

"I'll make a special trip to Austin this week to do it, and I'll wire you when I have it done."

"Fine. You're talking about us owning lots of ground in one big patch and really tying all that country up? From where Hoot has the ranch to clear past the Underground Ranch place on the west? And that would join the Erickson place up, too. Long will love it."

"You'll own it in a week."

They shook hands.

His other land agent only had some disconnected home places and the price on them had gone up with the expectations of a land boom being talked about, so he didn't make any deals there. He gathered the two cowboys and they went to Clare's Café for lunch. Things were quiet in town, he was happy to notice. All the signs were taken down, but moving around, Harp still felt some tension in the air.

"Well, the H Bar H bunch is back. I've been missing you guys," Harriet, the ample-butted waitress in her white uniform, said, then licking the lead pencil she used to write their food orders on her pad. "Meat loaf is the special today."

"Three specials, three coffees, and three pieces of pecan pie," Harp ordered.

"All right, guys, it will be coming up shortly."

"Learn much today?" Tyrone asked.

"Quite a bit. We may have us a real ranch coming. But it needs to be kept quiet until we make the deal."

Jim said, "Sounds good, boss man. You are going to need some new head drovers. Me and Tyrone want to apply for those jobs. We learned a lot last year and figure with good help we can get them up there."

"Boys, good help may be damn hard to find. I

agree you both can be candidates, but I want Long here when we decide. I will put you both down."

Around that time, he heard a man say aloud to his tablemates, "I see they let anybody in this gawdamn place. They even let boy killers eat here."

Harp stopped Jim from saying anything or getting up. Under his breath, he said, "He ain't worth anything. Stay put. Eat like nothing's happened."

The loud mouth went on, "Aw, hell, they think anyone can shoot a damn kid."

Harp and his men finished lunch and their pies. Quietly he said, "Start for the door. When you get there, hold it open for me."

Both men looked at him to explain. He whispered, "No matter what happens go outside, hold that door open, and stay there."

They went for the door and Harp stood, leaving a tip on the table.

Headed for the door, Harp caught the loud mouth by his shirt collar, jerked him up, drew the man's gun, discarded it, and with his belt also in Harp's grip rushed him, cussing a blue streak, out the door that his men held open. The charge carried the guy outside and tossed him on the ground past the boardwalk.

He struggled to get up, but Harp had his finger in his face. "Listen, if you don't shut your mouth about this matter, you will need a new face to wear, because I am bashing in the one you have. Now do you hear me?"

"I-I—" the man stammered, red faced.

"Yes, coming in a place, cussing at me, will get

you killed and make the world a better place without you. Now don't forget what I said."

"Yeah—yeah."

"I mean it. That boy died with his killer friends. I considered him one of them or he'd be alive today."

The man still on the ground was sitting up wiping his mouth with the back of his hand. "All right."

"That's better. Now, let's go to the ranch," he said to his own men.

On the way home, Jim was laughing. "Boy that was fast action, Harp. He never knew what came at him."

"I thought he was drunk and not able to move fast enough. But he is sober now."

"Damn sure sober now." All three laughed.

"He's lucky, boys, that it was me and not Long that did that. He'd been missing teeth instead of brushing the dust off his butt."

"Is Long coming back?"

"He better or I'll haunt him. He said he'll be back here by Christmas. That's what he told me when he rode off."

"What'cha figure he went looking for?"

"I'm not sure. But he and I have worked pretty hard since we were boys at ranching and being rangers watching for Comanche. I think he wanted to see new places and new people. We also made two large cattle drives in that time, and he wanted to be away from it all for a time."

"Folks thought him and that captain's wife were once close?" Tyrone asked.

"He said it didn't work out. No telling but I could

sure use him around here. Oh, well, I can handle it till he gets back."

They unhitched their horses, stepped in their saddles, and rode home. At the ranch they took his horse to put up, and he thanked the men for going along.

His dad came out on the porch where he washed up in the waning light of the day.

"How did it go today?"

"The State of Texas really needs money. Tommy Snyder found out that they are selling rangeland to adjoining landowners for two dollars an acre.

"He thinks we can tie up all that land over there. Twenty sections for twenty-seven thousand dollars. Land that ties into the Erickson Ranch, which is ten sections, and Grass Valley where Hoot is at."

"You serious?"

Harp nodded. "That would make one helluva ranch wouldn't it?"

"It sure would for that price."

"He's going to Austin to cinch the deal for us. He wants it quiet until he gets it stamped as rangeland down there."

"I still can't believe that those guys griped about you taking unbranded cattle. After this they may really hate you as the landowner next to them."

"You two staying out here in the cold all night?" Katy asked from the door.

"No, ma'am, we're coming."

They stormed in. He hugged and kissed her.

"You look unscathed." She set his full plate of food in front of him.

"I am. Had a good day."

"We have the wedding all set up for Saturday."
Katy sat down beside him and hugged his shoulder.

"That should make them happy."

"Oh, they are. What else?"

"I told Dad. Tommy found a crack in the state of
Texas's land sale. Adjoining landowners can buy
rangeland for two dollars an acre."

"And?"

"Start at Grass Valley go west of the Underground
House and tuck in the Erickson Ranch and we will
own a large continuous block of land."

"Is it all rangeland?" she asked.

"It will be if so designated."

"Boy, I am impressed. Your brother will like it
won't he?"

"He don't, he can lump it." They both laughed.

"He will like it and be impressed," his father said
quietly.

"You two make my head swim," Easter said. "I
can't keep up with all these land deals."

"I better get Reg to count it. Make sure we have
the money. We don't have this last purchase yet, but
Tommy is going to wire me when he has it done."

"Your dad told you two that money really counted
in this economy, and you two have done a real job
with it if this works," Katy said.

"We'll know in a week or ten days."

He went to bed with his wife almost too keyed up
to sleep.

CHAPTER 36

The next day Reg was busy working on the books when Harp walked in.

"I need a count of the sections we own now."

"Oh, I'd saw that it was over two sections and if you add Erickson's ten, then it's twelve. Why?"

Harp put his finger to his mouth to shush him. "I am looking at twenty more."

"Wow. I won't tell anyone."

"I think Texas needs money and they may have some fire sales."

"Katy calls you land barons." He laughed.

"It is all in a block with the current land we own."

"When will we know?"

"In two weeks."

Reg wheeled his chair around in a circle laughing. Back around he was still laughing. "You guys are sure making bells ring. Nice to be working for you."

"I hope it works."

Red came back from Diamond, said Doug figured

he'd make it, and he could now resume his role as foreman here at the home place. Chadron Turner became his jingle bob foreman. Everyone got ready for the big crowd coming to Chaw's wedding to Calamity.

Things were settling down. They almost had the consignment herd signed up with cattle and it was only November. That made Harp think about a second consignment herd. He rode over and talked to Doug one morning.

He found him working on books. "You ever think you need a bookkeeper, get one."

"Is there enough money in this game to do that?"

"Sure."

"Well, you are the boss." Doug put down his pen and closed the book. "What else is happening?"

"We have the consignment herd about full here and it's only mid-November. I think we may need another one."

"Four herds?" Doug shook his head in amazement.

"Yes, two thousand is enough in one herd. We were lucky with that three thousand but it was too many at the big river crossings."

"That's for sure. Can you man it?"

"I know I've got you and Chaw into jobs as foremen and you both will be needed here. But if two dumb boys made it to Sedalia, I can surely find some leaders for that many herds."

Doug chuckled and agreed.

"Really. How is this job going?" Harp asked.

"Very well for me. I like the *vaqueros*. They will almost do anything for you. They are all good hands. I think we have made many repairs to the operation. Finding bulls has been a chore, but I am replacing the longhorn crosses with Shorthorns and Herefords."

"And you haven't found a woman yet?"

Doug smiled. "I have some prospects."

"I hope you do find one. Katy and Lee are the center of my life."

"If you had not taken a chance on me on that drive, I'd still be bumming around. There is no end to the unemployed cowboys that come by here looking for work."

"Same at our house, but I don't see many I'd keep."

Doug agreed. "Kiss Katy and tell her I miss her."

After he left Doug he rode into town for the mail. While at the post office, getting everyone's mail, three ranchers asked if he had room for more cattle to take to Kansas.

"Give me ten days," he told each of them, mentally adding their numbers and found it came to over three hundred head. "I'm thinking of forming a new herd. Check back in ten days."

Johnny Crabbe, a man with silver temples and a longtime friend of his father's, nodded at his words. "I sure hope so. You two O'Malley boys have a real record of success in that business. Tell Hiram I said hi."

"Oh, I will. And I think I can manage another herd."

"Did I hear you say you had another herd forming?"

He looked up at the woman's voice. It was Anna Greg. Her perfume was in his nose. She looked very nice in black—still.

"How are you?" he asked, feeling as if he was the young cowboy coming to ask for her husband. He shifted the mail to under his other arm and took off his hat.

"Fine. How are you, Harper?"

"Very well, ma'am. How are the children?"

"They are fine. I was being nosey. I heard you tell the last gentleman you might form another herd to take to Kansas."

Why did she unnerve him so much with her presence?

"If you need cattle taken anywhere, Anna, I will take them for you."

"I know you are very busy."

"Tell me the numbers you have, and they will get to market. New consignment herd or not."

"Maybe you could come by and look at my cattle when you have time. Then you will know what I should sell."

He nodded numbly. "When is it convenient?"

She shrugged. "On Thursday?"

"Sure."

"Plan to eat lunch. I will have it ready. So nice to see you again, Harper."

What was it that was so alluring about her? It had

been a long time since he'd seen her. He felt like she had some power over him simply by talking to him. Why didn't her and Long ever make it together? He might never know, but he better figure out what it was she really wanted from him. Check and count her steers? That sounded vague. Why? What? He'd find out on Thursday.

He rode on home, gave the cowboy mail to Ira, left his horse with Holy Wars, and went on up to the house. Katy greeted him with a kiss on the back porch in the cool wind.

"Have a good trip?"

"Doug is doing fine. The town is quiet. I have more consigned cattle and may form a fourth herd. Oh, I saw Anna Greg in the post office. She has cattle that need to go to Kansas. I told her I'd go over and look at them and we'd fit them in even if I can't get another herd."

"How was she?"

"Still wearing black."

"Hmm, well, she turned down your brother. Guess she still misses her husband."

"Darling, I have no idea. But I will take her stock to Abilene."

"Oh, I would expect you to. Have you had lunch?"

"No, I got the mail and came on home."

"I can fix you something."

He thanked her. Why was Anna still on his mind? No telling.

Late afternoon Kate woke him from a nap. She had a yellow piece of paper. "I think you will want to read this. It's from your land lawyer."

He sat up and looked hard to focus on the wire.

HARPER O MALLEY THAT LAND HAS
BEEN DESIGNATED AS RANGE STOP I
LOOKED AT THIRTY UNITS STOP TELL
ME HOW MANY BY WIRE STOP TOMMY
SNYDER

He was talking forty thousand dollars. *Damn you, Long O'Malley. Why aren't you here right now when I need you?* If he bought it they'd need to borrow money to make four herd drives. This was the deal of a lifetime. Hell, yes.

"The boy is waiting in the living room for your reply. Is it good?"

"Yes. Wonderful. I will go in and tell him yes."

"Then Tommy made the connection?"

"That and more. Wow."

He quickly wrote a reply.

Tommy Snyder Austin Texas. Stop. Yes make the deal. Stop. Give me all details and if I need to come down there with the money. Stop. Harper O'Malley

"What does that mean?" she whispered.

"He lined up thirty sections designated as range-land."

Her brown eyes flew open. "Thirty?"

He nodded, then dug into his pocket for money. "Young man, here is a dollar for you bringing this to me and two more to send my reply."

"Wow. No one ever paid me that much. Thank you, sir."

"Now get back to town and wire mine back to him."

"Thanks, Mr. O'Malley. I will do that promptly."

Katy laughed as he fled the house.

"Good news?" Easter asked, coming from the kitchen, stirring a bowl in her hand.

Harp made sure they were alone in the house. "Tommy got thirty sections declared as rangeland."

She dropped her shoulders. "You are buying it all?"

"Yes. Don't feed that bowl to the chickens, Mom."

"I almost did that very thing."

All three were laughing as she set it on the dining table.

"What's happening?" Reg asked, wheeling in the room in his wheelchair.

"Harp just bought the rest of Texas," Katy said.

"Wonderful. How much?"

"Thirty sections," Harp told him.

"That is lots of land."

"What will you call the place?" his mother asked.

"Probably New Hell," Harp said, and laughed.

"Speaking of that, you remember that Chaw's wedding is all set for Saturday," Katy told him.

"You need me for anything? If not, I may go check on the cattle Anna wants to sell tomorrow."

"We are baking lots of cake . . . I can't go," Katy said.

"I won't take all day. Are we going to have enough seating?"

"We are borrowing benches that we will need. They will go back to several churches after the wedding. Red has told the hands that they have to return them after the reception."

"You ladies are handling it well."

"How much needs to be done to their house over there?" Katy asked.

"Those two are going somewhere after their wedding. We can take a crew, paint, and mop buckets over on Monday and spruce it up some."

"Will you need to go to Austin to settle the land deal?" Katy asked.

"I don't know yet. I asked in my wire to him."

"Do you feel good about it all?"

He hugged and swung her around. "Yes, I am excited. We bought Erickson's for a song and forty dollars a month. The old man figures that money each month will feed and cover his needs. That was all he wanted. I doubt he'll live for ten years more and he has no kin. We will look after him if he gets disabled."

Katy shook her head. "You do some wild deals I've never heard of, but you paid the old man some attention and he appreciates that more than all the thinking about selling a place and re-finding him a place."

"And we moved him."

"Yes, you did. Your brother is missing a lot isn't he?"

"He is indeed."

"He won't know half of what you've done when he comes home, will he?"

"No, but I am on the same path as we were before. Building a big ranch."

His mother piped in, "You really are doing that."

He thought so, too.

* * *

He left after an early breakfast. Why did he have a guilty feeling about going to see Anna Greg? She was just another woman. His ex-boss's wife. A woman he met almost two years earlier when he was on the payroll as a herd driver. He'd gone to find Greg and tell him he'd fired the cook.

He recalled her standing on the porch that day in an ironed starched dress. The captain's lady was her rank back then. He'd always figured she had earned that respect being Greg's wife. But there was some strain talking to her in the post office, and why did he feel that she wanted more than for him to look at cattle she wanted to sell?

He reached the ranch house mid-morning. As he hitched his horse, she came out on the porch in a starched dress—not a black one. This dress flattered her figure.

"Good morning, Harper. I feel I am imposing on you. I have some fresh coffee made. Have a seat on the couch and I will serve you some. Cream or sugar?"

"Black is fine."

He hung his hat and jumper in the hall. "Nice house."

"Oh," she said back over her shoulder. "I forgot you have never been inside before."

Back with a china cup and saucer, she set it before him on the coffee table. Then she took a seat beside him. "How is everyone at your ranch?"

"Fine. Busy baking and cooking for the wedding of one of my foremen named Chaw. He went with us to Sedalia."

"I recall that name. A local girl?"

"She lived over at Mason. A nice young lady. Calamity is her real name."

Anna laughed. "We are here alone. My children are at my folks today for a reason. I want to be very frank with you. I know you have a wife and you are very happy with her. But I thought, well, that when you came back from Sedalia and with Emory dead, well, I thought I could turn your head toward me."

"Oh."

She scooted closer. "Long was very kind, but he was not you. When I received your kind letter about Emory's demise I cried, and I remembered the broad-shouldered young man who told me, in my front yard, that he had fired the cook of the drive. That man was coming back home to Texas, and my hope for an alliance with you was very strong. But you found Kate. I have been heartbroken ever since."

"I never—"

"You never did a thing. I simply had a notion maybe you would part with her. Now you have a son and any relationship would probably not work. But would you consider having an affair with me?"

"No. Not because you're unattractive, not because I don't care for you, but because I have my wife and don't need anyone else in my life."

She slumped her shoulders. "I am sorry, but I had to do this today. I know I am shameless, but sometimes your heart overruns your better senses. I will be here. If she ever leaves you, you have my invitation."

From her dress pocket she took out a piece of

paper. Written on it: *Two hundred good steers. I can have them ready.*

"Anna—"

She rose shaking her head, tears streaming down her face. "I am so sorry but, Harp, I had to tell you my true feelings—please forgive me. I know I am a fool, but I can't help myself."

"Anna, we will take your cattle to Kansas. I can't even think about another woman. If I did, I'd think of you but—"

She was at the kitchen door. "I won't ever trouble you again. Please leave me to cry alone."

He rose and put on his hat and jumper. This was why his belly hurt coming over. He knew something was not right. The roan horse unhitched, he swung into the saddle. She was standing before the curtains in the bay window, handkerchief in her hand and waving good-bye.

He'd get lunch in Kerrville. Another thing that he needed to bury. Long was not him and he wasn't Long. Where was his big brother? Older maybe but not any bigger.

Long, come home.

CHAPTER 37

Katy asked him when he dismounted. "How is she?"

"Fine. She has some cattle she wants us to sell. I promised her we would handle it."

"No man in her life?"

"I don't think she is looking for one."

She encircled his waist. "She can't have mine."

He laughed when she hugged him. "She wouldn't want him."

"I am not sure of that. You are fast becoming a large landowner. There are lots of women looking for men who have money and land."

"Well, don't worry. I don't need any of them."

"Good. You have to be in Austin next Thursday to sign the papers. He sent you a telegram today. I answered you'd be there."

"Can you come? We will need to go to San Antonio by stage after the wedding and get down there by Wednesday."

"Yes. I want to."

"Great. Let's go buy half of Texas."

"You know what?"

"What?"

"People are going to hate you even more for buying this land than for stealing their cattle."

"Because it will land-lock them into our land eventually."

"Will they sell to you?"

"Some will, some won't. I can care less. They made no attempt to buy it. I did."

Kate shrugged. "None of them have the money to buy anything."

"My dear, I see in the next decade private land will have bob wire strung around it."

"Yours, too?"

"It will be the way to keep your grass for your own stock, to have grass like the sisters do, in case of drought."

"Just be more careful. I want you to rock your grandbabies."

"I plan to do that."

"I will have some white shirts and clean pants packed for you and I can be ready to go when we need to leave."

"Good."

"I want you to buy a new business suit when we are down there. You're going to have to go to important places, and I don't want anyone saying that you're some hick from Camp Verde."

"All right, fine."

"There are going to be more opportunities coming down the road for you."

"Like what?"

"Appointments to government boards. These Yankee carpetbaggers won't be here forever. Eventually Texans will run Texas again. You will be in that circle. Trust me you will be. A man with forty sections will be looked up to for those jobs."

"Anything else in my crystal ball."

She slugged his arm on the porch. "I am not a gypsy."

"But you know things like one."

"I am only thinking about you and preparing you for things to come."

"And for that I am grateful."

"Wait; don't go in just yet. Did anything happen to you today?"

He shook his head.

"No? I fretted all day that you were being challenged by someone today. I was not sure who but maybe your enemies thought badly about you."

"Maybe. I'm fine."

She shook her head. "It was nearly as bad a day for me as the one that made me wait longer at the store for you to arrive at Lee's Creek."

"Nothing happened to me."

"Good."

He followed her in. There was never any intention on his part to even consider Anna's offer. But Kate knew he had been challenged. She had some powers few individuals possessed. At times they were vague to her. Thank God she didn't know.

He wanted no one else but her.

But he had been challenged.

* * *

The Chaw-Calamity wedding was a hoot. Cowboys danced their boot soles off on the straw-floored barn. Many ladies liked to dance and their husbands didn't, so the ranch hands filled the dance cards of the young, old, fat, and skinny ones until the band about died from exhaustion.

He and Katy slipped off before midnight. No reason to tell her about the Greg woman and his encounter with her. He had Katy. That was enough. That Anna wanted him and not his brother, Long, was a shame, but too bad. He was taken.

The crew hauled benches back to churches past dawn.

Next they rode the stage to San Antonio, spent the night, and the next day went on to Austin. Tommy Snyder met them and by taxi they went to the Alhambra Hotel. They had supper in the restaurant and learned the signing was to be held over at the Texas State Land Office at 10 a.m.

Tommy was excited. "So far I have sold ten ranchers land adjoining their own. Most bought much less than you did. But I think it is just the start. More will come back next fall from Abilene and want more land."

"Tommy, what about the people land-locked inside our future ranch?" she asked.

"That will be up to them. Most, for lack of access to free range, will be forced to sell out."

"Will it cause a range war?"

"They won't have a leg to stand on."

"That won't stop hotheads from rising up."

"I agree. But in time they will be forced to move on."

"You have seen the maps. How many have places in that purchase?"

"A dozen, maybe less. Some are just squatters. Others will claim they filed a homestead on it but never sent in papers and will now say the records were lost. Just living on land will not give them a claim or right to be there."

"I will pay you to challenge everyone inside our borders. If they are legitimate I will observe their rights. If not I want them moved off."

"That's what I do for my money; I am a land lawyer. I expect them to protest in court even, but if they have a legal claim we will talk about them selling if they want to."

"That sounds right to me," Harp said, and Kate agreed.

The signing and transfer of money by check went smoothly. The land officer gave them a rolled-up map of the purchase and the land commissioner shook his hand to thank him.

"I understand you sold Texas cattle in Sedalia, Missouri, two years ago?"

"My brother, Long O'Malley, and myself sold eight hundred head of steers there in late summer. I guess we were the first cattle sale after the war. In fact Lee signed the peace about the time we got the drive to Fort Worth."

"Was it difficult?"

"I can tell you I got some gray hairs from it."

"How did two young men do that? You had no experience at driving cattle long distances did you?"

"We had experience. We'd fought the Comanche. My dad recovered many white children they stole. We were along with him. Herding a bunch of dumb cattle wasn't much worse than those times."

"Thomas said you even had the law on you up there."

"Yes, we did. They passed a law that no Texas cattle were allowed in Missouri, but the Saint Louis meatpackers said to let us come in because they had to have beef."

"They do now, don't they?"

"They still need them. I understood they ate every hawg and chicken up during the war. It will take years to get back enough to bother our cattle shipments."

"Mr. O'Malley, you should be right in the Texas history books with Crockett, Bowie, and the rest."

"Thanks, and thanks for letting us buy this adjoining land. We will raise more Texas beef on it."

Tommy, Kate, and Harp hurried away so as to not have to talk to any reporters. The news would spread fast, and there would be many angry people saying they never heard of this sale. A scandal was brewing, but they already had the state seal on their deed. They bribed no one and merely used the advantage of a law set down by the presiding Texas state officers.

They celebrated in a private dining room with Tommy and two associates who had sent him notice of this new law. They all three toasted Kate and Harp. Neither drank anything but tea. Still it was fun.

The next morning, the Austin newspaper head-
lines read:

Nineteen-Year-Old Cattle Baron
Buys Thirty Sections of Texas Rangeland
In Bexar County—for *Cash*
HE SAYS HE WILL BUY MORE !

Inside the coach rocking for home, she flicked
the newspaper with the back of her fingers. "Nineteen years old huh? Wait until he's twenty-five. He
may own the northeast quarter of the state."

"Easy, easy, we have to crawl to walk, sweetheart."
He held her in his arms. "You know all those
women back there in Austin we saw?"

"Yes."

"I didn't see one I'd trade you for."

"You know why?"

"No."

"Because I would not let you go that's why. Dang
you are such a neat kid, I am never letting you go."

"I don't feel that young."

"Life has been a drag on us both, I guess. I lived
for four years not having anything at all, and now
here I am with you and we have a great son. I thank
God every morning for delivering me from that hell
I was in."

"Amen. Long and I took a job that was supposed
to pay fifteen dollars a month if we got to Missouri
with the cattle. Sounded good. There was nothing
we could do to make that much money at home,

and what would be hard about driving cattle? We'd done that before."

Kate smiled. "When we get to San Antonio lets buy two big cans of peaches and eat them in our room."

"And get drunk on them like we did at Lee's Creek."

"Cowboy, you think of the neatest things to do in the whole world."

And they did.

Word got out by morning that they were at the Crockett Hotel. They came downstairs for breakfast and asked the clerk what all the noise was outside.

"They have a police line out there holding people back. They want to lynch some guy named *Harbor* who underhandedly bought a huge ranch from the carpetbagger government in western Bexar County."

"Send our bags that are up in our room to the H Bar H ranch in Camp Verde, Texas. Here is a twenty-dollar gold piece. Ship them and keep the change."

"What is your name?"

"H. O'Malley, but don't use it. Use the brand. Come on, darling, we are going out the back way."

At the livery he rented a buckboard and team, hitched quickly, and he paid them to go to the livery at Bernie and get it back. They'd take a stage from there to Kerrville.

Things worked smoothly. They made Bernie and left the team. He tipped the man two dollars to hold them for the livery coming after them. On the regular stage to Kerrville, he picked up a few newspapers to read about the riots. There, he hired a boy he casually knew to quickly take them home to the ranch.

The boy spared no whip, sliding corners and making his ponies run. He got them there so fast that Harp paid him five dollars and the boy about swallowed his Adam's apple.

Harp told him to cool them good before he went back to town. He agreed and unhitched them to walk out their heated condition.

His mom came rushing out. "Whatever is wrong?"

"Let's go in the house and we can explain it. Where is Dad?"

"He's coming from the barn on the run."

"How is my boy?" Katy asked.

"Lordy me, he's fine. Is that why you rushed home so fast?"

"No. We can talk better inside."

When Harp finished their escape story everyone laughed.

"I guess even real cattle barons can get into big trouble," Hiram said.

"They damn sure can." He'd never seen the likes of people that mad because someone bought some rangeland.

Finally he asked, "Long still hasn't come home yet?"

Hiram shook his head and pointed at the calendar on the wall. "We are fast running out of the days left in November. And people will quiet down about the deal. It won't be anything at all by New Year's Day I bet."

"I didn't do one illegal thing. They sent out word

to people they could find, with adjoining land, and they all had the option to buy it."

Hiram almost choked on his words, he was so upset. "None of them had the damned money."

"Now that is possible, too. But they won't offer this for long I bet. I think they had a short fall, and a quick deal like this is going to cover it. Tommy thought so, too."

"What next?" Hiram asked.

"Start hiring men. We are going to have four herds going north."

Hiram explained what he had heard. "Some ex-ranger named Charlie Goodnight is revamping supply wagons with a kitchen cabinet in the back gate of the wagon. He has a fly out back for shade and to cut off the rain. Oh, and he uses the back gate for the cook's table. It has folding adjustable legs with pins to level them. They call them chuck wagons."

"Sounds neat. Who does that in town?"

"Two or three guys," Hiram said.

"Talk to Ira and then get them set up and I'll look for another one good as they are."

"I can do that. Mom and I talked while you two were gone. We are concerned that Long hasn't come back yet. He knows how much work you have to do to get ready for another drive, and he's never left it all on you to do before. There is no way to track him down. We have no idea where he went. But he should have sent a two-sentence letter anyhow. We are worried."

"I've been concerned for a month now, but I don't know where to start looking."

"There isn't a place I can think to look. You keep working. You have lots of cattle to move. We can only hope and pray."

He thanked his dad and went to talk to his bookkeeper. There were lots more things to do. If a lynch mob didn't string him up first.

CHAPTER 38

November skipped into December. They even saw some snowflakes floating around one cold day that far south. Ten days into the month he had the second consignment herd full. The Clark brothers were building the first chuck wagon for the O'Malley brothers. Harp stayed close to the fireplace making more plans for the crews he still had to hire.

His foremen assured him there were lots of hands willing to ride for him since he paid for the trip back and they might get put on permanently at the ranches. He put an ad in the local paper, for applications, and he got a hat full.

Some he knew, some he'd never heard of before. He answered that some come in on a trial basis and most turned out to be good workers. He began to build a team and hoped his brother would be home by Christmas. He'd wait to see if he made it before hiring any more.

He rode into town to see the progress on the chuck wagon. Ira went along pleased he would have the first updated one in town. They were standing in the shop admiring the work the brothers had done so far when all hell broke loose.

The shots struck Harp's horse, which had turned around at the time the shot was fired. The animal reared in pain. Harp had his gun out and shot the man who was standing in sight with a smoking gun in his hand. The horse went over backward and Harp knew he'd been shot badly. He lay on his side pawing up hay and dust. Damn that. Now shooting his next best horse.

The man he shot dragged himself into a stall and wildly shot back. A second man turned and ran. Ira was so damn mad over them attacking him he chased him shooting, and his third shot stopped him. The man went facedown.

Harp told the man on the ground in the stall to drop his gun. Instead, he raised his pistol but before he could do anything, Harp shot him in the face. The interior boiled with stinging gun smoke, burning his eyes. What in hell was wrong with people? He did not recognize the man, and it made him so mad that they shot his horse. In the end he had to put the poor thing out of his misery.

The Clark brothers crawled out from hiding. They were shocked by the outburst. Both town marshals were there telling people to get the hell back and let them do their job.

Ira and the younger lawman dragged the shooter he shot out of the street and dropped him in the dust of the wide doorway to the shop.

"Who in the hell are they?" Harp demanded.

"Strangers," the main marshal said. "I never saw them before."

"Some SOB put a bounty on my head, but I guess the likes of them two won't tell us anything. Looks like they both have already gone to hell." Harp shook his head in disgust.

"I'll have the funeral home plant them," the marshal said. "Sure sorry it happened here, Mr. O'Malley."

"My name is Harp."

"Yes, sir, Harp."

"That horse they shot, I wouldn't have sold it for two hundred dollars. Ira, let's go get what supplies you need and go home."

"Yeah. They damn sure ruined our day."

"I bet you're mad. That was a good horse. We can drag it out of here and we'll have this wagon done this week. I am glad you like it. We will get your others done as fast as we can, but we are getting several requests to fix other wagons," the older Clark brother said.

"You find a good wagon, buy it for me. I need one more for next year's drive."

"Whew, you are busy."

Harper nodded and they left to get Ira's needs at the mercantile.

"You know, Harp, someone seriously wants you dead," Ira said.

"I find him, I will end his life."

Harp borrowed a horse from the livery, rode back to the ranch, and told the story to Katy.

"Who was it?"

"I guess someone whose toes we stepped on either branding mavericks or buying the last land."

She hugged him. "I'd stop them if I could. Would Hiram like a new pocketknife for Christmas?"

"Yes. What are we getting for Mom?"

"I'm still thinking. Christmas was never this nice in my life. I got a good taste of it last year, but I am in the mood this year to make it fun and a really happy time here."

"We always had Christmas, but it was a lot plainer growing up."

"We are blessed. Someone just rode up," she said. "It is Chaw. Wonder what he came for?"

"I'll put on a jumper and go see."

Harp did just that and went out on the porch to greet his foreman. "Hey, you have problems today?" They shook hands and Harp showed Chaw into the house.

"No, but I heard they shot at you in town today," Chaw said.

"Both are dead. No one knew them. Hang your coat up and come in the living room."

"Howdy Miss Kate," Chaw said politely.

"Howdy to you. Miss Calamity all right?"

"Oh, she's fine. We are doing wonderful."

"What brings you here?" Harp had him sit down on the couch.

"One of my boys was over at Oscar's Saloon. It's a hole-in-the-wall riffraff hang-around. He stopped for a beer and overheard a man offering to pay for someone to kill you."

"They tried this morning. Who was making the offer?"

"Ryle Beemish, who owns a place in your new land."

"Hear that, Katy?"

"You know him?" she asked.

"No. Heard the name, but now I intend to meet him."

"I'm glad I am not too late," Chaw said. "We can stop him."

"I really should get the law to do it. We go to lynching people even if we are hanging the right ones, we will get a reputation for forcing small outfits out and being killers. More than we already are."

"If the law can't, then by damn, we will."

"Chaw, thanks. I'd made up my mind to find the one behind all of this, and I think you just did."

"You have so much to do anymore. I am not sure how you can even think."

"I'll go into town and find that Kent Roberts, who testified at the trial. Let him handle this."

"I feel bad I didn't come sooner and tell you. This was my first chance. Hoot and I have met and we have plans to straighten out all the cattle that have been branded, owned by folks you bought out, and the rest of the livestock grazing our land."

"Sounds great. Thanks. Tell Calamity we hope she is happy."

"Oh, she's happy now that the Erickson house is repainted and she has her new curtains hung. And I am sure happy with my job."

Chaw thanked Kate for her offer to feed him

lunch, but he wanted to head back home. Harp walked the living room floor.

"Well you know the problem now," Katy said.

"How can I make it not look like the big landowner oppresses the small guys?"

She frowned at him. "He's hiring killers to murder you. You shouldn't feel bad."

He hugged and kissed her. "I guess I need to try to forget it."

"No. Go find that deputy and file your report. He can handle it."

"I'll do that tomorrow. I need to calm down some."

"Good. I would like to have my husband back. You have not been yourself in a while."

"I will try to restore him."

"Better."

The day dragged by and in the morning he and Tyrone rode to town. They found the new man Alan Jeffries who represented the Bexar County sheriff.

Jeffries listened and agreed that someone was hiring killers to get Harp. But, he said, proving it would be difficult even with a witness. Especially with it being one of his own employees offering to witness. A jury might consider he was being paid to lie.

Harp agreed. Jeffries promised he'd do some more investigating into the matter. Harp thanked him and they went back to the ranch.

"We never found much help there," Tyrone said to him when they were cutting across country to get back.

"I felt the same, but you can only do so much without evidence backing up the story."

"What can we do next?"

"Wait for Martin to hire someone else I reckon."

"That don't sound worth a hoot."

"I agree. But I need to get on with my life."

Tyrone nodded.

It was two days before Christmas when Harp went to town to get the mail and newspapers. He stopped by and checked with his banker. Jim welcomed him into his office and asked what he could do for him.

"Oh, I just stopped by to say Merry Christmas."

"Same to you. Everything going good in your life?"

"Aside from some men trying to shoot me, I guess I am fine."

"No lead on that?"

"Leads but not enough evidence. I don't know how to end it."

"I sure can't help you."

"I didn't come by for that. Just wondered what you knew about what business would be like in the next year."

Jim smiled. "The national debt, and the rush to get rich, will govern it. Some things look great. But that may be a paper fortune situation and collapse. People want to eat, and the beef business will continue. It's all Texas can ride on to help us."

Harp shook his hand and thanked him. He had to continue getting four herds ready to go to Abilene and keep settling the great land his purchase brought him. He headed back home to read his mail and newspapers.

He rode home without incident, a cold wind sweeping at him along the way. He began to wonder if his brother was even alive. While he knew Long was not a hand to write letters, no word in over three months was too long. A ranch hand took his horse and he went on into the house.

He had lunch with his father, mother, Lee, and Katy. He told them nothing was happening and spent the afternoon reading the newspapers, looking for a clue to the future. Later he talked to Reg about the books, and the bookkeeper confirmed they still had ample money to operate.

"I don't think we will have to borrow any, either," Reg added.

"Thanks. That is good news. If we do another trip north this next year and do good, we will be well situated in the business."

"Oh, yes, we will."

He thanked him, and Reg handily wheeled his chair back to his office.

Someone rode up and it was a youth. From the front windows Harp studied him and wondered what he wanted. He opened the door, and the young man reached in his pocket for a yellow paper wire.

"I have a telegram for you, Mr. O'Malley."

"Thank you." He took the paper and unfolded it.

HARPER O MALLEY WE ARE COMING
STOP SAVE US SOME CHRISTMAS CHEER
STOP LONG

What does it say?" Katy asked, and he handed it to her.

"He's alive anyway, Harp, he's alive." She jumped up and down. "Oh, thank God."

"What did you get?" his mother asked, rushing into the room.

"Oh, he got a wire from Long. It says *we* are coming."

"Who is *we?*"

Hiram broke in, "What's all the fuss in here?"

"Harp got a wire from his speech-making brother," his mother said.

"What does he say?"

"We are coming. Save some Christmas cheer."

"Did he marry a widow with ten kids?" Hiram asked. "Where was it sent from?"

"Fort Worth, yesterday."

Harp was laughing. Who could *we* be? They'd find out when he and whoever he had with him got there.

"This is such great news. I couldn't have a better Christmas gift," his mother said. She was crying. So was Katy, and Harp had to admit the wire was pretty great news. They would have to simply wait to see it happen.

Thank you, Lord . . .

TO MY FANS

Well, you've had a chance to meet and read my new series, The O'Malleys of Texas. Plans ahead are to switch back and forth between Chet Byrnes and the O'Malley Brothers.

It's all very exciting for me, and then throw in the fact that we have an option, with a production company, to film the first two Chet Byrnes books: number one, *Texas Blood Feud*, and number two, *Between Here and Texas*. You never know with an option, but these folks seem sincere and we will just have to wait and see how things turn out. So in the future a version of Chet Byrnes may appear on the silver screen. Meanwhile I will continue writing books on how I interpret the West for your reading pleasure.

I leave you my thoughts about the West. Some real brave folks made up the men and women who brought with them their family, religion, hopes, dreams, and ideas to a fresh new country, carving out ranches and even empires. Turn over that card and on the back side there were the criminals. Wanted, worthless ones who rode the tide west ahead of law and order, filled with greedy needs to rob, rape, steal, and kill anyone in their way. That fire from hell had to be put down, and the brave men and women who wanted a place to raise their families on that harsh land rose above them, and the West was a better place without the lawless elements.

Thanks. Until we meet again, may the good Lord bless and keep you.

Dusty Richards
P.O. Box 6460
Springdale, AR 72766
dustyrichards@cox.net

ACKNOWLEDGMENTS

I am dedicating this book to my college buddies
Dave Eastlake and Gene Miller, my former
ranching partners, Monty and Sumner Smith,
and one great lady, a cowgirl, rodeo director,
and a real friend, Pat Hutter,
my literary agent, Cherry Weiner,
who sells these books,
my editor, Gary Goldstein,
who over the years has encouraged me—
oh, yes, and especially, my wonderful wife,
Pat, who has really supported me in my writing
endeavors for over half a century.
Any questions, I am at dustyrichards@cox.net.
Thanks for being my fans.

Look for the next book in the
O'MALLEYS OF TEXAS *series!*

DEAD AIM

*From Western Writers of America Spur Award–winning
author Dusty Richards comes a thrilling new chapter
in the O'Malley family saga, a blazing American
epic of blood, bullets, and brotherhood set
deep in the heart of Texas . . .*

Long John O'Malley is only nineteen years old,
but he's no greenhorn. The oldest and boldest of the
O'Malley brothers, Long John cut his teeth tangling
with Commanche at the tender age of sixteen.
He risked his life to rescue a group of captive women
settlers—and forged his own destiny as a hero in the
making. Now he's taking on his biggest challenge yet:
riding shotgun on a wagon train across the hostile
Nebraska Territory. It's a treacherous trail, and it's
not long before the young Texan is earning his
paycheck by fighting off a tribe of bloodthirsty Sioux.
But the real test lies in the journey ahead—
a genuine ride to hell and back, from the
Rocky Mountains to Sante Fe and all the way home—
that will either make Long John O'Malley a
living legend . . . or a deadman.

**Coming in February,
whereever Pinnacle Books are sold!**

Visit us at www.kensingtonbooks.com